Seven words flew through the darkness, moving on wings of music and fire. . . .

Tom jolted awake in the dead of night, all but knocked from his bed.

All of the prayers he'd ever heard before had come to him as whispers.

This one had fallen with the force of a command.

The seven words echoed in his mind. They'd come from hundreds of miles away, from a place he'd never been, from a little girl whose name he didn't know but whose voice he could now never forget.

It was a cry for help, a plea made in terror. Seven simple words that would haunt Tom for the rest of his life.

Please, God . . . don't let them kill me.

Praise for David Mack and his bestselling *Star Trek* novels

"David Mack [keeps] the reader enthralled . . . jaw-dropping."

—SFReader.com

"Riveting writing of the finest caliber . . . a real page-turner."

—Sci-Fi Online

"A meaty, gripping story populated with strong characters."

—*TV Zone* Magazine

"Powerful stuff . . . David Mack's plotting shines."

—*Starburst* Magazine

***The Calling* is also available as an eBook**

THE CALLING

DAVID MACK

POCKET BOOKS
New York London Toronto Sydney

Pocket Books
A Division of Simon & Schuster
1230 Avenue of the Americas
New York, NY 10020

First Pocket Books trade paperback edition July 2009

Manufactured in the United States of America

10 9 8 7 6 5 4 3 2 1

Library of Congress Cataloging-in-Publication Data

Mack, David
The calling / David Mack.—1st Pocket Books trade paperback ed.
p. cm.
1. Psychics—Fiction. 2. New York (N.Y.)—Fiction. 3. Supernatural—Fiction. 4. Suspense fiction. I. Title.
PS3613.A272545C35 2009
813'.6—dc22 2009008657

ISBN 978-1-4165-7992-2
ISBN 978-1-4165-8072-0 (ebook)

This book is dedicated to the memory of Robbie Greenberger, who, at the age of twenty, was taken from us before he had a chance to follow his own calling.

All this time
I've been working them angels overtime
Riding and driving and flying
Just over the edge

—Rush, *Snakes & Arrows*,
"Workin' Them Angels"

1

Jung Lee didn't hear the bullet till it passed through his head.

Hot powder shot up from its ricochet off a concrete skylight housing. The dust stung Jung's eyes. The slim young Korean man winced against the pain, blinked his eyes clear, then turned to see who had ambushed him.

Backlit by the distant Manhattan nightscape were three figures, spread across the expansive terrain of the Brooklyn high school's roof.

Farthest away, perched above the roof's access door, was a pale-skinned man with close-cropped dark hair and not an ounce of extra fat. Loose shirt and pants. Hard muscles and hard eyes. He jumped down, landed on bare feet, and stole forward with the supple grace of a predator.

Flanking the barefoot man was a fragile-looking young woman with short red hair, a retro-punk sense of fashion, and half a dozen facial piercings.

On the right was a large bearded man dressed in a motorcyclist's riding leathers festooned with gang insignia. The biker aimed his handgun at Jung and fired three more shots, which tore holes through Jung's T-shirt and both sides of his hoodie—but left the Sentinel unharmed.

"So it's true," said the barefoot man. He flashed a malevolent smile. "You really are immune to metal."

Jung had never seen any of them before, but as they moved toward him, he knew who they were. There was no point in answering them. They hadn't come to talk—the Scorned never did. Jung reached behind his back and drew a pair of nunchaku. The two halves of the wooden flail were linked by a short length of coarse rope, making it a very quiet weapon as he swung it in a defensive figure-eight pattern and sidestepped away from the edge of the high rooftop.

The biker became a watery, almost transparent blur—and then he was three blurs, splitting up and charging at Jung.

The Sentinel dodged left and swung his nunchaku in a blinding pattern of arcs and snaps. The weapon passed through one blur, then another—and then a kick swept Jung's legs out from under him. He fell backward and rolled with the change. Arching his back, he absorbed the momentum of his fall and then sprang forward, back to his feet, narrowly avoiding the biker's clumsy stomp at his neck.

A snap-strike of Jung's nunchaku caught the biker in the side of the head. The leather-clad brute staggered backward. Wary of the red-haired woman and the barefoot man, who were moving to either side of him, Jung backed off, turning his nunchaku once more in a steady figure eight.

Bolts of electricity leapt from a cluster of cell-phone antennae on the roof's nearest corner. The high-voltage barrage enveloped Jung. Spasms rocked his body, and his tongue suddenly tasted like copper. The nunchaku tumbled from his hand. As the lightning ceased, Jung saw crackles of electricity dancing across the red-haired woman's fingertips.

The biker blurred and divided again, and all three blurs advanced on Jung.

Crushing blows pummeled Jung's gut and face. The biker reappeared from his blur-disguise and locked one arm around the Sentinel's throat.

A stabbing pain flared hot and sharp in Jung's back, followed by another. His howl of pain came up empty; at a loss for breath, he knew one of his lungs had collapsed.

"Ceramic knife," the biker taunted him. "Ain't that a bitch?"

The redhead stepped in front of Jung and placed her hand over his chest. Each crackle of electricity between her fingertips made his heart skip a beat.

Behind her, the barefoot man observed with dispassionate calm. "You know you can't win," he said to Jung. "But you can decide how you'll die. Quickly . . . or slowly." To the redhead, he said simply, "Fiona."

She jolted Jung's chest for a split second. A sound like the ocean roared in his ears. His skull felt as if it had ballooned to twice its size. His vision turned purple, and then he struggled to see through a swarm of slow-moving violet spots.

"That's the quick way," said the barefoot man. He nodded to the biker, who gave the knife in Jung's back a tiny but excruciating twist. A cry of agony lay trapped in Jung's aching chest. "That's the slow way." The trio's leader took a pack of cigarettes and a lighter from his back pants pocket. Fished out one cigarette and lit it. "So . . . if you'd like to end this right now, all you have to do . . . is tell me if the Called gave the girl any other Sentinels."

Struggling for air, Jung gasped, "I don't know."

The questioner lowered his square chin and narrowed his eyes. "Don't lie to me, Jung. We *know* who you're guarding—the one who can see the Bridge." Fiona stepped aside, and the barefoot man stepped forward.

Jung looked up and met his feral stare.

The punch hit Jung's face like a burning sledgehammer.

His cheek prickled with heat where the blow had fallen. The stench of his burnt goatee was sharp in the cool fall air.

"Let's try again." The barefoot man wiped Jung's blood from his knuckles by dragging them across the front of Jung's hoodie. "Are you her only Sentinel?"

Heroism would bring Jung neither glory nor a reward, but cowardice would inflict untold suffering on more souls than he could imagine. His survival was no longer important. Defending his charge was all that mattered now.

He twisted and pushed himself back onto the knife that was still stuck between his ribs. The biker lost his balance for a fraction of a second—long enough for Jung to get his hand on the man's holstered pistol and pull the trigger.

The shot cracked like thunder underfoot, and the biker let go of Jung's neck. The knife slid free of Jung's ribs and the pistol cleared its holster as the biker stumbled backward with a bullet in his foot. Jung snapped off a shot at the redhead, just as she lit him up with a burst of blue forked lightning from her hand.

His vision whited out with pain and shock. Clarity returned in a blink. He was on his knees with a smoking scar on his chest and a painful ringing in his ears. The redhead lay slain by the gruesome gunshot wound in her throat.

Three blurs raced toward Jung. He'd have time to shoot only one. A calm, quiet voice in his heart told him where to aim. He fired at the center target.

The blurs vanished. All that remained was the biker, staggering backward, hands pawing helplessly at his bloodied chest. His lifeless eyes were still wide with shock as he collapsed on the gravel-covered rooftop.

A hand snared Jung's left wrist in a searing, viselike grip.

Under the sleeve of his hoodie, the hairs on Jung's forearm crisped and shriveled, and his flesh cooked on the bone.

The pistol tumbled from Jung's grasp. The barefoot man kicked it away across the shadowy rooftop as he tightened his grip on Jung's arm.

The Sentinel bit down on his cry of agony, shifted his weight, and tried to throw his attacker. Instead, the enemy Seeker let go of Jung's arm, changed his stance, and caught Jung with a jumping kick to the head.

Jung fell semiconscious on the gravel. Where the kick had caught his face, a vicious burn began to blister. He shook his head and fought against the pain as he wobbled to his feet. Barely able to breathe and beginning to slip into shock, Jung knew he had little chance of stopping a Seeker whose touch could burn flesh.

"You're not the one I came for," the barefoot man said, circling him. There was a mocking quality to his voice as he added, "You could run. I'd let you go."

Jung wiped blood from his mouth, then said, "You know better than that." He was a Sentinel of the Called, the only defender standing between the enemy and an innocent. He wouldn't run.

The enemy Seeker came at him, jabbing him with kicks and punches. Jung tried to block and hit back, but his scorched left arm was a soft target, and his right arm soon was peppered with blisters from deflecting the Seeker's infernally hot hands and feet. Then both his arms were snared—

He heard bones break. Sharp cracks split the night air.

Sickening jolts of pain shot through his elbows and shoulders. It would have sunk him into shock if the horrific burning in his torso hadn't already done so.

The Seeker dropped Jung in a smoking, twitching heap on the roof.

Jung lay still, shivering despite the heat that radiated from his brutalized body. Out of the corner of his eye, he watched as the barefoot man laid hands on his slain comrades and reduced their corpses to charred skeletons.

Then the enemy Seeker stood above him, holding the ceramic knife. The man fished a disposable cell phone from his pants pocket. Tapped in a number. Waited for someone to answer.

"It's Tanager," he said. "I got him. Looks like he was working solo." He listened a moment, then replied, "Yeah, you're good to go. Grab the girl. Good luck." He hung up and tucked the phone away.

Squatting over the stunned Jung, Tanager stabbed the ceramic blade an inch into the fallen Sentinel's left pectoral muscle, slashed diagonally across Jung's chest to the middle of his right side, made a horizontal gash back to the left, then cut another diagonal wound to the man's right hip. Eyeing the crude, vaguely S-shaped lightning-bolt graffito—the mark of the Scorned—Tanager flashed a sinister smile, then locked his left hand around Jung's throat.

A rush of all-consuming fire and a crimson haze of pain filled Jung's body and mind. He silently begged God to forgive him for his failure.

"Ashes to ashes," Tanager said as he cremated a Sentinel of the Called with his bare hands. "Dust to dust."

Phaedra Doyle was fighting for her life, and she was losing.

Her attacker had struck from the shadows. The gangly eleven-year-old had heard the stranger's steps only seconds before he'd grabbed her from behind.

He'd said nothing as he clamped his hand over her mouth and nose, muffling her cries with a damp, medicinal-smelling rag. She'd seen enough movies to guess that the cloth being mashed into her face was drugged, so she struggled to hold her breath.

On coltish legs she'd been moving in quick strides through the John Jay High School parking lot, which tonight had beckoned as a handy shortcut between the Park Slope block where her friend Nora lived and her own tree-lined Brooklyn street. The lot's Fifth Street gate was always chained shut, but a few weeks earlier, vandals had detached part of the chain-link fence next to it.

Most of the time, Phaedra knew to stick to the sidewalks, but tonight a gruesome car accident at Seventh Avenue and Fifth Street had cut off her usual route home. She also wanted to avoid the men in hard hats working at the corner of Eighth Avenue and Fourth Street because the road crew had a habit of saying crude things to her, sexual things that made her afraid of them.

After slipping through the open Fourth Street gate, she'd been distracted as she strolled across the lot toward the gap in its fence—lulled by the brisk autumn evening, by the speed with which night had fallen now that daylight savings time had ended, by the new music blaring through her earbuds.

She'd paid no attention to the lone SUV parked against the lot's tall concrete western wall, just shy of the flood lamp's soft circle of orange-hued light.

Then had come the crush of a callused, thick-fingered hand on her face and a burly arm locked around her throat.

She thrashed in his grip, twisted back and forth. His hold tightened. Her awkward back kick at his instep missed, and she slumped, weighted down by her book bag and unable to regain her balance. He dragged her out of the light and into the shadows.

Help was so close, only a panicked shout away, but she couldn't pry his hand from her face. Desperate for air but afraid to breathe, she felt herself getting dizzy. Her strength was fading. Inhaling was risky—who knew what was on that rag?—but a cry for help was her only chance. If she was lucky, if anyone was close enough to hear, if someone in the apartment buildings whose sides faced the back of the school had a window open, then maybe she still had a chance to escape.

She sucked in a breath. Pulled through the rag, it was heavy with a cool perfume that smelled like a poison. The drug left a bitter metallic taste in the back of her mouth. Her vision softened and dimmed as she tried to scream.

Then her attacker's arm stiffened into a vise on her throat, and no matter how hard she pushed from her chest, no sound passed her lips. Without warning, her legs turned rubbery and failed her.

Collapsed in his grasp, Phaedra felt consciousness fading. He let go of her head, and it lolled backward. She stared at a blue-black sky streaked with clouds the color of cotton candy dragged through the gutter. As he lifted her through the open rear hatch of the SUV, her head pitched forward, hiding her face behind a fall of long, straight brown hair. She landed hard and lay dazed as the liftgate thumped shut.

The SUV's carpet had an oily smell, and it was rough and gritty with dried mud beneath her cheek. She heard one of the vehicle's side doors open. With a labored shuffling and huffing, the man climbed inside and clambered over the back of the rear seat into the cargo area with her. Insulated from the ambient roar of the city outside the SUV, Phaedra heard the sound of a zipper being undone. She couldn't get her eyes to focus through the drug-induced haze, but she felt the man lift the hem of her pleated skirt. Shame and terror welled up inside her.

A sharp jab in her thigh dispelled the druggy fog and cleared her senses for a moment. She looked down and saw a hypodermic needle in the man's hand. The needle's tip was stuck in her left thigh. He slowly pushed down on the plunger and injected half a syringeful of golden liquid into her body.

Then she got her first real look at him. Dark suit, white shirt, gray tie, black shoes—a generic New Yorker. What held her attention was his black gas mask, with its large insectlike lenses, through which she saw his unsympathetic eyes. It had a protruding round speaker that made her think of a pig's snout. Attached to the speaker's side was a large round filter.

"Don't fight it," he said, his voice muffled behind the mask's rubber face while a hollow echo of his words squawked from its speaker. The syringe emptied, and he pulled the needle from her leg and covered it with a plastic cap.

A dark circle of shadow pressed in on her, like the cold walls of a well into which she was sinking.

Her limbs felt heavy at first, then her sense of herself evaporated, as if she were made of mist and memories. Her field of vision shrank until all she could see was that grotesque mask looming above her.

Then, as everything else dimmed, something new appeared: a terrifying shape, a black figure made of smoke and fear. It wrapped around the man as if it were a cloak. Its form churned and changed as her focus softened—it grew wings, horrible and batlike, and they enfolded her in their demonic embrace.

The last glimmer of light faded from Phaedra's sight, and she realized with a sick, cold horror that this might be the end of her life.

As the man and his living shadow smothered her, she took refuge in a terrified, silent prayer: *Please, God . . . don't let them kill me.*

2

No one ever guessed by looking at Tom Nash that he was extraordinary, and that was just fine with him.

He was taller than most folks he met, well over six feet. He was also broad shouldered, lean, and weathered from years of hard work with his hands, much of it outdoors. He'd worked as a handyman most of his life—fixing cars and doing a little carpentry, a bit of plumbing, and some landscaping. He'd even earned a license to work as a locksmith, but there wasn't much call for it in Sawyer, Pennsylvania, thanks to a couple of big lock companies that had pretty much cornered the market.

None of that made him particularly special, though.

His truck certainly didn't set him apart. Plenty of folks in Sawyer and the local area drove pickups, and more than a few had their cargo beds capped like Tom's, to keep both thieves and the weather off the gear stored inside. Tom was sure there were probably a few whose mileage put his red beast's 98,000-plus odometer total to shame, but he didn't know anybody who owned one.

Tom made a left into his driveway and brought his truck to a stop in front of the garage door, which had been stuck shut for going on two years. He keyed off his truck's engine, which rattle-shuddered into silence, as if its parts had been spinning in a whirlwind and now were collapsing in a heap beneath the scratched and dented hood. One of these days the truck's death groans would be genuine, but he had no idea how he'd be able to tell the difference.

He got out of the truck, inhaled the cool night air, and walked to the house, where he found Scout, his neurotic but lovable border collie, lying in the dark on the front steps. She gazed up at him with her most remorseful expression.

"C'mere, girl," he said, patting his thigh. Scout whimpered in response. "Trouble, huh?" More high-pitched lamentations expressed the dog's dismay. "For you or for me?" Scout tucked her snout beneath one gray-speckled paw and hid her eyes. A tired grin tugged at the corners of his mouth. "No, don't tell me. It'd just ruin the surprise." He stepped over his cowering dog, opened the scraped and scuffed front door, and walked into his living room.

As houses went, Tom's was comfortable. It was on the small side, but it had two floors, a few small bedrooms, and two full bathrooms with showers. He and his wife, Karen, had made the down payment with money they'd inherited after his father died. Most of their furniture was secondhand stuff left over from their first few years of married life, when they'd lived in a small apartment. None of the pieces matched the house or one another, but taking a loan to buy furniture when he could barely keep up with the mortgage rubbed Tom the wrong way.

Especially with their first child on the way—an experience that was teaching Tom all kinds of new anxiety about the future.

The aroma of frying chicken lured him into the kitchen, where Karen—enormously pregnant and three weeks from her due date—was toiling over a deep skillet filled with hot olive oil, boneless chicken, and crispy sage leaves.

He stepped up behind her, laid his hands on her shoulders, and gently pressed his lips to her neck. "Hey there."

"Guess what your dog did today," she said while turning over a sizzling piece of chicken with a pair of tongs.

Not ready to take the bait, he kissed the other side of her neck. "Oh, not bad," he said, teasing her with a deliberate non sequitur. "How was your day?"

She flipped another chicken breast. The oil spat and crackled. "Your dog showed us why we can't have new furniture."

"You know, it never ceases to amaze me," Tom said. "When Scout does something useful, like chase a raccoon out of your garden, she's 'our' dog. But when she wrecks something, she instantly becomes 'my' dog."

Karen scowled jokingly over her shoulder. "Your point?"

"No point," Tom replied.

"Get used to it," Karen said. "Same rule goes for kids."

"Great." He started rolling up the sleeves of his red plaid flannel shirt. "Anything I can do to help out in here?"

She gestured with her chin toward the mountain of soiled pans and utensils in the sink. "You can get started on those."

The one drawback to Karen's amazing culinary gift was that she generated more dirty dishes than any three other people Tom had ever met. He was convinced that she could find a way to make a greasy mess out of the broiler pan and half the forks in the silverware drawer just to serve a bowl of cold cereal.

It took about a minute for the water from the tap to run hot enough to wash dishes. He started shifting things around, figuring out what he ought to wash first.

Beside him, Karen lowered the heat underneath a steamer filled with something green. "Did you finish that roofing job today?" she asked.

"Yeah," he said, squeezing some grapefruit-scented liquid detergent onto a scrubber sponge. "Won't get the check till next week, though. Deeley's always slow about paying up."

She took the skillet of chicken off the heat and set it on a hot pad on the counter. "And what about your *other* project?"

He lifted one eyebrow in wry amusement. "It went fine."

One thing about Tom's life made him extraordinary. Karen was the only other living person who knew what it was, and one of only three people he had ever trusted with his secret: for seventeen years, since he was sixteen years old, he'd been hearing other people's prayers.

Tom didn't know how it happened, or why it had happened to him. It wasn't something he could control. He couldn't choose whose prayers to hear or which ones or when. At first he'd thought it was a weird kind of telepathy, but he'd never been able to read other people's thoughts or send his thoughts to others.

His mother had decided he was crazy. Father Keir, an elderly history teacher at the Jesuit-run high school he'd attended, had told him it was a vocation—a spiritual calling—but one that had to be pursued with caution and discretion.

The only thing Tom knew for certain about his gift was that whenever he heard a prayer, he felt compelled to act. To get involved. To help in whatever way he could.

"So what was it this time?" Karen asked. "Another shut-in?"

He shook his head. "No. Just a regular guy." He left it at that, and Karen understood from the lack of details that the situation was one best kept private.

In this case it had been a fired teacher who'd prayed for help to fight his alcoholism. Tom had found the man at 6:45 a.m. sitting on the railing of an isolated bridge beside his parked car, with curses on his lips and vodka on his breath. Persuading him not to jump had been easy; getting him to meet Tom that afternoon when he'd dried out for a visit to a local AA meeting had been more difficult.

Fortunately, Tom had learned over the years that he could be very persuasive when it was for someone else's benefit. To his chagrin, his knack hadn't enabled him to haggle a better price when he bought his truck.

Karen sighed. She opened the cupboard and removed two large orange dinner plates. "Just tell me we didn't make another interest-free loan or give away something important."

"Nothing like that," Tom assured her. "I promise."

A sidelong glance told him that Karen was still a bit miffed about one of his recent acts of charity for a stranger. "This time," she said. "What about next time?"

"Won't know till it happens," he said. He rinsed a glass under running water hot enough to scald his fingertips.

She shook her head but said nothing as she used the tongs to lift a chicken breast out of the oil and put it onto a plate. After nine years together, she no longer needed to speak in order for Tom to know she was annoyed with him.

He turned off the water and dried his hands with a dish towel. "You think I'll do something dumb, right? Give away our house? Let a stray dog eat all our food?"

Karen's shoulders slumped, and a deep weariness infused her voice. "No," she said. "Not exactly. But I worry about you, Tom." She lifted the lid from the steamer, releasing a cloud of roiling gray vapor that billowed and dispersed beneath the oven hood. She spooned some broccoli onto his plate and handed it to him. "Don't forget to take some salad."

Tom set his plate on the counter next to a large bowl and served himself a small pile of tossed greens rich with the fragrance of balsamic vinegar. "What're you worried about? It's not like I do anything dangerous."

"No, but you snoop in other people's business. One of these days someone's gonna get ticked off."

Wouldn't be the first time, he mused, but he knew better than to tell her that. "Relax," he said. "I'll be okay."

Karen served herself dinner. "What if you're not, Tom? What if you get hurt? Or killed?"

"In other words," Tom said, "what'll happen to you?"

"Are you kidding?" she snapped. She slammed her plate down on the counter. Broccoli crowns rolled off the plate and fell to the floor. "Which one of us makes sure the bills get paid on time? Who keeps gas in our cars and food on the table? Which one of us actually has health insurance?"

Chastised, he looked at the floor and brooded over the answer: *You do.*

She picked up the fallen vegetables. "Honestly, Tom, if I had to raise our son alone, I could—and you know that." With a sigh, she tossed the dog-fur-covered broccoli into the sink. "But what the hell makes you think I'd *want* to?"

Tom put down his plate and stepped softly behind Karen. He rested his hands on her shoulders, then caressed her arms, which were hard and tense. "I never said that. That's not how I feel." He kissed the back of her head through her light brown hair.

She remained distant, closed off from him. "Don't," she said. "I need to be angry at you for a few more minutes, okay?" Pulling away from his touch, she rested her hands on the edge of the sink and leaned forward. "You know I believe in you, in *what you do*. I've always supported you—*always*." She laid a protective hand on top of her rounded womb. Tears shimmered in her eyes. "But right now, just this once, I need you to be here for *me*, okay?"

Tom felt ashamed for failing her when she'd done so much for him. He set his left hand on her hip and let his right hand gently stroke the side of her enlarged belly. "I'm sorry I worry you," he said softly in her ear. "I don't mean to. And you're right; there's no way I can know what's gonna happen. But that'd be true no matter what I did. It's true for everybody, all the time."

She set her right hand over his. He took it as a sign that he could keep talking. "But whatever it is that sends me on these errands, it's never given me more than I could handle. It's never put me in danger." With a gentle tug on her shoulder, he turned her to face him. "I'd never lie to you," he said, wiping a tear from her cheek. As she looked up at him with tear-reddened eyes, he added, "This is all gonna be okay. I promise."

"I believe you," she said, resting her head against his chest. Her voice trembled with fear. "But what if you're wrong?"

He wanted to tell her not to be afraid, that nothing would happen . . . but he knew that would be a lie.

Because sooner or later, something always did.

3

Seven words flew through the darkness, moving on wings of music and fire, racing westward against the turning world.

Like an arrow slicing through the ether, the words left the city behind, passed over suburbia, and soared over sparse stretches of undeveloped woodland. Stray thoughts rose from the Earth as if it were an endless spring of consciousness, a fountainhead of desire and dread, a geyser of hope and fear.

Guided by steady hands of spirit, the words broke through the barrier between the ethereal and the physical, pierced the clouds, and fell toward a landscape dotted with small houses.

So many ears could not hear what was spoken.

So many eyes could not see what was shown.

None bore witness save the one whose mind lingered now in the shade of dreams, a beacon shining in the gloom.

Most mortals could not hear the words that sailed on the ether . . . but a Seeker could.

The seven words sped like a feather on a gale then fell like a stone into the Seeker's soul, shredding the fabric of his dream and rousing him from a troubled sleep.

The message had been delivered. The words had been heard, and the Seeker would know what to do.

The rest was up to him.

Tom jolted awake in the dead of night, all but knocked from his bed. All the prayers he'd ever heard had come to him as whispers.

This one had fallen with the force of a command.

Seven words echoed in his mind as he scrambled from bed wearing just his frayed green sweatpants.

He hurried barefoot downstairs, ran through the kitchen, and hurtled out the back door to his autumn-browned backyard, where he stared eastward through tear-filled eyes, his chest heaving with ragged breaths.

That was where the words had come from.

He felt it. He *knew* it.

They'd come from over a hundred miles away, from a place he'd never been, from a little girl whose name he didn't know but whose voice he would never forget and whose life now depended on him.

It was a cry for help, a plea made in terror. Seven simple words that would haunt Tom Nash for the rest of his life.

Please, God . . . don't let them kill me.

Karen Nash turned her head and peeked through half-open eyes at the empty other side of her bed.

Gray predawn light behind the window blinds was barely distinguishable from darkness. She glanced at the clock on her end table. It was just after 5:30 a.m., about five hours earlier than Tom normally staggered to consciousness on a Sunday. *Never a good sign,* she thought, remembering all the odd hours at which his bizarre gift had made its demands on him.

She pushed off the sheet and comforter. In slow, stiff movements, she lowered her legs over the side of the bed.

Chronic backaches and hip pain had plagued her for weeks, and sitting up first thing in the morning had become a challenge. The enormous parasite inside her—which in polite company she was always careful to refer to as "the baby"—had made just about everything in her life difficult and uncomfortable. Even the paste that coated her tongue in the mornings tasted worse.

A gentle push on her back with both hands enabled her to sit mostly upright. *I don't know how I let him talk me into this,* she mused, looking down at her round belly—but then, despite all the discomfort and inconvenience, she couldn't help herself, and she smiled. She slid her feet into a pair of soft, well-padded slippers, sighed with relief, and started to stand up.

Her moment of bliss faded as a hot, sour surge of heartburn worked its way up from her stomach into the back of her throat.

After a visit to the bathroom to swallow some antacids and relieve her bladder, she waddled down the hall and descended the deep-plush-carpeted stairs in slow, plodding steps. The house was quiet. Normally when Tom couldn't sleep he'd camp out on the sofa and watch old movies on TV with the volume turned low, but there was no telltale blue flicker in the living room.

At the bottom of the stairs she stopped and listened. Then she heard it: a scrape of shoes on the asphalt driveway, followed by the hollow, metallic sound of the truck's liftgate being shut.

Now what? she wondered as she pulled open the front door. Chilly air not yet touched by the dawn made her shiver.

Tom was in the driveway, looking haggard but ready to travel in his slate boatbuilder jacket, dark green canvas shirt, faded blue jeans, and flat-soled sneakers. Scout trailed him and whined softly as Tom circled the idling truck, checking its tires. He passed through its gray exhaust cloud and saw Karen staring at him. She stood with her arms folded across her chest, a cold, dry whisper of a breeze rippling the silk of her maternity nightgown.

"Morning," he said flatly, as if his mind was elsewhere.

A weary blink and a frown was all the reproach she could muster so early in the day. "Where the hell are you going?"

He broke eye contact with her—another bad sign. "Long story," he said, and he opened the driver's side door.

It frightened Karen when he was taciturn, because it meant he was hiding something unpleasant. "Tom," she said, adding steel to her voice. "What's going on? Another errand?"

With one hand on the door and the other on the truck's roof, Tom slumped at the shoulders, and his head drooped. His sigh was muffled by the engine's idling purr.

He gently shut the door and turned back to face Karen. "Not exactly."

The way he said it gave Karen a completely different kind of chill from the one the wind inflicted.

She took measured steps down the front stairs and walked toward her husband. "Something's wrong, isn't it?" He stared at the ground and wore a forlorn expression. After a moment he nodded. "Tom, what is it? . . . Was it a prayer?" Another nod. "For God's sake, please talk to me."

He looked up. Now that she was closer, she saw that his eyes were bloodshot and his face ashen. "It wasn't like any prayer I ever heard before," he said. "It's life or death." He was quiet for a moment. In a haunted tone, he continued, "It was a girl. A child. . . . She asked God not to let them kill her."

"Let who kill her?" Karen asked. "Kill who?"

Tom shook his head. "I don't know. I don't know who she is or who they are. All I know is she's in trouble."

His fear was contagious. She grabbed his arms and tried to make him look at her. "Tom! You have to call the police."

"And tell them what?" He averted his eyes and stared toward the back of their house. "Besides, this isn't local."

She looked at the truck. "Where are you going?"

"East." He turned his head to face her. "New York."

Everything was coming so quickly that Karen had no idea how to react. It was like a nightmare coming true. "New York? Now? Tom, I could go into labor any day, you know that."

"I know," he said, like a guilty man making a confession.

She pressed on. "Why does it have to be you? And why now, so far from home?" She shook him. "Tom, I *need you here.*"

"Yes, you do." He reached up and grasped her cold fingers with his large, warm hands. "But right now she needs me more."

He gently pried her hands from his arms. His voice softened and took on a mellifluous timbre that Karen had always found impossible to resist. "I've always believed I hear prayers for a reason. That someone or something wants me to get involved." A note of fear crept into his voice. "There has to be a reason I heard this girl's prayer. A reason why it has to be *me.*"

"You don't know that," she said, desperate to make him stay. "Maybe someone else can do it."

"How?" Resolve hardened his tone. "As far as I know, I'm the *only* one who heard her prayer, which means I'm the only one who *can* help her. I can't walk away from this. Please believe me. However this happened, it wasn't a request—it's an *order.* I *have* to go."

There was something in his voice as he'd said that, some mysterious quality that Karen had heard only a few times before in all their years together. She didn't know what it was, but when it was there, he could talk her into anything. Besides, how many times had she told him he was doing God's work? She'd believed it then, and she still did, no matter how many times Tom had denied it.

His eyes were calm. She knew that he was committed.

"What you're doing could be really dangerous," she said, surrendering. "You know that, right?" He nodded in reply. "Promise me you'll be careful."

"I will," he said. "You know I will."

She started to cry. "And don't eat junk food. Remember your cholesterol and your triglycerides."

"I'll remember," he said with a put-upon smile.

"How long will you be gone?"

"No idea," he said. "As long as it takes."

Tears stung her eyes and traced salty trails down her cheek to the corners of her mouth. "I don't think I could take it if I lost you," she said, fighting not to collapse into a sobbing mess. *Damned third-trimester hormones,* she fumed. With his thumbs, Tom gently wiped the tears from her face as she added, "What if you don't come home?"

He cupped her face in his palms and fixed his blue eyes on hers. Then he said with absolute conviction, "I will *always* come home to you. That's a promise I'll never break."

And she knew it was the truth.

Her husband leaned forward and kissed her with tenderness, with love, and with sorrow. The morning air was cold on her back, but his body was warm beneath his jacket. She wished she could simply anchor him to the ground and forbid him to go, but that wasn't possible. She had known from the beginning that she shared him with something greater than either of them—just as she also had known that, sooner or later, this terrible day would come.

Their embrace parted slowly, and he took a step back. "Time to go," he said with a sad smile. He opened his door, got into the idling truck, and pulled the door shut. Scout, who had been lying flat on the browned front lawn, stood up and trotted over beside Karen as she watched Tom shift the pickup into reverse, filling the air with exhaust fumes.

The truck's engine rumbled as Tom backed out of the driveway into the narrow street. Karen laid one hand on Scout's head and skritched the dog's wiry fur as a wintry breeze blustered past, tearing loose a flurry of dried leaves from the large tree in the front yard. A lull in the truck's engine noise signaled a change of gears as Tom shifted it into drive. He bade farewell with one final, simple wave before he accelerated away.

Karen watched the truck grow smaller as it retreated down the long residential street, carrying the man she loved away from home and into the unknown. As much as she admired all the good deeds he'd done with his peculiar calling, she would have traded them all to avoid this moment.

Her husband was riding off into danger . . . and she was alone.

4

Dreamless darkness vanished in a blinding flash. Though her eyes were shut, Phaedra winced and lifted her arm to block the glare.

It felt to her as if only a moment earlier she'd been in the back of the SUV, the injected drug dragging her down into a pit of black. Now she was somewhere else. Someplace quiet. She shifted her weight and felt the spongy resistance of a blanketed mattress beneath her.

Clacks and thuds of metal bolts. Sounds overlapped with their own sharp echoes. Keeping her arm raised to shield her eyes from the intense white light coming from above her bed, she propped herself up on her other arm to face the source of the noise. She squinted while her vision adjusted to the flood of harsh light that surrounded her. Fear and shame prompted her to tug her tartan skirt down. To her left, a few diagonal yards from the foot of her bed, was a gray metal door. It opened out. The man with the gas mask walked in.

He carried what looked to Phaedra like a school-cafeteria fiberglass tray. On it was a paper plate with scrambled eggs and toast, a pint-sized carton of orange juice, a plastic spoon, and a paper napkin. He set the tray on a small, low table in the corner of the room, across from her bed.

His breathing came through the air filter in hisses and gasps, and his voice sounded mechanical when amplified by the mask's external speaker. *"We hope you slept well."* He pointed to the corner of the room opposite the small table. She followed his gesture to see an open doorway. *"Your bathroom is in there. We've given you the basics."*

She glared at him. His clothes were drab: gray suit, white shirt, boring tie, scuffed black leather shoes. He was taller than average. There was no longer any sign of the horrifying winged smoke-shadow that had surrounded him in the SUV, but she still felt the same sensation of fear when she looked at him.

She desperately wanted to run for the open door, but he stood in the middle of her path. *No way past him,* she admitted to herself.

"What's with the mask?" she asked in an accusing tone, trying to sound brave but unable to keep her fear from putting a tremor in her voice.

"We value our privacy," he said. He took a few steps toward the door, stopped, and turned back. *"We suggest you eat your breakfast before it gets cold."* He continued walking away.

She sprang from her bed to the desk, picked up the tray, and hurled it at him. It flipped over instantly and hit the floor several yards shy of his feet.

Not even close. Phaedra raged with disappointment. *Pathetic.*

The man stopped outside the door and looked back at the splattered eggs and spilled juice. *"We'll be back in a while to clean that up."* As he pushed the door closed, he added, *"Lunch will be served at one o'clock."* The thick metal door shut with a resounding bang. After a few seconds, the clacks and thunks of bolts and bars being locked into place reverberated through the door and echoed off the room's bare cinder-block walls.

She wanted to check her clothes to make sure everything was still where it should be, but she felt paranoid that the man was watching her, that he was a perv who'd hidden cameras all over this concrete dungeon. A sharp tug untucked the thin blue blanket from her bed. Draping it over her head, she huddled on the bed beneath her makeshift tent and, in a panic, inspected everything she had on. Nothing was torn, nothing was damp. No stains, no missing layers. As far as she could tell she wasn't hurt, but she still couldn't shake off her profound terror of violation. *Even if this creep hasn't touched me yet, that doesn't mean he won't,* she told herself. *He's gotta want something.*

The space beneath the blanket grew warm and thick with Phaedra's exhaled breath. She threw aside the blanket and inhaled cool, fresh air. Her cell had none of the moldy odors that made her think of basements. It had almost no smell at all, as if the room had never been used before. The only scent she noticed was from her pillow, which smelled clean like laundry detergent, but not the kind her mother used.

Suddenly, she missed that scent so much, more than she'd ever thought she could. Tears welled in her eyes as she wished she was home in her room, with her mother just a shout away. Despite all the times she'd griped about her chores and her homework and her curfew, she wanted them now. *Compared to this, washing dishes and doing geometry's not so bad.*

I have to get out of here, she told herself, repeating the thought as she dried her eyes with the side of her palm and got up. She tried moving the furniture around in the hope of maybe blocking the door, but everything except the small plastic chair at the desk was bolted down. Pushing and kicking at the gray door did no good, but she tried anyway until her hands and her feet hurt from pounding on the solid barrier.

Tired and thirsty, she decided to look at the bathroom. It was the same length as the outer room but only about half as wide. Inside, along the far wall and facing the doorway, was a small steel sink with the kind of fixtures that had to be held open to make the water flow. *That sucks,* she thought with a grimace. To her surprise there was no mirror above the sink, just a blank cinder-block wall.

To the right of the sink was a stainless-steel toilet and, beyond that, a metal-walled shower with a clear plastic curtain. In the middle of the floor was a large covered drain. On the wall opposite the toilet was a towel rod hung with a pair of forest green cotton bath sheets. More recessed lights dotted the ceiling. There was no sign of a camera, but Phaedra remained fearful of being watched.

What she didn't find anywhere in her cell was a switch for the lights. *It must be outside,* she figured. Her captor, she realized, decided when it was night or day for her. Then she realized that he would also be the one who would say whether she ever saw real daylight again.

She fought against that grim notion. *I bet Mom has every cop in the state looking for me.* Then she sighed, her hopeful defiance smothered by despair as she stared at her cell's gray walls. *Who am I kidding? This isn't a movie. Kids vanish every day and never get found. No one's comin' to save me. I'm screwed.*

Staring at the mess of her breakfast strewn across the floor, she realized that she was painfully hungry and that lunch wouldn't come until one o'clock. But worse than that . . . for all she knew, her next meal might also be her last.

5

A mile a minute rushed under the wheels of Tom's truck. He tightened his grip on the steering wheel as a curve in the New Jersey Turnpike brought the jagged skyline of New York into view. From a distance the city resembled the lower half of a shattered grin, dark teeth tearing the flesh of an early morning sky.

Tom had never liked cities. He'd found Philadelphia, Pittsburgh, and even Allentown overwhelming. As for New York, he'd never gone there and had never wanted to. Now it slowly grew larger on the horizon, its skyscrapers ominous even in daylight. They reminded Tom of gravestones in an old cemetery—huge vertical slabs all slammed up against one another with no breathing room between them.

Traffic thickened as he passed exit 12, and the roar of other cars competed with the music blaring from his speakers. It wouldn't be long before he reached the Goethals Bridge into Staten Island. From there he would be as good as lost. Even so, he would be glad to get out of this two-lane death race, which for the last forty-one miles had been hemmed in on either side by four-foot-tall concrete barriers.

He turned down the radio, which was tuned to a local classic-rock station, and stole glances at the ever-closer metropolis. *I must be nuts,* he admitted to himself. *I don't know where I'm goin', and I don't even know who I'm lookin' for.*

There had been times when he heard prayers he didn't think he was suited to handle—a plea from a woman overcome with regret after tossing her husband's golf clubs into a river was one memory that always made him grin—but this crisis was completely out of his league. Saving a kid in trouble was a job for the cops or the FBI, not a small-town handyman.

But he'd heard the girl's prayer, so here he was.

Another thing Tom wasn't much good at was praying. It was funny to him—he'd spent years answering other people's secret wishes to God but never saw the point of making one himself. As the city rose, dark and strange, from the horizon, fear twisted in his gut. He was alone out here and terrified that a young girl's life lay in his clumsy, callused hands.

Thinking back to his youth, he recalled the advice Father Keir had given him after Tom had convinced the old man that his ability to hear prayers was real. "No matter what good you try to do in the world," the skeptical Jesuit had said, "others will often suffer as a result, either by design or by neglect. Try to keep a thought for them when you put your gift to use. But remember this: if your purpose truly is from God, you should feel peaceful in its pursuit."

Tom struggled to pierce the mental fog of panic and shape his thoughts. He had a lot of words for what he was feeling right now—"scared" and "doubtful" topped the list—but "peaceful" wasn't one of them.

God, I don't know if You're listening. Some girl I've never met needs my help, but I don't know what I'm doing. If I blow this, somethin' bad's gonna happen to her, I can feel *it. I guess what I'm saying is . . . I need help. I need Your help. 'Cause I don't think I can save her by myself. So throw me a line, will ya?*

There was no answer to his plea—just the hum of the road under his tires, the drone of the engine, a twang of music from the radio . . . and his own fearful, troubled silence as the city loomed closer.

Getting lost in Brooklyn proved easier than Tom expected.

Before this trip, when he'd thought of New York, he'd thought only of Manhattan, a narrow island with tall buildings and lots of landmarks that he knew from TV but couldn't find on a map, such as Times Square or the Empire State Building. Now he saw that Manhattan was just a sliver of the city, one small but densely populated borough. The others—Staten Island, Queens, the Bronx, and Brooklyn—were huge sprawls of crisscrossing street grids. Home to more than eight million people, the city was bigger than anything Tom had ever seen before. He had no idea how to find parking there, much less a kid whose name he didn't even know.

I'm gonna run out of fuel soon, he worried, anxious of time's passage. *And God only knows what's happening to that girl while I drive in circles like a dumbass.* An hour of aimless turns led him past more churches and bars than he could possibly count until he was heading north along Flatbush Avenue, a two-way boulevard packed with short buildings and myriad small stores.

Small groceries and ethnic restaurants blurred past. Tom marveled at the sheer number of discount shops, luggage stores, and furniture outlets. More than a few spaces stood empty and abandoned behind graffiti-tagged metal drop-down barricades. In the middle of sardine-packed blocks sat old movie theaters that had been converted into houses of worship. Thrift shops, pawnbrokers, beauty salons, sliver-thin fast-food joints, pharmacies, and Army Navy stores—all topped by brick apartment complexes—huddled against squat, claustrophobic supermarkets.

Odd-angled intersections gave the rows of buildings a haphazard quality and made traffic hard for Tom to predict. Stopped at one light after another, he noted with amusement how many run-down buildings were crowned by brand-new satellite dishes. The sidewalks were jammed with people, all of them in a hurry.

This wasn't the glitzy glass and steel of Manhattan or the scary urban wilderness he'd seen a thousand times on television. If not for fleeting glimpses of the Manhattan skyline, he could almost have imagined he was in Pittsburgh or Cleveland or Allentown.

Then the avenue's character changed abruptly and completely. After he passed Ocean Avenue, he found himself driving through an oasis in the middle of the urban sprawl. Tom glanced at a sign on his right and caught the name Brooklyn Botanic Garden before he raced past and left it behind. For the next few minutes, the avenue was flanked by thick walls of trees that were still thick and mostly green, barely touched by the late-autumn weather.

As quickly as pastoral serenity had enveloped him, it fell away as he arrived at Grand Army Plaza. Traffic fed into the multilane rotary intersection from every direction. Tom felt paralyzed; there were so many ways that he could go, and he had only seconds to decide before the light changed.

Eastern Parkway, a major thoroughfare, cut across his path and passed the Brooklyn Public Library. Flatbush Avenue seemed to continue straight. Adding to his distraction was the plaza's chief attraction, a massive pale archway topped by three groupings of dramatic black statuary depicting soldiers, horses, and angels.

The light changed. He trusted his instincts and went straight.

Flatbush Avenue led him down a short, bucolic drive before sending him toward another multilane madhouse. By the time his peculiar intuition told him that he was going the wrong way, changing lanes to stay on the rotary proved to be a nightmare. Horns blared, and vile curses came at him from every direction and in multiple languages.

His neck was dripping with sweat and he was mumbling vulgarities of his own as a line of cars prevented him from making another last-second lane change, forcing him to endure another circuit of the rotary. In the hubbub, he missed the turn for the rotary and instead went north on the gentle curve of Plaza Street East. When it, too, turned south and transformed itself with no warning into Plaza Street West, he decided that whoever had designed these roads should be condemned to drive on them twenty-four hours a day for the rest of his miserable life.

To his relief, Plaza Street West led him onto Prospect Park West, a quieter, more residential street. He looked around; something about this place *felt* right.

He couldn't say exactly what it was that gave him an odd sense of déjà vu. The prayers he heard rarely came with images or details. A sense of direction and distance accompanied most of them, but Tom had no idea why or how that worked.

Now, however, as he drove slowly beneath the lofty, interlocking boughs of stately old trees and admired the meticulously maintained brownstone and brick town houses, an electric tingle raised the hairs on his neck. The sensation faded somewhat as he turned a corner onto an avenue lined with a dazzling variety of appealing little shops, restaurants, and bars, but it returned in full force as he returned to the tree-draped tranquility of the residential cross streets.

A flash of yellow on a lamppost caught his eye. He slowed down.

It was a letter-sized sheet of canary-hued paper with a photocopied portrait of a girl and a bold headline: MISSING. He was too far away to read the smaller text below the photo, but he noticed that every third or fourth post had been adorned with another yellow sheet.

He reached a break in the line of tightly sandwiched parked cars, pulled in, and stopped the truck. He got out and walked back a ways to a lamppost on which a yellow flyer had been taped. One look at the girl's photo was all he needed to be certain: it had been her prayer he'd heard.

He pulled the flyer off the lamppost and took it back to his truck. He slumped back in the driver's seat and studied the page.

The girl's name was Phaedra Doyle and she was eleven years old. She had been missing since the previous night. Her mother, Anna, had posted the flyers as a personal plea to her neighbors. The police knew about the case, it said, and anyone with information was being asked to contact them. The only phone number listed on the sheet was for the NYPD's Missing Persons Squad.

Tom knew better than to try dealing with the cops. Not

only would he have no way to justify his involvement with the case but he had learned the hard way that he might just end up making himself a suspect. It would be better, he decided, to try to make direct contact with the missing girl's parents.

He dialed 411, waited through the automated greeting, then answered the prerecorded prompts. *"What city or borough?"* asked the feminine voice.

"Brooklyn, New York."

"Business or residential?"

"Residential."

"Please say the person's first and last name."

"Anna Doyle," Tom said.

"There are multiple listings," the automated voice said. *"I'll get an operator to help you."*

Barely a second later, a human operator joined the call. The woman asked in a crisp, professional manner, *"You'd like a listing for Anna Doyle?"*

"Actually, I need an address," Tom said.

"Okay, sir. Do you know which street?"

"No," he said, then glanced at the open atlas on the seat next to him and noted where he was. "But I can narrow it down to Park Slope."

"Just a moment," the operator said. Tom heard the clack of computer keys. *"I have a listing for a Robert and Anna Doyle on Fifth Street in Park Slope."*

"That's it," Tom said, reacting to a fresh surge of intuition. He opened the glove compartment and dug out a ballpoint pen and a small white spiral-bound notebook. He flipped in a hurry to a blank page. "Go ahead," he said. The operator read him the complete address, which he repeated aloud as he scribbled it down. "Got it," he said when he had finished.

"The zip code and phone number will follow, if you need them."

"Thank you," Tom said, genuinely grateful.

"You're welcome." Another automated message kicked in, and Tom jotted down the Doyles' phone number as well.

A name, an address, and a phone number. It was more than he'd had just a few minutes ago. Now he needed to figure out how to approach a total stranger in an unfamiliar city.

Back home in Sawyer, he had a reputation that preceded him. Folks who'd never met him knew his name, had heard of his knack for showing up when someone needed a helping hand. Here in New York, though, he was just another outsider poking his nose in people's business.

Which makes me about as welcome as a repo man. He saw his reflection in the side-view mirror. *And I dress like . . . well, like a handyman.* He sighed. *I wouldn't let me in if I came knocking at the door. If I'm gonna do this, I have to look the part.*

On the sidewalk outside his truck, a young woman pushed a frilly baby stroller, and a man who Tom guessed was her husband walked beside her. Tom lowered the passenger-side window and waved to get their attention.

"Pardon me," he said to the man and flashed a low-key smile. "Can you tell me where I could buy a suit around here?"

6

Time was Anna Doyle's enemy. Seventy-two hours, the police had said. Most "nonfamily abductions," the duty sergeant had told her, were over in less than three days. It had seemed like cause for hope until Anna's incessant, desperate questions had led him to confess that in cases like this that ended badly, the child was usually dead within a few hours of vanishing.

Anna sat on the edge of her daughter's bed, paralyzed by a frantic desire to be in a hundred places and doing a thousand things. Afternoon light streamed in through the slanted window blinds, warm and golden . . . a mockery of the leaden, guilt-tinged dread that was crushing her heart.

She wanted to be out on the streets, grabbing every person she could find and shaking them by the shoulders until by some miracle she found one who could tell her where her daughter was, until she could find the bastard who'd done this and kill him with her bare hands. Damn the law, to hell with common sense—she wanted to kick in doors and search people's homes and empty every building one at a time until

Phaedra was found. She wanted her little girl's face on every TV screen twenty-four hours a day, seven days a week, until she came home. But all she could do was weep and scream with rage, alone inside her empty house.

I should've been there to walk her home, she castigated herself for the hundredth time. *She was too young to walk alone at night, I knew that. Why wasn't I there? Why?*

It didn't matter that Phaedra had bristled at even the merest suggestion that she needed hand-holding. "Jeez, Mom," Phaedra had protested just a few days earlier, "I'm *eleven years old.* I don't need a babysitter *all the time,* okay?"

Their empty house was stark proof that Anna had been right. So was the dry finality of the yellow copy of the NYPD missing-persons report she'd been given.

Eleven years old wasn't nearly old enough for Phaedra to face the world alone. It wasn't enough.

Phaedra's bedroom seemed to Anna like a poor choice of refuge from her grief. Every inch of it reminded her of her precious only child, of that fragile life she had carried inside her, who had shared her every breath for nine months, whose growing body had made Anna's blood her own—and who was ripped from her now, taken by force by a monster who couldn't possibly appreciate how unique and priceless beyond words Phaedra truly was.

But no other room in the town house held any fewer emotional traps. Uneven stacks of Phaedra's schoolbooks sat on the living room floor beside the sofa. In the TV room, one of her sweaters, still scented with her perfume, was draped over an armchair. Her folded soccer jersey lay on a chair in the kitchen. A pair of her sneakers rested beside the front door in the foyer.

There wasn't a room in the house that didn't echo with her absence. It went through Anna like a needle, stitching her every thought with anguish.

A menagerie of stuffed animals perched on the shelf above Phaedra's bed, gazing down with unblinking eyes and cipher-like faces that Anna invested with her own terror and grief.

Most forlorn of all was Phaedra's beloved plush toy rabbit, Clarence, who reclined against a rumpled pillow, looking woefully incomplete without the girl's arms wrapped around him.

Anna's eyes burned from more than twenty-one hours marked by uncontrollable crying jags and no sleep. She didn't want to sleep. Whenever she closed her eyes, she was haunted by visions of her daughter wounded or abused or dying. All that waited for her on the other side of slumber were nightmares—she *knew* it.

Instead she hovered by the phone, praying for it to ring, silently begging it to bring her any piece of good news, any reason to keep believing this would somehow not end in tragedy. She felt like a ghost haunting her own life, a gray shade watching herself go numb.

Recriminations surfaced when her thoughts became idle. *I should've spent more time with her,* she berated herself. *Why didn't I hire help? Why did I think I had to do everything? Bobby left us enough money. I could've paid someone to do the cooking and the cleaning so I could be there to walk her home.* Just when she thought her tears had run dry, she found more. *I should've been there. This is all my fault.*

The doorbell rang.

Its sonorous high-low chiming reverberated inside the house as Anna bolted from Phaedra's bed and scrambled downstairs. It could be Phaedra returned home without her keys. It could be the police with her daughter in tow. A neighbor with information. Maybe a local TV news crew willing to put Phaedra's picture on the air and get the word out.

She skipped the bottom two steps, dashed to the front door, undid its three locks and bolts, and pulled it open.

There was no one there.

The stoop, the sidewalks, and the street all were deserted. From corner to corner, she saw no one. For a moment she wondered if she had imagined the doorbell—then she looked down.

A padded yellow envelope lay on the stoop at her feet.

She reached down and picked it up. It was lightweight, sealed, and had nothing written on either side of it. There was a small bulge near its bottom left corner. Another look up and down the block gave no sign of who had left it there, but Anna had a paranoid sensation of being watched. She carried the envelope inside the house and shut the door. Then she lifted the package to eye level and brought it close to study it.

A shrill digital ringtone split the air. Startled, she dropped the envelope. She stumbled after the ringing parcel as it tumbled across the hardwood floor. Seconds later she caught it, ripped open its top flap, and pulled out a cheap prepaid cell phone. She pressed the TALK button. "Hello?"

"Mrs. Doyle," a man said, his voice unfamiliar and thick with an Eastern European accent that she couldn't place. *"Pay attention. We have your daughter, Phaedra."*

Anna's despair vanished; it was replaced by searing anger and absolute concentration on every word this man said. "Go on."

"Your husband, Robert, left you and your daughter a generous inheritance," he said. *"Life insurance, stocks, savings."*

She seethed. "He left us enough to get by."

"Don't be coy with me, Mrs. Doyle. He left you over twelve million dollars, plus that fancy town house you live in. So if you ever want to see your daughter alive again, it's time you learned how to share the wealth."

Anna imagined the man as some pale villain, then she calmed herself by picturing him dying in a barrage of police gunfire. The phone's plastic shell creaked in her crushing grip. "How much will it take to get Phaedra back?"

"All the cash," he said. *"The house you can keep."*

"How generous of you," she said with cold fury.

"First thing tomorrow," he said, ignoring her remark, *"have your lawyer liquidate your holdings and transfer them into negotiable bearer bonds."*

She interrupted, "I don't know what those are."

"Your lawyer will know." The man sounded impatient. *"Once we know you have the money, we will call you again on this phone with more instructions."*

Her jaw trembled from being clenched with such ferocity. It was an effort to relax her face enough to mutter, "Fine."

"One more thing. After we hang up, you'll be tempted to call the police or the FBI. Don't. We know everything they do. The officers who took your report last night were named Cleary and Indyk. Their sergeant's name was Bishop. And they told you to call a detective named Dellario if your daughter's not back by tonight. The last four digits of your report's case number are three, six, one, and nine. . . . Should I go on?"

"No," Anna said. Her voice was calm but her heart was filled with murder. "I get the point."

"If you call them, we'll know. And your daughter will die in pain . . . and in pieces. Get the money and wait for our call." He hung up, the line went dead, and the cell phone in Anna's hand switched back to standby mode.

Anna stood with her back to the front door and stared at the phone in her hand. She wanted to feel relieved that Phaedra was alive. *I should be grateful,* she told herself. *It's just about money.* But she wasn't grateful, and she wasn't relieved; she was furious. Her daughter was being used to steal everything her husband had left them. Bobby hadn't been born rich; he'd earned his money, and unlike many of his so-called peers, he'd always taken charity seriously. His generosity and compassion for others had been a big part of what had attracted Anna to him in the first place. And now a bunch of thugs were threatening Phaedra's life to steal her inheritance.

Anna wanted to call the police or the FBI, but the man on the phone had known enough specific details of her meeting with the cops that she didn't dare. If she defied the kidnappers and they weren't bluffing, she would never forgive herself. Tears ran down her cheeks. She felt powerless and terrified and enraged, and so completely overwhelmed that she wanted to scream. Taking a deep breath to calm herself, she leaned back and rested her head against the door.

Three sharp knocks from outside bounced her head off the door and forced a frightened yelp from her throat. Keyed up with adrenaline, Anna spun and yanked open the still-unlocked door.

A tall, fair-haired, clean-shaven man in a dark gray suit and the world's most boring blue tie smiled at her. He looked like an insurance salesman or maybe a Jehovah's Witness. His voice had a Midwestern flatness to it. "Hi," he said with a polite dip of his square, dimpled chin. Then he lifted his eyebrows slightly as he inquired, "Anna Doyle?"

All of Anna's years of living in New York told her to say nothing, to shut the door and lock it. But something about this guy, some quality that eluded her—perhaps the way he smiled or the timbre of his voice or some other intangible quality more felt than observed—told her to trust him.

"Yes," she said. "I'm Anna Doyle. Who are you?"

"My name is Tom Nash," he said.

Her suspicions lingered. "What do you want?"

"I've been asked to look for a missing person, and I think your daughter's disappearance might be connected."

Of course, Anna realized. *Boring suit, big smile. Private detective.*

"How did you find me?"

He reached into his jacket pocket, took out a folded sheet of yellow paper, and opened it to reveal one of the flyers she had posted. "I had your name and a neighborhood," he said. "So I called information and asked for your address." He refolded the paper and stuck it back in his pocket. "I'm sorry if I scared you by showing up at your door. I didn't mean to."

She couldn't help being amused by his low-key, "aw shucks" manner. "You're not from New York, are you?"

"No, ma'am," he said with another gentle smile. A cool breeze tousled his hair, but he didn't seem to mind.

Anna folded her arms to keep herself warm. "Look, if you're just here to score a quick buck—"

"I won't ask you for money," he cut in. "Fact is, I'm already working for someone else. I'm not here to scam you. I just want to help." He gestured past Anna toward her kitchen. "Would it be all right if I came in to talk?"

She had plenty of reasons not to let him in. He was a stranger. He could be lying—about who he was, about why he was there, about everything. She lived alone, and if he hurt her, it might be days or weeks before she was found. If something happened to her, then what would happen to Phaedra?

And the timing of his arrival, just after the ransom demand, was unsettling.

There was no logical reason to trust him. But she did.

"Come in," she said, and she ushered him inside.

Tom felt like a ridiculous imposter.

Anna led him to a small TV room, sat him on the sofa, planted herself in a chair across from him, and indulged him with patient answers while he asked her the kinds of questions he remembered hearing cops ask on TV shows: "When did you last speak to her?" . . . "What was she wearing?" . . . "What time did she leave her friend's house?"

He took notes as the dark-haired woman spoke, scribbling key details of her answers in his small spiral notepad. His blue ballpoint kept running dry and he would scratch it furiously in the margin to coax out the ink. Each time it happened, he felt a bit more foolish, but she didn't seem to notice.

"You say she left the, um . . ." He peeked at his notes.

"The Landrys," Anna said, filling in the name for him.

He expressed his thanks with an embarrassed smile and wrote it down. "Right. She left their house at seven o'clock?"

"That's what they told me," Anna said.

Tom flipped pages until he found the Landrys' address. "And you said they live just a couple minutes' walk away?"

"Yes, on Fourth Street, between Sixth and Seventh avenues."

He pointed to the block on his map of the local area. "Here?"

"Mm-hm, that's it." She got up wearily from her chair. "I'm guessing you'll want to see Phaedra's room next," she said, as if this was a bad thing.

He answered in a gentle voice, "If you don't mind."

Anna took a deep breath and let out a heavy sigh. Her tone was bitter. "The cops searched every inch of it yesterday."

Tom could tell that fact bothered her. "For what?"

"Proof my little girl ran away," Anna said. "Anything to avoid the hassle of actually looking for her."

He stood and took a slow half step toward her. "For what it's worth, I don't see it as a hassle." She looked up at him, the anger in her brown eyes fading. He added, "I'm here for just one reason, Mrs. Doyle—to help you find your daughter."

She nodded once and gestured with an outstretched arm toward the hallway. "All right, then. It's upstairs." Then she walked out of the living room, and Tom tucked his notepad in his jacket pocket while he followed her through the house.

Their footsteps echoed on the creaking hardwood floors. The inside of the town house was rich with the smells of lacquered wood, old books with leather bindings, and a subtle potpourri. Tom was no expert in antiques, but he had worked for enough people of means to know when he was in a wealthy person's home. From its furniture to its window treatments, the Doyles' home was sumptuous without being flashy. Its colors were muted and its lighting indirect, giving everything a soft glow of illumination with no harsh shadows.

At the bottom of the stairs, on a hutch beside the living room entrance, was a collection of framed photographs. Tom stopped to look at the pictures: Anna and a handsome young man, who Tom assumed was her husband, holding their infant daughter; the father caught in midstride, running behind Phaedra as she pedaled away from him on a blue bicycle; the man, Anna, and Phaedra huddled over a birthday cake with seven candles. Candid moments, fleeting episodes of happiness . . . all transformed by a moment's tragedy into bittersweet reminders. Tom's throat tightened with sorrow. *It could just as easily be my son missing someday,* he realized. *Or me missing from his life. How'm I supposed to keep him safe all the time? What if I'm not there when he needs me?*

Anna, who had started up the stairs, paused and looked back as she saw that Tom had halted in the foyer. "Something wrong?"

"No," he lied, blinking his eyes clear and composing himself. He picked up one of the photos, a family portrait. "Is this Phaedra's father?"

When he looked up for the answer, he saw tears in Anna's eyes and only then realized what he'd done.

"He was," Anna said, her voice unsteady. She wiped her eyes dry with the palm of one hand. "We lost him nine months ago." Tom set down the photo and moved to follow her upstairs. Instead of continuing ahead, she folded her arms across her slender torso and continued, "A drunk driver hit him. The doctors said it was over in an instant." A cynical grimace pursed her lips. "But when I wake up each day without him, it doesn't feel instant; it just keeps going, day after day after day. And now that he's gone . . . I just don't know what to do."

Her grief was raw and bitter and it pulled Tom down like quicksand. "I'm sorry," he said. "I don't know what to say."

Anna shook her head. "Nothing *to* say." She turned away and climbed the stairs. "Phaedra's room is at the end of the hall."

As he followed her upstairs, he thought of Karen's fear that someday one of his "errands" might end in disaster. He'd always insisted to Karen—and to himself—that there was nothing dangerous about what he did. Now he regretted not taking Karen's warnings more seriously.

He imagined her and his unborn son fending for themselves without him. Unlike Anna's late husband, Tom had no fortune to bequeath. If he passed, his wife and son would gain no inheritance—they would simply lose a husband and a father forever. *What if I make a mistake?* he wondered. *What if my luck runs out?* He tried to banish those questions from his mind, but Anna's tragedy had struck a deep chord inside him. *I'm no genius,* he admitted to himself. *Karen's right: sooner or later, I'll make a mistake. And then what?*

As he faced the worrisome fact that he had no answer to that question, Anna led him inside a sunlit second-floor bedroom.

Pastel blue walls and white trim gave the small room a soothing character. A shelf above the bed was crowded with stuffed animals of all kinds, but only one was on the bed, atop a pillow: a golden blond rabbit with floppy pink-felt ears, slightly crooked stitches that stood in for a nose, and black bead eyes. It radiated innocence, and its synthetic fur had the matted look of a well-loved companion toy.

Anna stood to one side, just inside the doorway, while Tom circuited the room, taking in its details. A faint trace of perfume lingered in the air.

The desk was topped with piled papers, some teen-oriented magazines, a pentagonal wooden jewelry box, and an old mug crammed with pens and pencils. A computer wire was stretched across the desk and dangled off the front of it. He asked, "Was there a computer here?"

"The police took it," Anna said. "To see if Phaedra made any suspicious online contacts."

Tom nodded and opened the door to the closet; its hinges squeaked. Inside, five identical school uniforms hung in a row. Behind them were several dresses, some blouses, and a handful of jackets of varying styles and weights for different seasons. Shoes were arranged in pairs on a metal organizer attached to the back of the closet door. Boxes of sneakers were stacked in one corner of the closet. In the other corner sat a violin case. "Tidy," Tom noted.

His comment drew a grin from Anna. "She always has been."

"You're lucky," Tom said, shutting the closet door. "My friends' kids treat their floors like big laundry piles." He took another look around and turned back toward Anna. "You're sure there's nothing missing?"

"Positive," she said. She pointed at the bed. "That's all the proof I need right there."

He looked at the bed and saw the empty gaze of the stuffed animal looking back at him. "The rabbit?"

"She calls him Clarence," Anna said. "She *never* travels without him, not even for a night at a friend's house. She's had him for years. I thought she'd outgrown him, but after her father died . . ." She shook her head. "Well, it is what it is. Believe me, if she ran away, Clarence wouldn't be here. He'd be with her."

There was no arguing with Anna's certainty. Out of curiosity, he walked to the bed and picked up the bunny. It was soft and rumpled and smelled like a perfumed old sock. More important, he could tell from the way its white muzzle fur had been carefully brushed that this toy was loved. He set the plush rabbit back on the pillow with care. "I believe you," he said.

He noticed that the light outside the bedroom window had grown dimmer and more reddish in the last few minutes. A glance at the clock confirmed that it was getting late. "I should get going," he said. "I still need to talk to the Landrys. Could you call and tell them I'm coming?"

"Sure," Anna said.

She led him out of the bedroom and back downstairs to the front door. He watched her undo the chain on the front door, retract the dead bolt, and twist the knob. She had opened the door barely a sliver when she hesitated and looked back at Tom with an expression of dread.

"What're you going to do if you find Phaedra?"

The question caught him off guard, in part because he hadn't thought that far ahead yet. After a moment's reflection, he said, "I'll call the cops. It's the law."

Anna's jaw clenched. Her eyes opened just a bit wider, and her grim countenance became one of fear. "Please don't," she said. "You can't."

Before he could insist that he had no choice, he saw just how frightened she was. "Why? What's wrong?" He watched Anna's emotional struggle play out in her twisting frowns and awkward, nervous fidgeting. She folded and unfolded her arms, shifted her weight from leg to leg, and let herself look at everything in the room except him. "Mrs. Doyle? Why can't we call the cops?"

Her voice was equal parts fear and fury. "Because the men who have my daughter will know if we do," she said, "and they'll kill her." She reached in her pants pocket and took out a slim disposable cell phone. "They left this on my doorstep just before you got here, and they used it to call me. They want every dollar my husband left me, by tomorrow, or Phaedra dies."

Fear churned a sickening swell of acid in Tom's empty stomach. "Ma'am, if there's been a ransom demand, you *have* to call the FBI."

"The kidnappers said they had people inside there, too," Anna said. Covering her eyes with one hand, she inhaled a deep breath and let it out in an angry sigh. "They know details from my police report. They even know the names of the cops who came here. If we call the law, *they'll know.*" She looked Tom in the eye. "Promise me: if you find her, you won't call the cops."

"I promise I'll do whatever it takes to get her home safe."

"No," Anna said, "don't change what I said." She poked his chest with her index finger. "Promise you won't call the cops."

"I can't," he said, regretting his words even as he spoke. Anna opened the door for him. He stepped out and looked back. "But I promise not to do anything that might put your daughter in danger. You have my word on that."

That pledge seemed to mollify her, for now. She crossed her arms and softened her tone. "You have my number," she said. "Call me if you find anything."

"And you have mine. Call if you need me, day or night."

She nodded her thanks. Then, with a slow push and a sad smile, she closed the door behind Tom with a heavy clack.

Tom ambled down the steps of the stately, narrow brownstone, turned left down the tree-lined street, and followed his map to the Landrys' home, two blocks west and one block north. Night would fall soon, and he wanted to finish up and find a place to spend the night. A place that wasn't the cab of his truck.

As he walked alone from one dim orange pool of lamplight to another, he shook off the paranoid sensation that he was being watched. *This whole mess has you keyed up,* he told himself. *Just relax and figure out one thing at a time.*

But he couldn't relax. If the kidnappers had told Anna the truth, then this situation had become even more potentially lethal than he'd feared. He might have to contend not just with whoever took Phaedra but with crooked cops, too.

"Whatever it is that sends me out on these errands, it's never given me more trouble than I could handle," he'd told Karen just the night before. "It's never put me in danger." He cast his thoughts skyward with a baleful stare. *God, if this is Your way of showing me You have sense of humor . . . I'm not laughing.*

7

NYPD detective Frank Kolpack was ready to kill someone for a cigarette.

He was on his eighth piece of spearmint gum in two hours. It wasn't helping one goddamn bit. Sure, he'd tried nicotine gum, just like every other recovering smoker he knew on the job, but he thought it tasted like shit—which, of course, hadn't stopped him from devouring the stuff. In less than a month, he'd gone from a pack-a-day habit with tobacco to a two-pack-a-day habit with the drugged gum.

Only one way to do this, he'd decided a few days earlier. *Cold turkey. No choice. Just gotta do it.*

It had sounded good in theory. But now he was slumped in the driver's seat of his Toyota sedan, which stank of stale cigarette smoke, and he was worried that at any moment he might start punching his dashboard and screaming obscenities just to vent the panic of his nicotine-starved brain. *Stay sharp,* he told himself, repeating it like a mantra. To keep his shaking hands occupied, he wound his empty spearmint gum wrappers around his left index finger, wrapping them tighter on each turn until he cut off the circulation and turned his fingertip blue.

Focus on the job, he commanded himself. *Eye on the ball.*

Peeking over the door's edge, he looked through the car window at the front of the Doyle residence. It had been over an hour since he'd watched the blond stranger knock on the door and go inside. The visitor had talked his way inside before Frank could find his digital camera and snap a shot of the guy. Now he had to wait for him to come back out. *Better this way,* Frank told himself. *Had his back to me before. He'll be facing me on his way out. Just don't miss the shot, genius.*

The sun had begun to set, steeping the tree-canopied street in shadow. Frank picked up his camera and took a test shot, just to make certain he had enough light to get the picture when the blond man came out of the brownstone.

The image in the viewfinder was crisp and well exposed. He was about to turn the camera off and put it back on the passenger seat when the front door of Anna Doyle's town house opened, and the man emerged.

Frank lifted the camera back into position, zoomed in, and waited for its autofocus to settle on the man's face. Just before it could lock on, the man turned around for a few more words with Anna, leaving Frank looking at the back of the guy's head.

"Come on," Frank mumbled, trying to hold the camera steady. "Wrap it up."

The man turned back in Frank's direction. Frank snapped a few good shots as the visitor descended the front steps of the brownstone, then he ducked low, provoking sharp twinges of pain in his lower back as he hid beneath the steering wheel. He heard the blond man walk away behind his car.

I bet I know where he's going, Frank mused. He sat up slowly and raised his seat to its normal position, mindful of the risk of being seen. The visitor was walking against traffic on Fifth Street, which meant that Frank would have to circle the block and try to pick him up on Eighth Avenue.

Frank turned the key in the ignition and shifted the car into drive. He pulled away from the curb. Drove a bit faster than was safe for the neighborhood. Cut someone off on Prospect Park West. Made a tire-squealing turn onto Sixth Street without signaling. Sped down the narrow residential road to Eighth Avenue, only to get stuck at the damn light.

By the time Frank merged into traffic on Eighth, the blond man had already crossed the avenue and was heading for Seventh Avenue. Figuring he could get ahead of his surveillance target, Frank changed lanes to make a left onto Fourth Street. Thanks to a road crew, passage to the street had been choked down to a single narrow lane, and because the city preferred to do its road work at night, a man in an orange reflector vest blocked Frank's car while a bulldozer jerked back and forth in a six-point about-face.

All Frank could do was seethe as the second hand of his watch ticked a slow circle on his wrist. He cursed under his breath and wished for a smoke.

Finally, the road crew waved him through the turn. He rolled to a stop for a red light at Seventh Avenue and saw the blond man moving at a quick step along the next block. Lagging about thirty yards behind him, Frank drove slowly down the block and turned off his car's headlights. The blond man arrived on another brownstone's doorstep. Frank pulled in beside a fire hydrant because it was the only gap in the street's endless line of bumper-to-bumper parked vehicles.

In less than a minute, the visitor talked his way inside the town house. As the door shut, Frank dislodged a yellow envelope from the narrow gap beside his seat. He opened it and pulled out a thick sheaf of photocopied pages.

It took him a few seconds to thumb through the standard forms and typewritten statements to find the responding officers' original report. Running his finger along the side of the page, he found what he was looking for: the address where Phaedra Doyle had last been seen. It was the same building into which the blond man had just been ushered.

So much for his visit with Anna being a coincidence, Frank decided. He dug in his pocket for his cell phone, pulled it free, and flipped it open. He speed-dialed the Russians and waited while it rang a few times.

Jarek, a slow-witted enforcer, answered the call. *"What is it, Kolpack?"*

Oh, goody, Frank brooded. *The ape's learned how to use caller ID.* "We've got a problem in Park Slope. Put the big man on."

Muffled noise from the other end of the line lasted for a few long moments. Then he heard the heavily accented voice of his longtime associate, Viktor. *"What's the problem?"*

"Anna didn't follow instructions," Frank said. "She called in some help."

Viktor's voice was gruff. *"Cops or feds?"*

"Neither. Looks like a private eye." He used his shoulder to hold the phone to his ear while he unwrapped a new stick of gum. "We have to deal with this. As in *now.*"

"Just tell us where he is," Viktor said, his deadly intentions implicit in his tone. *"We'll do the rest."*

Frank had already twisted half the length of the empty gum wrapper around his finger. "Don't kill him," he said between chews. "If you go dropping bodies, this turns into a homicide case, and that's the last thing we need. Just rough him up and send him packing."

"Relax, Frank," Viktor said. *"He's as good as gone."*

Tom left the Landry residence with a few more notes about Phaedra Doyle's pastimes and not much else. Night had already fallen, and a soft groan of cool wind rustled the leaves in the canopy of branches above the street, dappling the sidewalk with moving shadows in the dim lamplight.

A chill in the air gave him a small shiver. *Wish I'd bought a trenchcoat to go with this suit.* Shaking his feet to relieve the aching in his arches, he wished he had splurged on better shoes as well. *Just have to tough it out till I get back to the truck,* he told himself. He was looking forward to changing back into his regular clothes and finding a place where he could crash until morning.

There was just one thing left for him to do before he packed it in for the day. He was trying to figure out where, in the short distance between the Landrys' and the Doyles' homes, Phaedra could possibly have been taken. The avenues were all busy with pedestrian traffic, even on a weekend night, and the cross streets were generally well lit and packed from corner to corner with buildings that had not an inch of air between them.

He stopped at the corner of Fourth Street and Seventh Avenue and looked around. *The most direct route back to the Doyles' house would be the way I came,* he reasoned. *Then again, the streets out here are a grid, so she might have walked across on Fourth Street and then down Eighth Avenue instead of Seventh.* He crossed the avenue and continued east on Fourth Street.

Along the south side of the street, a short distance from the corner, he noticed a large, empty parking lot whose gate was wide open. Something about it commanded his interest. He stopped and studied it for a few seconds. Compelled to look closer, he slipped into the lot.

To his right was a tall, massive structure that stretched the length of the block from Fourth Street to Fifth Street. It was a high school, he recalled, having noted it on his way to the Landrys' building. Its foundation of weathered white concrete supported a blocky façade of faded red brick. Near the lot's entrance, a handicapped-access ramp with steel railings led to a pair of squat green metal doors beneath high squared arches. Majestically tall windows were fronted by black iron bars. Between the north and south wings of the building was a large gap, where a below-ground-level courtyard and some service areas were partitioned from the parking lot by a tall chain-link fence.

Opposite the school was a high blank cement wall. It was topped by an uneven length of chain-link fence in which a handful of tennis balls had become lodged. Behind that rose the concrete flanks of back-to-back apartment buildings, whose sides were marked by several columns of small windows.

Most of the lot was steeped in shadow. Its only illumination was spillage from the nearby streetlamps, the fixtures above the school doors, and, in the middle of the lot, a single floodlight mounted near the roof of the Fifth Street apartment building.

Tom stopped in the shadows and fished a small Maglite from one of his jacket's inside pockets. With a twist he activated the compact flashlight, and a few more turns of its headpiece focused the beam. He swept it over the lot's darkened areas, looking for anything unusual.

Beyond the fence, near the school, he saw a row of trash bins. Even without his flashlight, he would have known they were there; they exuded a powerful stench, a combination of rotting meat and decaying vegetables. He winced and wrinkled his nose. *Is there any corner of this city that doesn't reek?*

The narrow circle of light passed over a slick portion of asphalt that cast rainbow reflections. Tom crouched beside it for a closer look. It was an oil stain, a recent one. He sampled the oil with his fingertips; it smelled fresh, and there was a decent amount of it on the ground.

Looks like someone's engine has a leak, he figured. He was about to wipe his fingers clean on his pant leg when he remembered that he was wearing a suit. After a few moments of searching in vain for a stray napkin or paper towel, he smeared his fingertips clean on the sides of his black shoes.

Tom continued to search the pavement as he moved toward the back of the lot. It was completely walled off from the street by more chain link. He climbed some concrete stairs to find a gate. A heavy chain was wrapped around it and secured with a padlock. *Dead end,* Tom thought with a sigh.

Then he turned to leave, and his flashlight beam caught a gap in the fence at his feet. He kneeled down and tugged on the chain link. A large section of the lower corner lifted away easily. *More than big enough for a person to slip through,* he realized. *Which would make this a perfect shortcut for a kid.*

He started walking a methodical back-and-forth pattern, his beam sweeping the asphalt at his feet. Near the school's fence, outside the floodlight's reach, a few small metallic glints caught his eye. He stepped over to the closest one and aimed his light directly onto it.

It looked like a short piece of striped wire, or maybe two

wires twisted together: one silver, the other white. The ends of it were frayed, and it curled like a pig's tail. He pivoted slightly, and his beam revealed that he was only a few feet from the oil stain he'd seen minutes earlier.

Turning back, he reached down to pick up the wire—then he heard something that made him stop.

Footsteps. Getting closer.

He turned off his flashlight, stood, and looked to his right toward Fourth Street. Coming in through the lot's main entrance were two large young men. One was bald and wore a black tank top, black jeans, and combat boots. His companion wore a battered black leather jacket and sported a bleached crewcut.

They moved with a purpose, and Tom had a sinking feeling he knew what it was. He turned to make a run for the break in the fence—and saw the dark shapes of two more club-fisted young men slipping through it from Fifth Street. One wore camouflage; the other was wearing a dark tracksuit.

Cursing softly, Tom pocketed his Maglite and backed toward the school, determined to keep his attackers in front of him . . . for all the good it would do.

Within moments they surrounded him. The largest, the one with the bleached crewcut, slammed his hand into Tom's chest and shoved him back against the fence. His accent was heavy and Slavic. "You ask a lotta questions," Crewcut said. He pointed his finger at Tom's face. "Not smart." Then he glanced at his friend in the camouflage. "Show him why."

On his left, Tom saw Camouflage cock his fist. Tom raised his hands to defend himself.

The punch came from the bald guy on the right.

It was like getting hit with a brick. His head snapped left

with the blow, and time slowed as the dull meaty sound of impact echoed inside his skull. Tom had been in fights before, but he couldn't remember ever getting hit like this.

Another brutal blow caught him in the gut, right below his ribs, and knocked his breath from his chest. He doubled over, powerless to catch himself. Something hard smashed into his nose and mouth, sending a ruby flash of pain through his darkening vision. He fell sideways against the fence. His ears barely registered the ringing vibrations in the chain link as he hit the ground.

A salty froth of bloody spittle welled inside his mouth. Metallic-smelling currents of bright crimson poured from his nostrils. Then a mad flurry of kicks bashed his torso from both sides and left him no direction to roll for escape.

All at once it stopped. Two pairs of hands clamped around his arms and yanked him halfway to his feet. Another hand clutched his chin and lifted it. Crewcut held Tom's face. Tracksuit and Camouflage kept Tom propped up. Baldy paced behind Tom, who was in too much pain to turn his head to watch him. Then the bald man's beefy forearm reached over Tom's shoulder and locked around his throat.

Crewcut slapped Tom's face gingerly. "I was told not to kill you," he said. "And I'm supposed to make sure you can walk away when we're done." A sinister smirk possessed his face. "But no one said you have to be recognizable." The crewcut man dipped his hand into his jacket pocket. He pulled out a set of brass knuckles. "Smile. Then say good-bye to your teeth."

Slipping through the gap in the fence on Tom's right, on the far edge of his vision, was a silhouetted figure wearing a trenchcoat and wielding what looked like a long and slender club.

Unable to move, breathe, or cry out, all Tom could do was stare in horror as Crewcut slipped his brass knuckles into place on his right hand.

I'm a dead man, Tom realized.

Trenchcoat charged at Tom with an axe handle cocked high. It fell in a blur, and the next thing Tom heard was the crack of wood against flesh and bone—

—and Crewcut fell and rolled away as if he'd been hit by a truck.

Crewcut's three buddies dropped Tom and went after the Good Samaritan. Tracksuit threw a wild punch at Trenchcoat, who stepped clear and swung the axe handle in a graceful arc that broke Tracksuit's forearm with a wet snap. A moment later, Tracksuit's howls of agony echoed across the city, and lights snapped on in half a dozen apartment windows that faced the parking lot.

The newcomer with the axe handle stood between Tom and the thugs. The bald man said something in a foreign tongue to Tracksuit, who retreated toward the main gate. Then Baldy and Camouflage lifted their groaning friend with the crewcut to his feet and half carried, half dragged him away into the night.

Tom watched all this from the ground, on his back, too stunned to move. Then he got a good look at his rescuer.

It was a woman. A breeze billowed her trenchcoat, revealing her long legs and shapely torso, all clothed in supple black leather. Her elegant bronze cheekbones and beguiling, slightly Asian-looking brown eyes were framed by raven tresses. Her every movement exuded confidence, strength, and sensuality.

She looked down at Tom and extended her hand. "Y'all right, *papi?*" she asked in a sultry-sweet voice as she helped him up.

"I'm alive," Tom said. "Thanks to you."

He wiped a thick sheen of warm blood from his chin and upper lip. His new suit was filthy, and the shirt and tie were bloodstained. He wiped his hand clean on the front of his pant leg, then offered it to his new friend. "Tom Nash," he said with a weak but grateful smile.

"Erin Sanchez," said the woman, whose handshake was firm.

"Fine piece of hickory you got there," Tom said. "I'm lucky you came along when you did."

"Luck had nothin' to do with it." A mischievous smile brightened her face. "I heard you pray for help."

8

"Yeah, I'm a little scuffed up," Tom said, mumbling through bloodstained teeth into the cell phone tucked against his left shoulder. He reclined the driver's seat of his truck a few degrees. "But you should see the other four guys."

Karen didn't sound amused. *"Is that supposed to make me feel better?"*

"Hang on," he said, his nose and lips throbbing against the paper-towel-wrapped frozen gel pack in his right hand. A motley assortment of athletic cold packs were arranged against his torso, soothing the deep aches in his ribs. "I'm the one who got beat up, and I'm supposed to be making *you* feel better?"

"So you admit you got beat up."

"What is this? The Inquisition?" He moved the small gel pack to the bruise beside his right eye as he swallowed a bit of salty-metallic blood. "Yes, I took a minor ass kicking. On a scale of one to ten, I'd give it a four."

She sighed heavily. *"Fine, make jokes. But if you start feeling dizzy or sick, or if you vomit or start reacting to bright light or loud noises—"*

"Go to the ER and get treated for a concussion, I know." He had to smile. Even on maternity leave, she was first and foremost a nurse. "I'll be fine, honey."

"You say that, but half the time you don't know how to put a Band-Aid on correctly," she chided. *"I'd worry less if you were here, so I could help you."*

"Relax, I have help," he said. He debated how much to tell her about Erin; he wasn't sure if it would comfort her or trouble her more. "I met someone else like me, another person who hears prayers. That's who saved my butt."

"Saved you? As in you nearly got yourself killed?"

"I think you're not seeing the big picture here."

"No, I heard you—someone else who hears prayers. That's great. Now they can take over and you can come home, right?"

"Not exactly," Tom said.

Erin appeared at the truck's passenger door and tapped lightly on the window. Tom reached over and unlocked the door. Erin opened it, and a cool breeze followed her in. She closed the door and set two paper bags at her feet.

Finally, Karen asked, *"Does your friend have a name?"*

"Erin," he said, even as he noted the subtle fragrance of her perfume.

"And what does he do?"

It took Tom a second to realize that Karen had misheard the name as "Aaron."

"It hasn't really come up," he said. Rather than spend the next hour arguing with Karen about why it was no big deal that he was driving around New York at night with a sexy young woman, he decided not to correct his wife's flawed assumption. "To be honest, there's a lot I still don't know about what's going on."

"No kidding," Karen said. *"It sounds like you're already in over your head. Why don't you let the cops take over?"*

"Tempting, but it's not that simple," he said. "The ransom swap's tomorrow, and the mother's convinced the law can't be trusted. Calling them in might do more harm than good. Until we figure out what's going on, we can't risk it."

From the passenger seat, Erin glanced askew at Tom and raised a curious eyebrow. He imagined Karen making much the same face on the other end of the phone call as she said, *" 'We,' huh? So you and Aaron are partners now?"*

"For the moment." He frowned and set the semifrozen gel pack in his lap. "Anyway, I need to go. It's late, and we have a lot to do tonight."

"Be careful," Karen said firmly. *"No heroics, okay?"*

"Not a chance. I'm happy just to be walking right now."

She softened her tone. *"Call me in the morning?"*

"Count on it," he said. "Sweet dreams, love."

"Stay safe, sweetie. G'night."

"G'night." The connection clicked off as Karen hung up.

He closed his cell phone, connected it to the charger plugged into his dashboard lighter socket, and straightened his seatback. Rubbing his stiff neck, he asked Erin, "What's for dinner?"

The leather-clad Latina reached down, picked up one of the paper bags, and handed it to him. "Best egg rolls in Brooklyn," she said. "Dumplings aren't half bad, either."

He pried open the stapled-shut bag and was rewarded with the rich aroma of deep-fried food. Inside were two egg rolls in grease-stained wax-paper sleeves and a cardboard takeout carton with a narrow wire handle. "Healthy," he deadpanned, then he pulled out one of the egg rolls and offered it to Erin.

She waved it off and picked up her paper bag. "Got my own, thanks."

His hunger took over, and he tore away the wax paper and bit off a third of the crispy treat in one bite. It was almost too hot to eat, but it tasted so good, so perfectly greasy and decadent, that he just didn't care. *Deep-fried, carb-loaded goodness,* he thought ecstatically as he chewed with his eyes closed. *Exactly what I'm not supposed to be eating.* He felt guilty for a second, then took another bite.

He finished the first egg roll and felt it settle like a rock in his stomach, then he cast a sidelong glance at Erin. She pushed the last bite of her egg roll past her ruby-hued lips—which closed in a tight smirk around the tip of her index finger as she noticed his stare. She pulled her finger away and chewed for a second, then said with her mouth still half-full, "Not bad, eh, *papi?*"

"Fantastic," he said, mostly talking about the egg rolls. He reached into the bag, pulled out the second egg roll, then grabbed the carton of dumplings and opened it. More deep-fried sinfulness. He looked in the bag for a fork but found only a pair of chopsticks and a few napkins.

Holding up the chopsticks, he threw a quizzical look at Erin. "I don't know how to use these."

She narrowed her eyes, then plucked the sticks from his hand. In a flash, she produced a butterfly knife from her trenchcoat, opened it with a lightning-fast series of flips in one hand, and slashed at the chopsticks. With one stroke, she shaved off two narrow strips of soft wood, turning the sticks' flat ends to points. Planting them back in Tom's hand, she said, "Here. Go spearfishing."

Tom stared at the now-lethal chopsticks while Erin's butterfly knife danced closed in her hand and disappeared back into her coat pocket. "Thanks," he said, stabbing the sticks through a dumpling. As Erin pulled a cold-sweating can of root beer from her bag and popped the tab, he added, "So . . . we both hear prayers. What're the odds, huh?"

Her brow creased as she muffled a mocking snort of laughter. "You're kidding, right?" She studied his face and wrinkled her brow at his uncomprehending stare. As if she was stating the obvious to a complete moron, she added, "It's the most common ability we have."

Now Tom was lost. "Common?"

She recoiled slightly from his ignorance, as if it were contagious. "Well, what would you call it? It happens to all of us. Well, the Seekers, anyway—"

"All of us?" The more she spoke, the less Tom understood. "Who's *all* of us? Hell, who's *us*? What's a Seeker?"

His question left her speechless. She set her open can in the drink holder between them and shifted in her seat to face him. "You're serious? You don't know what you are? What *we* are?"

He turned his palms up, shrugged, and shook his head.

She blinked and shook her head in stunned disbelief. "That's crazy." Drawing a deep breath, she looked back at him, half-lit by a distant streetlamp and the headlights of a passing car. "Haven't you heard of the Called?"

"No."

"Well, that's what we are. I mean, it's what we're part of. There are lots of people like us in the world—people who hear prayers and try to help."

Tom felt as if the floor was falling out from under his entire life. It was both comforting and humbling to know that his gift wasn't as unique as he'd thought. Feeling his dinner churn in his stomach, he asked, "How many of us are there?"

"Like, an exact number? *Pfft.* No clue. Sages might know."

"Sages? What—"

Erin held up a hand to cut off his questions. "Sorry, I'm not doing this right. Never had to be the teacher before."

Tom cocked a curious eyebrow at her. "Teacher?"

"You know, like in those old kung fu movies?" She flashed a teasing smile. "When the student is ready, the master appears."

"And you're the master?"

"Compared to you, I am."

"And that would make me—"

"Grasshopper. Now gimme a second." She held up a silencing hand again. "Trying to remember how this goes."

Tom waited while she stared out the windshield for several seconds, collecting her thoughts. A few more cars cruised past on Ninth Street.

"Okay," she continued at last, "eighteen years ago I got schooled by a guy named Isaiah. Now it's my turn to school you. Breaks down like this: Me and you are part of a group known as the Called. The Sages are kind of in charge; they know about weird old stuff and make big plans. Seers help us tell who's human, who's one of the Called, and who're the Scorned. Sentinels guard people, places, and things, and the Seekers—that's us—go from place to place and help people." She shrugged. "Least, that's the big picture."

All he could do was stare at her, dumbfounded. Finally, he broke the spell of his confusion with a slow blink and said, "You've gotta be kidding me."

"Hey, I didn't make this up. I'm just the one tellin' you how it is."

"Have you ever seen any of this with your own eyes?"

She laughed into her fist for a second. With a sweeping

flourish of her hand, she replied, "I've seen things you wouldn't *believe.* You think people like us get cool powers? Wait'll you see what the Sages can do."

"Powers? What powers? You mean hearing prayers?"

"That's part of it," Erin said. "But I'm talking about the other stuff. Haven't you ever noticed that you've been good at getting people to do the right thing?"

He thought about it. "I guess. Not that it did me any good when I was trying to get a better deal on my mortgage."

"That's 'cause it don't work like that," Erin said. "We got a way of puttin' people at ease, givin' 'em a shove in the right direction—but it only works when we're doin' good. Try to use it for yourself, and it don't work."

Nodding, Tom said, "That sounds about right."

"Even this thing you an' me got goin'," she said. "How easy we get along? That's part of it, too. When we're doin' right, we got a way with people."

She was starting to make sense to him. They'd known each other for less than ninety minutes, but already she felt as familiar to him as an old friend. "What else can we do?" he asked, spearing another dumpling and popping it into his mouth.

"That's about it," she said. "We hear prayers, get involved, try to help people do the right thing. But we each have one special talent."

"Which is . . . ?"

"Everybody's different," she explained while he ate. "Nobody can tell you what your special gift is. That you gotta figure out for yourself."

"Well, I don't know about you, but except for hearing prayers and talking people into stuff, I've never had any powers."

Erin shrugged. "Maybe you're a late bloomer. Wouldn't be the first. We don't get all our gifts at once. You get 'em when you need 'em. But trust me, when the time comes for you to get your power, you'll *know* what it is."

"I can hardly wait." He speared his last dumpling. "And the Sages and the other guys? They have powers, too?"

"*Oh, yeah.* Sentinels get powers like ours, but they don't hear prayers. They go where the Sages tell them, and they guard people and places. A Seer's only gift is reading people's auras—telling Called from Scorned, Seekers from Sentinels, yada yada. And the biggest powers go to the Sages, who call the shots."

"So we work for them?"

She grimaced. "Not exactly. Sometimes we get orders from the Sages, but most of the time they let us do our own thing, 'cause Seekers are the only ones who hear prayers. Sages are the generals; we're the foot soldiers."

"If we're part of this big thing, does that mean we can call in some backup? Or some replacements?"

Erin shook her head. "No. Ain't exactly enough of us to go around, know what I mean?" She lowered her window, then crumpled her paper bag and tossed it into a nearby trash can. "Look, we better motor if we're gonna find this kid in one piece."

He protested, "Whoa! Hang on. How'd we get these powers? Why us? And you keep mentioning the Scorned—who are they?"

"Chill. We'll get to that later. Right now we gotta move, okay?"

"No, *not* okay," Tom said, angry. "You can't just dump all this in my lap and expect me to roll with it. I need to know what the hell I'm getting into here."

Erin looked flustered. "Fine." She sighed, looked out her window for a moment, then continued, "I *don't know* how we get our powers, okay? Maybe the Sages do. As for the Scorned . . ." She frowned. "They're a lot like us. Same castes—Seekers, Sentinels, Sages—and they have powers, too. But when we try to help people, the Scorned try to cut us off at the knees." She looked at Tom. "All you really need to know about them is that they're the enemy."

"How long has this been going on?"

"To hear the Sages tell it? Forever."

Tom shook his head in disbelief. "But what's it about?"

She rolled her eyes. *"Pfft.* Who knows? Some people call it good versus evil, or Heaven against Hell. I once heard a Sage tell Isaiah it had something to do with a bridge, but when I asked about it, they gave me the silent treatment." Fixing him with a stare, she added impatiently, "Look, it's been fun playin' Twenty Questions, but are you ready to go look for this kid yet?"

"Sure," Tom said, satisfied that Erin had told him as much as she could.

She took the paper bag from his hand, scrunched it, and chucked it with another NBA-worthy lob into the trash. Then she pointed forward. "Drive straight and merge onto Gowanus North."

Tom keyed the ignition, shifted the truck into gear, checked his blind spot, and pulled away from the curb. "Where are we going?"

"Over the bridge, into Manhattan."

There was no hiding his anxiety. "Why? What's there?"

Erin smiled. "If I'm right? The guys who beat the shit out of you."

"We're not looking to jam you up," the Internal Affairs investigator told her as he shut the door to the 71st Precinct's interview room. "We just want to talk."

Detective Katharine Bailey decided he was full of shit. IAB was *always* looking to jam someone up. *Damned if it'll be me,* she promised herself, sliding onto the hard gray metal chair on the far side of the bolted-down table.

"I'm Detective John Landsman," he continued, opening a leather flip-fold to show his shield. He was lanky with close-cropped but unruly black hair and thick glasses that made him look more dopey than bookish. He gestured at his partner, a short, curvy woman who wore her light brown hair in a stylish bob. "This is Detective Lisa Cadan." Cadan held up her own IAB badge and nodded at Bailey.

"Good for you," Bailey said. "Now what? We sing 'Kumbaya'?"

Cadan leaned against the wall on Bailey's right. She propped up one foot behind her. A border of black scuffs ringed the room at knee height, evidence of decades of people perching there in that pose. "Relax," Cadan said. "It's not you we're looking at." Even from a few feet away, the woman's breath stank of bad station-house coffee and menthol cigarettes.

"Great," Bailey said. "You just want me to help you screw someone else."

Landsman held out his open hands, palms up. "We just want you to help us tell the signal from the noise."

She wondered if he thought using wiretap slang made him sound cool. Squinting up at the sickly glow of a weakly stuttering fluorescent light, she folded her arms and said, "Cut to the chase. I have work to do."

"Detective First Grade Frank Kolpack," Cadan said, like it meant something.

Bailey shrugged. "What about him?"

"Tell us what you know," Landsman said.

"He's a douchebag," she said. "He's also having a hell of a time quitting smoking." She looked at Cadan. "Maybe he can give you some pointers."

Cadan folded her arms and swapped an irritated glance with Landsman, who continued, "Have you ever known Detective Kolpack to fail to log in evidence? Or to tamper with evidence before logging it in?"

Bailey looked back and forth between the pair. In fact, she *had* suspected Kolpack of those offenses and of planting drugs and weapons on quite a few suspects. But what she suspected and what she could prove were two very different things, and she didn't plan on sticking her neck out to IAB on a hunch.

"No," she said. "I've never *known* Frank to do that."

"What about scuttling a case?" Cadan asked. "Did you know his clearance rate on kidnappings is less than twenty percent? Less than thirty on homicides?"

Bailey rolled her eyes. "So what? Doesn't mean he's bent. Just a shitty detective." To Landsman she added, "Why don't you go get me a Coke?"

Unfazed, he replied, "If he's such a bad detective, why's he still on the job?"

" 'Cause being stupid isn't a crime. Luckily for you."

Landsman and Cadan stiffened but kept their poker faces. After a steadying breath, Cadan unfolded her arms, stepped forward, and asked, "Do you know if Detective Kolpack has a cell phone?"

"Of course," Bailey said. "We all do."

Cadan nodded and reached inside her jacket. She pulled out a letter-sized envelope and slapped it onto the interview table. A dozen grainy monochrome surveillance photos spilled from it in a fan-shaped overlap. "Then why's he going through four disposable cell phones a week?"

Bailey stared at the images on the table. Frank buying a stack of prepaid phones in a Bedford-Stuyvesant bodega. Talking on one in his car. Chucking one into a garbage bin in an alley. Variations on the theme.

She looked up. "Who's he been talking to?"

"Other disposable phones," Landsman said. "They all get ditched with minutes left on them, so kids find 'em and fill the logs with unrelated calls. Makes it almost impossible to get tap warrants."

"Shit," Bailey muttered. Frank was using classic organized-crime tactics. Anyone who'd ever done a tour in Narcotics knew the drill. It was so simple that even street gangs had taught themselves to do it. She sighed. "Why tell me?"

"Your LT said you and Kolpack get along," Cadan said.

"Did he?" Bailey said, unable to hold back a grim chuckle. "Leave it to a lieutenant to sugarcoat a shit sandwich." The next part she enunciated with care, to make sure the IAB half-wits would understand. "Kolpack and I do not 'get along.' He wants to get in my pants, and I"—she patted her holstered sidearm for emphasis—"would rather fuck my Glock."

"Thank you for that lovely mental image," Landsman said with unruffled sarcasm. "Your erotic predilections aside, do you think you could take advantage of Detective Kolpack's interest in you?"

"To do what?"

Cadan replied, "Watch for suspicious behavior. See if there's a link between the cases he buries and whoever's talking to him on those throwaway phones. Maybe tie him to something bigger."

Bailey narrowed her eyes. "In other words, you want me to do your job for you. And instead of working my own cases, you want me to spend my time taking notes so I can be a rat for yours." She pushed her chair back from the table and stood. "No thanks."

Landsman said in a flat, calm voice, "More people on the job in this precinct have caught bullets in the six years since Kolpack got here than were shot in the *twenty-six* years before that—combined."

Frozen in place, Bailey replied, "Could be a coincidence."

"Could be," Cadan said. "Probably isn't."

"All we're saying," Landsman added, "is that you might want to do yourself a favor and help us get a bead on this guy—before he sends a bullet *your* way." He opened the door for her and stepped out of her path. "Think about it."

She glared at the pair for a moment, then walked back out to the squad room, a low-ceilinged pen with one wall of barred opaque windows, too many desks packed into too little space, and the world's least comfortable chairs. She sat down at her desk and took a bite of her sausage pizza and a swig of her Diet Coke. Both were lukewarm. Now, in addition to being exhausted, she was disgusted, too.

The IAB detectives slipped quietly out of the room and made a beeline for the back stairs. Bailey frowned; they hadn't told her much about Frank that she hadn't already known or at least suspected. And they were right: if he was mobbed up, then anyone who followed him on a call would run the risk of seeing the wrong thing at the wrong time—and getting capped with prejudice.

Dropping the remains of her dinner in the trash, she reminded herself that for a cop there were only two things worse than being a rat.

One was being a cop-killer.

The other was being dead.

9

Phaedra Doyle had put nearly every inch of her cell to the test. It had taken pretty much the entire day—minus a break for lunch when the man in the gas mask had come back at one o'clock, as he'd promised—and she was no closer to finding a way out than she had been when she'd first woken up.

Worse, she was wiped-out tired and totally starving.

Looking around, she sulked at her failed attempts at sabotage.

She had pulled on the bed and kicked at its legs to knock loose the bolts that held it down. It hadn't budged.

The plastic chair at her desk wasn't tall enough to wedge under the doorknob and jam the door shut. Its back had cracked when she'd swung it at the door, and now the fracture poked her in the back when she sat in the chair.

Way to go, she chided herself. *No place to sit now but the bed.*

Adding to her failures, the bed now had no sheets. She'd pulled them all off and ripped them up. Not that she'd known why or for what. At first she'd thought she might twist the strips into a rope or make a trap or do something else useful. But she'd ended up with a bunch of ragged, irregular pieces of tattered fabric and no clue what to do next. The rags sat in a sad pile near the door.

Hanging from the shower head had only proved to her how sturdy it was. Pulling down the shower curtain had felt like a victory until she found that it was even harder to rip than the bed linens had been. Almost impossible, actually.

She'd quit while she was ahead and left the bath towels in one piece.

For all of a few minutes, she'd had a fantasy about tunneling out through the concrete floor or the cinder-block walls.

Then she'd realized that she didn't have anything to chip at the stone with. There hadn't been any utensils with her lunch—a lame turkey and cheese sandwich on white bread with mayo, a bag of baked potato chips, and a box of apple juice—and the ones that had come with her breakfast had been plastic.

The bolts and locks on her cell's door clacked and banged as they were undone from the outside.

Phaedra sat on the end of her bed—knees together, hands folded on her lap, chin tucked, brows knit with hatred—as she watched the door open.

Her captor entered carrying a tray. Once again there was no sign of the dark wings or evil smoke she had seen around him in the van. She was beginning to think she had imagined it all, that it had just been the drugs playing tricks on her.

But *something else* came into the room with him, she was certain of it. She couldn't see it or hear it; she couldn't say what it was. All she knew for a fact was that it was evil and that it was never far from the man in the mask. It was almost an odor—a trace of something sharp, like the stink after striking a match. And it was cold. A chill stippled her arms with gooseflesh.

While he crossed the room, she peeked through the open door, desperate to spot a clue beyond its threshold. All she saw was a dark corner whose walls and floor all were made of concrete. No windows, no clues to where she was.

He set the fiberglass tray on the table by her bed. His voice was flat and thin through the mask's speaker-snout. *"We hope you like pierogi."*

As he walked back toward the door, Phaedra shot a suspicious look at the paper plate of half-moon-shaped ravioli swimming in a gray-brown mushroom gravy. She called after him, "Do you have a name?"

He stopped and looked back over his shoulder. The mask's insectlike eyes and long filter made him look like a mad scientist's fusion of a pig and a bug. *"Of course we have a name."*

"What is it?"

A long silence followed. She expected him to argue with her, maybe get into some kind of debate about why he should tell her anything. Seconds dragged by while she waited for his reply, and he stared at her the whole time.

Finally, he said, *"Our name is Leon."* He stepped through the door, began to close it, then paused. *"We'll be turning off the lights in one hour. Breakfast will be served tomorrow morning at six o'clock. Good night."*

The door shut with a heavy thunk. Bolts and tumblers clanked back into their locked positions, then the room went silent once again.

Phaedra got up from the bed and plodded wearily to the table. Flopped into the cracked plastic chair. Picked at her dinner. In addition to the pierogi, she had been given a dry mixed salad with greens, tomatoes, and cucumbers. There were also two pieces of buttered bread and a paper cup of milk. As at breakfast, a plastic fork and knife sat side by side on a clean paper napkin.

She devoured the meal. The pierogi were heavier than the ravioli her mom served sometimes, but they tasted good and they were satisfying. Some were filled with meat, some with cheese. As for the salad, she would normally have eaten the tomatoes and cucumbers and left the greens, but tonight she was hungry enough to eat it all, even without dressing. She saved the bread and most of the milk for last.

After dinner she collapsed onto the uncovered bed and waited for the lights to go out. Time seemed to stretch out as she lay on her side, her back to the door, staring at the gritty texture of the cinder-block wall.

Though she was exhausted, her heart was pounding. She tossed and turned and flipped the pillow a half dozen times in search of a cool spot. She was used to having more pillows and her own bed and her knitted quilt blanket.

Then she realized what was really missing.

Her dismay came out in a plaintive whisper: "Clarence!"

She began to cry. Softly at first—just a sniffle or two as a few tears rolled from her eyes along the side of her nose and over her upper lip. Then she started to whimper and sob. Halting, choking cries of loneliness and fear doubled her over.

Dammit, don't cry, she told herself. *Don't be a baby. What if he sees you?*

It didn't matter what she told herself. She was so scared, and even though it wouldn't have helped her get away from Leon, all she wanted right now was her plush rabbit pal. That was why she couldn't get comfortable.

Without her matted furry friend tucked under her arm, she couldn't relax. There would be nothing between her and her night terrors. Fearsome visions that her imagination had conjured of her father's gruesome death and other dreams that she didn't understand but which chilled her blood all the same.

Then came the faintest click—and the room turned black.

Alone in the darkness, Phaedra wrapped herself around her pillow and tucked her face into it to muffle her howling cries.

She knew she would fall asleep sooner or later.

And that was exactly what she was afraid of.

10

After they parked the truck, Erin made Tom take off his blood-spattered white shirt and tie and put on a black T-shirt. Then she used a damp cloth to wipe the dust from his suit.

"There," she said, tossing the cloth back into the truck. "That'll do."

"Are you sure?" he said, twisting around to inspect the back of his pants.

"Fabric's dark enough not to show dirt." She smiled as she took off her trenchcoat to reveal a black leather corset, then shook her dark hair in a wild mane around her shoulders. "Besides, no one'll be lookin' at you, anyway."

In a matter of a few hours, she led him through half a dozen rowdy bars on the city's Lower East Side. He expected them to be deserted on a Sunday night. What they found were teeming throngs in their twenties and thirties, bobbing in packs to deafening, bass-heavy beats that were so loud Tom was fairly certain they could have stunned small animals. After visiting two bars, he was sure he'd been rendered hearing impaired for life.

Invariably, all the men were attired similarly to Tom, in some combination of a dark suit with a black T-shirt or a dark silk shirt underneath—a look that Erin had dubbed "mobster chic"—and the women all seemed to be contestants in a citywide hooker look-alike contest. And, as she'd predicted, everyone gawked at her and ignored him.

Skipping past the lines of people waiting to get into those bars and talking their way past the bouncers at the doors proved easy. All Tom and Erin needed to do was turn on their doing-God's-work charm and everyone cooperated nicely. Tom almost felt guilty about it until he remembered that he didn't want to set foot in these clubs in the first place.

Erin and Tom sat next to each other at the oval-shaped bar of a club called M1-5 with their backs to a red-velvet pool table. Liquor bottles were clustered in a miniature skyline on an islandlike shelf in the middle of the bar. Four bartenders worked in steady rhythms, trying to keep up with the demands of the customers who surrounded them, shouting for more drinks. Some patrons were refugees from the pack of wildly gyrating bodies in the back of the club.

Tom sipped his seventh ginger ale of the night and shouted over the pounding house music to Erin, "I don't think I've ever been to this many bars in one night without getting drunk. Or paid so much money to do it."

She twirled the swizzle stick in her club soda with lime and kept her eyes on the wooden booths that lined the far wall, which, like most of the club, were drenched in a deep shade of red. "If you don't drink, you have to tip well," she hollered back. "Keeps 'em from getting pissed at you." She sipped her drink, then added, "Be careful and look over your right shoulder. Tank top."

He cast a furtive sideways glance over his right shoulder. Stepping up to the pool table, cue in hand, was one of the men who'd attacked him in the school parking lot hours earlier. It was the beefy bald man in the black tank top, black jeans, and combat boots.

As Baldy lined up a shot on the nine ball, Tom turned away and pretended to sip his ginger ale. He tried to keep his voice down, but the blaring music made that a tricky proposition. He asked, "How'd you know where to find him?"

"The new Russian mob boys have their favorite spots, like everybody else," she said. "Back in the day, they used to hang in Brighton Beach, at the supper clubs in Little Odessa. These days, they like to play in the city."

Tom's jaw went slack as he realized how much trouble he had just brought on himself. Fearing Erin's answer, he asked, "Did you just say *Russian mob*?"

She threw a surprised look at him. "Who'd you think they were? Muggers? Did they want your cash?"

"No," he said, still processing this bit of new information.

"The one with the brass knuckles said he was told to go after you," Erin said. "Those *pendejos* were sent by someone else. And everything about them shouted Red Mafia." She speared the lime in her drink with the swizzle stick. "We're lucky they weren't better armed. Next time they'll come heavy."

Wall-of-sound power chords from the overhead speakers made Tom wince. He looked up at the high ceiling and gritted his teeth for a moment before he said, "Do I even want to ask how you know so much about the Russian mob?"

"Stay in this game long enough and you learn things," Erin said. "Either that or you end up dead." She sipped her drink and peeked quickly over her shoulder, then continued. "When

I started out, I was just a kid. Prayers I heard were simple, easy stuff—milk runs, y'know? Then one day I was a few weeks shy of eighteen, and I ended up hitchin' a ride down to D.C. to spring some girl from a drug dealer who was pimpin' her out. Long story short, I ended up in deep shit, and I had to crack some heads." She shrugged. "Guess what I'm saying is this thing we do, it ain't for the faint of heart." Another quick look back and she nudged Tom's elbow. "Let's go while he's busy."

She dropped a ten-dollar bill on the bar and got up, and Tom followed her. Behind them, Baldy had his back turned while he lined up his next shot. Erin cut like a knife through the crowd, parting the sea of inebriated young flesh on her way to the front door. Then she and Tom were outside on the narrow sidewalk, free of the stifling heat of bodies and the oppressive hammer of house music run amok.

He drew a breath of cool autumn air polluted with car exhaust and reeking of garbage and stale urine. Looking up and down the poorly lit block of decaying, graffiti-strewn buildings clad with rusted iron fire escapes, he asked, "Now what?"

"He'll be in there awhile," Erin said. "Let's get the truck and camp out a few doors down. When he leaves, we'll follow him." She started walking.

"What'll that get us?" he asked, falling into step beside her.

"Dunno," she replied. "But right now, he's all we've got."

The prepaid cell phone on the end table shrilled in Frank Kolpack's ear, waking him in a shocked frazzle from a booze-induced nap on his sofa.

Another high-pitched digital shriek felt like an axe splitting his head. He rolled over with a groan and spilled the rest of his vodka and cranberry in his lap. "Goddammit," he grumbled, catching the empty cocktail glass before it fell to the floor. Head pounding, crotch damp, mouth full of sour aftertaste, he set the glass on the coffee table as the phone cried again for his attention.

He muted the old movie playing on the television, picked up the phone, and answered, "Go."

"I thought you said the private eye was working alone," Viktor said.

Frank rubbed his eyes. "Why, what happened?"

"A woman," the boss said, anger adding a tremor to his voice. *"With an axe handle. Sent my boys home in bad shape. She put Gregor and Yuri in the hospital."*

He heaved a sigh, then said, "I'm sorry, Viktor. That's terrible." Actually, he thought it was hilarious, but he knew not to bust Viktor's chops at times like this.

"You know we can't let this go," Viktor said.

"Of course not," Frank said. "Bad for business. How can I help?"

"Do you have any photos of this bastard?"

"Yeah, hang on." Frank sat up. Getting off the couch was the last thing he wanted to do right now, but duty called. His head swam as he stood. "I took a few snaps of him with the digital while I was watching Anna's place." He shuffled across the matted, crumb-flecked carpet and ignored the quasi-medicinal odor wafting up from his vodka-soaked lap. "I can e-mail them to you," he said as he picked up the camera from its place on his cluttered bookshelf.

"Good," Viktor said. *"That will do."*

A flick of his thumb activated the camera. He watched the preview screen as he searched for a good shot of the blond man. The last picture in the series was the first one he saw, and it was obscured by a motion blur. "Gimme a sec to find one I didn't botch," he said, scrolling back through the sequence of photos he'd taken. An acidic belch burned his esophagus and left him tasting bitter cranberry juice.

"How dignified," Viktor deadpanned.

"Glad you liked it." He thumbed through a few more digital images saved on his camera's memory card.

All the pictures he'd taken of the blond man were messed up in ways that blocked the subject's face. A lens flare. A dark smudge. More motion blurs. Everything around the man was in focus. But not him.

Not good, Frank thought as realization set in. The other images on his camera were fine, with no sign of distortion. Only the blond man's photos had been tampered with. *Time for a change of plan.* "On second thought, Viktor, sending your guys after him again might make him suspicious."

Exasperated, the Ukrainian boss shot back, *"Then what do you suggest?"*

"Let me put an independent contractor on this one," Frank said. "Someone who can't be tied to you. Let's keep your hands as clean on this one as possible."

He heard murmurs of agreement over the line, then Viktor said, *"Yes, that would be best, considering the plan for tomorrow."*

"Exactly," Frank said. "Forget about this. I'll take it from here."

"If you insist," Viktor said. *"Let me know when it is done."*

"Will do."

They said good night and hung up. Frank waited a few seconds to make certain the line was clear, then he keyed in a number from memory. While he stood and listened to the phone ringing on the other end, he stared at the occluded image on his digital camera's preview screen and scratched an itch on his neck.

The call was picked up, and Frank heard a woman's voice.

"Done already, Frank?"

"Not yet," he said. "There's a new wrinkle. Someone new's been Called."

She sounded annoyed. *"So?"*

"I need Zev and Dillon, right now."

"Again? So soon? We can't keep loaning them out to you, Frank. They have their own responsibilities."

He swallowed a host of curses that were crowding his thoughts and forced himself to keep a civil tongue. It wouldn't do him any good to make her angry. "I wouldn't ask if it wasn't important," he explained. "We're close on this one."

"Maybe we should cut our losses."

"No!" he protested. "I can pull this off. We can accomplish both objectives. All I need is twenty-four hours and a little more backup."

Silence. He waited for her to say something, *anything*. Every second that passed kicked his tension level up a few more notches.

At last she replied in a weary voice, *"All right, Frank. Zev will call you in a few minutes. Anything else this evening?"*

"No," he said, grateful for the consideration she'd already shown him. "That's it, I promise. And thank you."

"Good night, Frank." She hung up.

He pocketed the phone and went straight for the drawer where he kept his cigarettes. It was empty. *That's right,* he remembered. *I threw them away. Cold turkey.* He swore softly toward the ceiling, then collapsed back onto the couch and waited for his phone to ring. It was going to be a long night.

"Careful," Erin said. "Not too close. Keep a few cars between us and him."

Tom slowed down and let a couple of cars slide into the

lane ahead of his pickup as they approached the turn for the Brooklyn Bridge. "How many?"

"Three or four," she said, opening the glove compartment. Rooting through its clutter, she added, "Usually I'd say two, but we're so high up in this heap of crap, I could see his ass from Jersey."

Easing through the left turn off Centre Street and entering the bridge's on-ramp, Tom asked, "Doesn't that mean he can see us, too?"

"All that *pendejo* sees are lights in his rearview." Erin pulled a pen and a napkin from the glove compartment. "This capped truck of yours looks like an SUV. We'll fit right in." She thrust her arm forward, finger pointing. "Merge!"

A dozen yards in front of him, the left lane was closed for maintenance. He stepped on the gas and jogged right into the middle lane, cutting off a row of cars, whose drivers honked their horns at him, long and loud. A glare of headlights filled his rearview mirror. Low girders blurred past overhead, and the lights of Brooklyn stretched out ahead of him on the far side of the moonlit East River.

As the din faded behind them, Erin shook her head. "Want me to drive?"

Tom snapped, "*No,* I don't want you to drive." She rolled her eyes, smoothed the napkin on the dash, and began scribbling notes on it with the pen. He asked, "What're you doing?"

She looked up at Baldy's car, a black BMW, and said, "Writing down his license number, make, model, and color. And his tail-light design." Glancing at Tom she added, "In case we lose him."

"We're not gonna lose him," Tom said, returning his focus to the moving traffic all around them. "Mind if I ask a stupid question?"

"Go ahead," she said, still writing and drawing.

"What if he'd taken the subway instead of driving?"

"I'd have tailed him on foot and called you to join me when I knew where he was going." She folded the napkin and stuffed it into her coat pocket.

Minutes passed without conversation as they kept their eyes on the BMW. The road droned beneath the truck's tires, and Tom considered turning on the radio before deciding he didn't need the distraction.

He glanced at the dashboard clock and mused that twenty-four hours earlier, he had been home and safe, asleep in his own bed, next to his wife. Now he was in New York City tailing a violent Russian mobster and hoping not to get shot in the process. *I must be out of my mind,* he decided. *Who would send* me *to do this?*

"I thought of another question," he said.

Erin threw a sidelong glance at him. "Shoot."

"Do we work for God?"

She averted her eyes toward the river. "What god?"

"I don't know. Any god."

All trace of humor left her voice. "If we do, I haven't met him."

Silence fell like a curtain between them.

Soon the bridge was in his rearview mirror, and their target had led them down Adams Street, a broad multilane thoroughfare flanked by pristine high-rises. One looked to Tom like a commercial tower, another like an apartment complex. Government buildings rubbed shoulders with corporate headquarters. Even late on a Sunday night, traffic was brisk and busy.

Within a few blocks, the neighborhood lost some of its luster, and the traffic thinned out. A light up ahead turned red, and the BMW stopped in the left lane, turn signal blinking. "Fall back," Erin said. "Don't give him a good look at us."

Tom tapped the brakes and slid into the left lane behind an SUV, a few vehicles behind Baldy's car, giving them some cover. He activated his left turn signal, which clicked in sync with the blinking dashboard icon. "Good?"

"Perfect," she said.

They followed the BMW onto Atlantic Avenue, a semi-industrial stretch of road that got more depressing the longer they followed it. Soon the car turned right down Fourth Avenue and passed into a grid of streets that looked very familiar to Tom. "Park Slope," he muttered. "Back where we started."

"Maybe," Erin said. "Just keep an eye on him and watch the lights. If we get stuck at a red, we could lose him."

Getting the feel of the timing of the streetlights came easily to Tom. He had no trouble tracking the car through several turns—across Seventeenth Street to Prospect Expressway, which then became Ocean Parkway, and then left onto Beverley Road and into a patchwork of smaller streets—to a quiet residential road lined by attractive two-story houses. Tom turned off the truck's headlights to draw less attention as the traffic melted away.

About a block and a half ahead of the truck, the car turned down a long driveway beside a large Victorian-style house. Tom pulled over to the side of the road and put his truck in park. He didn't dare turn off its engine; on a quiet street like this one, its clattering death rattle would wake half the block.

The BMW's lights went dark, and Baldy got out. His car's taillights flashed and its alarm chirped twice as he locked the doors with his keychain remote. He went inside the house. Seconds later, lights blinked on in the windows.

Tom let out a long, low whistle as he admired their surroundings. "Nice neighborhood. Being a thug must be good business."

"Always has been," Erin said. She pointed at the curbs on both sides of the street. "Cans are out. Tomorrow must be trash day." She smirked. "Lucky us."

He didn't like the sound of that. "Why is that lucky?"

"Saves us the trouble of pokin' around behind his house lookin' for it. All we have to do is let him bring it to us." As if on cue, the side door of the house opened, and Baldy walked outside and around a corner into his backyard. Moments later he returned dragging a dark green rubber trash can with a beige lid down his driveway. "Bingo," Erin said.

Baldy stood the can at the corner of his driveway and the curb, wiped his hands on the sides of his black jeans, and lumbered back into the house. As soon as the door closed, the lights inside switched off.

"Okay," Erin said, perked up with excitement. She opened her door and got out of the truck. "Pull up to his driveway," she added, then gently shut the door with a soft clack. Before Tom could protest, Erin jogged across the street and over to the man's house. By the time he had shifted the truck into gear and caught up to her, she had extracted a bulging black trash bag from the can.

He lowered his window and asked, "Now what?"

"Open the hatch."

"No. My truck hauls tools not trash."

She rolled her eyes. "It's not trash; it's a bag of clues. Now open the hatch."

Ten minutes later, in an empty parking lot behind a closed fast-food joint on Church Avenue, Tom stood half-blinded in his truck's headlights and stared down at the most disgusting pile of clues he had ever smelled.

"This was a great idea," he said to Erin, who squatted beside the wide-strewn garbage and picked at it with the ballpoint pen from his glove compartment. "Now we know he owns at least one cat and doesn't use flushable litter."

Still focused on her exploration of the ammonia-reeking mound, Erin replied, "Sometimes we get our hands dirty, *papi*. Get used to it."

He reached down and pulled his black T-shirt up over his nose. It didn't do as much to block the stench of cat feces and rotting fish as he hoped. Squatting beside Erin on the edge of the trash circle, he said through his ineffectual gas mask, "Are we learning anything? Anything useful, I mean."

Raised eyebrows and a tilt of her head expressed her doubts. "Maybe," she said. She speared one envelope and set it aside. "Phone bills tell you their numbers and who they talk to." Poking the pen through another, smaller envelope, she made a tsk-tsk noise and shook her head. "Somebody needs to teach our friend to shred his bank statements." Another stab. "And his pay stubs."

Tom eyed the pay stub as Erin pushed it off the pen, and he picked it up. " 'Baba Yaga Club,' " he said. The name jogged his memory. He held out his hand. "Can I have the pen?" She gave it to him, and he used it to push a few bits of slimy crud out of the way, revealing a soggy matchbook. He flipped it over with the pen. The matchbook's cover read BABA YAGA CLUB and featured a crude drawing of a wart-nosed old crone that Tom figured was meant to be an archetypal witch. Along the cover's bottom edge was a street address. " 'Avenue X, Brooklyn,' " he read. "Is there really an Avenue X?"

"Yeah, down in Gravesend." Erin plucked the matchbook from the mess with her fingernails. "Near Brighton Beach. Big spot for Russians."

Standing and stretching the dull ache of fatigue from his legs, Tom asked, "What are the odds a guy like him can afford to live in a swanky neighborhood and drive a Beemer with a job at a bar?"

"Pretty good," Erin said, gathering up the envelopes she had liberated from the muck, "if the bar's a front for laundering money."

Mustering his best sarcastic tone, he asked, "Hmm . . . you don't think there might be something *illegal* going on at that club, do you?"

They locked eyes, smiled knowingly, and replied in mocking unison, "No . . . of course not."

11

Baba Yaga occupied a dingy one-story building that sat within spitting distance of the elevated F train tracks and a stone's throw from the sprawling Coney Island train yard. Its walls had been painted a once deep but now faded purple. A rectangular sign stretched the length of the small blocky structure, dominating the upper third of its façade. Weathered plywood masked what Tom assumed were windows. A graffiti-tagged, solid-metal security gate covered its main entrance.

To the left of the club—behind a brand-new twelve-foot-tall chain-link gate topped with barbed wire—a dark and narrow alley led to an unlit, enclosed small rear lot. A gleaming black town car was parked in the alley.

Across the deathly quiet street, all the stores were shuttered for the night. It was the same eclectic mix of businesses that Tom had gotten used to seeing huddled together in the city: a liquor store, a shoe repair shop, a sushi restaurant, a bagelry, a deli, a produce market, a Chinese takeout joint. Unlike other parts of New York that Tom had seen so far, this area had aboveground electrical wires on wooden utility poles, with wires fanning out from transformers above the street.

Flanking Baba Yaga were an Italian restaurant and a dental clinic, both also closed and hidden behind grim steel barricades.

"Nice area," Tom said. He threw suspicious glances up and down the dark, deserted avenue. "I wonder if my truck'll still be there when I get back."

"Chill," Erin said, inching toward the alley gate and toting her trusty axe handle close at her side. "West Third Street's safe. It'll be fine."

She peeked around the corner. "Car's empty." Testing the padlock on the gate, she noted, "It's open. Someone's in there." She lifted the latch and pushed the gate open just wide enough to slip through. "Come on."

Tom wanted to tell her not to go inside, but it was too late—she was already creeping down the alleyway. He followed her, gently closing and relatching the gate behind him before skulking through the shadows to catch up to her. Odors of urine, garbage, and motor oil wafted through the alley on a chilly breeze.

They stopped at the corner of the building. Erin posed as if listening for something. She whispered to Tom, "Sounds like people inside, talking. Maybe two or three. I can't tell." A sideways nod. "We need to get closer to the door."

He and Erin turned the corner and walked all of two steps before they came face-to-face with three snarling Dobermans. The muscular black dogs tensed, eyes gleaming beneath brows knit with rage, and the light above the club's rear door cast a pale shine on the saliva spilling through their bared fangs.

A sick, hollow feeling churned in Tom's gut as the canines

prowled forward and spread out around them. "Maybe we should go," he whispered.

"Relax," Erin said, keeping her voice hushed. "We can handle this." She held up her palm to the closest dog and said in a soothing tone, "S'okay, puppy. We're all friends here. Be cool . . ."

Her words trailed off as the dog relaxed and backed away. It laid down, licked its chops, and rested its head on its front paws.

Meanwhile, the other two dogs continued growling and moving closer.

Looking askance at Tom, Erin said, "Give it a try."

Perplexed but willing to trust her, Tom stretched out his open hand toward one of the two advancing Dobermans and said in his softest voice, "Hiya, pooch. No need to fight. Let's just be buddies, okay?"

The dog reacted by growling more loudly and taking another step forward.

"Crap," Tom said, pulling his hand back. His mouth went dry with fear.

Erin stepped between him and the dogs, one hand out, palm up, like a traffic cop halting cars. She whispered to the two Dobermans for a few moments. Then they, too, ceased their snarling and slunk away to lie down beside the first dog.

She put her back to the wall of the club and motioned for him to do the same. He did as she directed, then leaned close to her and said, "First, thanks. Second, what the hell just happened?"

"Remember what I said about us each having a special talent? Well, mine is talking with animals. Guy who schooled me could read languages he'd never been taught. And so it goes."

Flummoxed, Tom asked, "So what about me? What's my talent?"

"Beats me," Erin said with a shrug. She smiled. "But at least we can rule out talking to animals." Turning serious, she pressed her index finger to her lips, signaling him to stay quiet. She turned her head toward the door to listen. "More talking," she whispered. "Definitely Russians."

She grabbed Tom's sleeve and pulled him away from the wall. "They're coming." He went where she led. They scrambled across the small enclosed lot and ducked behind a large trash bin in the corner, near its high rear wall.

As he and Erin crouched low and pressed themselves into the foul-smelling sliver of space behind the garbage container, Tom heard the club's rear door open. Men's voices spoke in a rapid Slavic patter. The door slammed shut.

Tom took a chance and peeked out from behind the bin to see the men. There were three of them. One was an older man, trim and well groomed, attired in a dark tailored suit over which he wore a long gray wool coat. Walking ahead of him toward the town car was a brute who looked like a brick wall in black trousers and a green Windbreaker. But it was the third man who held Tom's attention.

It was the camouflage-wearing thug who had helped attack Tom in the parking lot hours earlier. He seemed to be contrite as he accepted a lecture from the man in the suit. They walked together toward the town car.

In the alley, Brick Wall opened the gate. Then he clicked his remote to unlock the town car, which flashed its lights and honked its horn in response.

Camouflage and the Suit stopped beside the car. Brick Wall opened the driver's door and got in. The Suit placed a paternal hand on the younger man's shoulder. He spoke for a few moments while gesturing subtly with his free hand, and Camouflage nodded in understanding.

The town car's engine purred to life. Its headlights snapped on. Erin yanked Tom back behind the Dumpster a split second before the car's lights would have exposed him.

"Thanks again," he muttered.

"De nada," she said, hugging him to her supple, athletic body. He felt her chest heave against his back with her every breath, and he noted the viselike press of her clenched fingers on his arms. As practical and tactical as he knew her actions to be, something about the moment felt erotically charged.

Thank God something in this bin stinks, Tom thought. The urge to gag and vomit gave him something to think about besides Erin's lean, elegant legs.

Grit crackled under the town car's tires as it backed out of the alley and stopped in the street. Tom heard a car door open, followed by footsteps and the closing of the gate. The subtle click of a lock snapping shut echoed in the alley.

More footsteps, a closing door, and then the car drove away into the night.

"You can let go of me now," Tom said, leaning forward.

"If you insist," Erin said, giving him a playful shove. They stood and dusted themselves off. "Let's go have a look inside."

She stepped around him and walked back to the club's rear entrance. He caught up to her as she was setting up to try to kick in the door. "Hold up," he said, sticking out his arm to block her path. "There's a better way."

He stepped to the door, reached into one of his jacket's inside pockets, and took out a small, tightly rolled sheepskin sheath. Erin watched with keen curiosity as he unrolled it to reveal a selection of fine-grade locksmith's tools. Tom selected the implements he felt were best suited to the door's lock and went to work.

"Well, look at you," Erin said. "Where'd you learn to do that?"

"Back home I'm a bonded locksmith," he said, deftly manipulating the teeth and tumblers inside the lock, which gave up its secrets and opened with ease. He looked back at Erin and added with a smile, "Of course, it's more of a hobby these days." A turn of the knob and the door was open.

They stepped in out of the cold and shut the door behind them. "Look for a light switch," Erin said. Tom found one next to the door and flicked it on.

Overhead, two long fluorescent tubes in a rectangular shell flickered and hummed to life, revealing a windowless backroom office with cheap furnishings. Two beat-up, brown faux-leather-upholstered chairs sat on either side of an L-shaped Formica countertop in the near corner to their left. He counted at least four ashtrays—two glass, one metal, one plastic—filled with cigarette butts, their filters pinched almost flat and stained a rich brown. Half-used matchbooks littered the room, which was cursed with the acrid reek of stale smoke.

Supporting the countertop was a quartet of short filing cabinets, one at either end and two near the corner. Three taller filing cabinets stood along the back wall on the left side of the room, under an old-fashioned circular wall clock.

Tom took in the office's other details. Cinder-block walls and a concrete floor. An unfinished ceiling crossed by naked, rusting pipes. In the corner to his right, an ugly old sofa with ripped fabric upholstery. On the opposite side of the room from him was another door, which he assumed led to the rest of the club.

He looked at Erin. "Now what?"

"Start pokin' around," she said. She began poring over the loose papers on the countertop. "Check the filing cabinets."

The first two cabinets that Tom pawed through were filled with hanging file folders packed with documents written in Cyrillic characters. "It's all in Russian," he said. "These could be signed confessions and I'd have no clue."

She nodded. "Makes me wish Isaiah was here. He'd know what they said." She opened the other two filing cabinets and started thumbing through the sheafs of paper they contained. "More of the same," she said.

Tom stepped over to the farthest tall filing cabinet and opened its top drawer. "Payroll documents," he said. "Employee records. I bet the IRS would love to get a look at this."

Erin closed her filing cabinets and walked over to join him. "Might be useful," she said. "But it's a lot to go through, and we don't have the time."

"I know," Tom said, closing the last drawer of the first cabinet.

He reached over and pulled on the bottom drawer of the middle tall cabinet—and it refused to open.

"Locked," he said.

"Promising," Erin replied.

She watched as he dug out his tools again and picked the lock. "These guys oughta buy a safe," he said while he worked. "At least that'd be a challenge for me."

"Careful what you wish for, *papi*."

The lock twisted free, and the bottom drawer rumbled open.

It was filled with brand-new boxes of bullets marked *.357 SIG*.

"Interesting," he said. What he'd meant was "unnerving."

He closed that drawer, stood, and opened the middle one, which contained two orderly rows of factory-condition compact black semiautomatic pistols.

Erin's eyes widened. "SIG Sauer P229s, designed for .357 rounds," she said. "Serious hardware."

Tom slid the drawer shut and dreaded what he might find as he opened the top drawer. It slid out to reveal an assortment of cylindrical objects that he suspected and Erin confirmed were—

"Silencers."

"Great," Tom said. He tried opening the last of the tall filing cabinets. It, too, was locked. "Wonder what they've got in here," he added as he began picking the lock with calm precision, listening for the soft clicks of contact. "Nukes?"

"Never know," Erin said.

The lock turned over, and he stepped aside to put away his tools as Erin opened one drawer after another. They were packed with new still-in-the-plastic prepaid cell phones. He reached in and grabbed one.

"Someone gave Phaedra's mother one of these this afternoon," he said, studying the feather-light, wafer-thin phone in his hand. "It was exactly this model—it was even this color." He showed it to Erin. "Coincidence?"

Her eyebrows arched with disbelief. "What do *you* think?"

He tucked the phone into his jacket's side pocket. "I think we need to find out who we're dealing with."

The F train thunder-rattled behind Zev Kujan, hurtling northward away from Coney Island. Aftershocks of the subway train's passage shook the concrete platform under the gaunt man's tired feet and sent tremors through the metal-and-wire-mesh safety wall against which he was leaning. When the train vanished at last into the night, all that remained was the city's ever-present background roar, the steady white noise of distant traffic.

Only a few people had left the train. It was late, the Avenue X stop was hardly one of Brooklyn's hot spots, and Gravesend was far from any neighborhood that might be remotely mistaken for hip or trendy. Most of those who had gotten off walked north on the platform toward the exit.

One person, however, walked away from the exit—toward Zev.

He didn't bother to look. He knew who it was.

Dillon Tanager joined him at the railing and stared in the direction of Zev's gaze. "I got your message," he said.

"Apparently." Zev turned a sidelong glance at the Seeker, who was a bit shorter than he was but far more powerfully built. The man had a grace to his movements, the product of many years of intensive martial-arts training. His face was lean and square with a strong jaw and a thin brow, unlike Zev's, which was marked by sunken cheeks and thick eyebrows topped by a high forehead.

Lifting his chin at the street below, Dillon asked, "Where are they?"

Zev pointed at the Baba Yaga Club. "In there."

The Seeker checked his watch. "For how long?"

"About ten minutes," Zev said.

Dillon took a pack of smokes from his jacket. "Alone?"

Zev shrugged. "Far as I can tell."

Dillon nodded and tapped the pack against the side of his hand. He opened the flip top and plucked out one cigarette. "How'd they arrive?"

"On foot," Zev said. "Came up Avenue X from Third Street."

The cigarette dangled from Dillon's lips as he stuffed the pack back into his pocket. "Armed?"

"Not sure. Too dark over there."

The Seeker took a lighter from his jacket's other pocket and lit his cigarette with a snap of his fingers across the Zippo's flint wheel. A long, slow inhale was followed by an escaping plume of smoke, whose sharp odor was enough to mask the stench of festering restaurant garbage from the street below. He took the cancer stick from his mouth. "You got a good look at them, right?"

"Yes."

"And . . . ?"

Zev knew better than to make Dillon ask obvious questions. "Two Seekers of the Called," he said to his comrade in the Scorned. "No doubt about it."

"That's all I need to know," Dillon said. He reached under his jacket to the small of his back and pulled out a black semiautomatic pistol. With fast, well-practiced motions, he ejected the clip, checked it, slammed it back in, and pulled back the slide to chamber a round. He made sure the safety was on.

Cocking one eyebrow, Zev asked, "What's with the gat? Hands of fire not good enough for you?"

Dillon returned the pistol to the small of his back, under his belt. "It's gonna be two Seekers against one," he said. "And who knows what powers they have? The sooner we cap these two and get back on the road, the better." He took another drag off his cigarette. "Stay here and keep your eyes open." Then he was away, moving at a quick step for the exit, leaving a pungent gray smoke trail twisting in his wake.

Zev turned his gaze back to the deserted street below the elevated train. He sighed. Violent confrontations weren't something he enjoyed, but he understood that they were necessary sometimes.

It was, after all, a war.

Unlike the cheap old piece-of-crap locks on the club's back door and its filing cabinets, the brand-new padlock on the parking lot's gate was giving Tom some trouble.

"Hang on," he said to Erin, concentrating on the delicate sensations his fingertips were detecting through his tools. "I've almost got it."

The lock's inner workings caught and turned, then released the prong. It sprang open in his hand, and he pulled it free of the chain.

"There," he said, reeling in the slack links, which clanged against the steel fence post. He opened the gate, stepped through, and looked back.

Erin wasn't there. A quick whistle turned his head.

She was outside the gate, leaning on the club's front wall and holding her axe handle against her right shoulder.

"Thought you'd never get out," she said with a teasing smile.

He looked back down the alley, then at Erin. "How'd you . . . ?"

"Climbed a pipe in the back, walked over the roof," she said. "Been here for about a minute while you fiddled with that thing." She pushed off the wall and lifted her chin toward the end of the street. "Let's breeze."

Tom pulled the gate shut. "Hang on, I should relock it."

"Why?"

"Y'know, to cover our tracks," he said.

"Waste o' time," she said. "Leave it." She stepped past him.

Then he saw a man walking up the block behind her. The guy was still a dozen yards away, jaywalking across the street. His hands were stuffed in his jacket pockets. He kept his head down but his eyes facing forward.

As Tom started turning to follow Erin, he saw the man quicken his pace—and reach under his jacket, behind his back, to pull free a—

"Gun!" Tom shouted to Erin, pulling her toward the row of parallel-parked cars across the street. They ducked and sprinted as bullets started flying.

Thunderous bangs were answered by firecracker echoes.

Erin dived over a car's hood, with Tom a step behind.

Bullets shattered the car's side windows. The windshield spiderwebbed with cracks as slugs punched through it.

Stinging shards peppered Tom's face as he tumbled to cover on the other side of the vehicle.

The car's alarm whooped and shrilled. Its headlights flashed till more bullets shot them to bits. Its tires ruptured with deafening pops.

"C'mon!" Erin said, scrambling on all fours down the line of cars. Tom followed her. He winced as bits of glass jabbed into his palms.

The barrage followed them, demolishing car windows, covering the sidewalk with broken shards, and filling the air with more shrieking alarms.

Each shot sounded closer than the last.

A close ricochet off a fire hydrant grazed the back of Erin's right thigh, tearing through leather and flesh to leave a bloody streak.

The shooting stopped with a hollow, metallic click.

Erin sprang to her feet, and Tom tried to keep up.

Just a few feet away, on the other side of a honking, flashing parked car, the gunman ejected an empty clip and reached into his jacket for another.

Erin, her face flecked with tiny cuts from glass shrapnel, flung her axe handle at him.

It spun through the air, a wooden blur.

The new clip was half out of the gunman's pocket when the hickory club hit his face and knocked him back a step.

Blood gushed from his nose. The clip fell from his hand.

She charged, one foot pushing off the car's bumper, and leapt at him, taking him down with a flying tackle.

Tom climbed over the car's hood, leaving bloody hand prints. Every fleeting contact drove glass shards deeper into his palms.

In the middle of the street, Erin landed two solid punches in the gunman's face. He caught her bare forearm as she tried to land a third.

Then came an audible sizzle. Smoke curled from between his fingers.

Erin landed an uppercut on the man's jaw, and he let go of her. She rolled one way; he rolled the other, reaching for his pistol's reload clip.

Tom snatched the axe handle from the pavement.

The man jammed the fresh clip into his handgun. Aimed at Erin.

With no time to think, Tom made a golf swing with the axe handle. Hit the man's gun hand as he fired, sending the shot wide and knocking the pistol from his grip, over the parked cars onto the sidewalk.

Tom brought the hickory down for another blow—and the man caught it, stopped it dead. He yanked on it, pulling Tom within his reach.

Erin's foot slammed into the man's crotch.

He doubled over and lost his grip on the axe handle, which Erin plucked from Tom's hands. "Move!" she yelled to Tom, who followed her.

They sprinted back toward the unlocked gate to the alley. Their attacker stumbled through a narrow gap between two parked cars, scrambling to retrieve his pistol from the distant, glass-sparkled sidewalk.

The gate rattle-banged open as Erin slammed through it and dashed down the narrow alley. Only as Tom trailed her into the shadows did he remember that they were running headlong into a dead end.

Dillon felt ready to throw up. Nausea filled his gut from the kick to his balls, his right hand throbbed from getting smacked by the axe handle, and he was pretty sure his nose was broken from stopping the hickory with his face. The cacophony of car alarms filled the street, making his headache worse by the second. He sucked a salty sheen of blood from his teeth.

It hurt to bend down. He groaned as he picked up his Beretta with his left hand. Then he lurched across the street, toward the still-open gate to the dead-end parking lot behind the Baba Yaga Club.

Far off but getting closer, sirens wailed in the night.

Time to wrap this up and get gone, he decided.

He walked with calm purpose through the open gate. His steps crunched softly over the loose bits of gravel that littered the pavement.

At the end of the alley, the lot extended to the right behind the building. Most of it was hidden from view around the corner. *That's where they'll try to jump me,* he figured. He put his back to the wall on the left and raised his gun.

A deep breath steadied his shaking hand.

Staring with one eye down the barrel, he kept the targeting sights lined up as he inched past the corner. His finger tensed on the trigger.

A blur from the rear left corner of the lot—something flew at him from behind the reeking, overfilled Dumpster.

He ducked. An empty bottle missed his head and smashed on the wall behind him.

He fired two shots into the corner. Slugs zinged off the trash bin.

Then came a mad flurry of barks and growls, and three massive black shapes lunged at him from the dark.

He tried to turn the Beretta, to switch targets, but he was too slow.

The dogs rammed into him. His back hit the wall, and his breath left him.

One Doberman clamped its jaws around his left wrist. Another sank its teeth into his right arm below the elbow. The third was on top of him, going for his throat, and he fought with his knees and legs to keep it at bay.

They thrashed their heads like sharks in a feeding frenzy. They stank of dog sweat and garbage breath.

Beyond the wild fray, the two enemy Seekers ran past him out of the alley, and he cursed himself for walking into a trap.

Blood poured down his arms, and he screamed in rage as he twisted and struggled to break free. The third dog sank its fangs into his right thigh.

Pumped with adrenaline, he forced his arms together and clamped his aching right hand onto the neck of the dog chewing through his left wrist.

The dog howled as its flesh began to burn, and its open mouth freed his left hand. He wrapped his left arm around the second dog. It, too, yelped in pain and fear as it felt the fire in Dillon's flesh.

Both animals thrashed and flailed in his grip.

Then they twitched. Went limp. And smoldered.

He threw them aside. The third dog still refused to let go of his leg.

Stubborn little shit, Dillon raged as he grabbed the beast by the nape of its neck. Within seconds he reduced it to a heap of burnt fur and bones.

His two targets were long gone, and he was in no shape to go after them. He'd have to take a different tack next time.

He fished in his jacket for his cell phone and tapped the speed dial for Zev.

It rang only once before Zev picked up. *"What happened?"*

"I'm hurt," Dillon rasped. "Bring the car to the alley. Fast."

"On my way," Zev said. He hung up.

The car alarms whooped, and the keening of sirens got closer by the minute. It was time to leave, before people started asking questions that Dillon wasn't ready to answer. He crawled down the alley to the gate, pulling himself with his mauled arms and pushing himself with his one good leg.

A screech of brakes and a long scrape of tires on asphalt. Zev's beat-up Chevy sedan skidded to a halt in front of the alley. The Seer was out of the car in a flash. He opened his passenger-side door, then ran to Dillon and wrapped his arms around the wounded Seeker's chest. In a blur of pain and motion, he deposited Dillon into the shotgun seat and slammed the door shut.

Then he got in on the driver's side and simultaneously closed the door, shifted the car into drive, and stepped on the gas. They lurched forward and sped down Avenue X, into the night, away from the sirens.

Zev threw nervous looks in the rearview mirror. "What's Plan B?"

"They set a trap for me," Dillon said. "I'll return the favor." He eyed the bloody mess he'd made of his seat and door. "But first . . . I need a doctor."

12

Alone in the dark, Phaedra didn't want to sleep. She talked to herself to stay awake. Played mental games. Counted backward from a thousand.

Anything not to sleep. Not to dream. Not without Clarence.

Had it been minutes? Hours? Was morning close? She had no idea. She'd never liked wearing a watch, and her MP3 player had been taken away by Leon.

It was darker in her cell than any place she'd ever seen. It was pure black. Nothing gave off any light. There were no windows, no clocks—nothing to give her a clue about how much night was left.

She tried waving her hand in front of her face but couldn't see even a hint of movement in the darkness. Even as she felt the air move on her face, all she saw was an unbroken wall of empty blackness.

This is what it's like being blind, she realized.

Her other senses had kicked into overdrive when the lights went out. Her breathing sounded louder than usual. She was certain that she could feel every detail of texture on her mattress. And even though she had thought earlier that the room had no odor, she had become certain after lights-out that she could smell the synthetic fabric of her mattress, the stale perspiration in her clothes, the oil that was building up in her hair, and even the chlorinated water gurgling in the bathroom toilet.

The toilet, she thought all of a sudden. *What if it got clogged? And something blocked the bathroom's floor drain?*

It would be a big mess. Even bigger if she could add the shower's water to it. She imagined Leon having to clean it up. If she did enough damage, he might have to put her someplace else for a little while. Maybe she'd get an idea of where she was—the street or the neighborhood or even just if she was still in the city.

The key was to clog up the floor drain. It was pretty big.

I need something to stuff into the drain holes, she reasoned. She thought about using some of her clothing, but without a change of clothes handy, that seemed like a bad idea.

Then she remembered the bed sheets she'd torn up. They were still in a pile by the door. *I can follow the wall to the rags,* she reasoned.

She slipped out of bed and crawled on all fours to the wall. Then she kept her left hand against it as she began a slow lap of the room.

Anything to keep her mind occupied. To keep her in motion and awake.

Soon her right hand landed on the pile of torn bedsheets. *Bingo!* She used one long piece to bundle the rest together, then dragged it behind her as she continued crawling, past the door, around the entire room, into the bathroom.

Finding the drain was harder. It was in the middle of the room, which meant taking her hand off the wall and wandering aimlessly in the dark. She searched with her hands, making wide circles as she scuttled forward.

One fingertip caught on the edge of a hole in the drain cover. She huddled herself above it and felt around the outside of the drain. Then she ran her palm over its entire surface to get an idea of how many holes it had. She counted three rows, one inside the other, and a single hole in the center.

Okay, I think this'll work, she thought, and she started pushing wads of ripped bedsheet into the holes. She twisted the fabric to get each piece through, then she let them unwind until they were wedged in place.

It was slow work. Phaedra worked her way around each row, stuffing up one hole at a time, then moving on to the next. When the outer row was finished, she started on the center row, and then the inner row and the middle opening.

At last she had plugged them all, and had a few rags left over, which she layered on top of the blocked drain. *Now the shower drain,* she decided.

She crawled until her hands found the wall with the towel rod, and she followed it, with her shoulder against it, until she felt the towels brush her face. She pulled both of them down and draped them over her neck.

Then she turned around and crawled back to the shower, where she scrunched one of the towels into a wad and set it over the drain.

A little hair on the drain always makes the tub at home fill up when I shower, she thought. *Let's see what this does.* She stood and sidestepped out of the now curtainless shower stall. Her hands probed the wall until she found the control lever for the shower and rotated it to the on position. A spray of cold water coursed unseen from the shower head and doused her arm.

Working from memory, she inched back along the rear wall until she bumped against the toilet. She circled around it and felt her foot kick over the roll of toilet paper next to it. Fumbling and groping in the darkness, she found the roll and unspooled the whole thing into the toilet. Then she pressed the flush lever and dropped the second towel into the bowl for good measure.

She was already backing away as she heard the slap of water overflowing the toilet and spreading across the floor. Stumbling blindly through the darkness, she collided awkwardly with the wall. Filled with an irrational fear of the water she imagined flooding across the floor, she hurried as fast as she could with her hands pressed against the wall, following it around the corner into the main room and back to the bed. She climbed on top of it and pressed herself into the corner.

Cowering on the thin, bare mattress, Phaedra clutched her pillow to her chest and listened to the soft patter of spilling water and the drone of the shower. It was almost hypnotic, and she felt her thoughts drifting as the sounds washed over her.

There would be no way to avoid falling asleep now, she knew. She was too tired, and with the bed the only reliable dry ground, she had little choice but to stay put. As she began sinking down into the well of slumber, she prayed she wouldn't have to face the night terrors that had haunted her since her father's death.

But she knew she would.

13

Tom watched Erin struggle to unlock the windowless gray metal door of a bleak-looking concrete building. They were on Dupont Street, in an area she'd said was called Greenpoint. "Got a safe house there," she'd explained, in between giving him turn-by-turn driving directions.

Gunfire still echoed in his ears, and his hands were still shaking from the adrenaline rush of being shot at. Fear had tied his stomach in a knot and refused to let it go. The long day had caught up to him, and he was fighting to stay awake.

The lock finally turned, and Erin slammed her shoulder against the door to push it open. On her third attempt it swung inward with a whiny creak.

He glanced nervously back at his pickup, parked across the street, as he followed her inside. "Will my truck be safe there?"

"Relax," she said, pulling him inside, clear of the door. "Who'd steal *that*?"

She slammed the door shut and left them in the dark. Then she flipped on a light switch and kept walking.

Inside the squat building was a wide-open loft converted from an industrial space. The floor was polished concrete stained to an earthen shade and sealed in a glossy sheen. Erin's footsteps snapped with sharp echoes as she crossed the room.

Exposed beams and planks served as a ceiling, which was supported by a row of broadly spaced iron poles.

The room had no windows, but simple lights were recessed between the ceiling beams and hidden by high sconces on the redbrick walls, which were decorated with a handful of abstract paintings.

Steam radiators were spaced a few yards apart on one side of the room. Pipes ran from floor to ceiling in the corners, and undisguised electrical conduits snaked along the floorboards to a number of AC outlets.

Near the entrance, on a large square of reddish ceramic tiles, was a kitchen area that featured a long countertop against the wall, a deep double sink, a huge stainless-steel refrigerator with a built-in ice maker, several wall-mounted cabinets, and a wide cooking island that included a flattop grill and a bar-style sitting area with some tall stools. Residing on the countertop were several more stainless-steel appliances: a toaster, an espresso machine, a blender, and a microwave oven.

There were few furnishings in the sprawling main room: one worse-for-wear old sofa, a trash-salvaged coffee table, and some pine-board shelves on cinder blocks. At the far end of the room was an open doorway that Tom hoped led to a bathroom, and next to it was an elevated area behind a wall of windows and a French door. As Erin switched on another light and climbed the stairs to the raised space, Tom saw it was a small loft with some low dressers and a digital clock on a headboard shelf behind a queen-sized bed.

Erin tossed her trenchcoat on the bed, dropped her axe handle in the corner, then sat on the bedroom steps to take off her boots. "Make yourself at home," she said, directing Tom to the sofa with a tilt of her head.

Tom slipped off his boatbuilder jacket as he walked to the beat-up old couch. He was about to sit down when he spied a stray coil poking up through the seat cushion. "I think I'll stand," he said, draping his jacket on the sofa's back.

She undid the laces of one combat boot and then the other, then chucked them both into the middle of the floor. He watched her wiggle her toes and sigh. Then he was looking at her legs. "That's better," she said, snapping his eyes back to her face. She stood. "You hurt?"

"Scrapes and bruises," he said, remembering the cuts on his palms, which had stopped bleeding, and the scratches that flying shards of glass had left on the back of his neck. "Nothing major." Between those and his earlier injuries, he expected to be in pain; instead, he felt numb.

With a weary but still fluid stride, Erin walked toward the open doorway. "C'mon, let's get patched up," she said, nodding for Tom to follow.

The safe house's bathroom was as polished as the rest of the space was raw. Granite tiles covered the floor and three-quarters of the high walls; the upper part of the walls and the ceiling were finished in pristine white. Green marble served as the vanity countertop and as a platform around the deep spa bathtub and the glass-walled shower area, which were made of spotless white porcelain.

Twin rectangular washbasins sat on the vanity, mirror images of each other, with side-mounted faucets that featured single-lever controls for water flow and temperature. A massive mirror dominated the wall over the basins, and a row of teal-painted cabinets provided ample storage beneath them.

"Have a seat by the tub," Erin said, opening one of the cabinets.

Tom stepped past her while she fished around under the sinks. "I don't mean to pry," he said, "but what do you do for a living?"

"Nothing," Erin said. "Hard to do a nine-to-five when you don't know what you're doin' day to day."

"Tell me about it," he said, taking a seat on the tub's wide elevated platform. "So if you don't work, what do you do for cash?"

She stood, holding two small plastic bins packed with first-aid supplies, and shrugged. "I get an allowance from the Sages."

"Enough to pay for a place like this?"

Settling down on the tub's platform next to him, she said, "No, just spending money." Waving at the room, she continued, "None of this is mine; the Sages just let me use it. Folks like us live off the grid most of the time. Safer that way." She opened one bin. "Why? Where do you live?"

"Small town," Tom said. "In a little house with a big mortgage."

Erin tsked and shook her head. "First thing the Sages would tell you is sell that place and get into a safe house somewhere."

She arranged tubes of ointment, rolls of gauze and medical tape, and a pair of small scissors in a neat line on the platform next to her.

"I like my house," Tom protested.

"You *won't* like being found by the Scorned."

He pointed at the hand-shaped burn on her right forearm. "Speaking of the Scorned, is the guy who did that one of them?"

"What gave it away?" she asked, squeezing hydrocortisone onto the burn. He could smell the medicine. "Cut me off some gauze."

He reached past her and picked up the roll of fabric and the scissors. Unspooling several inches of the sterile bandage, he said, "So, you don't work. But if you did, what would you do?"

"Dunno," Erin said, spreading burn cream all the way around her arm. The question seemed to make her uneasy. "Never really thought about it."

With a snip of the scissors, Tom cut loose a couple of feet of gauze. "You never wanted to be anything? Not even before you got Called?"

"Dropped outta high school at sixteen," she said. "Not like I had a lotta options, y'know?" As Tom offered her the strip of gauze, she nodded to her arm and said, "You mind? Hard to put it on one-handed."

"Sure," he said. Taking care not to put any pressure on her burn, he gingerly wrapped the gauze in slow, loose loops around her arm. "You don't want it too tight," he said, making the final pass under her arm. "Hold it here."

She pressed one finger on the end of the gauze while he cut two lengths of medical tape.

"A veterinarian," Erin said.

He looked up, confused by the non sequitur. "Huh?"

"When I was seven," Erin said. "I wanted to be a vet. My family had this cat, and some kids broke its leg throwing rocks at it. My mom and I took it to the vet, and he put a cast on it.

On the way home. I told my mom that's what I wanted to be when I grew up." She smiled, but there was a melancholy look in her eyes. "A week later, for Halloween, my mom dressed me up in a little white lab coat with my name stitched on it, and I carried the cat while I went trick-or-treating."

Tom heard longing and sorrow in Erin's voice, the remnants of a lost dream. At a loss for words, he simply nodded in understanding, then looped the tape around her bandage to hold it in place. "There," he said. "That ought to do it."

"One down, one to go," Erin said, standing up. "Still have to fix my leg." She unbuckled and unzipped her leather pants.

His voice shook like he was hitting puberty again. "I, uh—"

Before he could get any more words out, she dropped her pants to her ankles, stepped one foot free of them, then kicked them away.

As if it was the most ordinary thing in the world, she stood in front of him wearing nothing but a black leather corset, a minuscule pair of black silk underwear, and black socks. She lifted her right foot onto the tub platform to elevate her thigh, which bore the raw red gash of a grazing bullet wound.

Pointing at a hand mirror hanging on the side of the sink cabinet, she said, "Could you hand me that?"

He retrieved the mirror and gave it to her. She held it under her leg to get a clearer look at the wound, then grinned at Tom. "Beauty, ain't it?" She laid the mirror on the tub platform to free up her hands. "Looks worse than it is. I'm more upset over what that *cabrón* did to my pants."

She stepped over to the sink and washed her hands.

Eager to think about something other than Erin's current state of undress, Tom set his eyes to studying the bathroom's tile as he said, "I guess this wasn't your first time getting shot at."

Over the sound of running water, he heard her laugh. "No," she said, "but I'm guessing it was yours." She turned off the water and faced him while she toweled her hands dry. "Don't worry. You'll get used to it."

"I doubt that," he said, unable to shake the memory of point-blank gunshots.

She returned to the tub and lifted her leg as before. "Don't sell yourself short," she said. "Bet you're capable of lots of things you never dreamed of." She picked up the tube of antibiotic ointment, squeezed some onto one fingertip, and gently worked it into the wound on the back of her thigh. Then she unwrapped a sterile bandage, set it into place on the wound, and taped it down. Wiping off her hand with a towel, she told Tom, "Take your shirt off."

"No, that's okay, I'm fine," he said. Pointing at his superficial wounds, he added, "They're just scrapes."

"Turn around then," she said. "Still ought to clean 'em up. Don't want 'em getting infected." Unable to argue with her, he turned around. Again he heard running water, and a soft splash of excess water being wrung from a washcloth. Then he felt a soothing, moist warmth on the back of his neck.

"Your wounds are deeper than you think," Erin said, her voice soft and close to his ear. She dabbed gently at his neck, patted his torn flesh with tender care.

The closer she got, the more aroused—and nervous—he became.

"You, uh, know I'm married," he said.

"I know," she said. "That's another thing folks like us don't usually bother with. Makes things too . . . messy."

She gently pulled the collar of his shirt away from his neck and swabbed under it with the washcloth. Drops of warm water trickled down his back.

He closed his eyes and swallowed hard. "Didn't you ever think about . . . you know . . . having a family?"

"No," she said, reaching forward to mop his sweaty brow. "Never had any desire for a husband or kids. Of course . . . I do have *desires.*" With a salacious grin, she peeked over his shoulder at his lap. "Guess you got a few of your own."

Tom was on his feet and out of the bathroom in a matter of seconds.

He spent the longest minute of his life pacing in the middle of the main room and taking deep breaths. Panic had left him with a serious case of dry mouth, so he crossed to the kitchen sink, rotated the lever for cold water, and drank in greedy gulps right from the faucet. As he straightened and sleeved his mouth dry, he heard Erin's footfalls as she emerged from the bathroom.

"Time for bed," she said.

Words formed a traffic jam in Tom's brain. "Uh-huh."

She nodded at the old sofa. "You can crash out here if you want," she said, "but I hear that loose spring can be hard to sleep on." Padding slowly up the stairs to the loft, she untied her leather corset. At the top of the stairs, she threw a look over her shoulder. "Though it's only fair to warn you . . . if you join me, you won't get much sleep in here, either."

Tom felt as if he was seeing Erin clearly for the first time. She was trying so hard to project an air of seduction, to act the part of a femme fatale, but what he saw in her eyes wasn't lust or even attraction—it was a mix of sadness, vulnerability, and most of all, loneliness.

She turned out the bedroom light and let her corset fall away, revealing a primitive-art tattoo on her lower back as she slipped under the bedcovers.

Tom's stare traveled from the darkened bedroom to the jagged spring in the sofa cushion and back again. He shut his eyes and sighed.

"It's gonna be a long night," he muttered to himself.

14

Anna Doyle haunted her kitchen, cell phone in hand, her eyes on the microwave's clock. It was 6:59 a.m. on a gray Monday morning.

Her black coffee had gone cold since she'd last taken a sip—and she couldn't remember when that was. Unable to sleep, she had sat up at the kitchen table all night, imagining worst-case scenarios then banishing them from her mind with fantasies of Phaedra's homecoming, which felt like hollow wishes.

When she rubbed her eyes, the skin on her face felt oily. Her dim reflection on the front of the microwave showed her how flat and greasy her hair had become overnight. She couldn't remember the last time she'd eaten, but still she had no appetite. The hum of the refrigerator filled the empty silence of her home.

Then it was 7:00 a.m.

She lifted her phone, selected her lawyer's cell phone number from her contacts list, and pressed TALK. It rang while she held the phone to her ear.

Pick up, she prayed. *Pick up* . . .

A loud click was followed by a low rumble and the voice of Marc Cimbal, her family's longtime legal and financial counselor. *"Hello? Anna?"*

"Hi, Marc. I hope it's not too early to call."

"Not at all," he said. *"I'm on the train."*

"Good. I was afraid I'd wake you."

She could almost hear his good-natured grin as he replied, *"An early bird like me? Not a chance."*

Anna stood and paced, because sitting still was too difficult. "What time do you get in?"

"I'll reach Grand Central by quarter of, and I'll be in my office by eight," Marc said. *"Why? Do you need to come in?"*

She took a breath, then said, "No, I need you to do something for me."

"Name it."

"I need you to liquidate all of my assets immediately. As in today."

"Anna, are you crazy? That'd be a huge financial mistake. Never mind the tax liabilities—the trade fees would be astronomical. Not to mention it'd be a red flag for auditing when we do your taxes next year—"

"There's more," she cut in. "I need them transferred into bearer bonds, at least twelve million dollars' worth, and in my hands by end of business."

His sigh sounded like a roar of wind over the phone. *"Now I know you've lost it. Bearer bonds are almost impossible to get in the United States. The IRS knows people use them to evade taxes and launder money."*

"There must be some way to get them," Anna said, growing desperate.

"Well," Marc said, dragging out the word to fill a long

pause. *"I didn't say 'impossible.' I said 'almost impossible.' I might be able to wire your assets to an account in the Caymans, then use them to buy Eurobonds."*

"Fine," Anna said. "If it works, do it. But I need something physical in my hands by the end of the day."

He let out a doubting groan. *"I don't know. It might take a few days to—"*

"Today," Anna repeated. "In my hands."

She sensed his suspicion level rising. *"Anna, what's this about? Are you in financial trouble? Because I can help with—"*

"It's not like that," she insisted. "I just need the money." She stared out the window at two small brown birds on a bare branch. "Will you help me or not?"

"You're asking me to act against your financial best interest," he said. *"Ethically speaking, I have to tell you not to do this."*

Pressure pounded in her temples. "It's my money, Marc. Just do it."

"At least tell me why." Behind his voice, she heard the *bing-bong* tone that announced the closing of the train's doors. *"I can't help you do something illegal. You know that."*

"What I'm doing isn't illegal," she almost shouted.

"Fine, then you won't mind telling me what it is."

Anna didn't want to have this conversation, but she didn't have time to waste. She had to hope that the truth would satisfy him.

"I'm paying my daughter's ransom."

"Jesus!" he hissed, as if talking through his teeth. The background noise faded away, and his voice sounded closer—she pictured him cupping one hand over the phone to shield their conversation. *"Are you serious?"*

"She vanished Saturday night," Anna said. "I got the ransom

call yesterday afternoon. They said if I don't deliver twelve million in bearer bonds by the end of business today, they'll kill her."

"Have you called the FBI?"

"No, and I'm not going to—and neither are you."

"Anna, you have to—"

"The kidnappers know everything about the report I filed for Phaedra," she interrupted. "Names, case numbers, *everything*. They said they have people inside the police, the FBI, everywhere. If I call in the feds, they'll kill my little girl."

He exhaled heavily. *"Do you know who they are?"*

She rolled her eyes. "They didn't leave their name and number, no."

"No, I mean, in general. Did they sound Italian, Asian . . . ?"

"Russian," Anna said. "They sounded like Russians."

"All right," he said. *"Rounding up twelve million in one day won't be easy, but I know some people. I'll call you when it's done."*

"Thank you," Anna said. "And Marc—hurry, please."

"I will. Wait for my call this afternoon."

They said good-bye and hung up. It was 7:04.

There was nothing more Anna could do until she had the money. She was exhausted, distracted, and trapped in a state of perpetual panic.

I ought to take something to help me sleep, she told herself.

Then she imagined her little girl, held prisoner somewhere dark and lonely.

She downed another mouthful of cold coffee.

Phaedra had nowhere to hide. The birds were everywhere.

Large, nasty blackbirds with rasping squawks swooped at her, pecking at her head and her hands and her neck with their beaks, scratching at her arms and her face with their talons. Their mad cawing swallowed up her cries of terror.

The island was bare, treeless, and tiny. It was little more than a sandbar in the ocean, a patch of charcoal-colored dirt under a leaden sky. No matter in what direction Phaedra ran, the birds continued their merciless siege.

She tripped over her own feet in the deep sand and fell on her arms. A murder of crows landed on her back and speared her with their beaks. Thrashing and twisting, she shook them off and staggered away, her hands over her face.

Running blindly, she stumbled into the surf. It was ice cold.

Shock sent her backward, away from the dark, frigid water. Her feet felt numb. When she pulled her hands from her eyes to see where she was going, she saw that her palms were red with blood.

The island was swarming with birds. Every inch of land was covered in black feathers and scratch-squawking beaks.

In unison, they all took wing and raced toward her.

She screamed—and the clouds were rent by a shaft of sunlight. Thunder rolled as the birds disintegrated in the blinding white glare.

She awoke screaming and shaking, bathed in sweat and coiled around her twisted pillow on the bare mattress in the cinder-block room.

Overhead, the lights were on and painfully bright. The room echoed with the metallic clacks and impacts of the door's bolts being unlocked.

Averting her gaze, she saw that the floor of the entire cell was submerged beneath two inches of faintly chlorine-scented water. *That's it?* She was disappointed; she'd hoped to awaken to water as high as her knees.

The door swung open into the corridor outside her cell, and water flooded out, drenching Leon's ugly brown leather shoes. He stood there in his enormous black gas mask and another of his boring plain suits—brown, this time, with a white shirt and a gold-and-red checkered tie—while he surveyed the mess.

"Well," he said through the mask's snout-speaker. *"You've been busy."*

She was silent as Leon waded into the room. Water sloshed over his shoes and darkened the hems of his pant legs as he walked toward her, shaking his head.

"We were bringing you breakfast," he said. *"That'll have to wait now."*

He took a pair of handcuffs from his jacket pocket and reached toward her. She cowered and retreated from him, but it wasn't Leon she was really afraid of—it was the smoky black demon-shadow that lurked above and behind him every step of the way, echoing his every movement.

Her back hit the cinder-block wall. She turned her head away and shut her eyes. A handcuff closed with a cold, hard click on her wrist. As Leon reached down and locked the other ring of the cuffs to the metal frame of the bed, Phaedra sensed a clammy, toxic presence surrounding her. She held her breath; it was like being submerged in a pool of dirty water.

The gross sensation went away as Leon backed off. Now that Phaedra was stuck in one place, he went into the bathroom, leaving her unattended. Moments later, she heard him pulling the rag strips from the floor drain, followed by a deep sucking gurgle as her homemade pond started to shrink.

He stepped out of the bathroom holding the two sopping-wet green towels. They dripped steady streams as he carried them out of her cell and threw them aside. Then he moved out of view. She heard the sounds of feet climbing stairs and of doors opening and closing.

Even though she was cuffed to the bed, the fact that the door to her cell was open made her feel more free than she had minutes earlier. She fiddled with the handcuffs, to see if there was any way to work them free of the bed frame. Instead, she ended up tightening them another notch around her wrist.

Leon returned with a plunger in one hand, a wide squeegee mop in the other, and a trash bag draped over his shoulders and around his neck. He went back into the bathroom. Phaedra listened to the steady thump-suck pattern of Leon's plunging of the clogged toilet. The rustling of plastic and the wet slap of something heavy echoed from the bathroom.

When her captor passed through the room again, he was hauling the trash bag with both hands. He set it outside her door, then walked back to the bathroom. More sounds of tedious work followed. Soon, he was back, squeegee mopping the floor, corralling the floodwater out of her room and toward the now-opened drain.

And everywhere Leon went, his demon-shadow followed.

Phaedra had no idea how long she had watched and listened to him working. Finally, he finished, took his mop and plunger, and went upstairs again.

He came back minutes later carrying the tray with her breakfast, and he set it on the desk by her bed. Three small pancakes and two sausages on a paper plate. A paper cup of orange juice. One paper napkin and a cafeteria-style plastic spork. A diner-style single-serving plastic container of artificial maple syrup.

"We regret to inform you that your breakfast is now cold," he said. *"But under the circumstances, we can't feel that bad about it, since it was hot when we first brought it down."* His words were gently spoken, but his shadow seemed to seethe whenever it got close to her.

He nodded to the bathroom. *"We just want you to know, we don't blame you for what you did. We should have expected that. It was foolish of us to leave you so much to work with."* He reached for her wrist, and she cringed again while he unlocked the handcuffs from the bed. *"We've left you twelve squares of toilet paper. That should be enough for the day. Let us know at lunch if you need more."* Tucking the cuffs back into his jacket pocket, he added, *"If you want to take a shower tonight, tell us at dinner and we'll bring you a towel for twenty minutes."*

She massaged her aching wrist and glared at Leon as he and his shadow walked to the door. He stepped out and started to push it closed.

Just before it shut, he paused, poked his gas-masked head back in, and said with obvious sarcasm, *"Bon appetit."* Then he closed the door, and she heard the percussion of bolts being slammed back into place on the other side.

Long after he was gone, Phaedra was still shivering in terror. Now she knew the thing she'd seen in the truck on the night she was kidnapped hadn't been a hallucination. There were no drugs in her system now.

Whatever that evil, smoky thing had been, she was certain it was real—and that it wanted her dead.

15

"T*hen I stubbed my toe taking out the trash,"* Karen said. *"That's your fault, too."*

"Naturally." Tom paced beside his truck with his cell phone pressed to his ear and his face frozen in a tired, long-suffering smile. "What else?"

"The blueberry pancakes were burned," his wife groused. *"That never happens when you're here."*

He covered his free ear as a car with a bad muffler drove by. "Did you remember to turn down the heat before you spooned out the batter?"

"Don't try to make this about me," Karen said with mock anger. *"You're the one off in New York playing detective with your new friend, instead of being here to make the coffee with that dash of cinnamon I like. Oh, and you'll never guess what your stupid dog did last night."*

"If she's *my* dog again, I'm not sure I want to know."

"No, you don't. But we're buying a new couch."

"Understood." A cold breeze pushed through the parking lot. Tom raised his jacket's zipper from half-mast to the collar. "I'm sorry I'm not there, honey. Aside from your toe and the coffee and the pancakes and the couch, are you doing okay?"

She let out a resigned sigh. *"I'm fine. But I'd feel better if you were home."*

"Believe me, so would I."

"Are you and Aaron still getting along?"

He felt a guilty twinge as he once again let Karen's flawed assumption go uncorrected. "We're doing fine," he said. "But we have a long day ahead of us."

"Well, I won't keep you, then. Tell Aaron I said 'hello.' "

"I will," Tom said, grimacing at his lie of omission.

"And don't go thinking you can eat like a bachelor just because I'm not there. You still have to watch your cholesterol, so no junk food. *Right?"*

"Right," he said. "Gotta go. Love you."

"Love you, too. Stay safe."

"I will. Bye."

"Bye." She hung up.

He flipped his phone closed and reached for the driver's door of his truck. Pulling it open, he winced and groaned as the bruise and the scratch on his ribs throbbed and burned. His hand went to the sore spot inflicted by the sofa spring, which had stabbed him in the back all night long.

Pushing through the discomfort, he climbed into his truck. Erin was in the passenger seat, digging into her McDonald's breakfast. As he settled into his seat and pulled his door shut with a pained grunt, she tossed a paper bag in his lap.

"Got you a McMuffin and hash browns," she said.

Great, he thought, eyeing the bag with a sour frown. *More temptations.* He nodded once to Erin. "Thanks. Coffee?"

She pointed at the two cups in the drink holder on the island between them. "Front one's yours," she said through half a mouthful of egg and cheese. She swallowed, then added, "How's wifey?"

"She's good." He took his breakfast sandwich from the bag. The paper around it crinkled loudly as he folded it back. Then he stopped and looked at Erin. "We need to talk about last night."

"No, we don't," she said. "Nothin' to talk about." She took another bite of her breakfast and chewed.

"I'm not so sure," he said. "If there's nothing to talk about, why do I feel like I have something to hide from my wife?"

Erin shrugged. "You tell me."

"Are you saying you really don't get that what you did last night wasn't cool? 'Cause it wasn't. That can't happen again."

She held up her hand in the universal pose for stop. "Chill! I was just tryin' to do you a favor, okay?"

"I don't think last night was about doing me any favors."

Scowling, she shot back, "What's that supposed to mean?"

"You barely know me. So why're you in such a hurry to take me to bed?"

She reacted with a dismissive shrug. "You're a good-lookin' guy. Thought we could have fun."

"A gorgeous gal like you must have lots of options. Unmarried ones."

"You just don't get it." She put down the last bite of her sandwich. "People like us . . . we ain't s'posed to have husbands and wives and kids. We're s'posed to stay mobile, free to drop everything and go wherever we're needed, anytime, day or night. How you gonna do that with a wife and a rugrat? Huh?"

He looked away, out the windshield at traffic. "I've done okay so far."

"Yeah—*so far.*" Easing back a bit, she continued, "Doin' what we do, we make enemies—bad ones. The kind that'll come lookin' for you. The kind that'll kill that wife and kid of yours if they find 'em. I'm tellin' you this as a friend: the best thing you could ever do for them is leave 'em."

"Not gonna happen," he said. There was a dark note of truth in what she'd said, but it rubbed him the wrong way. "Maybe that was the right choice for you, but not for me."

His offhand remark seemed to strike a nerve. Anger flashed in Erin's eyes. "I didn't *have* a choice." Her rage faded and was replaced by sorrow. Tom could see in Erin's expressions that she was struggling to decide what she ought to say next. A tear rolled from her eyes, and she palmed it from her cheek. "When I was Phaedra's age . . . the Scorned came looking for me, too. I don't know how they found me—I didn't even know what I was yet. But they killed my parents and my kid sister before a Sentinel could stop them."

Erin's tough-girl façade began to make sense to Tom. Her attempts at casual, fleeting intimacy seemed tailor-made to provide her the illusion of companionship without exposing her to the risk of further emotional loss. And he suspected that the death of her family hadn't been the last such tragedy she'd endured.

After a long and doleful silence, she added with quiet conviction, "That's our enemy, Tom. It's what they do. If you love your family . . . let them go."

He looked her in the eye. "No. I love my wife, and I'm gonna love my son. They're my *life.* I won't leave them."

She turned away and nodded. "Fine," she said, signaling her surrender. Then she looked back. "But ask yourself this, and be honest. If you'd heard a prayer like Phaedra's ten years ago, would you still have gotten married? Would you still be starting a family if you'd known your calling could be life or death?"

Picturing that scenario, he realized that he had taken his quiet life in Sawyer for granted—and that he probably never could again.

"I don't know," he said. "Maybe not."

"That's all I'm saying," she said with a half nod.

"And all *I'm* saying is maybe what *you* really need is a better way to make new friends."

That bit of truth earned Tom a sullen glare.

He and Erin sat and finished their greasy breakfasts in mutually resentful silence while early morning traffic rolled by on Atlantic Avenue. The sky brightened quickly from dull gray to an off-white shade of overcast.

After they finished, Tom gathered up the trash, got out of the truck, and walked the refuse over to a nearby garbage can. When he returned, Erin had his New York City road atlas open. She was staring at a map of Brooklyn.

He folded his arms. "So what's our next move?"

"No clue," she said. "Swap's today?"

"Tonight, yeah."

She propped her arm on the door and rested her head on her hand. "Doesn't leave us much time."

"Well," Tom said, thinking out loud, "what do we know so far? Guys who sound Russian say they're holding her, and they want twelve million bucks. When I started poking around, four Russian guys beat the crap outta me. We've linked at least two of them to that club in Gravesend. So the next lead we work is the club."

Erin threw him a confused shrug and head shake. "What does that get us?"

An idea took shape in Tom's head. He grinned.

"More than you'd think," he said. "If you know how to ask."

Frank Kolpack found driving in molasses-slow Monday-morning traffic on the Jackie Robinson Parkway to be rage inducing enough without his also having to listen to Viktor Nemikov's furious ranting.

"They went through everything!" Viktor shouted, his voice distorted over the disposable cell phone's hands-free speaker. *"Searched the whole place!"*

"Calm down," Frank said. "Did they take anything?"

Viktor screamed back, *"How the hell should I know?"*

"Ask Dmitry," Frank said, trying to sound reassuring. "He keeps your inventory. He'll know if something's missing."

"Later. What are you going to do about this?"

Recoiling from the sheer stupidity of what he was hearing, Frank replied, "What do you expect me to do?" The traffic ground to a halt. He sipped his coffee while the boss continued his tirade.

"I pay you to be my eyes and ears. Find out who did it."

He shook his head. "Viktor, I can't investigate it unless you report it, and we both know why that's a bad idea."

Viktor bellowed, *"They burned my dogs!"*

That caught Frank's attention. "They what?"

"Burned them!" Viktor said. *"Cooked them to a crisp, all three of them, and left them for the flies. What sort of monster hurts a dog?"*

Frank rolled his eyes in dismay. *The sort whose hands burn flesh.* "All right," he said. "I'm on top of it."

"I want these bastards in my hands tonight."

Ahead of Frank, the line of cars inched forward again. He

let his foot ease off the brake. "Eyes on the prize, Viktor. We already *have* a date tonight."

"You're sure that's happening?"

"Positive," Frank said, pushing down on the brake as the sea of cars came to another stop like setting concrete. "My people tell me Anna's lawyer is already moving her assets into Eurobonds on the London Exchange. By the time Wall Street closes today at four, she'll have the cash in hand for the swap."

Viktor made a dismissive noise as if he was clearing his throat. *"All this effort for such a simple deal,"* he said. *"A wire transfer would be faster."*

"And traceable," Frank reminded him. "Bearer bonds aren't."

"Yes, yes," Viktor said, brushing off the lesson. *"Of course, it won't matter how the money gets delivered if Leon doesn't keep his mouth shut."*

Frank shook his head. He hated it when Viktor started getting cold feet. Any little setback could spook the man. It drove Frank insane and made his hunger for a cigarette all the more intense. His right hand curled into a fist.

"It *could* go wrong," he admitted. "But it won't. Once the money gets to the swap, we're golden. Leon's cool—just make sure *your* people stick to the script."

"And if Leon does something stupid?"

"He won't," Frank snapped, stepping on the gas as he switched lanes and cut someone off in the process. The driver behind him gave him a long and angry honk. Frank flipped his middle finger over his shoulder.

"How can you be sure?"

After a disgruntled sigh, Frank said, "Because he's a professional. You can trust him. I guarantee it."

"If you say so, I believe you," Viktor said. *"But it feels to me like there are too many variables that are out of our hands. I don't like it."*

"Relax, it's all taken care of." Traffic sped up, so Frank stepped on the gas and enjoyed being back in motion. "If Anna calls in the law, we walk away," he continued. "The phones are clean, and no one's seen our faces. Whoever shows up to the swap'll be the only witness, so we pop 'em and grab the cash. There's no downside to this for us, Viktor. If it goes sour, we walk away and lose nothing. If it pays out, you're up twelve million—minus my finder's fee, of course."

"Of course."

"Bottom line, Viktor: the situation is under control. Just tell your people to stick to the plan, and everything'll be fine."

"Very well," Viktor said. *"But the man who killed my dogs has to pay."*

"Absolutely," Frank said. "Good-bye and have a good day, Viktor."

"Good-bye," the Russian grumped, then hung up.

Frank pushed the END button on his cell phone and enjoyed the relative silence in the car, which, despite having three brand-new pine-tree-shaped air fresheners—one on the rearview mirror and one on each backseat coat hook—still reeked of old cigarette smoke.

He rolled down the window to get some fresh air. It was cold but it felt good, since talking to the Russians always made his ears burn with rage.

If he'd had a choice, he wouldn't have involved the Russians in the ransom scheme at all, but the fact was he needed them. Controlling a situation as volatile as a swap would take manpower—and possibly firepower, if the cops got involved—since Anna was almost certain to demand the exchange happen in a public place. Naturally, he already had such a location in mind.

His cut of the ransom would be only three million, but that was the price he paid for staying out of the fray. Giving up nine million dollars rankled him, but it seemed like a worthwhile investment to let the Russians handle the heavy lifting. Because if anything did end up going wrong, it would be their asses on the line instead of his, and if there was one thing Frank Kolpack believed in above all else, it was minimizing risk to himself.

That was just good business.

The front door of the Cobble Hill apartment building opened with a barely audible vibration after the third time Erin leaned on her friend's buzzer. She pushed through the front door and then the vestibule's inner door in quick succession, while they were still unlocked.

Tom followed close behind her as they stepped quickly down the hallway to the stairs. As she started climbing, he stopped at the bottom stair and looked up through the space between the switchback flights.

"What floor did you say he was on?"

She paused and looked back. "Fourth."

"Is there an elevator?"

"Buildings with less than six floors don't have to have elevators in New York," she said and resumed plodding upward, two stairs at a time. Grumbling under his breath, he worked hard to keep up with her.

Each floor brought its own parade of odors. The ground floor had smelled of garlic; second floor, incense and pot; third floor, cigar smoke and cat urine.

They arrived on the fourth floor, which stank of old socks. Erin figured it was Tom's good luck to have been gasping for air after finishing their rapid climb, since it meant he was breathing through his mouth. She led him to an unmarked door with chipped green paint and thumped the side of her fist on it.

From behind the door, someone growled in a thick Welsh accent, *"Right! I'm coming, already."*

Then came a seemingly endless clatter of bolts being retracted and chains being removed, ultimately leading to the knob turning and the door swinging open.

Standing there was a tall but paunchy man in his late twenties, sporting an unkempt beard and long, unwashed bleached hair. He was barefoot and wearing nothing but a pair of gray briefs. A pelt of blond fur covered his chest, abdomen, and legs. Squinting, he poked his head forward to get a closer look at his visitors.

"Erin, is that you?"

"Morning, Rhys," she said, wincing at his body odor.

He scratched his chest and yawned. "What time is it?"

"Five of eight."

His face twisted with horror. "In the *morning?* I just went to bed! What're you doing here?"

She nodded at a small laptop tucked into a corner of his combination living room and kitchen. "Need to use your computer."

He rubbed his palms against his eyes. "Is that all?"

"That's all," she said.

Waving them inside, he said, "Fine, let yourselves out when you're done."

Erin led Tom into the apartment, which was just as she'd

remembered it from her last visit, many months earlier. Dirty plates and mugs everywhere. Unwashed clothes all over the floor. A sink full of mold-covered pans.

Tom took it all in with an air of mild horror. "Jesus," he said. "Last time I saw a place that looked like this, the Red Cross was serving doughnuts."

"Call them," Rhys said, staggering to a collapse on a sofa strewn with old newspapers. He mumbled as he passed out, "I like doughnuts."

Seconds later, the snoring started.

"There's your computer," Erin said to Tom. "Show me what you've got."

He stepped past her, tiptoed through Rhys's minefield of junk and leftovers, and took a seat at the small table where the laptop lay waiting. She stood behind Tom and watched as he opened the portable computer, which hummed and clicked to life. With practiced ease, Tom navigated through its menus, launched a Web browser, and typed a query into the search engine. A page full of results popped up, and he skimmed the list quickly before clicking on one.

"What're you doing?" she asked.

"I searched for 'New York City property records,'" Tom said. "As I figured, the top result was the online version of the official city register. We can use that to investigate property deeds and stuff." Opening a new window, he typed in more search terms. "Now I'm looking up the New York State Division of Corporations. That'll help us find information about who owns that club."

As he began copying information from one screen and pasting it into the form fields in another, he glanced at Rhys and asked softly, "What's *his* story?"

"Musician," Erin said, assuming that explanation would be all the information Tom would require. She'd assumed wrong.

"What kind of musician?" Tom asked.

A smile tugged at her mouth. "Washboard in a jug band."

Tom stopped typing and turned his head to meet her gaze. "Washboard? In a jug band?" He looked at the saw-snoring Rhys, then back at Erin. "He makes a *living* doing that?"

"Hell, no," Erin said. "He has a job pumping septic tanks on Long Island."

If Tom had a joking response to that revelation, he kept it to himself. He turned and went back to work. A minute later, he said, "Okay, here we go." Pointing at various details, he narrated his findings for Erin. "This is the city's online register. We start by plugging in the address we know, for the Baba Yaga Club. The register tells us who owns it. . . ."

She read over his shoulder, " 'Baba Yaga, LLC' . . . dead end?"

"Not by a long shot," Tom said. "Now we put that into the database for the state's Division of Corporations. That should give us a list of corporate officers and maybe the major shareholders." More typing, more waiting. Then a new screen of information appeared. "Okay, it looks like Baba Yaga's a shell company for something called VKN Land Parcel Corp. Let's see what the state has on them and see if the city has any property registered to them."

While they waited for the computer to produce more search results, Erin said, "Have to admit—I'm impressed, *papi.* How'd a small-town guy like you learn to do this stuff?"

"Please. I'm from the suburbs, not Amish country." He looked over his shoulder at her and smiled. "Besides, once you buy a house, you learn nobody has any secrets." New data appeared on the computer screen. Tom studied it for a moment, then said, "All right, VKN's corporate info goes to a lawyer, who's probably a front. *That's* a dead end." Switching to the screen with the city register, his tone changed. "This, on the other hand, is exactly what I'm talking about. More than three dozen properties registered to VKN, all of them in Brooklyn."

"They're all over the place, though," Erin said, scanning the addresses. "That's a lotta ground to cover by tonight."

Tom held up a finger. "Maybe not. We can probably rule a lot of these out. Multiunit apartment dwellings can go—too many possible witnesses for them to keep Phaedra there. Most of the commercial real estate is also too high-profile. What we're looking for would be an industrial or manufacturing space, preferably not in use right now. Someplace you could hide a kid."

Working from her memory of various neighborhoods and intersections, Erin eliminated most of the addresses on the screen, until only nine remained. She scribbled them down on a piece of scrap paper and handed it to Tom. "These are the ones to check."

"Okay. You know how to find all of 'em?"

"No problem," she said.

"Great, let's go." He closed the laptop, got up, and followed her to the door. As she opened it, he hooked a thumb in Rhys's direction and asked, "Want to say good-bye to Rip Van Winkle?"

She looked back at Rhys's gangly form, which was drooped over the couch in a pose that made him look as if he'd melted. "Rhys! We're going!"

Facedown in a sprawl of week-old newspapers, Rhys groggily mumbled a reply that sounded like "Burpf."

Tom looked concerned. "Is he okay?"

"He's fine," Erin said, leaving the apartment. "Let's go to work."

16

Katharine Bailey walked into the detectives' squad room on the second floor and shambled to her desk as if it were just another morning.

She pushed through the creaky wooden swinging gate and noticed that the cage on her left was empty for a change. "Hey, Bob," she said, nodding to Detective Halper, who had his feet propped up on his desk while he read his folded-over copy of that morning's paper. "Slow night?"

"For a change," Halper said, too engrossed in the sports page to look up.

The rest of the squad room was filled with similar portraits of apathy: Detective Ohara half-asleep at his desk, face propped on his hand, a hint of drool in the corner of his mouth; Detective Whitfield flinging pencils point-first into the ceiling tiles; Officer DeSantis kicking off another day in his anticrime rotation with a breakfast of black coffee and aspirin.

Bailey slumped into her chair as Lieutenant La Salle emerged from his office and did a double take in her direction.

"Do my eyes deceive me?" La Salle said, his sarcasm quotient at an all-time high. "Am I really seeing Detective Bailey putting in unpaid overtime?"

She half smirked, half glowered at her commanding officer. "Just digging till I see daylight, Lou. I've got a week of overdue fives to fill out."

"What else is new?" La Salle said with a sardonic smile. "You've been a week behind since you got here." He shambled toward the stacked grid of mail slots, pulled a handful of envelopes from his mailbox, and shuffled through them. "Long as you're doin' favors, want to sit in for me at CompStat today?"

"No, sir," Bailey said, launching an automated DD5 form on her antiquated desktop computer. "Getting too close to the bosses gives me a headache."

"Me too." La Salle chucked his mail into the trash. "Are those just filler fives, or can I actually expect you to close one of those today?"

She shrugged. "You know the drill, sir. 'Pinks are free—' "

" 'But blues cost money,' " he said, finishing the aphorism. "Tell me something I don't know." Disgruntled and tired-looking, he wandered away into the squad's coffee room, where the plastic radio on top of the fridge squawked out a steady twenty-two-minute loop of news, weather, and traffic.

Bailey looked at the clock. It was 8:25 a.m. The desk across from hers was empty. Prairie-dogging her head up over her blocky computer monitor, she called to Ohara, "John! Seen Frank this morning?"

"He's out on a canvas," the Asian-American detective said. "Had me clock him in. Why?"

"I just needed his notes on last week's OTB collar," she lied, ducking back behind her monitor. She pushed some papers around on her desk and tapped at random keys until she was sure the other detectives were ignoring her.

Affecting as casual an attitude as she could, Bailey got up and circled around to Kolpack's desk. No one else in the squad looked up. She slid into Kolpack's chair and let her eyes scan the dense clutter of his desktop.

Incomplete reports, half a cup of the previous day's coffee, a crooked stack of case files dating back months. Two pencils with broken tips. Three packs of spearmint chewing gum—one at either end of the desk, one by the phone, all open.

She tugged on the top desk drawer. It resisted, so she pulled harder. It opened. There was nothing suspicious in it that she could see. *No help there,* she mused. The desk's lower two drawers proved equally fruitless.

As she eased the lower one shut, she noticed out of the corner of her eye that someone was watching her.

It was Detective Whitfield. "Lose something?" he asked.

"Looking for a spare notepad," she said. "Frank hoards 'em whenever supplies come in."

Nodding toward his desk, Whitfield said, "C'mon, I think I've got one."

"Great," Bailey said, feigning relief as she got up and followed him.

He opened his top desk drawer, fished out a brand-new spiral-top notepad, and lobbed it to her. "No charge."

"Thanks, Carl, you're a lifesaver." She held up the pad, smiled at Whitfield, and carried her trophy back to her desk, where she stuffed it into a drawer with five others.

She sank into her chair. *Fuckin' cops. Can't mind their own business.*

She felt self-conscious and more than a bit ashamed of herself for snooping in Kolpack's things. *What did I expect?* she asked herself. *Did I really think he'd leave a smoking gun in his desk?*

Still, she knew that she'd had to look; she'd needed to be sure. Something about Kolpack had felt off for a long time, and Bailey had been aware of it well before her chat with IAB the previous evening. It wasn't that she had ever seen him do anything obviously illegal; what bothered her was the feeling that he was always pursuing a hidden agenda.

All she was really looking for was a reason to break the code of silence, something rock solid that she could hand off to IAB without branding herself a rat.

Trust was a matter of life and death for people on the job. From the officer making a traffic stop to the Emergency Service Unit trooper going through a door, the one thing that made it possible for a cop to face the dangers of his daily life was the knowledge that the cop next to him would have his back—both on the street and in court.

Sometimes that meant saying a perp got a faceful of bruises falling down a flight of stairs while fleeing police custody. That your partner confiscated a baggie full of pills from the suspect's pocket. That the snub-nosed .38 had been visible on the floor inside the car the entire time, not dropped there during your search of the vehicle. That the shooting was righteous because you were sure the skel had been waving a gat, not a cell phone.

All lies. But for good reasons. Not just to save cops' asses but to protect the public from dirtbags who would've gamed the system and taken a walk otherwise. The skels and the lawyers had their tricks, and so did the job.

Of course, there was a line. A limit. There had to be.

Bailey didn't know yet whether Kolpack had crossed it. But until she found out, she'd have to follow her gut.

And her gut told her that Kolpack wasn't to be trusted.

17

Anna told herself the same thing every time she paced by the phone in her kitchen: *Don't call him yet. It's too soon. Give him time.*

Her eyes flitted between the window, where a gathering storm darkened the day by slow degrees, and the clock over the stove, which seemed to move in slow motion. She prayed for time to march on swifter feet even as she felt dead on hers.

Acid burned in her stomach, stirred by fear and fury. In a perverse way, Anna was grateful for the cramping pain in her gut. It was helping her stay awake, despite the leaden sensation in her eyelids. Focusing on the twisting agony in her stomach kept her in motion; it kept her sharp and ready.

Don't pick it up, she commanded herself as she passed the phone again. *Just leave it. It's not even noon.*

A faint pattering of rain left wet streaks across the window.

She couldn't help herself. Her left hand plucked the phone from its cradle and her right hand pressed the redial button.

The other end of the line rang while anxiety gave the hot knife inside her stomach a fresh twist.

Marc sounded worried when he answered his cell. *"Anna? What's wrong? Did something happen?"*

"No, nothing's happened," she said, hoping it was true. "I just wanted to check in, get an update. See how we're doing."

Now he was flustered. *"I'm working as fast as I can,"* he said. *"But you ought to know you're losing a bundle on this. Between fees, taxes, and a dip in the share prices, we'll be lucky to clear eleven million."*

"Marc, the kidnappers want twelve, you know that."

The lawyer grumble-sighed. *"Something tells me they'll settle for less, as long as you're in the ballpark."*

Anna wished she could breathe fire over a phone line. "And you're willing to bet my daughter's life on that?"

"You're the one betting her life, Anna. Do you really think thugs like these will make a fair trade? Because, to be honest with you, I don't. I think if you show up to meet these guys with a briefcase full of bearer bonds, they'll just take the money and kill you and Phaedra." He let her seethe a moment before he added, *"I'm begging you, Anna—call the FBI while there's still time."*

She shut her eyes and tried to squeeze the throbbing pain from her forehead. "If I do that, and they kill my baby, I . . ." Her voice deserted her for several painful seconds, then she recovered a small measure of composure. "I couldn't live with that, Marc. I have to do this." Strengthening her resolve, she added, "Tell me you'll have the money ready on time."

"I'll have it," he said. *"I'm working trades on three exchanges to make it happen. If all goes well, I should be able to start picking up the bonds by one thirty, and I'll have them all by four."*

"And you'll call me as soon as you have them?"

"Yes. But I'd feel a lot better if you called the feds."

Anna rolled her eyes at Marc's stubbornness. Then her gaze fell upon a scrap of paper she'd left on the kitchen table. She picked it up. On it was a phone number and a name: Tom Nash. His promise echoed in her thoughts: *I'm here for only one reason, Mrs. Doyle—to help you find your daughter.*

Her mind was made up. "We're not calling the cops or the feds," she told Marc. "But I am calling in some help."

18

Rain slashed across the truck's windshield. Tom squinted past the fast-thumping wiper blades and kept his eyes on the traffic as Erin said, "Turn right up here."

"Where the hell are we?" he asked, unable to spare a glance at the road signs while weaving around a driver making a U-turn in the middle of the intersection.

She looked out her storm-blurred window. "Somewhere in Crown Heights. Get ready to make a left on Lefferts."

Tom strained to see anything ahead of them besides a fuzzy kaleidoscope of tail lights and traffic signals. "How many properties do we have left to check?"

"Just one," Erin said. "If it's still standing."

He nodded with a grim frown. All the properties purchased by VKN that they had visited that morning had been demolished. A few had been converted into working parking lots, but most of them were little more than deep excavations filled with heavy construction machinery and surrounded by plywood barriers.

The next light came up fast out of the gloom. "Turn here," Erin said, and he steered the truck east on Lefferts Avenue. Most of the street's features were obscured by the gray veil of the downpour, but what little Tom saw made him think that was probably for the best.

Erin stared out her window, watching the building numbers. She checked the list in her hand and said, "I think that's it, up on the right, just past the merge."

Tom slowed down and let a few cars pass him on the right, then he switched lanes for a slow cruise past the three-story building. Its lower half was redbrick, the top a weathered beige concrete. A short flight of stairs parallel to the street led to a small landing in front of its boarded-up main entrance; a long, shallow-angle cement ramp led away from the door on the other side of the landing. Next to the building was a fenced-off empty parking lot filled with garbage.

"Well, at least this one's still here," he said. Noting the boards that covered its windows and doors, he added, "Looks like nobody's home."

"Maybe we're just supposed to think so," Erin said. "If you were looking to hide someone you were holding for ransom . . ."

"Yeah, I'd say it fits the bill for that," Tom said.

She pointed at the intersection ahead of them. "Go right on Utica, and swing around to the next block. Then pull into the White Castle lot."

"Got it," Tom said, nudging his directional to signal for the turn. He guided the truck through two right turns onto East New York Avenue and then made another quick right into the fast-food restaurant's parking lot. A van pulled out of a spot against the building, and he moved his truck into it as soon as it was clear.

He turned off the engine, which slammed and banged its way to silence.

"Maybe it's time for a tune-up?" Erin said with a hint of amusement.

"Actually, we're saving up to buy a hybrid."

Opening her door, she replied, "Sexy." The truck filled with the soft roar of pouring rain as Erin grabbed her axe handle. "Ready?"

He took the keys from the ignition. "Hang on. Are we gonna break into this place in broad daylight? Even if it's raining, someone's gonna see us, aren't they?"

"There's a back door facing the parking lot," Erin said.

"Which is still visible from the street," he replied. "What if someone calls the cops? And what if Phaedra's in there, and we get arrested for kidnapping her?"

Erin frowned and bobbed her head. "Okay, good point." She started emptying her pockets and stuffing things under the passenger seat. "Leave anything that can identify you here. License, phone, video membership card—anything with your name on it or linked to something with your name on it." She pointed at the car keys in his hand. "Like those. If we get pinched, just shut up and follow my lead." When she was done, all she had was her axe handle and her butterfly knife.

Tom gathered up his wallet and a leather flip-fold that held his credit cards and driver's license, which he kept separate from his wallet—a lesson he'd learned the hard way after getting mugged years earlier during a trip to Pittsburgh. He shoved the whole lot under his seat.

He checked his jacket pockets. All he had in them was his locksmithing kit and his Maglite. "Ready," he said. Erin got out of the truck and shut her door. Tom opened his door, used his keys' remote control to lock the truck, then stepped out into the downpour. He tossed his keys under his seat and shut the door.

They jogged across the restaurant's parking lot toward the Lefferts Avenue exit. Erin kept her axe handle tucked close at her side under her trenchcoat. Tom hunched inside his canvas jacket, which was soaked through within seconds.

Rain beat down on the city, its white noise almost deafening. The sidewalk shimmered with the reflections of passing cars' headlights. There were no other pedestrians out that Tom could see.

He and Erin moved quickly west up the avenue, to the chained and locked gate of the abandoned building's parking lot. Erin stood watch while he picked the padlock and undid the chain. Less than thirty seconds later, they were scampering across the trash-filled lot toward the building's rear entrance.

The back door turned out to be a garage secured behind a steel drop-down barricade. Tom made quick work of the two padlocks that held it closed, then Erin helped him lift the barricade a few feet, just enough for them to slip under.

Once inside, they stood up. The susurrus of the storm was muffled, making the dribble of water falling from their drenched bodies to the concrete floor sound that much louder. Tom shook his arms and squeezed the excess water from his hair. Erin seemed content to stay wet while she looked around.

The inside of the building had been all but gutted. As Tom and Erin crept forward, their steps echoed between the few bare support timbers that remained in place. Overhead, between exposed steel crossbeams, sagging floorboards showed off their rot. Junk and debris were scattered everywhere in the musty-smelling space, which was steeped in shadow. Lengths of wire drooped from what was left of the ceiling, and under every boarded window was a patch of shattered glass.

The steady siege of rain on the windows' plywood coverings filled the eerie, desolate space with a hushing roar, and groaning winds moaned through the floors above them.

"That must be the front door over there," Tom said, pointing at the boarded-over entrance and stepping over a pile of loose scrap wood.

Erin nodded, then froze as a high-pitched chittering sounded from the darkness. Tom stopped, looked back at her, then searched out the source of the noise. A huge pack of the largest rats he'd ever seen skittered past, along the edge of the shadows.

"Holy shit, they're big," he said.

"Sí," Erin said, recoiling from the rodents.

"What're you afraid of? Can't you talk to them?"

She arched her eyebrows. "Some animals can't be reasoned with. Rats hate people." She pointed to a nearby flight of stairs. Without any walls or backing, it looked like the skeleton of its former self. "Let's head upstairs," she said.

They reached the stairs. Tom grabbed her arm to stop her. He pointed at a series of fresh footprints in the heavy gray dust that coated each step. "Someone's been here," he said. "Pretty recently."

"Prints heading up and down," Erin noted.

He nodded and wondered aloud, "Maybe someone visiting the girl?"

Treading with care, they inched their way up the stairs. Every shift of their weight prompted long, loud creaks from the tired, semirotten stair frame.

The second floor was another yawning expanse of forlorn darkness and cobwebbed debris, but with a few walls still partially intact. The floorboards groaned under their feet as they skulked forward, following the footprints.

A legion of broken medical-looking machines, some vandalized, were scattered about. Some lay on their sides, others were piled in heaps. Old metal bed frames, stripped of their mattresses, had been upended in seemingly random locations, most of them blocking the easiest passages to the other stairwells. "Looks like a riot went through here," Tom said.

"Prints head back that way," she whispered. "To the west staircase."

He gestured for her to lead the way. Brandishing her axe handle openly, she stole forward, wary and alert as they wove a path through the maze of clutter. At the west stairs, she paused, checked up and down, then looked back at Tom. "They head upstairs," she said softly. "Something's blocking the next flight down."

He sidled past her, activated his flashlight, and aimed it down into the shadows. "Chairs," he said, keeping his voice low. "Someone piled this staircase with them." He turned the beam upward. "Whoever we're following, they went this way." He started upstairs and was reassured to hear her follow him.

The top floor of the building was more intact than the first two. Most of the internal walls remained in place. Sheets of linoleum had peeled back to reveal the old flooring beneath them, and some of the antiquated wiring and plumbing was still visible through a handful of minor breaches in the drywall. Like the lower floors, however, it was also impenetrably dark.

He looked at Erin. "What do you think?"

"Looks like a dead end," she said, "but we should check all the rooms on this floor to make sure."

"Agreed."

They explored the corridor side by side. Tom checked the rooms on the right and Erin scouted the ones on the left. Room after room held nothing but chipped paint, crumbling plaster, torn-up linoleum, and piles of broken wooden furniture. Wind wailed through the building's empty spaces.

Tracking the footprints with his light, Tom led Erin down a connecting passage that linked the floor's two main corridors in an H shape. He pointed at the floor in the middle of the small corridor. "Look at that," he said. "The footprints just stop." Aiming the beam at the wall in front of the dead-end trail, he saw an unusual graffito—a simple lightning-bolt icon so freshly drawn that its paint was dripping:

"Mark of the Scorned," Erin said.

Tom stepped forward for a closer look. A quick, sharp slice of pain bit into his ankle. He felt a wire snap.

"Down!" he shouted, hitting the deck. Erin dived to one side.

Ceiling timbers and loose wood tumbled down on top of them.

A rain of dark gray dust followed the wood, coating Tom and Erin from head to toe and filling the short passage with a thick, choking cloud. Tom coughed, checked the bruises on his forehead and arms, then asked Erin, "You okay?"

"I think so," she said, then hacked out a few hard coughs of her own.

He started to push his way free of the mound of cumbersome wood when a new smell filled his nostrils. His eyes went wide, and he froze as he recognized it.

"Kerosene!" he said, stumbling over the timbers, which he could barely see in the dusty gloom. His hand found Erin's arm, and he pulled her along. "Run!"

He got all of three steps. Then everything exploded into searing red thunder before it smashed down into dull black silence.

Dillon reclined in the passenger seat of Zev's car and permitted himself a satisfied smirk. Through the rain-washed windshield, he watched fireballs blast through the plywood covering the third-floor windows of the abandoned clinic.

"We should have brought marshmallows," he said to Zev.

The Seer shook his head. "I can't believe they walked right into it."

Admiring the glow of spreading flames, Dillon replied, "They saw what they wanted to see."

Tracking the enemy Seekers hadn't been all that difficult. It had been obvious to Dillon that they were looking for the abducted girl and that some blunder or other had led them to Kolpack's cohorts in the Russian mob.

Figuring they would investigate the club's owner next, he had availed himself of the same public resources that they were certain to use. Thinking the way they would, he'd ruled out all but a handful of the Russians' properties and discovered that this one was the last with a building still standing.

Then all that had remained had been to set the trap.

Reddish orange licks of fire jumped from the third-floor windows, which belched black smoke into the dreary gray downpour.

Sirens wailed, rising in pitch as they drew near. In the side-view mirror, Dillon saw the sapphire and ruby flashes of emergency lights. Police cruisers and fire engines were speeding down Empire Boulevard to meet the blaze.

"Time to go," Zev said, starting the car's engine. Nodding at the growing inferno across the street, he added, "Nice job, by the way. It's a work of art."

"Thanks," Dillon said, raising his mummified left hand and casting a dour grimace at his bandage-swaddled right arm and leg. "Not bad for a gimp."

Zev pulled away from the curb and accelerated away from the burning building. "Still, it would've been nice to see you beat those two in a fair fight."

"That's the great thing about a trap," Dillon said, tugging his baseball cap over his eyes for a long-overdue nap. "When it works, you don't have to fight."

A jackhammer was pounding inside Tom's skull.

The roar and snap of flames jolted him awake. He and Erin were on the floor in the middle of the short passage, which was blocked at either end by a wall of fire. Searing heat stung his face as he sat up. Oily black smoke rolled along the ceiling.

He reached over to Erin, stretched to make contact, and became light-headed. His mouth was sandpaper dry, and his guts churned with nausea. It was a battle to keep his eyes open and focused. He crawled to Erin's side and shook her.

"Erin! You with me? Wake up!" She didn't stir.

A boom and a furnace blast of hot air turned his head.

Rickety walls were crumbling before the advancing fire, and the stacks of broken wooden furniture were fueling it, tempting it forward like bait.

Then he remembered the kerosene and the wire and the maze of junk between them and the exit, and he knew that they'd walked into a trap.

"Dammit," he muttered, pulling his damp jacket over his head. He yanked Erin's wet trenchcoat from her body and wrapped it around her head, then grabbed her arms and hefted her over his shoulder in a classic fireman's carry.

He was grateful that she was lean of frame and lighter than she looked, because her weight on his back was still enough to make his knees fold for a moment. Struggling to his feet, he noticed water vapor rising from their rain-soaked clothes, evaporating in the blistering heat.

Gotta move fast, he realized. He retraced their steps down the short corridor and ducked into the last room before the fire-blocked intersection.

Flames licked through the doorway as he entered, and he heard another arm of the blaze punching through walls a room or two behind him. Through rough holes in the wall in front of him, he glimpsed the black, smoke-filled but not yet ablaze north corridor. *Hope this works,* he prayed.

He braced his left foot, lifted his right, and started kicking at the rotted drywall, timbers, and studs. Gasping for air, all he tasted was smoke. A painful fit of coughing seized his chest and scorched his throat, but he fought on. Each kick knocked down more of the wall, widened the gap, toppled the support studs.

In the north corridor, the flames were spreading, as if to cut him off. He lunged forward through his hard-fought gap in the wall and stumble-sprinted away from the fire, toward the west stairwell. Rich columns of smoke rose from the lower floors, obscuring his vision. Descending into the stinging clouds, Tom cringed as another deep explosion shook the building.

The second floor was darker than night. *Have to get back to the center stairs,* Tom told himself, even as he tried in vain to remember the path they had taken through the labyrinth of bed frames, smashed furniture, and broken machines. He knew he'd have to hurry, because the entire building was heating up like a crematorium, and Erin's weight was starting to become more than he could bear.

There was nowhere to go but forward, into the darkness.

He charged ahead and almost immediately collided with something hard. Sharp pain spiked up from his shin, and he lost his balance for a moment. It took all his strength not to fall on his face and drop Erin.

Then the darkness gave way to fire and thunder.

A storm of burning floorboards, crossbeams, and debris rained down around them as sections of the third floor collapsed onto the second. Towering spirals of flame swept through the suddenly cavernous space, surging bright and hot as they devoured the oxygen.

Tom saw the path through the maze clearly now—because every inch of it was on fire. He tightened his grip on Erin and started running.

The conflagration seemed to reach for him at every turn. It was so bright that he couldn't see, so hot that it baked away his sweat faster than his body could make it. He felt each sting of pain as the fire stabbed him with its white-hot talons.

Wood cracked like rifle shots as the floorboards and walls

were rent by the blaze. Tom felt the floor start to sag as he cleared the maze and dashed into the center stairwell.

He made it two steps before the skeleton of a staircase collapsed beneath him and Erin, dropping them both in a jumble of snapped wood and old nails onto the concrete first floor. The hard landing left him stunned, winded, and disoriented.

Another profound rumble from above. Tom draped himself over Erin.

An avalanche of blazing wreckage from the second and third floors crashed down onto the first. Tom looked out from the partial shelter of the stairwell to see that there was no safe path back to the rear entrance of the building—he and Erin were surrounded by a raging inferno.

Beside him, she groaned and teetered on the edge of consciousness.

Searching desperately for the nearest exit, Tom saw the front door just a few yards away, but it lay on the other side of a sea of flames. The crisscrossed planks that barricaded it were already on fire.

If only we could reach it, Tom lamented. *But there's no way. It's impossible.*

Then the flames parted.

At first he thought it was a mirage. Then he looked closer, eyes wide, and marveled at the miracle in front of him—not at the path that had opened through the blaze but at the *shape* of that path. As it spread and swept upward in two symmetrical curls, the flames wavered and the light from the inferno shimmered with spectral details—hard edges and fine lines.

Wings, majestic and feathered, with a span of at least twenty feet, all but invisible except in the blaze. They tensed, then flapped forward, clearing the way.

A voice that Tom couldn't hear but felt with every shred of his being commanded him: **Go.**

Startled out of his awestruck paralysis, he hauled Erin to her feet. "C'mon!" He sprinted forward, and she staggered close behind him. With the last of his strength, he threw himself at the smoldering planks covering the front door and crashed through them in a storm of sparks and splinters.

Tom gasped as the rain hit him, grunted as he struck the concrete landing outside the front door, and groaned as Erin landed on top of him.

He looked at his soot-stained friend and asked, "You okay?"

"Little crispy," she said. Glancing back into the hell from which they'd escaped, she added, "Could've been worse."

The next sounds they heard were the clacking of semi-automatic pistols being primed and a voice through a bullhorn shouting, *"Freeze!"*

Tom tilted his head back and noticed the two dozen or so cops that had surrounded him and Erin. "It's worse."

As the cops closed in with nightsticks, handcuffs, and stun guns, Erin whispered to Tom, "Say nothing to them—not even your name."

"But—"

"Not even your name," she repeated. "Trust me."

Two cops pulled her off Tom and dragged her onto the sidewalk. A second later, two more cops did the same to him. Lying facedown on the pavement with a knee in his back, Tom winced as icy handcuffs snapped shut and bit into his wrists.

"You're under arrest," the cop said, "for arson."

19

The downpour slowed to a drizzle while Frank aimed his camera at the UBS ground-floor offices across the street. Through the enormous windows facing Park Avenue, Frank had a clear view of Anna Doyle's lawyer, Marc Cimbal, shaking hands with a trio of bank executives. Frank zoomed in and focused on the brushed-aluminum briefcase in the lawyer's left hand.

So far, so good, Frank mused.

It was the lawyer's second stop of the day. His first appointment had been only one block away, at Deutsche Bank. Frank hoped there wouldn't be too many more stops. It was almost one thirty, and he was ravenous for lunch.

Never used to get this hungry when I smoked, he brooded.

Inside the bank, the lawyer and the bankers stepped away into the private offices. *To the vault,* Frank figured, putting down his camera. He dialed Viktor on his disposable cell phone and activated the speaker.

While it rang, he fished a fresh pack of gum from his jacket pocket and tore off a third of the wrapper. He had two sticks of spearmint out and half-unwrapped by the time Viktor answered. *"Yes?"*

"Viktor, it's Frank. Everything's in motion."

"You're sure?"

"He's visiting his second international bank of the day. I'd say we're definitely on for tonight." He pushed both sticks of gum in his mouth. The minty sweetness was a poor substitute for the bitter rush of tar and nicotine.

Frank folded the paper and foil gum wrappers into thin strips and absentmindedly wound them tourniquet tight around his fingers as Viktor asked, *"How soon should I put my people in position?"*

"Tell everyone to hit their marks by five fifteen," Frank said. "They should be set to go before Anna comes for the swap, but we don't want them loitering long enough to get noticed by the NYPD."

"Understood."

"And remember, this is all about speed. In and out. Nobody should move unless they have to. If your guys are quick and keep a low profile, we all win."

"Yes, yes," Viktor said, impatient with being lectured. *"Five fifteen. My people will be ready. Call if the plan changes."*

"Will do. Talk to you later."

Viktor hung up without any fanfare. Frank did the same.

Rain tapped softly on the roof of Frank's car. The damp chill of the day seeped in through a million unseen routes, along with exhaust fumes from the traffic rolling past. He passed the long, empty minutes winding and unwinding the paper and foil strips around his left index finger.

About the time that his gum started to run out of flavor, movement inside the bank caught his eye. He picked up his camera, pointed it at the windows, and focused once more on the lawyer, who shook hands again with the bank executives before making a fast exit. The man had a nervous aspect to his character; his eyes darted from side to side, as if he was expecting an attack at any moment.

I'd be nervous, too, if I was carrying that much cash all by myself, Frank thought with a malevolent smile. He briefly pondered whether he might be able to get away with mugging the short, mustached man in broad daylight. Before he could concoct a scheme to make it possible—and avoid incurring Viktor's wrath by doing so—his cell phone rang.

Holding his camera steady with one hand, he used the other to turn on his phone's hands-free speaker. "Go," he snapped.

"It's done," Dillon Tanager said.

He looked down at the phone. "Details."

"They walked into a trap," Dillon said. *"And it blew up in their faces."*

"How'd you leave them?"

"Dead or in custody."

Frank felt a headache coming on. "Wait a second—you didn't *confirm* the kill? Did you see the bodies or not?"

"We weren't waiting around for confirmation," Dillon replied. *"Lights and sirens were coming. We had to leave."*

"Goddammit." Frank put down his camera and heaved an angry sigh. "You were supposed to kill 'em, not get 'em arrested!"

"We did what we could. On a slab or in a cell, they're your problem now. We're outta here." A loud click signaled the end of the call.

A primal scream worked its way up from Frank's diaphragm, and he let it loose with enough fury to draw spooked stares from pedestrians on the sidewalk. He pounded the side of his fist against the dashboard several times in quick succession and cursed himself for not keeping an emergency pack of smokes hidden somewhere in the car, because he really wanted—*needed*—a cigarette.

He seized the steering wheel in a white-knuckle grip and hollered at his car's roof, "Why must everyone in the world except me be *totally fucking useless?*"

It would be too suspicious to call in looking for a report about the blond man and his friend. He would have to abandon his surveillance of Anna's lawyer and go back to the precinct house in Brooklyn and check the day's logs for collars and DOAs. *That's why I get paid the big bucks,* he thought, cracking a sour smile at the gallows humor as he keyed the ignition.

He pulled out into traffic. *Back to work.*

By the time Tom reached the desk officer at the 71st Precinct, he had already been treated for smoke inhalation by an ambulance crew, given a bumpy ride in an odd-smelling white-and-blue police cruiser, been brusquely searched three times—once on the sidewalk, again after being pulled out of the cop car, and again in a small drab room just past the precinct's front entrance—and been read the Miranda warning ("You have the right to remain silent . . .") four times.

He gave the New York cops credit: they were nothing if not thorough.

They didn't have much of a sense of humor, though.

"Name," the desk officer said.

Remembering Erin's instruction to say nothing, he replied, "John Doe."

That earned Tom a long, hostile glare from the desk officer. "The law says you have to identify yourself to me, sir. What's your name, and how old are you?"

Tom's pulse was racing as he lied, "I don't remember."

"You don't remember?"

Tom had never been arrested before, and it took a lot of effort to hide the fact that he was in stress overload. "Amnesia. Bumped my head on the sidewalk."

The desk officer barked across the room at the cop who'd arrested Tom. "Witwicky! Does he have any ID?"

"Sorry," Officer Witwicky said. "All we got off him were locksmith's tools and a flashlight."

The desk officer flashed a cold stare at Tom. "So, you're a locksmith, eh? Maybe you've been fingerprinted somewhere." He stamped Tom's booking sheet, initialed it in three places, then handed it to Witwicky as he told Tom, "Go ahead and play dumb. We'll know your name soon enough."

Another officer led Erin into the grim, barren room and presented her to the desk officer.

"Name," the officer said to her.

"Jane Doe," she replied, and Tom almost laughed.

The desk officer scowled at her. "Let me guess. You've got amnesia, like your husband over there." She shrugged. He waved her on and glowered at her arresting officer. "Okay, Levitt, see if AFIS knows who she is."

The patrolmen led Tom and Erin into the next room, where a man in civilian clothes sat at a small table. He monitored a laptop computer attached to a flat, compact device with a smooth glass plate a few inches square.

The civilian stood and snapped on a pair of white surgical

gloves. He nodded to Tom. "Left hand first, please, starting with your thumb."

Fighting to keep his hand steady, Tom offered it to the technician, who yanked it toward himself. Working in slow rolling motions, the man guided each of Tom's fingertips over the glass panel while watching images of Tom's prints appear in real time on his laptop monitor.

As soon as the civilian finished taking Tom's prints, Witwicky ushered Tom to the far end of the room, where a digital camera was mounted on a tripod facing a plain gray wall. Pointing to a yellow line painted on the floor a couple of yards in front of the camera, Witwicky said, "Stand there."

Tom took his place at the line while another civilian technician stood behind the camera, checked the settings, and pressed the shutter. The flash left spots swimming in Tom's eyes. "Turn to your right," Witwicky said.

He pivoted right, and the technician snapped another image. "Now face the other way." Tom turned about-face, and there was another flash. "All right," Witwicky said. "Now you get to wait upstairs in the cage till the—"

"Hang on," interrupted the fingerprint technician.

Rolling his eyes in annoyance, Witwicky replied, "What is it, Fallis?"

"Problem with the live scan on his prints," Fallis said. "They're not reading right. All we're getting is smears."

Levitt ushered Erin toward the camera and shook his head at Witwicky as they passed each other. "Our tax dollars at work."

Witwicky guided Tom back to the fingerprinting station and asked Fallis, "Did he have something on his fingers? Maybe the glass is smudged."

"I don't think so," Fallis said. "The optics look clean." Tapping keys on his laptop, he added, "I mean, I got a good set from—" He stopped, poked more keys, then stood up and stared in disbelief at his computer. "Now *her* prints are messed up, too." He ran a hand over his shaved head. "I don't get it."

Flashes caught Tom's eye, and he turned his head to watch Erin go through the motions in front of the camera. As soon as they finished snapping shots of Erin, Levitt escorted her back to the fingerprinting station, where she stood next to Tom.

Witwicky looked agitated and sounded impatient. "So what's the problem?"

"I don't know," Fallis said. "All the other prints we took today look fine." He threw an imploring look at the cops. "Can one of you put a few fingers on there so I can run a test?"

"Put your own fingers on it," Witwicky said.

The technician sulked as he alternated between the scanning machine and his laptop, entering his fingerprints and putting his software through its paces.

While Fallis worked, the photographer stepped over to the cops and handed them two photo prints. "Look at these," the man said.

The officers stared at the photos with their eyebrows arched in disbelief. Levitt asked, "What'd you do? Kick the tripod and stick your thumb in the way?"

"Gimme a break," the photographer said. "You were right next to me when I took these. It was by the book."

"So what happened?" Witwicky snapped.

"No idea," said the photographer.

Tom snuck a look over the cops' shoulders. The two photo sheets each showed three images. One page was pictures of him, the other of Erin. Every image was blurred, flared, or smudged beyond any chance of recognition.

Levitt grimaced. "That's just messed up."

Fallis cut in, "Okay, I just got a clean scan on my prints, and AFIS reads them fine, so let's try it again."

As the cops nodded for Tom to step toward the fingerprinting machine, Erin whispered to him so softly as to be almost inaudible, "Don't worry."

Finger by finger, they did the whole process again for Tom, then for Erin. Meanwhile, the photographer and another technician popped off half a dozen test photos, all flawless.

Fallis watched the print scans appear on his screen. From where Tom stood, they looked like two sets of solid-black ovals. "Dammit," Fallis muttered, then pinched the bridge of his nose. "They're messed up again."

Witwicky and Levitt took Tom and Erin back to the camera. They each took their turn saying "cheese," then waited for the results. Minutes later, the cops held in their hands two more sheets of unrecognizable images—they had been pixilated to the point of looking like cheap mosaics.

Levitt was losing his temper. He shouted at Erin and Tom, "Are either of you hiding a cell phone?" They both shook their heads no. "Do you have pacemakers? Some kind of implants? Something that's doing this?" All they could do was shrug and shake their heads again. "Search 'em," Levitt snapped at Witwicky, then he harangued the technicians. "We're gonna do it again and *again*, until you clowns get this right. Understand?"

Fallis and the photographer traded bored looks. "Sure," Fallis said. "We get paid by the hour. Long as you cough up the OT, we'll stay all night."

Roughly halfway through Tom and Erin's latest pat-down search, a sergeant entered and bellowed, "What the hell's going on? I got ten skels waiting to get booked, and these two are still here?"

"Glitches with the print scanner and the camera, Sarge," Witwicky said.

"Nice of you guys to tell me," the sergeant said. He pointed at Tom and Erin. "Put those two in the cage upstairs, run 'em through again later. And if you can't get this junk working in the next five minutes, you're gonna have to dig out a Polaroid and some old-fashioned ink and paper and *get this line moving.*"

Levitt said, "You got it, Sarge."

Tom and Erin were held against the wall while the cops slapped handcuffs back around their wrists. "Neat trick," Tom whispered to her.

"All part of the magic," she said. Then they were yanked away from the wall and led upstairs.

Something's protecting us, Tom thought. Remembering the shape he'd seen in the fire less than an hour before, he understood: *We have guardian angels.*

20

The disposable cell phone on Anna's kitchen table was ringing, and she was too terrified to pick it up. She knew it was the kidnappers calling. All of her hoping for a miracle, for a sudden fairy-tale ending, had yielded nothing but an afternoon of dread and silence and now this shrill noise echoing through her empty house.

She took a breath, steeled herself, picked up the phone, and pressed TALK.

Her voice quaked as she said, "Hello?"

The gruff Russian-sounding man replied, *"You have a good lawyer, Mrs. Doyle. It seems he will have all of your money ready on time today."*

"So he tells me," she said quietly, while seething inside.

"And that brings us to the next step." She heard the flick of a lighter and a puff of exhaled breath over the line. *"The exchange."*

"I'm listening."

"We like your lawyer's briefcase. Tell him we want all the bearer bonds placed in that case, and its three-digit combination set to nine-nine-nine."

"Fine," Anna said, rising from the table. She paced out of the kitchen into the living room, which was bathed in steel blue light from the overcast afternoon.

"At five thirty p.m. today, bring that briefcase and the phone we gave you to the south end of Times Square: Forty-second Street between Broadway and Seventh Avenue, in front of the subway entrance."

"All right, then what?"

"Then we'll call you with more instructions. And, Mrs. Doyle, remember the rules: no cops, no feds, no tricks. Be there with the money, or your little girl dies."

Before he hung up, she begged, "Let me talk to her! Let me know she's all right, please!"

"Five thirty," the man said, then the line clicked and went dead.

She hurled the phone at the couch and buried her face in her hands. Even though she'd never held a gun in her life, she fantasized about bringing one to the swap, just so she could put slug after slug into the monsters who'd taken Phaedra.

Wiping tears from her eyes, she pressed her palms together at her chin as if she were about to pray. *I still can't believe this is happening. Why us? Why Phaedra?* Drifting through the room, she noticed how carefully she stepped around the stack of schoolbooks Phaedra had left by the couch. *My God,* she realized. *I'm already treating the house like a shrine.*

It was true, and it frightened her. She looked around and saw that she hadn't moved anything except a few glasses and a coffee mug in the kitchen since she'd learned of Phaedra's abduction. *It's like I'm trying to freeze my life in amber so it won't change. So that she'll always be alive somewhere.*

Hope asserted itself, and Anna shook off her fear. *Stop that. Phaedra is alive somewhere, right now, and she's coming home. She is coming home, no matter what it takes.* She reached down to pick up the books, to carry them up to Phaedra's room and put them away where they belonged . . . but she couldn't do it.

Dammit.

She wanted to call Marc to confirm that he was almost done gathering the money, but she had already bothered him four times since that morning. Bugging him again wouldn't speed the process, and it might even slow him down.

Even more urgently, she had tried three times in the past hour to reach Tom Nash, the unusual private investigator, but he hadn't answered his phone. She'd left three increasingly frantic pleas asking him to help with the ransom exchange for Phaedra, but time was running out, and as far as she could tell, Tom had fallen off the face of the Earth.

Going to the swap alone was the last thing Anna wanted to do, but if she had to, she would. One way or another, her little girl was coming home.

21

The interview room was just about the most depressing place Tom had ever seen. It was dimly lit, and its scuffed floor, scraped walls, and decrepit drop-tile ceiling exhibited more shades of gray than he could count.

Only slightly more colorful were the two NYPD detectives sitting on the other side of the bolted-down metal table.

Detective Joe Figursky, a fireplug of a man with a tree-trunk neck, pushed a sheet of paper across the table for Tom's inspection. "You gotta admit, not givin' us your name looks bad," he said with a heavy Brooklyn accent. "I mean, look at it from where I'm sitting. You come crashin' out of a burnin' building, along with your little friend, and you got no explanation for what you're doin' there. What'm I s'posed to think? You tell me."

Tom stared at the piece of paper but said nothing. He knew he was in over his head; leaning back in his uncomfortable metal chair, he wondered who might be watching through the dark two-way mirror on the wall behind the cops.

"You're not doing yourself any favors here," said the second detective, Roy Thorne. He talked as if he might be from someplace like Connecticut or western Massachusetts. Sliding more papers in front of Tom, he continued, "Your accomplice was carrying a butterfly knife when we picked her up. That's a concealed deadly weapon."

Another sheet of paper was pushed forward. "You were carrying locksmith's tools," Thorne continued, "which explains why the parking lot gate and rear entrance of the building were found to be unlocked. That means we've got you both on breaking and entering, and criminal trespassing. Not to mention arson." He leaned forward and lowered his voice. "Are you sure you don't want to talk to us before she does? Because only one of you will get to make a deal."

That coaxed a morbid half-smile from Tom. *As if Erin would tell these guys anything.*

Figursky seemed offended by Tom's reaction. "You think this is funny?"

"Not really, no," Tom said, his fear masked only by his exhaustion.

Thorne sat back and folded his arms. "Then why don't you tell us what you were doing in that building?"

Tom considered all the ways that telling them the truth would only get him in even more trouble. "I'd like a lawyer, please."

A snort of laughter from Figursky. "You don't really think it's gonna be that easy, do ya?"

"I think it's the law," Tom said. Trying to sound brave, he said in a shaking voice, "I want a lawyer, and I won't answer any more questions till I get one."

Thorne backed up his chair with a deep, loud scrape across

the black-and-white-checkered tile floor. "Fine. One useless public defender, coming up." He got up, left the room, and slammed the door on his way out.

Across from Tom, Figursky leaned forward on the table and grinned. "Just us now, pal. Me an' you. So no more games. Why'd you torch the building?"

If Tom had learned anything from years of watching late-night television, it was that there was never anything to gain from talking to a cop without a lawyer. Whatever he said would get twisted, misinterpreted, and turned around to make him look guilty, even if he wasn't. And he was, a little. So he kept his mouth shut.

"C'mon," Figursky said. "Talk to me and maybe I can go to bat for you. But keep givin' us the silent treatment, and you're goin' down hard, I guarantee it."

For a brief moment, Tom considered what would happen if he tried telling the cops about the links between Phaedra's kidnapping, the thugs who attacked him in the school parking lot, the Russian club in Gravesend, and the abandoned building that had just burned to the ground.

Don't be stupid, he told himself. He remembered that the cops didn't even know yet about the kidnapping—all they knew was that Phaedra was missing. Worse, they'd have only his word and Erin's about the altercation in the parking lot and the links to the Russians, and considering his and Erin's current status, he figured the cops would consider them less than credible as witnesses.

Besides, he reasoned, *even if they find the Russians, they'll just deny everything. They probably have prefab alibis for situations like this.*

Figursky stood and circled around the table. Planting one hand on its edge and the other on the back of Tom's chair, he leaned down close to Tom and gave him a faceful of his onion breath. "Think you're smart, don'tcha? Playin' it cool? Lemme tell you how this is gonna go down, genius. We've got your stupid ass dead to rights comin' outta that blaze. You're lookin' at five years minimum. If you're really smart, you'll talk to me before that lawyer gets here, and maybe we can cut your time in half for cooperatin'. So what were you doin' in there?"

Unable to help himself, Tom replied, "I'm on a mission from God."

The detective shoved himself up and away, shifting the chair sideways beneath Tom. Disgusted, the squat, burly man plodded back to his chair, apparently not even suspecting that Tom had sort of been truthful with him.

Not that Tom could even consider telling the cops the unvarnished facts. Trying to explain that he had driven more than a hundred miles to New York because he'd overheard Phaedra Doyle's prayer for help wouldn't accomplish anything except to get him committed to a local mental institution.

The door opened, and Thorne returned. "Legal aid's jammed," he said to Figursky. "The DA wants our little firebug and his gal pal shipped to Central as soon as we get prints and photos. They'll give 'em lawyers over there. Sit on him while I find someone to take 'em over to Schermerhorn."

"Sure thing," Figursky said. Thorne stepped out and let the door close. Figursky smiled. "What do you want first? The good news or the bad news?"

"The good news," Tom said.

"It's a light day at Central Booking. You'll be in and out in nothin' flat."

"And the bad news?"

"Since you don't have a name, you won't be postin' bail—which means in about two hours, you and your friend'll be on your way to Rikers Island."

Frank got out of his car in a bad mood. He'd fought dumbshit traffic all the way from Manhattan back to the 71st Precinct, then got stuck settling for a space in the far back corner of the lot, along the wall. *Nothing like a long walk in the rain,* he groused to himself as he hurried through a steady drizzle.

Inside the precinct house, it was bedlam as always. Phones ringing nonstop because the uniforms were too lazy to answer them, a six-person backlog in the booking rooms, and a parade of skels and their insignificant others in the lobby. Frank shoved his way through the little people and flashed his shield at the desk sergeant, who buzzed him through the secure door to the first-floor offices.

He circled back to the sergeant. "Sanford, what'd I hear about a fire?"

"The old clinic on Lefferts," Sanford said. "Looks like arson." He pointed up with his pen. "Two collars, guy and a girl."

Sweeping his hands over his head to squeeze the rain out of his dark hair, Frank asked, "Who caught it?"

"Witwicky and Levitt made the collar; Fig and Thorne have the ball."

"Okay, thanks." Frank slipped out of the sergeant's nook and moved quickly down the corridor, past the patrolmen's locker room and the briefing room, then up the stairs before he reached the shift commander's office. He wasn't in the mood to get stopped for idle conversations, not today.

He took the stairs two at a time to the second floor.

At the top of the stairs, the door to the detectives' squad room was open. He shambled in, still dripping water all over the place, and reached over the chipped and weathered wooden banister to buzz the swinging wooden gate. It opened ahead of him with a loud squeak, drawing reflex glances from the other detectives in the room and the skels cooped up in the cages.

He threw a look at the day's catch. It was the usual mix. Some meth heads, a couple hookers, a drunk and disorderly, a DUI, a known wife beater. "Howdy, scumbags," he grumbled on his way past them.

Arriving at his desk, he settled heavily into his chair and nodded past his monitor to Bailey, who was engrossed in her mountain of paperwork. "Hey, Bailey. Thought you were on the four-to-one today."

"I am," she said. "I'm off the clock." She looked up and gave a tired shrug. "Just trying to catch up for a change."

"Trying to make the rest of us look bad? You do a shift off the clock and Lou's gonna want us all to do one."

She rubbed the tip of her thumb with her index finger, back and forth. "World's smallest violin, Frank."

"Yeah, yeah." He let the banter trail off as he noticed Thorne get up from his desk and walk to the interview room. As Thorne opened the door to poke his head in, Frank leaned his chair back to get a look past him at the man in the box—only to find his view obstructed by that lumbering blockhead Figursky.

So much for subtlety, Frank decided.

He got up and walked to the other side of the squad room as casually as he could. His first stop was the coffee room, where he grabbed a paper cup of burnt-smelling black java that he had no intention of drinking.

On his way out, he detoured just far enough to put himself next to the interview room's door, and he stole a glance through its narrow vertical window.

The suspect at the table was the blond man who'd visited Anna Doyle's apartment the previous day. He'd had a change of clothes, and he looked a bit more beat up than the last time Frank had seen him, but it was definitely the same guy.

Frank's jaw clenched as troubling scenarios plagued his thoughts. *If this guy was checking out Viktor's properties, there's no telling how much he knows. If he puts me or Viktor in the spotlight, it could blow the whole deal.*

There was no time to waste. Frank had to know how much the blond man had learned, and how big a threat he was really going to be. If he didn't know anything, Frank could let the system deal with him. But if he knew the truth, a more *permanent* solution would be in order.

Resolved to do whatever he had to, Frank opened the door.

Tom's head snapped up as the door of the interrogation room opened. Someone new walked in, a male detective in his forties. His damp dark hair showed the first touches of gray. He was lean, in good shape but not exactly muscular, and maybe a couple of inches taller than Tom. In his youth he might have been good-looking, but his face was weathered. The years hadn't been kind to him.

"Fig," the new detective said, walking toward his colleague seated at the table. "I need you to step out for a few minutes." He handed Figursky a manila folder. "I'm looking at this mope for something bigger." Something about the man's voice gave Tom a chill inside, as if he'd swallowed an ice cube.

The fireplug-shaped Figursky opened the folder and skimmed its contents. His brow creased with suspicion. "Pretty thin, Frank." Handing back the folder, he added, "Besides, Roy told me to stay here."

"Don't worry, I won't let your little fish get away," Frank said. He nodded toward the door. "Take five. I'll keep an eye on him."

Reluctantly, Figursky got up. "Fine, but if Roy blows a gasket—"

"I'll deal with it," Frank assured him. "Go."

Figursky shrugged, then left the interrogation room.

Frank stood and stared at Tom while he waited for the door to slam shut. As the impact echoed off the cinder-block walls, the cop said in a voice both low and menacing, "I'm Detective Kolpack. You and I have a lot to talk about." He walked to the table and sat down in Figursky's vacated chair. With calm precision, he laid down the manila folder with its bottom edge parallel to the side of the table. "I'm guessing you've already asked for a lawyer," he said.

Tom nodded. The threat posed by the detective was palpable.

"We've noticed you at the home of Anna Doyle," Frank continued. "And also at the home of Paul and Nancy Landry. I'm guessing you're aware of the fact that Mrs. Doyle's daughter, Phaedra, is missing."

This time Tom remained absolutely still. He didn't even blink.

"Though I have to wonder . . . what's the connection between your visit to the Doyles' home and your dramatic exit from a burning building?"

Another cold sensation bloomed in Tom's gut. It was a

sense that something was wrong, but he didn't know what, exactly, was prompting the warning. Worried that he might implicate himself in Phaedra's kidnapping, he kept quiet as Frank continued asking questions.

"I'm even more curious about why you and your friend weren't carrying any ID, and why you won't identify yourselves. Got something to hide? Scared a warrant check might turn up some priors?" Frank opened the folder, flipped over a few standard forms, and lifted up a blurred, shadowy photo. "Or maybe you'd like to explain why your mug shot and fingerprints never seem to come out right."

A freezing tingle teased Tom's ears, and he heard a dull buzzing, like a phone left off the hook. He blinked and looked at Frank. "What'd you say?"

The detective's reply sounded deep and distorted, as if it had been recorded and played back too slowly. "I asked why your photos and prints never come out."

"I don't know," Tom said, only half lying.

The man across the table went silent and fixed Tom with an angry stare for several long, anxiety-fraught seconds. Then he reached inside his jacket—and pulled out a pack of chewing gum. "Quitting smoking," he said as he plucked two sticks of gum from the pack. As if he'd needed to explain himself to Tom.

His fingers moved with speed and dexterity, unfolding the paper and foil wrappers and extracting the pale gray spearmint sticks, which Tom could smell from across the table. The detective folded the two sticks in half and pushed them into his mouth. Between chews, he said, "Why don't you try telling me everything you know about the disappearance of Phaedra Doyle?"

Frank continued asking more specific questions—had Tom ever met Phaedra, could he account for his whereabouts on

Saturday night, did he drive a truck or SUV—but all of Tom's attention was on Frank's hands, and on what they were doing with the gum wrappers. It was clearly a well-practiced habit.

First, the cop folded each piece of paper into a long strip one-quarter its original width. Then he did the same for each piece of foil. Next, he twisted the paper and foil strips together in tight braids, as if he were joining two strands of electrical wire. Then he wound the two braids into one continuous piece. Last, he began coiling the spiral twist around his left index finger, wrapping it so tightly that the tip of his finger began turning blue. After a few minutes, he removed the tiny tourniquet and cavalierly tossed it aside, onto the floor, forgotten.

A feeling like a rush of cold water over Tom's skin snapped his attention back to Frank, whose voice once more sounded like a recording played at half speed. "If you know something about Phaedra, you'd better talk—because right now we're looking at you as our number-one suspect."

Tom knew that Frank's statement was a lie. He knew it in the way that he knew fire was hot to the touch, or that he knew red from blue, or light from darkness.

I can detect lies, he realized. *That's my ability.*

Emboldened, Tom decided to test his power without delay. Leaning forward, he asked accusingly, "What do *you* know about Phaedra's disappearance?"

Frank recoiled. "Only what I've told you."

Another lie, Tom realized. He'd heard it like a sour note, felt it like frostbite on his ears. "You're involved, aren't you? Do you know where she is?"

That question jolted Frank from his chair. He was up and backing away. "I don't know what you're talking about."

Lying and panicking, Tom knew with a cold certainty.

"Are you the Russians' mole? The one who's tipping them off?"

Frank lunged forward and grabbed his case folder, slapped it shut in a jumbled mess. "We're done, scumbag," he said with shaken bravado.

As the detective made his way to the door, Tom played a hunch.

"Are you one of the Scorned?"

The detective stopped. Threw a look back at Tom that was both fearful and murderous. His stare was intense, intimidating, unblinking.

So was Tom's.

Frank's hand twitched above his sidearm.

The door opened. Figursky stuck his head in, and Frank's hand flinched away from his pistol. "Hey," Figursky said. "Lou says the techs are ready for another shot at prints and pictures. And Roy's back with pizza."

"Great," Frank said, pulling open the door and stepping past Figursky. "I'm starving." He cast one last baleful glare at Tom as he made his exit.

Figursky walked in and pulled Tom to his feet. "Time for another trip to booking," he said. Leading him out of the room, he asked, "Feel like talking yet?"

"No, thanks," Tom said. "I think I just heard all I needed to know."

Bailey had kept her eye on the interview room's door since Frank had gone inside and sent Figursky out. Something weird was going on, she was certain of it.

Through the closed door's vertical sliver of a window, she caught a hint of movement. Curious, she got up and started making her way across the squad room.

Just then, Thorne backed through the squad's squeaky wooden gate while balancing two large pizza boxes in one hand and carrying a stuffed-full paper bag in the other. "Lunch is served," he announced, carrying the box to an unused desk in the middle of the room. He upended the paper bag and dumped out a mess of paper plates, napkins, plastic forks, and single-serving spices.

A feeding frenzy commenced. Men in cheap suits swarmed around the pizza, whose sweet aroma filled the entire room. *Good,* Bailey figured. *That'll keep 'em busy for a while.* She skirted the group's outer edge and snuck past the coffee room on her way to the interview room.

As she neared the door, Figursky stepped into her path and cut her off. She ducked into the coffee room and stopped at the water cooler while she listened to Figursky talking to Kolpack, though she couldn't make out what they were saying.

Bailey poked her head through the coffee room doorway and saw Kolpack leave the interview room. She slipped out of the coffee room and into his path.

"Hey," she said. "Got a second?"

Kolpack cast an anxious glance over his shoulder. "What is it?"

Behind Kolpack, Figursky waved a pair of patrolmen, Witwicky and Levitt, through the gate to collect their suspects. Levitt unlocked the women's cage and summoned a young, attractive Latina clad in leather. Witwicky walked into the interview room with a pair of handcuffs at the ready.

"Remember that OTB collar last week?" Bailey asked Kolpack.

Looking back at her, he hesitated, frowned, scratched his brow, then replied, "Yeah, sure. What about it?"

"Could I get a look at your notes on that one? Mine have a lot of gaps, and I'm trying to get caught up on my fives."

Witwicky emerged from the interview room with a tall fair-haired man in custody. He led him toward the gate, where Levitt was waiting with the Latina.

"Fine," Kolpack said to Bailey, apparently distracted and bothered.

"Great," she said. Nodding at the tall male suspect, she inquired, "So what's that about?"

"Missing person," Kolpack said. She waited for him to offer something more, but that was apparently all Kolpack had to say on the matter.

Lieutenant La Salle emerged from his office and made a beeline for the pizza. He tossed aside the empty top box and grabbed a slice from the second box. He called across the room, "Bailey! Kolpack! Get a slice now or go hungry!"

The wooden gate creaked in protest as Witwicky and Levitt led their pair of suspects out of the squad room and back to the first-floor booking area. The entire time, Kolpack's predatory glare never left the male suspect's back. Bailey sensed an undercurrent of violence in every aspect of Kolpack's demeanor.

Bailey asked, "Who's the missing person? Do you like this guy for—"

Kolpack walked away from her as if she weren't even there, never mind talking right to him. He passed by the pizza and was through the gate, out of the squad room, and down the stairs before Bailey knew what to say.

She shook her head and wandered over to the pizza box.

There was one slice left, and she snagged it. It drooped in her hand and practically oozed onto the paper plate. Eyeing the greasy mess, she realized it was little more than a pile of fondue on a triangle of soggy dough. But at least it was free.

Back at her desk, she set the molten-cheese disaster off to one side and sagged back into her chair. Then she looked at the open file on her computer monitor and exclaimed, "Sonofabitch! He left without giving me his notes!"

"That's Frank for you," Thorne said.

Everyone else nodded.

Figursky, his huge mouth packed with half-chewed pizza, added, "What's up his ass today, anyway? You see the way he dogged those two perps down to booking?"

"No shit," Thorne said. "It's not even his case. So what's his beef?"

"Don't look at me," Bailey said. "I don't even pretend to know what's going on in his head." Muttered agreements traveled around the room.

Everyone went back to work, business as usual—everyone except Bailey, who was too distracted to concentrate on mundane cases anymore.

She drummed her fingers on her desktop. Why had Kolpack inserted himself into someone else's case? Interviewed someone else's suspect? As far as she knew, he hadn't caught any missing-persons cases recently. So what was he playing at? She thought about the intensity of his focus on the fair-haired man and couldn't help being suspicious about whatever it was that Kolpack wasn't saying.

The IAB investigators had told her that Kolpack had things to hide, maybe even connections to organized crime. She had told herself that if it was true, if he *was* a criminal, she didn't want to know about it, any of it, but her instincts as a cop told her that what she wanted didn't matter anymore.

Now she *needed* to know.

Frank shadowed the two suspects as the uniformed patrolmen walked them through another turn in the booking rooms. He kept an extra-close watch on the blond man.

This guy's more dangerous than I thought, he brooded. *The sooner I deal with him and his friend, the better.*

Fallis, the fingerprint technician, looked up and noticed Frank watching him. Probably assuming that Frank was monitoring the process, Fallis pointed at his laptop screen, then at the blond man and the woman in leather, before giving Frank a big thumbs-up.

At least we have that much on them now, Frank assured himself.

The blond man and the leather-clad Latina were led across the room to stand for their booking photos. Frank moved on down the hall, past the sergeants' break room with its odors of Chinese food and burned coffee, then past the locker room, which stank of stale sweat, holster leather, and gun oil. He stopped at the shift commander's door and knocked.

From behind the door, Captain Eichorn called in a low groan, "*Come in.*"

Frank turned the knob and swung the door open as he stepped in. Eichorn was at his desk, meaty hands holding either side of his large bald head, which was so odd looking that it always made Frank think of a Crenshaw. A jumbo container of generic ibuprofen sat on the desk in front of him.

Without looking up, Eichorn asked, "Who are you, and what do you want?"

"It's Kolpack, sir. I—"

"Get out."

"It's important, sir."

Eichorn sighed, opened his eyes, and studied Frank. "Make it quick."

"Levitt and Witwicky are walking a John and Jane Doe pair of perps through booking. Fig and Thorne are looking at 'em for an arson, but I think they might be linked to a missing-child case over in the seven-eight."

"You *think?* Based on what?"

"A confidential source," Frank lied, concentrating on overcoming the captain's ironclad incredulity. Like most of the Scorned, he could make normal people believe pretty much anything if he said it with enough conviction.

The captain was a hard sell, though. He threw a grim look in Frank's direction, reclined his chair, and heaved another heavy sigh from someplace deep inside his blubbered torso. "For the sake of discussion, let's say I buy that line of bullshit. Do you have enough to charge them?"

"Not yet," Frank said. "I want to sweat 'em a little. Put the fear of God into 'em so I can bring 'em around."

A rueful laugh shook Eichorn's chest. "And you plan to do that by . . . ?"

"Keeping them here overnight," Frank said.

Eichorn rolled his eyes. "Oh, for God's sake, Kolpack." He got up and lumbered to the window. "Forget it. They're Central Booking's problem now."

"Not until we send them," Frank insisted. "Captain, if I'm right, and these two are tied to that missing little girl, every minute matters. The sooner I shake 'em up and break 'em down, the better the odds we'll find that girl alive."

Frank watched the captain mull that over. All that really mattered to Frank was that the two troublemakers be kept in custody until after the ransom delivery, but in his experience, the less they moved around, the better. Keeping them in the squad-room cage would be the simplest solution and, in his opinion, the best one.

"Sorry," Eichorn said. "I'm not using up a favor for you. They're going to Central. If you want to question them, drive out to Rikers tonight. Better yet, let the seven-eight do it, since this one's on *their* dime." The captain slumped back into his chair and picked up his phone. "Now get out."

"Yes, sir," Frank said. He stepped quickly out of the office, cut through the briefing room to a side corridor, then ducked out a door to the parking lot. Rain pelted his face and shoulders as he hustled across the lot, dodging between sardine-packed cars on his way back to his vehicle in the far corner. By the time he got to his car, he was soaked again—not that he'd had much chance to get dry.

He didn't care. Rain was the least of his problems right now.

He unlocked the car and got in. Slammed the door shut. Fished in his pocket for his personal everyday cell phone. Dialed a number from memory.

The line rang while the rain played a drum solo on his car's roof.

His old buddy Andy Polumbo from the 42nd Precinct, now a correction officer on Rikers Island, answered. *"Frank! Long time, man. Whassup?"*

"I need a favor," Frank said, watching runoff pour over his windshield. "Are you and Calvin still running the Rikers Island fight clubs?"

"Yeah, but on the downlow," Andy said. *"That piece in the* Voice *nailed our nuts to the wall."*

"I know," Frank said, recalling a recent exposé by the *Village*

Voice that had uncovered evidence of guard-run, gladiator-style fights between inmates at the Rikers Island facility. "Anyway, I just wanted to give you a heads-up about some fresh fish coming your way."

Andy sounded intrigued. *"New fighting fish for my tank?"*

"No. I want 'em gutted and served as sushi."

"Got it," Andy said. *"How do I find these fish?"*

"Look for a pair of John and Jane Doe firebugs from the seven-one."

"Will do. But just so you know, the prep fee for sushi has gone up."

Frank suppressed two dire needs: to light a cigarette and to punch someone, anyone, in the face.

"Fine. What's the rate?"

"Twenty-five per fish."

It was easy math. Fifty thousand dollars to kill both enemy Seekers. A reasonable sum, he figured, considering how much was at stake.

"Deal. I want it done tonight, *capisce?*"

"Done."

"Thanks," Frank said, then he pressed END and dropped the cell phone on the passenger seat, happy just to have that disaster dealt with.

Across the parking lot, a door opened. Witwicky and Levitt led the blond man and the Latina out of the precinct house in handcuffs and guided them through the rain into a waiting white NYPD van. They slid the side door closed with a bang and tested it to make sure it was locked.

Levitt went back inside while Witwicky handed the van's driver a clipboard with the transfer order and waited while the driver signed the necessary forms to take custody of the prisoners. Then the patrolman went back inside the precinct.

Half a minute later, the van driver radioed in to Central Dispatch that he was under way to Schermerhorn Street. The van pulled away from the building and left the parking lot, on its way to Brooklyn Central Booking.

Frank offered the departing van a middle-finger salute. *Adios,* he thought, bidding his enemies a silent and malicious farewell. *And good riddance.*

Phaedra was desperate with hunger by the time she heard Leon unlocking her cell door. Metal parts clacked and banged as bolts were retracted and turned. The door swung outward, away from the cell. Leon stepped into view.

"Took you long enough," she said, her voice sharp from hunger. "Did you forget about me or something?"

Though his face was still hidden by the freaky gas mask, his head seemed to be bowed, as if he was ashamed. *"Our apologies,"* he said, sounding like a cousin of Darth Vader through the mask's snout-speaker. *"We didn't mean to leave your lunch until so late in the day. But we've had other matters to attend to."*

He turned, picked up a tray from beside the door, and carried it inside to the desk. The bat-winged smoke shape shadowed him every step of the way.

She retreated into the corner and watched him set down the fiberglass tray. Another paper plate, paper napkin, and paper cup. On the plate was a cheeseburger surrounded by golden-brown French fries. The cup was filled with milk. Next to the plate were single-serving packets of ketchup, mayonnaise, and mustard.

"Enjoy," Leon said. Then he walked away into Phaedra's bathroom, stalked all the while by his demonic echo. A few moments later, he returned. *"We see you need a few more squares*

of toilet tissue. We'll get that for you. Let us know if you wish to shower today and we'll bring you towels." Cocking his head to one side, he looked at her untouched meal. *"Is there something wrong with your lunch?"*

She shook her head in fast, fearful motions.

"Is it not to your liking? We might be able to get you something else."

As long as Leon's uglier half was looming over them, she had nothing to say. She closed her eyes and wished she had Clarence. Nightmares stayed away from her when she had her bunny; he was magic.

When she peeked through squinted eyes, the only person she saw in the room with her was Leon. She slowly exhaled a deep breath of relief.

"Are you all right?" Leon asked.

She didn't answer as she slunk over to the food and began wolfing it down. The burger was juicy, and the fries were still almost hot. It tasted homemade, not like fast food. She washed down a big mouthful with some milk, then sleeved her upper lip dry. The entire time, Leon stood by the door and watched her. When her lunch was almost gone, she glanced in his direction.

"Everything was satisfactory, then?"

Phaedra fixed her sullen, suspicious glare on him.

He stepped out and began to shut the door but paused as Phaedra asked in her most accusing tone, "Why are you so nice to me?"

In the pause before his answer, the shadow shape swirled back into existence above and behind him. His reply chilled her to the bone.

"Because we'll be spending the rest of your life together."

22

The Seekers were in danger. Bound to them yet separated from them, the Watchers were dismayed as their mortal charges were carried closer to a fate they clearly dreaded.

There was precious little the Watchers could do to intervene. Their effect on the material realm was restricted to the most intangible of interactions. Shifts in temperature, subtle manipulations of photons, magnetic fields, and charged particles, and alterations in the bioelectric activities of organic minds—these circumscribed the boundaries of their earthly powers.

Saving the Seekers from the inferno had required the Watchers to exert their most direct form of influence in the physical universe. Because of the unique nature of fire—both living and inanimate, a reaction on the threshold between matter and energy—it was as close as humans came to experiencing the Watchers as they were.

The Seekers' current dilemma demanded a more delicate intervention.

Hayyel radiated his dismay to Armaita. *We must help them.*

The second Watcher caught flashes of perception from her mortal bondmate. She applied that understanding to interpret the dense web of energies and particles through which the Seekers traveled. *Ahead of them,* she told Hayyel. *Those signal devices guide the humans' movements in the physical realm.*

What shall I do? asked Hayyel.

Prevent the signal ahead from changing its state, Armaita instructed. *I will adjust its counterpart to match it . . . when the time is right.*

Correction Officer Larry Daikeler knew that talking on a cell phone while driving was illegal in New York. He also didn't care, because he was driving a DOC van—who the hell was gonna stop him?

"Nah, man, we can't play at my house tonight," he told his pal Steve Glassman. "The wife's pitchin' a fit. Can we move the game to your place?"

"I dunno," Steve said in his droning voice, which was deep and nasal at the same time—no mean feat. *"My roommate's comin' home early. . . ."*

"You suck," Larry said, ribbing his old amigo. He guided the van through a lane change as he crossed the J. J. Byrne Memorial Bridge into Queens. "Why don't you call Pete and see if we can move the game to his place?"

"Why don't you call him?"

Accelerating past a line of cars, all of them speeding to make the light at the end of the bridge, Larry replied, "Because I have to drive a pair of scumbags out to Rikers and then drag my ass all the way back to Schermerhorn to punch out for my OT. So cut me some friggin' slack, will ya?"

He strained to see the upcoming traffic signal through the rain and mist. Oncoming cars' halogen headlights blinded him for a second.

On the phone, Steve gave in. *"All right, I'll call Pete and set it up."*

"Thanks, man. You're a prince. See you guys at six."

Larry lowered the phone from his ear. He glanced down for only a moment, to thumb the END button and put the phone back in standby.

The light ahead of him at the intersection of Greenpoint Avenue and Van Dam Street was still green. He stepped on the gas and barreled through the intersection.

Then came an apocalyptic slam of impact that he felt but never heard.

The rest was a blur.

Exhaust fumes in the back of the van were giving Erin a headache. Her trenchcoat was pulled open to accommodate her hands being cuffed behind her back, leaving her vulnerable to the dank, cold air seeping in through cracks in the rusted floor as the transport vehicle hurtled down darkening, rain-slicked streets.

Next to her in the rear seat, Tom sat in the same pose, hands behind his back, face fixed in a mask of frustration and fear. The past day had taken a brutal toll on him—Erin could see it from the look in his eyes. She was worried about him.

At the front of the van, on the other side of a welded metal security grate, the lone driver was chattering nonstop on his cell phone. It troubled Erin that he was paying more attention to his conversation than to the traffic around them.

Tom half-turned his head toward her and muttered, "This is

just great." She rolled her eyes in his direction, and he continued. "Anna has to ransom her daughter in ninety minutes, and we're on our way to jail. I don't suppose you have a Plan B for getting us out of this?"

"No, but we'd better think of one," Erin said. Noting landmarks blurring by outside the van's metal-mesh-covered side windows, she added, "We're less than twenty minutes from Rikers. If we end up in there, that's it."

Alarmed, Tom replied, "What do you mean, 'that's it'?"

"As in, we go in there, we're dead. If you're right and that cop Kolpack really is one of the Scorned, he'll make sure of it. Now that we know he's involved in the kidnapping, he has to get rid of us."

Tom shut his eyes, sighed, and let his head droop forward. "I guess all we can do now is pray for a mirac—"

Thunder struck with a million bits of shattered glass, a jolt of impact, and a groan of wrenched metal. Sideways momentum pinned Tom and Erin together. They moved in slow motion while the world spun around them in a blur.

Another loud, violent shock sent the van tumbling. Erin and Tom bounced and rolled inside the passenger compartment. They struck the sides, the seats, the roof, the buckled-in window gratings. Flurries of glass danced around them.

Metal screeched against pavement. The street scraped by beneath the van as it came to a halt. Erin's stunned ears barely registered a distant thud of collision. A car horn was blaring—one long, piercing drone that wouldn't stop.

Erin and Tom lay crumpled together in the wrecked van. With their hands cuffed behind them, they'd had no way to break their falls or shield their faces. The stinging of several nicks began to flare on her forehead and cheeks. Dull aches and throbbing bruises filled her whole body. A ferric tang of blood teased her tongue, and she realized that her teeth had cut the insides of her lips.

She tried to figure out which way was up and reorient herself, only to lose her balance and fall against the roof of the van, which she then saw was lying on its left side. Above her, the side door of the van had been bashed halfway open. Turning to check on Tom, Erin's every movement was answered by the grinding of glass motes under her feet.

Tom was on his knees, head bowed. He groaned, then looked up at her. His face, too, had been peppered with flying glass and was marked by dozens of tiny cuts. Bright red blood trickled from his nose. He smiled at her. "As I was saying . . . a miracle."

"Not unless we slip these cuffs and get outta this van, it ain't."

"Right," he said, getting to his feet. "I need something small and metal to pick the cuffs. It has to be flexible, like a hairpin or a paper clip."

She turned her back to him. "Inside my coat, under the lining in the back, along the seam."

Nodding, he scuttled in a tight half circle and turned his back to her. As he lifted her coat and began probing the fabric, he asked, "You planned ahead?"

"No," Erin said. "Ripped it climbing a fence a few weeks ago, and I don't know how to sew."

"Got it," he said, detaching the safety pin. "It's big. That's good." Looking over his shoulder at her, he added, "Give me a few seconds. I have to open the pin and make some bends in it to pick the double locks on these cuffs."

In the distance, Erin heard the first faint cries of a siren. "We've got a minute, tops," she said.

"I'm working as fast as I can," he said, his voice tense with concentration. "I used to pick handcuffs for fun, but never behind my back."

From the cab of the van, Erin heard the driver moan. Outside, voices began puncturing the eerie postaccident silence.

The sirens were getting closer.

With a click and a jangle of chain, she heard Tom free himself from his handcuffs. He turned and started working on hers. It took him only a few seconds, and then her right hand was free. "I'll do the other hand later," he said. "Let's go."

They shimmied past the edges of the seatbacks, then climbed up the front row of seats to the open side door above them. Tom pulled himself over the edge first, then reached back to help Erin out of the van, onto its upturned side. They pushed themselves off the van and landed on their feet in the street.

Multiple vehicles had piled up in the intersection. A crowd of gawkers had gathered on the nearby corners and sidewalks. Drivers trapped in snarled traffic on the bridge and surrounding streets honked their horns in a cacophonous din.

Radiators hissed, and injured drivers and passengers filled the night with pained cries. The asphalt was dusted with several hues of shattered safety glass liberated from windshields, scraps of metal torn from the van and other vehicles, and one shredded tire.

The sirens were louder now. Several blocks away, red and blue lights flashed through the rain and threw their light far ahead of them on wet streets.

Erin took a breath to clear her head from the effects of being whipped around on a blunt-force carousel. The chilly, moist air was sharp with the scorched-metal odor of overheated brake pads and venting car-engine fumes.

Searching the scene of destruction, she noticed a motorcyclist stirring back to consciousness beside his downed but still intact red Ducati. "C'mon," she said to Tom, leading him toward the bike. "We're outta here."

"Wait," Tom said, stumbling along a few steps behind her. "We're not . . . ?"

"Yes, we are," she said. She pointed at the top case mounted on the back of the bike, behind the passenger seat. "Open that, see if he has a second helmet."

Tom, still looking a bit dazed, did as she asked. Erin, meanwhile, stopped in front of the Ducati's owner and plucked his helmet off his head. "We need your bike," she said. "Nothing personal."

She didn't wait to see if he had a problem with it. Turning back to the bike, she saw that her hunch had been right: Tom had found a spare helmet in the top case. "Put that on," she said, "then help me stand the bike up, fast." She donned her own borrowed helmet and joined Tom in pushing the heavy bike upright. Once it was up, she climbed on and told Tom, "Throw a leg over and hold on, *papi.*"

Glancing over her shoulder, she squinted into the fast-approaching headlights of two ambulances, a fire engine, and a pair of police cruisers.

Tom mounted the bike, planted his feet on the rear foot-pegs, and took hold of Erin's waist.

Erin thumbed the kill switch and turned the key. The gauges and warning lights flashed, and the needles were pinned to the red lines as the bike ran its self-check. Then the gauges settled back to zero. She squeezed the clutch with her left hand, used her left foot to shift the bike into neutral, then pulled the clutch in again as she pressed the starter.

The Ducati's engine turned over with a roar, then relaxed to a purr.

She kicked it into first gear, twisted the throttle, and let go of the clutch. The bike rumbled forward, and she dodged through the slalom course of smashed cars. Clearing the mess, she steered down a service road that ran parallel to the bridge they'd just crossed and went full throttle.

As the bike's engine roared and the tachometer needle spun toward the red line, Erin barely heard the loudspeaker warning from the cops behind her.

"You on the motorcycle! Stop now!"

She ignored them as second gear kicked in.

The road was slick and poorly lit. It had been a while since Erin had been on a bike. She hoped she remembered how to handle it at speed. As she shifted into third, she ducked behind the bike's windscreen.

In her side mirrors, she saw the wild spray kicking up off her rear tire. *Maybe that'll slow the cops down.*

Ahead of her, past some railroad tracks and an intersection, the road dead-ended at the river. "Hang on!" she shouted back to Tom, then accelerated through a tight right turn. They picked up speed on their way past a dilapidated building connected by a jungle of rusted pipes to a cluster of enormous, silo-like oil tanks.

Police floodlights bathed the dark street in harsh light and cast Tom and Erin's shadow a hundred yards in front of them. Barked orders from the cops' loudspeaker were drowned out by the roaring wind and the growl of the engine as she kicked it into fourth gear.

Air slammed against her, cold and hard.

The bike gained speed quickly and opened its lead on the

police cruiser. That was when Erin heard the first pops of gunfire and saw divots kicking up from the road on her left—and realized that the cops were shooting at them.

Hurtling down the broad lane beside the railroad tracks, Erin saw another dead end looming ahead of her. A junkyard of some kind, filled with mountains of sand and scrap metal and populated by cranes and smelting plants.

Can't go in there, they'll block us in. She veered right, up a gravelly slope that threatened to drag her into a wipeout. Fighting for control, she downshifted for power and kept the bike steady as she leapt it onto the tracks.

The cross ties thudded in a steady rhythm under her tires, shaking her like a cheap motel's massage bed.

She chanced another look back. The cops weren't giving up. They powered up the gravel slope and swerved onto the tracks behind her.

A squeeze, a kick, and a twist, and she took the bike into fifth gear, hauling ass toward the Dutch Kill swing bridge. Rust had eaten through most of the white paint on its metal frame, bubbling and scarring it like acne. The concrete blocks of its no longer functional drawbridge mechanism were festooned with crude graffiti.

Bullets zinged off the bridge's rust-blemished steel and tore chunks from its gang-tagged concrete. Erin put the bike in its top gear and pushed it to the limit.

It took all her concentration to keep the bike centered on the narrow plank path between the rails as she crossed the bridge. Halfway across, a muffled crash from behind made her check her mirror. The cruiser's tire had broken through a rotted walkway plank. The car fishtailed and spun to a precarious stop, its nose poking through a gap in the bridge's frame and tilting ominously downward, toward the reeking, polluted sludge of Newtown Creek.

Erin kept the throttle pinned as she and Tom raced away from the far side of the bridge, still between the tracks. They passed a freight yard stacked high with multicolored metal shipping containers, then shot through a long straightaway between a pair of massive industrial buildings.

Up ahead, beyond the Pulaski Bridge and the sprawl of urban decay that defined the south end of Long Island City, she saw the lights of a Long Island Rail Road passenger train rumbling toward them.

Tom pointed over her shoulder and shouted, "We can reach the street before it cuts us off."

"Not the plan," she hollered back, steering left, off the tracks, and through a wide open lot behind some kind of factory that dwelled in the bridge's shadow. She slowed as they looped behind the building, onto a narrow strip of road that skirted the edge of the creek.

Once they were safely out of sight from the road or the bridge, she stopped next to a gap in the concrete barrier wall and shifted the bike into neutral.

She removed her helmet and looked back at Tom. "End of the line. Off."

He doffed his helmet and wearily dismounted the bike. "Why'd we stop?"

"The cops'll be looking for us on this," she said. "We ditched that car, but there'll be more—and helicopters, too. We have to lose this bike now." She pitched her helmet over the wall into Newtown Creek. "Help me push this thing."

Tom grabbed the right handlebar and Erin took the left. Working together, they heaved the Italian motorcycle over and through the break in the wall. It plunged into the oily black waters and vanished. As an afterthought, he chucked his helmet in after it. Then he eyed the industrial wasteland that surrounded them and smiled facetiously. "You always take me to the nicest places."

"Rather be back in the van?"

He arched an eyebrow and tilted his head. "Point taken. Now what?"

"We hoof it back to Brooklyn. If we split up, we can walk over this bridge without getting noticed. Then we can meet up on the other side and go from there."

"Won't they be looking for us?" he asked.

"Sure, together on a motorcycle. Right now we have two things going for us: it's raining, and it's getting dark."

"And one thing working against us," Tom said. "It's almost four fifteen."

"Well, then," she replied. "Hope you got your walkin' shoes on. 'Cause it's a *long* way back to your truck."

A devilish grin lit up Tom's face.

"Maybe not," he said.

Frank had just returned to his desk with a mug of bitterly scorched black coffee in his hand when Lieutenant La Salle stormed out of his office and shouted as he crossed the room, "Figursky! Thorne! Your arson suspects are on the run!"

Every head in the room turned toward the two detectives, who sat in stunned silence as the lieutenant descended on them. All Frank could think was, *I knew it.* He got up and sidled toward Figursky's and Thorne's desks, which faced each other.

Thorne asked the lieutenant, "What happened?"

La Salle slapped a folder onto Thorne's desk. "Traffic accident. A truck clipped the van taking your perps to Rikers." He opened the folder and flipped pages. "They slipped their cuffs and grabbed a motorcycle. Followed the river and ditched a pursuit car at the Dutch Kill bridge. No telling where they are now."

"Did we put out a BOLO?" Figursky asked.

"Not yet," La Salle said. "Dispatch wants to know if we have any photos that don't look like this." He lifted two booking-photo sheets from the folder.

Edging closer, Frank saw the images printed on them. They were totally pixilated and obscured by light and dark streaks. He sighed with irritation through his nose. *The Watchers are getting clever. They messed with our eyes. Made us think the photos were okay when they weren't. Bet the prints are fucked, too.*

Raising another sheet of paper, La Salle added, "And just FYI, I'm asking Captain Eichorn to fire Fallis, because the prints were botched again, too."

"Crap," Figursky muttered.

Frank lowered his chin and shook his head, disgusted.

"Since we need to get something out there A-sap, I've called in some help," the lieutenant said, waving someone into the squad room. The gate gave a long, semimusical creak as Detective Audra Moore, one of the NYPD's on-call forensic sketch artists, pushed it open and walked in. She carried a slender computer bag at her side, its strap slung diagonally across her chest.

The detectives greeted her with a low chorus of mumbled "hello"s and friendly nods. Figursky got up from his desk and offered her his seat.

"Thanks," Moore said to him as she sat down. She opened the clasp on her bag and pulled out a state-of-the-art laptop. Opening it, she asked, "Which of your fugitives do you want to start with?"

"The woman," Figursky said, at the same time that Thorne said, "The man."

Moore looked to La Salle for direction. He said, "The man."

Clicking an icon to launch a composite-drawing application, she asked, "Who spent the most time with him?"

Figursky replied, "I did. Spent almost an hour sitting across from him in the interview room."

"Good," Moore said. "We should start with the shape of the face."

"Kinda squarish," Figursky said.

Thorne cut in, "No, no—it was more oval."

Ohara interrupted, "I thought his hairline gave it a heart-shaped look."

And on it went, with each detective remembering the face just a little bit differently than everyone else did, to the point where Frank was certain that the enemy Seekers' Watchers had been working overtime to cloud the detectives' perceptions. For all he knew, no one had heard their voices the same way, either.

"Maybe we should start with the basics," Moore said. "Hair color?"

"Light brown," Figursky said.

"Gray," Thorne said.

"Blond," Ohara said.

Moore cast suspicious looks at the detectives. "Eyes?"

"Green."

"Brown."

"Blue."

She reclined her chair and looked at La Salle. "Is this your idea of a joke?"

"No," La Salle said, glaring at his detectives. "And whatever the explanation for this is, I'm not laughing."

Frank couldn't take it anymore. He reached into his jacket pocket and clandestinely keyed the speed dial for his own squad-room extension. A moment later, his phone rang. He walked back to his desk, picked up the phone, keyed his cell phone back to standby, and improvised his way through a one-sided conversation with the dead line.

"Seventy-first Precinct, Detective Kolpack. . . . Yes, I am. . . . Okay. . . . Are you sure? . . . Can you prove that?" He looked at his watch, as if he was concerned about the impending shift change. "Does it have to be right now? . . . All right, then, where?" Scribbling gibberish on a notepad, he pretended to be taking directions. "Right. . . . Mm-hmm . . . okay, got it. . . . We'll talk about that when I get there. . . . Bye." He hung up, tore the sheet of faux notes from the pad, and stuffed it in his pocket. "Lou," he called to La Salle, "I gotta step out. Tip from a CI on the Robeson case. Could be bullshit, but I want to check it out."

"Go ahead," La Salle said, waving Frank on his way.

Frank quickstepped to the exit and pushed through the gate while the artist made a futile attempt to elicit a description of the female fugitive. Had he been in a more charitable mood, Frank would have told her not to bother.

Descending the stairs two steps at a time, he plotted his next move.

If they're free, they'll probably try to help the Doyle woman, he reasoned. *So the best place to find them'll be at her house.*

He wasn't sure yet what excuse he would use for shooting them, but he was certain he'd think of something—he always had before.

Bailey only partially paid attention as Kolpack answered his phone call. But as his conversation continued, she was certain she heard something odd.

It took her a moment to realize it was a dial tone.

Coming from the earpiece of Kolpack's phone.

She said nothing and kept her eyes on her desktop full of work, while a few feet away, Kolpack continued his phony phone discussion and secured permission to go meet a CI that Bailey was pretty sure didn't exist. Across the room, the forensic artist was getting nowhere in her effort to untangle the mutually conflicting descriptions being provided by the rest of the squad.

Kolpack hung up his phone and made a swift exit from the squad room.

Bailey spent a few seconds wondering what excuse she would use to leave and follow Frank. Then she decided that no explanation was the best choice of all. She got up, lifted her jacket from the back of her chair, and calmly walked out. As she'd hoped, no one paid any attention to her departure.

A quick check of the stairs revealed no sign of Kolpack. Stepping lightly, Bailey made her way down to the first floor and checked the corridor. She caught a glimpse of the tail of his jacket as he cut through the briefing room, probably as a shortcut to the parking lot.

Treading softly, she slipped down the hall and stayed on his trail, through the briefing room, and then to the parking lot door. She caught it before it closed. Easing it open, she peeked outside. The rain had started to taper off, leaving the cars glistening with beads that caught the glare of the lot's floodlights.

Kolpack jogged to his car and got in. The sedan's headlights came on as the engine turned over. He pulled out of his space and cruised toward the exit onto New York Avenue.

As Kolpack passed the precinct's side door, Bailey made a mental note of his license plate number then skulked quickly to her own car, a beat-up blue hatchback.

She used her remote to unlock the doors and start the ignition as she approached. By the time she slid into the driver's seat, the car was ready to roll. She shifted into drive and headed for the exit.

Turning onto New York Avenue, she saw Kolpack's sedan a few cars ahead, his progress impeded by a red light. For once, Bailey was grateful for the aggravations of local traffic, bad weather, and an early nightfall.

It would make it harder for Kolpack to notice that he was being followed.

23

Tom figured that if anything could persuade one of the many cars zooming past him and Erin to stop, it would be Erin leaning out from the curb under a streetlamp, her arm extended and thumb raised, her trenchcoat open and fluttering in the chilly breeze to reveal her shapely leather-clad figure.

Apparently, I figured wrong, he decided as yet another line of cars rolled past, filling the avenue with the white noise of tires on rain-soaked streets. The sky was already dark in the east and fading to a violet-streaked indigo in the west. *At least it's stopped raining,* he consoled himself.

"Great plan," Erin said as the last car disappeared down the road. She dropped her arm and resumed walking south with Tom at her side.

He shrugged. "If we could just get someone to stop . . ."

"Don't count on it," she said. "Nobody picks up hitchhikers in New York."

When they'd first crossed the bridge, he'd suggested heading back to her nearby safe house on Dupont Street. Then she had reminded him that her keys to the safe house were locked inside his truck, several miles away.

Tipped off by a telltale glow on the wet pavement, Tom looked back and noted, "Another car coming." He smiled sheepishly at Erin. "One more try?"

She sighed, stopped, and stepped to the curb. As she opened her coat, struck a pose, and raised her thumb, Tom noticed that she was standing right next to a sizable puddle in the road.

Inching away, he said, "Um, Erin? I don't think you—"

"I know how to hitch rides," she said.

He raised his hands in surrender and took three steps back to make himself less conspicuous. Backed up against a wall, he watched Erin lean forward into the car's headlight beams. Like the other cars before it, it showed no sign of slowing down. Then it surged through the massive gutter pond and sent up a miniature tsunami, soaking Erin from head to toe and knocking her back half a step.

The station wagon slammed on its brakes, turning the pavement red with reflections from its taillights. Erin stood motionless and dripping. A few seconds later, the car's white reverse lights switched on.

Erin turned her head and smiled at Tom. "Pity's a wonderful thing."

He stepped forward to join her as the car backed up and eased over to the curb. It came to a stop in front of him and Erin. The passenger-side window lowered with an electric hum, revealing its driver, a white woman in her mid-forties. "Oh, my God," she said, aghast. "I'm so sorry. I didn't mean to do that."

"S'okay," Erin said. "Just water, right?"

Tom leaned down into the passenger window. The inside of the car smelled like cheap perfume, mothballs, and stale coffee. "Evening, ma'am. We hate to impose, but seeing as you were kind enough to stop—"

"Oh, no," the woman said, shaking her head. "I don't pick up hitchhikers."

"Neither do we," Tom said. "We're not hitchhikers, just stranded travelers."

Still wary, the driver replied, "Stranded?"

"We parked our truck in a different neighborhood and caught a ride into Queens with some friends of ours," Tom said. "But they left us in the lurch, and now we're late for an appointment."

The woman started raising the window. "Well, you can call a cab."

Clinging to the rising edge of the glass, Tom spoke quickly. "We have no cash, we were mugged—look at our faces. Please help us. It's life or death."

Just as the window was about to pinch his fingers into the door frame, it stopped, then lowered an inch. The woman's face betrayed her conflicted feelings. Picking up a pair of strangers when she was alone had to seem like a bad idea, Tom knew. He could only hope that the persuasive power that enabled him to coax people into doing the right thing would be on his side at that moment.

"Where are you two going?" she asked.

He looked at Erin, who answered nervously, "Corner of Utica and Lefferts."

The woman sucked air through her clenched teeth. "I don't know," she said. "That's pretty far out of my way."

"Ma'am, we wouldn't ask if it wasn't really important," Tom said.

She frowned. "For all I know, you could be escaped convicts."

Closing his hand around the handcuffs hidden in his jacket pocket, Tom flashed his most disarming grin and said, "Do we *look* like convicts?"

The driver's worried gaze lingered for a moment on Erin, but then she relaxed a little and said, "I guess not." She pressed a button on her armrest, and the car's doors unlocked with a muffled chorus of thunks.

Tom opened the passenger door. "God bless you, ma'am. You're a saint." He held the door open for Erin. "You know the way, so you ride shotgun."

Erin ducked into the car. Once her legs and the flap of her trenchcoat were safely in, Tom shut her door, then opened the rear passenger door and climbed in behind her. As soon as his door closed, the driver relocked the doors.

"You never know who might be out here," she said, shifting into drive and merging back into traffic.

Spying Erin's knowing smirk in the side-view mirror, Tom replied, "Ain't that the truth."

Anna paced in her kitchen. She was dressed and ready to travel, with a warm sweater under a lightweight raincoat. Her dark hair had been pulled into a loose ponytail to conceal the fact that she hadn't washed it in two days.

The coffee mug shook in her hand as she plodded back and forth between the dining table and the refrigerator. It had been nearly forty-five minutes since Marc had phoned to say that he had finished his whirlwind tour of New York's biggest international banks, where he'd called in a host of quasi-legal favors to turn her assets into bearer bonds. She had volunteered to meet him and take possession of the bonds for the swap, but he'd insisted on picking her up, for her safety.

So she waited.

She'd left six messages on Tom Nash's cell phone since the morning, but he still hadn't called back. *Maybe I was wrong to trust him,* she thought. *I let him get my hopes up for nothing.*

The phone rang. She grabbed it, hoping again that it was Tom. "Hello?"

"Anna? It's Marc. I'm outside."

Masking her disappointment, she replied, "Okay. I'll be right out." She hung up and took a moment to collect herself. As she walked out of the kitchen, her hand closed around the disposable cell phone in her raincoat pocket, just to make sure she still had it. She put on a brave face as she opened the front door.

Outside, the rain had turned to mist, light yet endless. At the bottom of her front steps, a black limousine was double-parked. Its rear door was open. Marc sat inside the car behind the driver, waving for Anna to get in.

She descended the steps, ducked between the parked cars, climbed in beside Marc, and closed the door. The inside of the limo was warm and smelled strongly of its leather upholstery. As usual, Marc's year-round tan was a rich golden hue, and his mustache was as impeccably groomed as his tailored Armani suit. The metallic briefcase was on the floor at his feet. Anna nodded at it. "Is it all there?"

"Yes," Marc said. He picked it up and opened it, revealing the thick stack of gold-embossed papers inside. "The combination's been set to nine-nine-nine, like you asked." As he closed the case, he added, "But I have to beg you one last time not to do this, Anna. Please call the FBI while you still can."

"It's too late for that. There's just over an hour till the exchange, and I can't—" She corrected herself. "I *won't* take any risks with Phaedra's life."

"Then what about your own life?" Marc shook his head in dismay. "Don't you realize how dangerous this is? Think about the kind of people you're going to be dealing with, Anna. They sound like mobsters. You think they'll really hand over Phaedra just because you paid the ransom?"

"It's the only chance I have," she said.

He looked away from her, out his window, and thought for a moment. Then he turned back. "You said a few hours ago that you were calling in some help. Did you follow through on that?"

"I tried," she said. "I left messages all afternoon, but he never called back."

"Who?" Marc asked.

"A private detective," Anna said. "His name's Tom Nash. Came to the house yesterday and said he was working on a case that he thought might be related to Phaedra's kidnapping."

Marc looked horrified. "And you *believed* him?"

"I know, it doesn't make sense. But if you met him, you'd understand."

"I doubt that," Marc said. "Did he give you a business card? Show you a PI's license? Give you any references?"

Recoiling from the sudden inquisition, Anna said, "No, he didn't."

"How much money did he ask you for?"

"Actually, he said he didn't want my money, that he was already working for someone else. So if you're worried that he was scamming me, he wasn't."

Crossing his arms and massaging his brow, Marc said, "Has it occurred to you that he might be working with the people who took Phaedra?"

"Marc, don't take this personally, but you're being paranoid." Leaning forward, she said to the driver, "Can we go now?"

The driver looked into the rearview mirror for Marc's consent. The lawyer nodded once, and the driver shifted the car into gear and drove away from Anna's brownstone, starting their trip into the city. As they made the turn onto Prospect Park West, Anna's hands began shaking.

Looking at Anna's hands, Marc asked, "Are you all right?"

"I'm on my way to bring twelve million dollars in a briefcase to a bunch of low-life thugs who could kill my daughter at any moment. What do you think?"

He opened a panel on the limo's wall and took out a cut-crystal cocktail tumbler. Gesturing to a drink well built into the wall beneath the cabinet, he said, "Five flavors of courage. Pick your poison."

"Gin," she said. "And make it a double."

She watched shadows blur past outside the car while Marc lifted a bottle, pulled the stopper, and poured a generous measure of clear liquid into the glass. He handed it to her, and she took it.

The glass was heavier than she'd expected. She sipped the gin and found it smoother and less medicinal than most she had tasted.

"Thanks," she said, though her hands continued to tremble.

He set the bottle back in its place in the drink well. "If you want to thank me, promise me one thing: don't hand over the money until they show you Phaedra."

"What if they refuse?"

"In that case," he said, "promise me you'll run like hell."

Frank pulled over and stopped across the street from Anna Doyle's brownstone. All the lights in the building seemed to be off.

He checked his watch. It was just past four thirty.

I bet I missed her, he fumed. He picked up his disposable cell phone and tried calling the woman's home phone number. It connected and rang several times with no answer. He hung up as a double ringtone signaled that his call was being routed to voice mail. *Shit. I missed her. Now what?*

His hands drummed anxiously on the steering wheel. He reached into his pocket and pulled out his last two sticks of gum. His fingers moved as frantically as his thoughts—tearing away the paper, then the foil, pushing the spearmint sticks into his mouth. He folded the paper and weighed his options.

I can stay here and wait for the blond man and his friend to show up. He dismissed that idea. *Forget that. If the Doyle woman's not here, they won't be, either. They'll probably contact her directly.* For a moment he dared to hope that the enemy Seekers had gone to ground to avoid the law. Then pessimism took hold again. *Who'm I kidding? If they're loose, they're a threat.* He wondered how Viktor and his men might react if the two Seekers interfered in the ransom grab.

Badly, he admitted to himself. *I'd better damage control this now.*

He picked up his phone and dialed Viktor.

The boss answered. *"What is it, Kolpack?"*

"Just checking in," Frank lied. "Are your men ready?"

"They're on their way," Viktor said. *"Some are there now. The rest will be in place by five fifteen, as we said."*

"Good." He began twisting the strips of folded foil and paper around his index finger. "I just wanted to give you and your men a quick update."

Viktor's tone turned cagey. *"About what?"*

"There might be two more guests at this little party," he said. "The ones your boys failed to take out last night."

"You said you were handling that," Viktor said defensively.

"I did what I could." The tip of his finger began to turn cyanotic. "The bad news is they might make this messy. The good news is they're not the law, so we're all still in the clear."

"But these people know who we are, yes?"

"Well, not exactly," Frank said. "I mean, I doubt they have your name."

"But they are the ones who broke into my club?"

He loosened the wrapper from his finger. "Probably, yes."

"If they've connected my people to the club and the ransom demand, they could tell the police. We can't let that happen, Kolpack."

Frank began to regret having told Viktor anything. "I agree that would be bad, Viktor, but what do you expect me to do about it?"

"You know what these two look like, yes?"

"I'm probably the only person who really does."

"Then we need you at the ransom exchange."

Alarm straightened his posture. He tossed aside his twisted gum wrappers. "Hang on, Viktor. I can't be anywhere near the swap, you know that."

"What I know is that there are two threats to this plan that my people can't pick out of a crowd, but you can. Either you help us, or I pull my people back."

"Viktor, be reasonable. I—"

"We're past the point of no return, Kolpack. You're in, or it's off."

He covered his eyes with one hand and scrunched his face in utter frustration. Viktor's demand made perfect sense, but being anywhere near the ransom grab without an alibi was a risk that Frank had hoped to avoid.

"All right. I'm in, goddammit. I'll be there in an hour."

"Don't be late," Viktor said, and he hung up.

Frank tossed the cell phone onto the passenger seat. Then he punched the dashboard twice, three times, and again until the knuckles of his right hand were raw and bloody and the face of the dash was cracked and splintered.

This was not how he'd imagined his day would go.

Maybe I can still salvage this, he reassured himself. *If I'm lucky, the Seekers won't show, and Viktor's men can grab the cash. Then we're done.* His reflection in the rearview mirror didn't look hopeful. *When have I ever been lucky?*

He drew his Glock 26 from its shoulder holster, checked the safety, ejected the clip, and confirmed it was fully loaded. Then he slammed it back into the pistol and holstered the weapon. With his right hand, he confirmed that his two backup clips were where they should be.

Okay, then. He shifted the car into drive. *Let's party.*

Bailey had no idea why Kolpack was driving over the Brooklyn Bridge.

Of course she'd had no clue why he hightailed it to a tree-shaded block in Park Slope, either, but at least that had been a short drive from the precinct. After watching him beat the hell out of his car's dashboard, she'd figured he would head either to a bar or back to the seven-one.

Instead, he'd taken Flatbush Avenue to Atlantic and followed it west, then hooked a right onto Adams Street.

And now they were on the damn bridge, heading into Manhattan.

At least we're going against traffic, Bailey mused.

It was four forty-five, and already the weekday rush-hour exodus from downtown had begun. Cars in the bridge's eastbound lanes were bumper to bumper and creeping like molasses all the way across the East River. A faint but persistent misting rain wasn't making the situation any better.

Keeping an eye on Kolpack's silver Toyota from four cars back and one lane over, all that Bailey could do was ask herself the same unanswerable question over and over: *What the hell are you up to, Kolpack?*

Tom watched a mechanic named Samir poke inside his truck's driver-side door with a slim jim. The swarthy youth had been at it for several minutes while Erin and Tom watched from a few feet away at the edge of the White Castle parking lot. *I could've had that door open in ten seconds,* Tom thought with a sigh.

He didn't want to be rude since the man was doing him a favor—though, in truth, Samir was really doing Erin a favor. She'd been the one who'd walked over to the auto-repair shop behind the gas station on Remsen Avenue to sweet-talk him into letting her and Tom back into "their" truck.

It didn't surprise Tom that Erin had had a far easier time enlisting Samir's help than he'd had convincing the woman in the station wagon to drive them here. Like most men probably would, Samir had taken one look at Erin and turned to putty in her hands.

Finally, the door's lock released with a dull pop. Samir pulled the slim jim free and opened the door. "Voilà," he said in his unusual, exotic accent.

"Thanks," Tom said, shaking Samir's hand. Then he reached under the driver's seat and retrieved his wallet. He opened it and handed Samir a twenty. "We really appreciate your help, man."

" 'Twas nothing," Samir said, tucking the bill under his oil-stained coveralls. Then a moment of suspicion overtook him. "You sure this is your truck?"

Tom flipped open his wallet and showed the man his driver's license. "See?" Nodding to the glove compartment, he added, "Wanna see my registration?"

"No, no," Samir said, backing away. "You're very welcome. Safe travels."

With a push of his thumb on a button, Tom unlocked the truck's other door. Erin opened it and checked to be sure her possessions were still under the passenger seat. "Loan me a few bucks?" she asked. "I'm starving."

"So am I," he said, forking over another twenty. "Hook me up with some sliders, some cheese sticks, and a Coke, will ya?"

Erin plucked the bill from his hand. "You buy, I fly."

"Keep the change," he said.

"Always," she replied, tossing him a mischievous smile. She jogged away across the slick, neon-lit parking lot to the fast-food joint's entrance.

Tom tucked his things back into the pockets where they belonged, then climbed back inside his truck, where *he* belonged. It felt good to be back in his own space. He'd had a very long day out of his element, and anything familiar was a welcome relief. He took a moment to breathe—

And his memory put on a horror show.

Bullets flying in the night.

A burning building falling in on him.

The click of handcuffs closing on his wrists.

He blinked and pushed back against his fears, against the certainty that he was out of his depth and sinking fast. *Crooked cops? Mobsters? What the hell have I gotten into?* He held his breath till his heart stopped trying to slam its way out of his chest, then he palmed the sweat from his face.

He exhaled and gasped for air, forcing himself to draw new breaths slowly.

The memory of a child's voice restored his focus.

A simple plea. Seven simple words he could never forget.

Please, God . . . don't let them kill me.

Through the restaurant's windows, he saw Erin ordering at the counter.

His cell phone vibrated inside his pocket.

He fished it out. The display said he had six new voice-mail messages. A quick check of the incoming-call log showed they were all from the same number—Anna Doyle. He played the first message.

"Tom, it's Anna. My lawyer's gathering the money for Phaedra's ransom, but he doesn't want me to go through with it. Please tell me you're close to finding her. And if not, say you'll be here to help me get her back. I really don't want to do this alone. Please call me."

The next four messages were all variations on *"Tom? Are you there? It's Anna. I have to leave soon. Please call me. Hurry."*

He played the last message. *"Tom, I'm on my way into the city for the swap. The kidnappers told me to wait in front of the subway entrance on Forty-second Street between Broadway and Seventh Avenue at five thirty. If you get this before then, please call me. . . . God, I hope you're out there. Call me."*

Erin walked out of the restaurant with a paper bag in each

hand as Tom selected Anna's cell-phone number from the call list and pressed TALK to dial.

The phone rang only once before she picked up. Her voice was filled with both hope and fear. *"Tom?"*

"Yes," he said. "I just got your messages."

"Where the hell have you been?"

"Long story," Tom said. "Where are you now?"

"We're in lower Manhattan, heading up Sixth Avenue."

"Who's 'we'?" Tom asked as Erin opened her door and got into the truck.

"I'm with my lawyer."

"Okay." He glanced at the dashboard clock. "It's quarter to five. I can reach you before the ransom drop. Is there somewhere we can meet?"

"Hang on, I'll ask." He heard muffled sounds on the line as Anna conferred with her lawyer. Beside him, Erin opened one paper bag and pulled out two medium-sized sodas, which she set into the drink caddy between them. Finally, Anna said, *"Look for me in front of the library at Fifth and Forty-second."*

"Fine. Wait for me there. If anything happens before I reach you, call me."

"I will," Anna said. After a pause, she said with some hesitation, *"I don't mean to sound skeptical, but . . . do you have some kind of plan?"*

"Not exactly," Tom admitted. "But I think it might be safer for you if I take the briefcase to the swap."

"I don't think my lawyer will like that," Anna said.

"He and I can talk about that later," Tom said. "For now, all I want to do is keep you out of danger and help you get your daughter back." His stomach growled as Erin opened the second paper bag, filling the truck's cab with the aroma of deep-fried treats and burgers steamed over onions. "Do you trust me?"

"Yes," she said. *"But I don't want you facing these thugs alone."*

Tom looked at Erin. Misty light spilling across her window gave her a saint's halo, and he thought of their guardian angels. "Don't worry," he told Anna. "I won't be alone."

24

With its majestic façade of floodlit marble and granite, towering Greek columns, and elegant statuary, the New York Public Library gave Tom the impression of an ancient temple surrounded by the modern world. It felt as if it had a touch of the eternal, an aura of permanence in a city devoted to perpetual reinvention.

Erin walked beside him as they neared the building's front steps. Heeding her advice, he had parked a few blocks away, both as a precaution and as a matter of necessity, since there was no parking anywhere on this stretch of Fifth Avenue, which was jam-packed with rush-hour traffic. Yellow cabs darted between lanes, and buses struggled to leapfrog past one another. Horns blared to drown out curses.

A few dozen pedestrians were scattered on the library's stairs and the plaza beside it. Some were solo, others in pairs or small groups. Almost all of them carried umbrellas, but no one was using them now that the rain had stopped.

On the bottom step, halfway between the library's white stone lions, stood Anna and an impeccably dressed man in his forties, who Tom guessed was her lawyer. The man was holding a metallic briefcase.

Nudging Erin, Tom nodded to Anna and said, "That's her."

Anna's face brightened when she saw Tom emerge from the crowd. She touched her lawyer's arm and whispered to him. The man nodded once.

Tom and Erin stopped in front of them.

The lawyer spoke first. "The swap is in ten minutes," he said, sharp and all business.

"We came as soon as we could," Tom said. "And nice to meet you, too."

Stepping between them to referee, Anna said, "Marc, this is Tom Nash. Tom, this is my lawyer, Marc Cimbal." The two men exchanged curt nods.

Tom gestured to Erin. "This is my associate—"

"Eva," Erin cut in. "Eva Morales."

"Nice to meet you," Marc said. "Now that we're all introduced, maybe you'd like to tell me your plan."

Tom shrugged. "Pretty simple, really. I'll carry the briefcase to the swap." He half paused as he stopped himself from saying Erin's real name. "Eva will follow me at a short distance as my backup."

Marc replied, "How do we know your offer's not just part of a scam to take Anna's money?"

Erin shot back, "Because we're not that smart."

"*That* I can believe," Marc said. "So that's it? That's your plan? You think you can just walk into a deal like this and finish it with a handshake?"

Erin said, "They probably plan to whack the courier and

split with the money before anybody knows what happened. Our job is to make that impossible."

Directing his incredulity at Tom, Marc asked, "How?"

Taking a pair of handcuffs from his pocket, Tom said, "With these." Pointing, he added, "Hand me the case."

Marc looked to Anna, who nodded her permission. The lawyer frowned as he handed the aluminum briefcase to Tom, who closed one cuff around the case's handle with a soft click, then locked the other onto his left wrist.

"When I get to the swap, I'll tell them that if they want the case, they need to free your daughter," Tom said.

The lawyer asked, "What if they want the case first?"

"I'll tell them I don't have the handcuff keys," Tom said. "Which happens to be true." He nodded to Erin. "I'll tell them only my partner has the keys." He omitted the fact that *neither* of them actually had the keys, since they were using a pair of cuffs he had picked open during their escape from the van. Speaking to Anna, he added, "No matter what, they don't get the case till you call and tell me that Phaedra's safe. Whether we give them the money or call the cops at that point is up to you."

Waving her hands, Anna said, "Don't try to be heroes. If they let my daughter go, just give them the money. No cops."

"If that's what you want," Tom said. He sensed that Marc was just as unhappy about Anna's decision as he was.

The lawyer looked Tom in the eye. "The moment they have the money, they'll try to kill you. You know that, right?"

"Yeah," Tom said. "I know."

"Don't give up the case until you know Phaedra's safe," Marc said.

"I won't."

Erin touched Tom's arm to get his attention, then tapped her wrist. "Eight minutes."

"Right," Tom said. "We have to go."

Anna handed him the prepaid cell phone she'd received from the kidnappers. "You'll need this," she said. "They said they'd call me on it when I reached the subway entrance."

"Okay," Tom said, pocketing the phone. "Wait here for my call."

She stepped forward and took his right hand in hers. "I'm putting my daughter's life in your hands," she said, then looked up through the tears in her brown eyes. "Please bring my baby home."

"I will," Tom said, fearful that he was promising more than he could guarantee. He gave Anna's hands a comforting squeeze. "I *will.*"

He let go of her hands, nodded to Marc, and merged back into the crowd, walking toward 42nd Street.

Erin was at his right shoulder. "Pick up the pace," she said in a confidential tone. "I'll fall back about thirty yards and keep an eye on you."

Lowering his voice, he asked, "Why'd you tell her your name was Eva?"

"I never tell people my real name unless I have to. And if you want to live very long in this fight, you'd better learn to start doin' the same."

Before he could respond, Erin dropped back several paces and began disappearing into the five o'clock crush of bodies marching toward Times Square. The press of people, none of them making eye contact, all in a hurry, made Tom claustrophobic. The subway station was only two blocks away, but for Tom the short walk felt like the Bataan Death March.

It was a relief to finally cross Broadway. He turned in a circle and took in the neon chaos of Times Square. Dizzying heights of steel and glass were bathed in a rainbow of electric hues. Floods of people surged in every direction, competing with an armada of cars, buses, and trucks for right of way.

Tom spread his arms to make sure anyone observing him would see the briefcase in his left hand and the disposable cell phone in his right.

He waited. People flowed past him and poured through the subway turnstiles like rainwater rushing down a sewer.

What if they're not looking for me? he wondered. *What if they refuse to deal unless it's Anna making the drop?* Looking around, he tried to find Erin but didn't see her anywhere. *Where'd she go?* Suddenly, he felt exposed and alone.

A clock on the side of a nearby building showed the time as exactly 5:29. In a blink it changed to 5:30.

The phone in his hand rang.

He stared at it, paralyzed, afraid to answer it.

A breath steeled his nerve. He pressed TALK and lifted the phone to his ear. Acid churned in his stomach as he said, "Hello?"

"You are not the Doyle woman," said a man with a Russian accent.

"I'm delivering the—"

"Our instructions were specific. No cops, no tricks."

"It's not a trick, and I'm not a cop," Tom said. "The money's in the case. If you want it, deal with me."

At the other end of the line, the Russian caller discussed the situation with someone, but their conversation was muffled and in Russian, leaving Tom with no idea what they were saying. All the while, he stood as an obstacle in the midst of a rolling river of people. Someone brusquely shoved past him without a second look.

Then the caller returned. *"Pick up the envelope."*

"What?" Tom searched the ground. "What enve—" He saw it, right at his feet: a plain white envelope with no markings. He kneeled and plucked it from the wet pavement. It was unsealed, so he lifted the flap.

Inside was a single yellow MetroCard.

"Go inside," the Russian said. *"Go down the escalator. Wait at the bottom."*

"For who?"

"You have thirty seconds." The caller hung up.

There was no chance to argue and no time to think.

Tom followed the rush-hour tide into the Times Square subway station.

Erin slipped past Tom while he pivoted in a circle in front of the subway entrance. *It's better if he doesn't know exactly where I am,* she decided. *He can't give me away to the Russians if he can't see me.*

She turned the corner onto Seventh Avenue. The entryway to the Times Square subway station had walls of glass in a maroon-painted metal grid, making it possible for her to keep an eye on Tom, who was still on 42nd Street.

Jeez, he looks lost, she thought, watching him turn about in confusion. Alert for any sign of danger to Tom, she eyed the fast-moving throngs of people as they pushed into the station. Minutes passed, and he continued to wait.

Then he lifted the prepaid cell phone to his ear. *Wish I could hear what he's saying.* The conversation seemed terse, at least on Tom's side.

A burly blond-haired man jostled Tom while pushing past

him. Erin tensed, shocked that the Russians would make a play for the case out in the open. Then she saw that Tom was okay. He kneeled, picked up an envelope, and took a MetroCard from it. Then he looked askance at his phone and tucked it back in his pocket.

He turned and entered the subway station.

She gave him a five-second head start, then hurried in the side entrance, fishing her own MetroCard from her back pants pocket. Elbowing in front of a pushy little man with a goatee and a bald spot, she swiped through the turnstile and dodged a commuter collision on her way to the escalator.

Peeking past the expansive hairdo of the woman in front of her, she caught sight of Tom near the bottom of the escalator. He had that lost look again.

As she neared the bottom, a deafening thunder of tribal percussion drowned out every other sound. Less than ten yards from the escalator, across from a Roy Lichtenstein art deco mural, an eclectic trio of young men—one African, one Hispanic, one Asian—pounded with drumsticks on overturned plastic containers, counterpointing one anothers' rapid-fire beats.

Around them, hundreds of blasé New Yorkers swarmed in a near-solid mass, racing in four directions to different platforms in the city's busiest subway hub.

Unintelligible voices squawked over an antiquated PA system mounted on the high ceiling. The few people who weren't in a mad frenzy to get somewhere milled inside a laughably small music-and-electronics shop, congregated inside a glass-walled ATM vestibule, or waited in line at a newspaper kiosk.

Frozen in the middle of all that madness was Tom. To his credit, he avoided looking directly at Erin as she walked in front of him, crossing his path on purpose so that he'd know she was there and had his back. Wanting to stay close to him but also out of sight, she shouldered her way into the record store.

The tiny shop's overhead speakers belted out the latest urban-fad anthem but not loudly enough to drown out the machine-gun rhythms of the plastic-can band outside or even the din of its own flat-screen high-definition televisions, which ran continuous loops of advertisements for crap no one really needed.

Erin staked out a place near the entrance and surveyed the scene.

There were at least ten cops within shouting distance on the Grand Central shuttle platform and patrolling the concourse. They had maintained a robust presence in the Times Square station ever since the 9/11 attacks.

Four National Guard troops wearing bulky body armor and carrying assault rifles stood against one wall, up the stairs about fifty feet from the ATMs, across from the kiosk between the entrances to the 1, 2, 3 train platforms.

The Russians were harder to spot, but Erin noticed them soon enough. She counted at least a dozen men, all wearing long coats, who had distinctly Slavic features and who were positioned around the station.

One read a newspaper while leaning against a painted steel support beam.

Two pretended to enjoy the plastic-drum corps.

One filled out deposit slips in the ATM vestibule. Another watched his back.

Two browsed magazines at the kiosk up the stairs but never looked at what they were "reading." One window-shopped in front of a knockoff clothing store.

One lurked near the bathrooms and checked his watch.

Two talked and studied a large subway map on the wall.

Another rambled in a solo conversation on one of the four antiquated pay phones attached to steel girders in the middle of the concourse.

Each had an identical curly wire running from the transceiver in his left ear, under his collar, to a battery pack concealed somewhere on his lower back.

If they're that well equipped, it's a good bet they've got guns, she figured. She pondered her options; she'd lost her axe handle in the fire, and the police had confiscated her butterfly knife. She needed some kind of weapon, fast.

Keeping her eyes on the Russians, she slipped out of the record store, walked quickly up the stairs to the news kiosk, and picked up the tallest, widest magazine they had. "I'll take it," she said to the clerk, handing him a five.

As he counted out her change, she rolled the magazine into a long, sturdy tube. *Paper's just thinly sliced wood,* she reminded herself. Rolled up tightly enough, even an ordinary magazine could be a solid, dangerous weapon.

It wasn't much, not against men with guns, but it was all she had. She hurried back and looked around for Tom, to make sure he was all right.

Then the Russians made their move.

Tom stood on the edge of the labyrinth known as the Times Square subway station and tried just to stay out of the way. At eye level, everything was shiny and freshly painted. Overhead, corroded pipes snaked every which way, and old paint peeled from the high ceiling and exposed angled girders.

The crowd surged past him, moving headlong to countless destinations, filling the air with body heat and the dull thunder of several thousand footsteps.

Of course, he could barely hear the crowd noise through the ear-splitting din of the trio hammering on empty plastic buckets a short distance away. Then he felt the disposable cell phone in his hand vibrate. Lifting it to his ear, he heard it ringing. He answered it. "Hello?"

There was no response.

Something poked him hard in the back.

"Hang up," said a man with a scarred forehead and a Russian accent. "Don't move."

Thumbing the cell phone back to standby, Tom felt his pulse quicken. He glanced sideways, back up the escalator, and saw a man with a single unbroken eyebrow at the top, staring at him with a cold expression.

The man behind Tom tried to grab the briefcase from his hand. Yanking it back from Scar, Tom winced as the handcuff bit into his wrist.

"No," Tom said. "You don't get that till the girl goes free." He tucked the phone back into his jacket pocket.

"You don't make the rules here," Scar said.

"The rules just changed," Tom said. "I don't have a key for these cuffs, but my friend does. When the girl's safe, I'll call for the key."

"Wrong," Scar said. "Give us the money now, or the girl dies."

A cold sensation traveled down Tom's spine.

Risking the Russian's wrath, he turned and faced him. "What'd you say?"

"There's no time," Scar insisted. "Give me the money, and I'll tell you where to pick up the girl, safe and sound."

Every other sound in the station was normal, but Scar's voice was deep and muddy—and an icy tingling stung Tom's ears.

"You're lying," Tom said.

Scar's stare never wavered. "Hand over the case, or we'll kill her."

Freezing pain filled Tom's sinus, as if he'd taken a sudden, deep breath of deep-winter air. "You're still lying," he said, piecing the situation together. "You won't let her go . . . but you won't kill her." Insight dawned. "You don't even *have* her, do you?"

"Of course we do," Scar protested, in yet another ice-cold lie.

"No. You don't." Scar flinched, and Tom realized with alarm, "This is no swap—it's a *heist.*"

The Russian looked anxiously up the escalator, summoning the man with the unibrow to join him. Tom backed away. Scar grabbed Tom's collar.

"Last chance," the Russian said. "Give us the case."

"No," Tom said, reaching up to pry the man's hand from his jacket.

The next thing Tom felt was a crushing blow to his left side, just below his ribs. Agony shot through his gut, and his knees started to buckle. Scar yanked Tom forward and pushed him toward the wall.

Before Tom could slump to the concrete floor, Unibrow stepped off the escalator and helped Scar prop him up. Speaking loudly for passersby, Scar said to Tom, "You should have gone easy on the vodka, brother." To his accomplice he added, "Maybe we should help him walk this off."

Tom could barely breathe. The two men pressed close on either side of him, and he was sure he felt the muzzle of a gun nestled against his back under his jacket. They pushed him away from the escalator, through the crowd, deeper into the station. "Shut up," Scar warned him. "Or else."

Pushed through a sea of strangers, Tom's mind drew a blank. He had to do something quickly. He and his Russian captors were heading toward a platform where a train marked with an S inside a gray circle was arriving in a clamor of shrieks, clacks, hisses, and bumps. A wall of people, all with their backs to Tom's predicament, crushed forward in anticipation of boarding.

A pair of New York City cops, their faces slack with boredom, flanked a round pillar and watched the crowd trudge past. Tom threw a desperate look in their direction, praying for eye contact. He wasn't sure they could see him.

The female cop glanced at him. It was a fleeting look—just long enough for Tom to silently mouth the word "help"—then she turned away, oblivious of him.

Dammit.

The subway train's doors opened with a rumble. Passengers inside rushed out, passengers outside shoved their way in. The Russians prodded Tom toward the far end of the platform, where a red railing was the only barrier between them and the dark netherworld of the subway tracks.

Oh, shit.

The Russians slowed. Scar touched his ear, drawing Tom's eye to the tiny device in the thug's ear, and the wire running from it under his collar.

Unibrow let go of Tom's arm as he and Scar reached under their jackets. A man's voice shouted, "Freeze! Police!"

Tom hit Scar in the face with the briefcase.

Then the bullets started flying.

Erin dodged through an onslaught of commuters as she tried to catch up to Tom, who was being all but dragged across the concourse by two Russians she hadn't seen before. The other twelve all were taking note of their accomplices, who were forcing Tom toward the Grand Central shuttle train platform.

Tom and his handlers passed a pair of cops, one of whom seemed to look in Tom's direction. At first, Erin thought the cops were as clueless as ever—then the female cop nudged her partner and nodded toward the pair of Russians hauling Tom away from them. The cops unfastened the safety loops on their sidearms and started following Tom and his escorts. The male cop keyed the radio transmitter mounted on his shoulder and spoke into it.

What the cops didn't see were two other Russians—the one who had been on the pay phone and the one reading the newspaper—who fell into step behind them. One had his newspaper draped over his hand, and the other had one hand buried in his jacket pocket.

The other ten Russians on the concourse remained vigilant but held their ground. The Russian near the bathrooms touched his ear and spoke into his jacket cuff. One of the Russians carting Tom pretended to scratch behind his ear.

Erin saw the ambush taking shape. She tightened her grip on her rolled-up magazine and used the crowd for cover as she closed in on Phone Guy and Newspaper Man.

On the edge of her vision, she saw more cops approaching from the other ends of the concourse. The four National Guard soldiers were on the move, too.

As the soliders passed through the center of the station's hub, the rest of the Russians began shifting their positions as well.

Erin was within arm's reach of Newspaper Man.

Everything was about to get ugly. She felt it in her gut.

Several yards ahead, the two cops following Tom and his captors cautiously drew their Glocks and gripped them with both hands. They raised their weapons and aimed at the Russians' backs.

The male cop shouted, "Freeze! Police!"

Tom's captors stopped.

Newspaper Man and Phone Guy aimed their SIG P229s at the cops.

Erin shouted, "Gun!" and stabbed the tip of her rolled-hard magazine with all her strength at the base of Newspaper Man's skull.

He dropped like a wet noodle but squeezed off one wild shot by reflex. It tore through the neck of a middle-aged woman a few feet away. Her blood showered a dozen people behind her. Hundreds more started screaming.

One of the Russians with Tom spun and snapped off a shot that dropped the female cop.

With a hard but clumsy swat of the briefcase, Tom knocked out the second man and broke free.

Phone Guy put a bullet into the male cop's back, then realized that Erin had clipped his wingman. He turned and started to swing his gun in her direction.

She landed a magazine jab between his eyes, another on his windpipe. As he staggered and gasped, she grabbed his wrist and kneed his pistol from his hand.

A shot ricocheted off the steel girder next to her, and she ducked for cover.

Two more shots hit Phone Guy's chest, and he dropped.

Then a stray bullet punched through the fleshy part of Erin's thigh, and she was down and bleeding on the concrete.

In the time it took Tom to knock Scar flat with the briefcase, the Russian's backup man had drilled four bullets into the female cop behind them.

Farther back, more shots thundered as Erin took down two more men with pistols. Then a new trio of cops rushed up behind her, guns blazing in Tom's direction. He hit the deck and protected his head with the metallic case.

Unibrow twitched inside a hail of bullets, and half a dozen innocent bystanders got caught in the crossfire. Crimson pools started spreading on the filthy gray concrete. Panicked civilians fell all over one another trying to clear the area, only to find themselves bottlenecking at the exits and corridors.

Tom peeked from under the case and saw that Erin had been hit. He scrambled to his feet and started toward her. Then came another nightmarish staccato of gunfire and frightened screaming.

No one knew which way to run, but it didn't matter, because there was no right way to go: six more men in long coats unloaded on the three cops, perforating their bulletproof vests with ease.

Staying low, Tom winced at the flurry of blinding muzzle flashes and deafening bangs. *How many Russians are down here?*

The National Guard troops fired back. A stutter-buzz of automatic weapons drowned out the wails of terror and anguish echoing through the concourse and felled the six exposed Russian gunmen.

Three men in long coats—two in the glass-walled ATM vestibule and one by the bathrooms behind the record store—produced military-style submachine guns from under their coats.

Bursts of bullets shattered the vestibule windows, eviscerated more civilians, and peppered the soldiers with an armor-piercing barrage. Fine red mists erupted from three of the troops' vests and helmets.

As they fell, the fourth soldier ducked behind a steel girder, about-faced, and returned fire toward the bathrooms.

A steady stream of lead from his rifle blasted apart the windows and widescreen television of the record mart before taking down the lone Russian behind its corner. Then the guardsman pivoted around his meager cover to fire at the two Russians in the ATM vestibule.

While the firefight raged, Tom crawled toward Erin. She saw him getting close and waved him off. "Run," she hissed in a sharp whisper. "I'm okay! Go!"

The thought of leaving her behind sickened him, but he had no choice. He saw the wound in her leg and knew she wouldn't be able to go with him.

He looked left toward an exit and saw another man in a long coat touching his ear and looking in Tom's direction.

Straight ahead, down a long passage next to a series of chrome-railed ramps and platforms, two more long-coated men pushed through the fleeing crowd and moved in Tom's direction.

The only route of escape was past the gun battle on his right.

The guardsman resumed firing into the ATM vestibule, where cash dispensers spat sparks across the glass-covered floor. He pulled back to cover, and the two Russian gunmen fired back at him. Then two cops lying prone on the slightly elevated adjacent section of the concourse opened fire with their pistols and killed the Russians in the vestibule.

The Russian duo in the passage ahead of Tom broke free of the crowd.

Tom took a deep breath. The air was thick with the acrid pall of expended gunpowder. He coiled himself, then exploded into a run.

He sprinted past the blood-drenched ATM vestibule and the shattered, smoldering wreckage of the electronics store.

The cops ignored him. The Russians came after him.

One of the cops shouted, "Stop!" Another yelled, "Gun!"

And the shooting started again.

Tom dashed to the other side of a row of steel support girders as bullets zinged off them and kicked up dusty divots near his feet. In two leaping steps he climbed the short stairs to the elevated level of the concourse and sprinted past two platform entrances and a news kiosk, toward another exit at the far end of the station.

Then he skid-stumbled to a halt.

Standing beyond the turnstiles at the far exit was one of the men who'd attacked him in the parking lot the night before. The man had traded in his camouflage for an all-black ensemble and a knee-length leather duster, but it was definitely him.

The man reached under his coat for a pistol as he vaulted over a turnstile.

Tom ran left and ducked as he heard shots fired. Bullets ripped into the kiosk, tattering stacks of newspapers and magazines. Tom fled down a steep flight of stairs onto a train platform—only to find his escape route blocked by several hundred people in a slow stampede away from the gunfire.

He knew the Russians would be right behind him. It felt wrong to put innocent people in danger by pushing into the crowd, but there was no turning back. "Coming through!" he shouted, sprinting down the platform.

To his surprise, the crowd cleared a path ahead of him. He repeated his warning call as he forged ahead. Each time it was like parting a sea of bodies.

He threw a nervous look over his shoulder. The Russian formerly known as Camouflage led two of his cohorts onto the platform in pursuit of Tom. They tried to shout their way through the wall of bodies as he had, with far less success.

If fear had a smell, Tom was in the thick of it. The people around him were shouting and shoving, slamming like frightened cattle into one another and him.

Halfway along the platform the crowd thinned as people surged down a staircase. Tom was tempted to follow them until he saw someone standing at the bottom of the stairs, as stationary as a rock in a river, staring up at him: a blond man with a small wire from his ear to his jacket collar.

Tom slipped past the staircase and craned his neck to look over the crowd to the end of the platform. Two pairs of men moved up either side of it in his direction.

From the tunnel behind them came a gust of warm, mildly foul air, followed by an uptown-bound number 2 express train hurtling up the center track.

Looking back, he saw Camouflage and his two thugs closing in.

Another sickening rush of tunnel breath pushed in from behind them, heralding the approach of a downtown-bound number 3 train on the opposite platform's center track.

He couldn't go forward, back, or down, and the local track offered no hope of escape. There was only one way out that he could see.

Tom backed up to the edge of the platform and shouted, "Move! Get out of the way!" Terrified commuters scrambled from his path, further congesting the platform on either side of him, momentarily slowing the Russians' approach.

There was barely enough room, but he had no choice.

He sprang forward, took three running steps, and jumped over the center track as the silver blur of the uptown train raced toward him from the left.

It was so close that the train's rush of air pushed him a hair off center.

He landed hard and twisted onto the opposite center track, barely clearing the electrified third rail. His knees smacked against the track ties and his head hit the platform.

Behind him, the 2 train rumbled past, an earthquake on wheels.

Blaring noises reminded him to move.

The number 3 train was bearing down on him, its horn trumpeting, its brakes screaming in protest. It was going too fast to stop.

Dazed and aching from his botched landing, Tom scrambled to his feet, hefted the briefcase onto the platform, and planted his palms to push himself up. To his surprise, it was harder than he expected.

The train was yards away, a behemoth of noise and steel.

Two men on the platform—one in blue jeans and a leather jacket, the other in a Wall Street–style suit and overcoat—grabbed Tom's arms and pulled him up. His feet cleared the edge barely in time to avoid getting sheared off by the train. Tom and his rescuers collapsed onto the platform.

Bullets exploded through the train's fragile metallic skin over their heads.

An angry percussion of semiautomatic gunfire ripped through the crowded train, leveling passengers and turning the windows white with fractures.

People started falling around Tom on the platform, some wounded, some dead, before he could shout to the others, "Down!" The rest of the crowd hit the deck as if his words had flattened them with brute force.

He pushed himself to his feet and sprinted for the nearest staircase. Bullets followed him, tearing across the wall under the stairs. Tiny shards of ceramic tile stung his neck. Tom grabbed the railing and swung himself through a hard about-face then sprinted up the stairs. More shots pinged off the metal railings beside him.

At the top of the stairs he broke right, away from opposite platform's staircase, from which he heard the clatter of running steps and angry shouts in Russian.

Up another short flight of steps was an exit turnstile, but it was chained shut. To the left of that was a chrome-railed staircase leading down, and beyond that a pair of escalators. *No cover on an escalator,* Tom realized. *Better take the stairs.*

Shots tore a line across the tiled wall over the stairs as he descended two leaping steps at a time. It was a long way to the first landing and switchback. A few steps shy of the landing he vaulted over the center handrails to the next flight of stairs, narrowly dodging another flurry of bullets that sparked off the landing.

He bolted off the second flight as more bullets rained down from directly overhead, blasting holes in the concrete around him. Another wide-open level lay before him, crowded with more commuters fleeing blindly from the gunfire.

Men with guns emerged from four different staircases and all turned in his direction. One pointed at him, and they began pushing through the crowd.

He spun and scrambled down the next flight of stairs,

jumped down the last five steps to the 7 train platform, and zigzagged left to duck another fusillade of shots from the three Russians descending the steps above him.

Then, from the level above came bellicose shouts of "Freeze! Drop your weapons!" The next sound was the furious stuttering of automatic rifles.

Tom threw a look back as he ran. All of the Russians twitched in a storm of bullets, which filled the air with a rosy mist.

He kept running as hard as he could, determined to leave the carnage behind. There were two staircases that led up and off the 7 platform. The first was packed with people pushing past one another. The second was at the end of the platform and largely empty. Tom bypassed the first staircase and sprinted up the second.

Damn, that was close, he thought as he leapt for the top step.

Something hit him in the face hard enough to stop him cold.

He winced in agony as someone twisted his left wrist and locked his arm in a viselike grip. As Tom blinked through the pain, Frank Kolpack unlocked the cuff on Tom's wrist, freeing the briefcase.

Frank caught the falling case by the cuffs, then released Tom and elbowed him in the chin.

Tom fell down the L-shaped staircase to its midpoint. He landed hard and looked up. Frank shifted the case to his left hand and turned away, then halted as a woman called out in disbelief, "Kolpack? What the fuck are you doing?"

Struggling back to his feet, Tom saw an attractive thirtyish woman who wore an NYPD detective's shield on her belt. He recognized her—she was one of the cops from the precinct in Brooklyn.

She fixed her wary stare on Frank as he turned to face her.

"Sorry, Bailey," Frank said. Then he drew his pistol and fired.

It wasn't the first time Frank had fired on another cop, but it was the first time he'd ever done so with witnesses.

Bailey dove for cover on the landing between the two staircases, half a step ahead of Frank's aim, behind a table stacked with religious literature.

Bullets tore through Bibles, ricocheted off steel girders and chrome railings, and slammed into nearby civilians. Then everyone screamed and ran from Frank, half the crowd going in one direction, half running the other way.

He snapped off another shot at the blond man on the stairs below him, but the enemy Seeker had already ducked around the corner. Bailey tried to roll out to return fire. He threw another shot at her, forcing her back under cover.

Time to go, Frank decided. Clutching the briefcase, he ran from Bailey, up the incline to the transfer tunnel to the Eighth Avenue trains, firing blindly backward as he went. Within seconds, he'd caught up to the closest of the fleeing civilians and pushed past them, turning them into human shields for his retreat. People scrambled out of his way and froze, terrified of getting shot.

This wasn't how Frank had wanted the deal to go, but his carefully wrought plan had been flushed the moment the Russians turned it into a bloodbath. There hadn't been much chance that any of them would survive a running shoot-out with the NYPD and the National Guard in the concrete maze of the subway station.

As for his rival all but handing the briefcase to him, that had seemed like a stroke of luck until Bailey got involved. Then Frank had been forced to make a split-second decision:

play the good cop and hand over the money, then hope that none of the Russians survived to implicate him and Viktor in the scheme, or make his own play for the case and earn twelve million dollars instead of three.

Twelve million dollars was simply too much to let go. And all he had to do to keep it was get out of this station—and out of New York—alive.

Tom stumbled back up the steps, pulling himself forward with one hand on the railing while wiping blood from his nose with the other hand. He peeked around the corner and saw Frank Kolpack flee into the crowd—then a pair of blind shots from Frank made Tom jerk back behind cover.

A near miss blasted off part of the corner and stung Tom's eyes with dust. Then the shooting stopped. On Tom's right, Bailey sprang to her feet and aimed her pistol in Frank's direction—and at the fleeing crowd.

The thought of seeing more innocent people gunned down was more than Tom could handle. He leapt in front of Bailey, held up his hand, and shouted, "Hold your fire!"

She blinked as if she'd been slapped, then pointed her weapon at the ceiling.

Then Tom was running, too, chasing Frank through the retreating crowd.

As Tom ran up the incline, the muscles in his legs burned, his knees ached, and knifing pains stabbed between his ribs.

After several strides, the path leveled out into a straightaway longer than a football field. Tom still couldn't see Frank, who was a couple of dozen yards ahead of him, but he saw Frank's wake in the crowd as the fleeing cop pushed and shouldered people out of his path.

"Look out!" Tom yelled. "Coming through!" People stepped aside or turned enough to let him pass, helping him close the gap to Frank.

Then Frank looked back at Tom and fired a few more random backward shots, which ripped through multiple people in the densely packed corridor and all but brought the crowd to a shocked halt.

Tom's voice boomed in the narrow, low-ceilinged tunnel: "Everyone, down!"

In unison, the entire crowd dropped to the floor.

The only people left upright in the tunnel were Tom and Frank, who hurdled over the crouched and prone civilians, and—Tom realized as a bullet flew past his head from behind—Detective Bailey, who was chasing them with her semiautomatic pistol leading the way.

Frank fired one wild shot at Tom, who twisted in midjump over a woman down on her hands and knees. The shot missed.

Then a trio of shots rang out from behind Tom, the first striking sparks from a steel beam over his head, the next blasting a scar in the white-tiled wall, the last so close that he felt the breeze on his neck.

At a full run, Tom could barely catch his breath. The tunnel seemed to blur past him as he closed the distance to Frank. Even though the cop had a longer stride, Tom was faster than him.

The end of the tunnel sloped downward, though the grade was shallower and shorter than the one Tom had climbed at the other end. As Frank raced from the transfer tunnel, someone shouted for him to drop his weapon. He snapped off one shot to his left, then turned right and dashed for a nearby staircase to the trains.

Tom emerged from the tunnel and glanced left to see a uniformed cop down on the ground, clutching a bloody wound in his leg. On the other side of the tunnel, a wall of people surged upstairs from the downtown platform, preventing Frank from making a swift descent, so he veered away right and kept running.

Another gunshot from behind turned Tom's head as Bailey came out of the transfer tunnel at a full run and stayed close behind him and Frank.

As far as Tom could tell, the only things that distinguished the Port Authority station from the Times Square facility was that its ceilings were lower and its steel girders were painted blue instead of puke green. Both sides of its concourse were lined with clothing stores whose display windows were populated by the worst-dressed mannequins Tom had ever seen.

The slightly curved tunnel ahead stretched for several hundred feet. A row of broad steel girders spaced ten feet apart ran down the center of the tunnel. Frank weaved from one side of the girders to the other like a slalom skier, keeping them between himself and Bailey, who continued to harass him with gunfire. To Tom's dismay, all of Bailey's shots struck bystanders instead of Frank.

Ricochets from Bailey's weapon shattered a clothing-store window, left a mannequin partially decapitated, and turned a fluorescent light into a shower of sparks and splinters.

Frank slid across the tiled floor to cover behind the railing and safety barrier for the first staircase to the uptown platform. He leaned out and snapped off four shots at Tom and Bailey, who both ducked behind girders.

Each impact rang out, bright and metallic. Then Frank's gun clicked empty. He ducked back to cover and ejected his clip.

Bailey peppered the railings with several shots as Frank slammed a new clip into his weapon.

Tom took advantage of the moment to advance one girder closer to the staircase. Then he cringed as two more bullets from Frank pealed against his new shelter.

Another round of covering fire from Bailey halted Frank's barrage, and Tom dashed in a crouch to the next girder, less than ten feet from the stairs.

From the platform below came the deep rumble-clatter of a decelerating train, the rising shriek and falling whine of brakes, and a great hydraulic hiss.

More bullets chimed against Tom's steel refuge, then against Bailey's.

Tom peeked around the girder and saw Frank scramble down the stairs. He went after him, nearly colliding with the oncoming wave of commuters climbing the stairs. As he reached the platform, he heard the *bing-bong* tone that preceded the closing of the train's doors. There were too many people in his way. The doors shut a second before he could follow Frank onto the A train.

He pushed through the crowd alongside the train, following Frank, who was walking forward inside the rear car, slipping through the knots of riders inside, and then passing through the door at the end to move into the next car.

Then the train's brakes released with a pneumatic gasp, and the train lurched forward, creeping at first but building in speed.

"Move!" Tom bellowed, his voice shaking the ground as if it had been amplified by a massive concert speaker. People on the platform scurried out of his way as he sprinted beside the train, gaining enough ground to reach the gap between the last two cars, then pacing it as the train sped up.

Behind him, he heard Bailey shout, "Stop!"

He ignored her and leapt off the platform, diving over the top of three metallic springs that drooped in the narrow gap between the cars—put there to prevent someone from doing what he was now trying to do. Knowing he wouldn't reach the inner safety barrier of three rubber-sheathed chains that guarded the passage between the train cars, he reached back as he fell and took hold of the uppermost outer spring.

As the train picked up speed with Tom dangling in the gap between cars, he began to suspect that this might not be the best decision he'd ever made. But he refused to let Frank get away. The Russians didn't know where Phaedra was, but Frank did—and the crooked cop obviously wanted the ransom for himself. Once that money was gone Phaedra's life would be forfeit, Tom was certain of it. That case full of cash was her only hope.

The train hurtled into the tunnel, and everything went dark for Tom as his eyes adjusted to the deep shadows. Electric blue sparks flashed under his feet, revealing a blur of tracks. All he heard was the roar of the train inside the tunnel. It was like standing next to a jet engine.

Got to get inside the train, Tom told himself. More blue lightning underfoot reminded him that certain death was just a mistake away.

The inner barrier looked almost close enough for him to reach. He struggled to find a foothold on the bottom coil. His foot slipped, and he clung desperately to the top spring.

Probing with his toe, he found a shallow indentation around one of the currently dark lights built into the end of the train car. He planted his foot onto the thin lip, then made a stretching reach with one hand toward the inner safety barrier.

The train pitched as it sped through a curve, and he lost his grip and plunged forward. His hands, slick with sweat, slid off the top chain. He snared the bottom chain in a panicked clutch and found himself inches away from being pinched by the scissoring movements of the two subway cars. Another blinding strobe of cerulean light showed his feet barely clearing the tracks.

Bright fluorescent light spilled over him as the door of the car on his right opened. He heard sounds of panic from inside. Silhouetted above him, two men fled through the door, heading for the last car of the train.

Tom called out to them, "Hey! Little help?"

The men stopped, and the one in front pointed down and shouted to the other, "Grab him, quick!" They reached down, and each man took one of Tom's arms. Heaving and fighting to keep their balance, they pulled him up from under the safety chains and steadied him between them. The second man, who looked as if he worked construction, asked, "You all right, buddy?"

"Yeah, thanks," Tom said. He stepped past them, slammed open the door of the car they'd just left, and moved forward as quickly as he could through the packed subway train. "Everyone, make a path!" he shouted. "And stay down!"

The passengers pressed to the sides of the car, whose interior was a curious combination of scuffed linoleum flooring, bright yellow-and-orange plastic seats, faux-wood panels, and an alternating series of off-center aluminum floor-to-ceiling poles that looked custom-made for strippers in training.

Pulling himself from pole to pole, Tom worked his way forward. The car rocked under his feet like a ship at sea. Even inside the train, the roar from the tunnel was deafening.

As he neared the next door, he saw through its window that

Frank was a full car length ahead of him, shoving passengers aside and pistol-whipping the ones too slow to get out of his way. Tom moved into the next car as Frank left it, and he repeated his plea for passage, "Coming through! Stay down, folks!"

Fifteen seconds later, Tom entered the next car while Frank was still a few feet shy of the far door. Frank looked back, saw Tom, and broke into a full run, slamming through a cluster of twenty-somethings blocking the door.

The youths fell in a pile behind Frank, blocking the door like a human Gordian knot. They shouted Spanish obscenities at the cop, who continued his mad dash into the next car.

As the door began to slide closed, Tom hurdled over the tangle of kids and stuck his arm in front of the door. He pushed it open and ignored the angry shouts that the twenty-somethings were now directing at him.

Frank was halfway across the next car and heading for the conductor's compartment at the far end, with several dozen cursing riders in his wake.

Tom followed the trail that Frank had blazed through the crowd. Then another high-speed curve rolled the train left, throwing both of them against other passengers who were smart enough to be hanging on to something.

"Stop running, Frank!" Tom shouted over the metallic whining and grinding of the train.

One of the passengers, a muscular Filipino man, jumped to his feet and tried to grab Frank. Tom didn't know if the man was acting of his own accord or if he had been influenced by Tom's command to Frank.

Either way, a moment later, Tom wished the man had stayed in his seat.

Frank elbowed the Filipino man's face, breaking his nose.

Then he leveled his gun and shot the man point-blank in the chest.

The would-be Good Samaritan fell backward into the arms of his fellow passengers, whose faces now were stippled with his blood.

The cursing in the train turned to screaming.

"Who else wants to be a hero?" Frank yelled as he backed toward the far door. He shot an overweight man in a cheap suit. "You?" Put a bullet into a girl who couldn't have been a day over nineteen. "You?" Drilled two more shots into the backs of a couple who were retreating in Tom's direction, along with everyone else in the car. "How 'bout you two?"

Moving in a terrified stampede, the riders slammed into Tom, forcing him backward as they ran for the door behind him, suffocating him with their sheer weight of numbers.

Frank wore an evil grin as he fired three more shots into the fleeing crowd. "Yeah! Look at all the fuckin' heroes!"

Tom was trapped. He couldn't breathe, couldn't reason with the mob. And on the other side of them, Frank was running again, getting away.

Fighting the crush of bodies was too much. Tom couldn't move . . . then he saw it.

A simple cord with an old, red-painted wooden knob on the end. Hanging from the low ceiling, just a few feet away. The emergency brake.

He put everything he had into one Herculean push for freedom. Thrusting his arm out as he jumped, he grabbed the cord. His weight did the rest.

Violent deceleration threw everyone forward to the floor. The lights flickered as sparks surged up from the tracks on either side of the train.

The tunnel resounded with the ear-splitting screech of a hundred tons of steel grinding from a wild rush to a dead stop.

Free of the panicked press of bodies, Tom staggered forward and lunged over and through them. He trampled a few people even as he tried not to, then ran for the far end of the car, hoping he could stop Frank before it was too late.

The lights stuttered, strobing the motion of falling bodies as the train slammed to a stop under Frank's feet. He fell forward and hit the sliding rear door to the conductor's compartment, which divided the train in half.

The train ceased moving with one final jolt.

Frank lifted his foot and kicked the handle of the unlocked door. The door banged open, and Frank stepped inside to face the slender, middle-aged conductor.

Pointing his Glock in the man's face, Frank barked, "NYPD! Open the doors! All of 'em!" The conductor hesitated. Frank fired a warning shot past the man's head, out the window. "Now!"

Shocked into motion, the conductor jabbed at the buttons on the control panel in front of him. All the doors shuddered open, filling the train with a deep rush of ambient noise from the tunnel. To make sure the doors stayed open, Frank pistol-whipped the conductor in the head, knocking him out.

He opened the forward door and looked back to see the blond man coming toward him fast. He snap aimed and fired. The enemy Seeker ducked and turned as three shots ricocheted off metal poles and hit other people.

Two shots left in the clip, Frank reminded himself. He retreated into the next subway car and pushed his way to the nearest door, on his left.

The blond man scrambled through the conductor's compartment.

Frank jumped from the train to the downtown-express track. It was a longer drop than it looked like. He landed hard and lost his balance, thrown off by the weight of the briefcase, and caught himself a hair shy of kissing the third rail.

Knees bruised from the impact, he struggled to his feet and ran in the dark toward the distant lights of the 59th Street subway station. Before he got that far, he knew he would pass at least one entrance to the catacombs: the network of abandoned subway tunnels beneath the city—his underground path to freedom.

Behind him, feet crunched heavily on gravel. Throwing a look over his shoulder, he saw the other Seeker in a crouched landing pose on the tracks. The fair-haired man leapt up in pursuit of Frank.

They raced through the sweltering dark. Every running step brought the other man closer to Frank. *I'll never get a cleaner shot than this,* he reasoned.

He made a spinning stop, aimed, and pulled the trigger, certain he was about to put two bullets in his foe's chest.

The shots went wide and wild, caroming off the steel girder beside the man, who faltered for a second and looked as surprised as Frank felt.

Then the other Seeker charged.

Frank had no time to reload. He turned and kept running.

His foe grabbed his collar.

As the man spun him around, Frank committed himself to ending this fight the only way he knew how: as the last man standing.

Tom felt as if he were sucking fire into his lungs with each running gasp for air. They passed the front of the A train and plunged headlong into the shadows.

He stretched his right hand ahead of him as he neared Frank. The distance between them shrank with each stride.

His fingers brushed the edge of Frank's jacket collar. With one more burst of speed, Tom closed his fist around it and yanked Frank to a halt.

Frank spun around and swung the briefcase in a high, wide arc. It slammed against Tom's shoulder and head, knocking him sideways against a girder. Stunned and stumbling, Tom focused on not stepping on the third rail.

A distant rumbling gained strength as it drew closer.

Frank dropped the case and came straight at him. Tom raised his hands to defend himself. The cop threw a punch. Tom tried to block it—only to see his hands pass through Frank as if the man were a ghost.

Something hit Tom's jaw from the right and sent him staggering toward the third rail. Shaking off the surprise and the spots in his vision, Tom looked for a second attacker but found only Frank circling him and looking to strike again.

Frank raised his foot as if to stomp on Tom's.

Tom retreated half a step, and something kicked the back of his knee.

His leg buckled under him. He landed on his knees in the trench between the track ties, which was filled with muck and filthy water.

Another punch hit the back of Tom's neck.

Stunned, he fell face-first to the tracks.

The tunnel boomed with thunder as a train roared by on his left, spitting flurries of blue-white sparks into the darkness and strobing Frank's movements. The cop stepped to Tom's right and drew back his foot for another kick.

A blast of sparks from the passing train filled the tunnel with blue light.

Then Tom saw Frank's reflection in the filthy water. If the reflection was true, Frank wasn't beside Tom. He was in front of him and deceiving Tom with an illusion, an image of himself displaced just far enough to catch Tom off guard.

Frank's foot snapped forward. It happened fast, but the flickering light made it look like slow motion.

Trusting the reflection, Tom sprang to his feet and lunged into what looked like empty air with his arms wide. He collided with something solid.

Half a second later Tom felt the jolt of impact as he and his foe landed hard on the tracks, and the illusion behind him vanished. Pinned on the tracks, the victim of Tom's blind tackle, was Frank Kolpack.

The last car of the downtown local train sped away, the din of its passage receding behind it. Shadows rushed to fill the void left by fading sparks.

Frank kneed Tom in the groin. Tom howled in agony, and Frank pulled one arm free and landed a crushing right cross on Tom's chin. Tom fell sideways.

As he slumped to the tunnel floor, he punched Frank in the groin as hard as he could. The detective doubled over like a jumbo shrimp, then lurched away from Tom, abandoning the fight to crawl toward the briefcase.

All Tom wanted to do was lie still until the pain stopped, but he couldn't let Frank have that case. Forcing himself up off the muck-and-trash-covered track bed, Tom scuttled on all fours after Frank.

He hurled himself forward as Frank reached for the case.

Tom wrapped his right arm around Frank's throat and used his left hand to lock his hold in place.

Frank pushed up and back then rolled, flipping them over. Tom fell on his back with Frank on top of him. The detective threw multiple elbow jabs into Tom's ribs. Each hit sent a jolt of pain through Tom's body.

Then Frank jerked his head forward and slammed it backward into Tom's face. Something inside Tom's nose snapped, and a stabbing sensation pierced his head like an ice pick. Grabbing Tom's right arm with both hands, Frank pried it loose enough to steal a breath, then he sank his teeth into Tom's wrist.

Tom let out an enraged scream as Frank escaped from his grip and scrambled forward on all fours, once again heading for the briefcase.

The man was inches shy of grabbing the case's handle when Tom went after him, his temper flaring, and launched himself at his enemy with a primal roar.

He tackled Frank into the narrow, wastewater-filled gulley between the track ties and forced the crooked cop's face into the vile, polluted muck.

In a fearsome display of strength, Frank pushed himself up from the puddle, even with Tom's dead weight on his back. Then he clawed his way forward and closed his fingers on the case's handle.

Tom brought the side of his fist down on the base of Frank's skull. During the seconds that the man lay stunned from the rabbit punch, Tom dove forward and grabbed the case's handle.

A warning horn trumpeted through the tunnel. Lights shone in Tom's eyes. A downtown-bound express train was bearing down on him and Frank.

Frank flailed and grasped the handcuffs dangling from the case's handle. He struggled to get out from under Tom, who refused to let go. Rolling side to side in an effort to shake Tom loose, Frank forced Tom onto his back. But Tom held the briefcase out of Frank's reach and snaked his right arm around the cop's throat.

"What're you doing?" Frank exclaimed, choking out the words.

"You're *not* getting that case!"

Another frenzy of elbow jabs and wild thrashing broke Frank free of Tom for a second. He tried to seize Tom's arm in a bid to wrest the case from him. Tom responded by yanking away the case, then smashing it across Frank's face.

Frank fell on his back in front of the approaching train and tried to scramble clear. Tom grabbed Frank's right ankle. The cop fell flat on the tracks. "It ends here, Frank," Tom said, fighting to hold his enemy in harm's way.

"Only for you," Frank said, kicking Tom in the shoulder with his left foot. Free to move, the cop somersaulted over the third rail onto the parallel local track, leaving Tom alone in the path of the express, which blared its horn as its brakes engaged with a bone-rattling metallic screech.

Tom pressed himself as deep as he could into the slime-filled trench between the track ties and held the briefcase in front of his face for whatever protection it might offer. All he heard was the high-pitched protest of overtaxed steel, and he lost sight of Frank as the train rolled over him and blanketed the tracks with blue sparks and a scalding hydraulic gasp.

Something metallic and forceful scraped against the top of the briefcase.

Then everything went eerily silent.

Tom lowered the briefcase, which now bore a gouge from some low-hanging piece of metal on the train's undercarriage. There was no sign of Frank. And the briefcase filled with Anna's fortune was still safe in Tom's hands, which meant there might yet be a chance to save Phaedra. But first he had to get out of the tunnel without being arrested again. Then he had to find Erin and come up with a plan to save Anna's daughter before it was too late.

From somewhere beyond the express train stopped above him, he heard the shouts of police and rescue workers moving into the tunnel.

He crawled out from under the train. Every part of his body hurt. He could barely stand, his vision was blurry, and vertigo left him reeling. He wasn't sure he could walk more than a few feet without passing out.

Move it, he commanded himself. *If you're slow, that girl dies.*

He turned and ran, losing himself in the subterranean gloom until he was in too much pain to take even one more step. Then he ran some more.

Phaedra's voice echoed in his memory and kept him moving, kept him pushing on through the pain, the fatigue, and the darkness. Seven simple words.

Please, God, don't let them kill me.

25

Bailey stood back as the ESU team bashed in the door of Kolpack's home.

The jamb splintered with a sharp crack as the battering ram struck the door above the lock. As the door swung inward, the ESU trooper with the ram stepped back. Three of his submachine-gun-toting teammates charged inside and deployed themselves in a cover-and-search formation, with two men checking the rear corners while one scouted ahead.

"Frank Kolpack!" shouted the lead trooper. "Police! We have a warrant for your arrest!" More men surged into the house, weapons braced at their shoulders, all wary of engaging a fellow cop in a firefight. Searchlights danced over the front of the house, courtesy of two helicopters hovering overhead—one from the NYPD, the other from a cable-news channel. Their rotors thudded like dueling drumbeats.

IAB investigators Landsman and Cadan flanked Bailey, who held the search and arrest warrants. Behind them, a dozen NYPD vehicles—a mix of cars and vans, plus an ESU truck—

filled the shadowy residential Bay Ridge street with flashes of red and blue from their roof lights.

Scores of patrolmen and sergeants manned a cordon around the house, and shift commanders from two precincts were on hand, along with the deputy commissioner for operations. Outside the yellow-tape perimeter were five TV news crews, a legion of reporters representing every print publication in the city, and a growing crowd of local spectators.

What a circus, Bailey mused. At times such as this, she sometimes wished she had never sought a detective's shield. She wished she'd applied to join the ESU team instead. Of all the jobs in the NYPD, it was the one that most closely resembled the life she'd enjoyed for eight years in the Marine Corps.

Minutes dragged by while the ESU team searched the small two-story house and its basement. Muffled shouts and thuds filtered out through the open front doorway. Then the leader's voice crackled over her walkie-talkie, *"All clear."*

"All right," Bailey said. "We're up." She shook off the damp chill of the night and led the IAB detectives into the house, where the ESU team milled about with their weapons slung across their chests. Aside from some disarray that she figured had been inflicted by the searchers, the inside of the house was orderly and spare in its furnishings, which were covered by a thin layer of dust. All the windows were locked, and the entire house had a stale, musty odor.

Small details caught her attention. The magazines on the living-room coffee table were several months old. In the kitchen, the cupboards and the refrigerator were barren. All the trash baskets in the house were empty. There were no clothes in the closets, no towels or toilet paper in the bathroom.

She walked into the bedroom, which contained an uncovered mattress, a digital alarm clock on the floor, and nothing else. Cadan and Landsman stepped into the room behind her.

Bailey shook her head and rolled her eyes toward the ceiling. "It's a dummy address," she mumbled. "Nobody's been here in months."

Landsman replied, "Then where the hell is he?"

"Could be anywhere," Bailey said, stepping between the IAB detectives and leading them back toward the living room. "Probably living under an alias." She let out a mirthless chuckle. "Assuming that 'Frank Kolpack' isn't an alias."

"Sonofabitch," Cadan muttered.

Ahead of them, television noise blared from the living room. Bailey hurried back into the room and snapped at the gathered cops, "Who turned on the TV?"

"No one," the ESU leader said. "It came on by itself."

She thought about that for a second. "Kolpack probably set it to turn on and off every night, to keep up the illusion for his neighbors." Looking back toward the bedroom, she added, "I'd bet the alarm clock goes off every morning, too." She nodded at the ESU team leader to get his attention. "What's in the basement?"

"Old newspapers and about a thousand cockroaches," he said.

"Delightful," Bailey said. She turned back to Landsman. "Did we get anything from the Russians who survived the firefight in Times Square?"

"Only that they were after a briefcase with about twelve million bucks in it," Landsman said.

"Which is probably the same case I saw him steal from a courier," Bailey said. "So he's armed and on the run with twelve million dollars. That's just great."

Cadan eyed the abandoned residence with a glum frown. "He must've been planning his exit strategy for months—maybe even years."

"I guess that's it, then," Landsman said, planting his hands in his jacket pockets and strolling toward the door. "Unless someone picks him up in the next few hours, my guess is we'll never see him again." He walked out of the house, and Cadan followed close behind him.

If someone had told Bailey that morning that she'd never see Kolpack again, she'd have called it a cause for celebration. Now it felt like a slap in the face.

She wasn't a religious person, but she hoped God was listening as she prayed for one simple favor.

Let that bastard cross my path one more time. That's all I ask.

Tom eyed the briefcase on the floor in front of the passenger seat of his truck and asked himself if all he'd done today was really worth it.

He sat in the driver's seat and opened the first-aid kit that he always kept in the back with his tools. His clothes were still soggy and reeking from the fetid, polluted slime-water in the tunnels. The stench filled the cab of his truck. He guessed that the odors might never come out.

For a moment, he was saddened to think that he might have to sell his truck when he got home, but then he realized that no one would ever buy a vehicle that smelled like this. *Guess I'll have to burn it,* he decided.

As he tried to unbutton his shirt, his hands refused to cooperate. They were shaking too violently to get a grip on the buttons. Rubbing his palms together and flexing his fingers against one another didn't help much. The harder he fought to steady his hands, the more the rest of his body began to shiver as well.

He realized that it wasn't the cold night air that was making him tremble.

His breathing was fast and shallow. He leaned forward and rested his head on the steering wheel for a few seconds while he fought to calm his shell-shocked nerves. He squeezed his eyes shut to force back tears of panic.

Dammit, he raged in silence, tucking his hands into his armpits. His mind raced through a frantic replay of the past twenty-four hours. Between the attack in Gravesend, the fire in the clinic, the van accident, and then the battle in the subway, he'd come within inches of death four times in a single day.

That's four times I almost made Karen a widow.

Four times I almost left my son without a father.

He sat back and opened his eyes. In need of an anchor, he pulled his wallet from his jacket pocket and flipped it open to his favorite photo of Karen. It was several years old, from before they were married. He'd shot it in the kitchen of her old apartment, and the light behind the window curtains had made the image look soft and dreamlike. He touched a fingertip to the photo, traced the shape of Karen's face, and wondered if he could just give Anna back her briefcase full of money and call it a day. Then he wondered if he could live with himself if he did.

Pull it together, man, he told himself. *Get your head back in the game.*

He tossed his wallet on top of the dash. With his jaw clenched in both pain and determination, he checked his reflection in the rearview mirror. Brown dried blood caked his nose, which was swollen and turning purple. Myriad tiny cuts dotted his chin, cheeks, and the back of his neck. A purple-green bruise covered half his forehead. His lower lip was split down the middle.

Touching a sore spot on the right side of his head, he found a big, aching lump. Struggling to steady his hands, he undid the buttons of his bloodstained shirt, opened it, looked down, and winced. Violet bruises covered his chest.

With some gauze pads and a bottle of water, he tenderly cleaned the grime and polluted water from his torn-up palms and wrist, then from his torso and face. Steady aches reminded him of the huge abrasions on his knees, elbows, and back.

As he reached over and riffled through the first-aid kit for some disinfectant spray, he grimaced at the bite mark Frank had left in his right wrist.

He sprayed the alcohol-based disinfectant across his open wounds, squeezing his eyes shut and screaming through gritted teeth at the hideous stinging pain it caused. Then he spritzed his palms and bit back more screams.

It took several seconds of deep breathing before he calmed down enough to continue. He fished a tube of antibiotic from the kit and gingerly applied it over the bleeding cuts. As he pulled out a roll of gauze bandages, some medical tape, and some scissors, there came a tapping on the passenger window. He looked up.

It was Erin. He unlocked the doors. She opened hers and climbed in beside him, eyes wide. "Jesus, *papi*! Y'all right?"

"I've had better days," he said through clenched teeth.

She watched him tend his wounds for half a minute. Then she noticed his still-open wallet on the dash. After a brief hesitation, she reached over and picked it up. Looking at Karen's photo, she asked, "This your wife?"

"Yeah," Tom said.

"She's cute."

He thought about how much he'd rather be at home. "I know."

Erin shifted her glance between Tom and the photo, as if she were reading his intentions from his bloodied face. "Thinkin' of bailin' on me?" When he didn't answer right away, she continued, "I'm not judgin'. I still get the shakes when shit gets bad. And it got ugly down there tonight."

"It wasn't just tonight," Tom said. "It's all of it, from getting my ass kicked by the Russians to people shooting at me. . . ." His hands started quaking again.

"I get it," she said. "This is way more than you signed on for."

"Damn right," Tom said.

She nodded. "Ain't gonna tell you what to do, okay? I'm just gonna say that we don't always win. Just 'cause we answer a prayer, that's no promise it'll have a happy ending. Sometimes, you gotta pick your battles. Know what I mean?"

He looked at her, stunned. Was she telling him to throw in the towel? The mere suggestion galvanized his will. "Yeah, I know what you mean," he said, plucking his wallet back out of her hand. "And this is one battle I plan to win."

"Glad to hear it," she said with a wry smile, and he realized she had played him. She tapped her foot against the briefcase, which was partially covered by Tom's sludge-stained jacket. "At least you held on to this."

"Barely," Tom said. "Remember Kolpack? That cop I told you about?"

"The one from the Scorned?"

"Yeah. He got ahold of it. Nearly got away, too."

Erin looked as if she couldn't believe it. "You went after him?"

"Yup," Tom said, cutting off a strip of bandage.

"You chased a man who had a gun."

"And a freakin' weird power," Tom said. "You see him in one spot when he's really in another." Pain made him wince and inhale sharply through his teeth as he pressed the gauze into place.

She shook her head. "*Papi,* that wasn't brave. That was stupid."

"No choice," Tom said, unspooling more sterile fabric and cutting off a small piece. "If he'd taken the case, Phaedra'd be dead by now. I'm sure of it."

"What're you talking about?"

"I'm saying the Russians don't have the girl," Tom replied. "They never did. They only *said* they did so they could steal Anna's money."

He could almost hear the wheels turning in Erin's head as she mulled that over. "So, if the girl wasn't kidnapped for ransom—"

"Then someone has other plans for her," Tom said.

Erin nodded. "And you think Kolpack knows who that someone is."

"And then some," Tom said, laying down the second bandage over a raw patch on his arm. He reached for the medical tape. "Let me finish plugging my leaks, then we can head back to Brooklyn to check out a lead." Tearing off strips of tape to secure his bandages, he nodded at Erin's leg. "Who patched you up?"

"Paramedics," she said with a shrug.

"How'd you dodge the paperwork on that?"

"They've got a subway station filled with dozens of casualties. After they fixed my leg, I said I needed to use the john. Fifty-fifty chance they don't even know I'm gone yet." She sniffed the air and wrinkled her nose at Tom. "By the way, no offense, but . . . you stink."

Choosing not to dignify that with a response, he dabbed antibiotic ointment into the bite wound on his right wrist. "Cut me off another strip of gauze, will ya?"

She did as he asked, then leaned over and lightly wrapped the cloth bandage around his wrist. The heat of her proximity and the musky scent of her perfume were enough to make him freeze in place. Looking up, she smiled. "Relax. I'm just bein' nice." She finished dressing the wound, taped the bandage in place, then leaned back into her own seat. "Whenever you're ready."

Tom buttoned his shirt and stole another look at his harrowed reflection in the rearview mirror. Glancing at Erin, he asked, "Are all your days like this?"

"No," she said with a tired sigh. "Just most of 'em."

He turned the key in the ignition, then paused before putting the truck in gear. "You know how you said that the trick with the photos and the fingerprints at the police station was 'part of the magic'?" Erin nodded, so he continued. "Well, I was wondering . . . have you ever seen the magic stop bullets?"

"No," Erin said. "No one has." She studied the look on his face, and her brow creased with concern. "Tell me you're not serious."

"I don't know," he said. "Down in the tunnel, there was a moment when I was sure Kolpack had me. He couldn't have been more than ten or twelve feet away; he was aiming right at me, but he missed by a mile."

"You sure it wasn't a near miss?"

He shook his head. "No way. Both shots hit the girder next to me."

"Crazy," Erin said. She thought for a moment. "They hit the *same* girder?"

"Yeah," Tom said.

"Almost like it was magnetized?"

"Exactly like that," Tom said.

She tilted her head and arched an eyebrow. "I dunno. Maybe it's possible. I mean, I never heard of nothin' like that before, but everyone's magic is different." Turning her head and throwing him a dubious look, she added, "But I wouldn't count on that happening again if I was you."

"Don't worry," he said, shifting the truck into drive and pulling away from the curb. "I won't."

Phaedra sat on the bed in her cell and made a futile attempt to ignore Leon, who sat in the cell's only chair and stared at her from beneath his gas mask.

He had been there for several minutes without speaking a single word. His silence was more frightening than anything Phaedra could imagine him saying.

She had thought he was bringing her dinner when the door to her cell had opened with its usual metallic clatters and bangs. Instead, he had left the door open wide behind him, shambled in limping steps to the desk beside her bed, pulled out the chair, and slouched into it like a broken man.

As ever, his smoke specter loomed above and behind him, dark and cold. Phaedra tried to avert her eyes, but the sensation of being stared at was too creepy. Whenever she turned her head, there was Leon. The snout-speaker of the mask amplified his long, labored breaths.

Unable to gaze too long at Leon's mask or his lurking shadow presence, she studied his hands. His knuckles were raw, bruised, and torn.

He sighed. Through the speaker it sounded like a heavy crackling.

"This would be so much easier if we could just kill you," he said.

At a loss for a reply, Phaedra pulled her knees to her chest and pressed her back into the corner. Leon's head drooped forward, as if he were passing out.

He sprang from the chair, grabbed it by its seatback, and threw it at the wall. The plastic chair snapped and broke with a crack like a rifle shot. It fell in a twisted heap on the floor.

Leon paced beside her bed, massaging the back of his neck with one hand. *"Travel light,"* he said. *"That's our motto. Always has been."* He pivoted and reversed direction, taking short steps. *"Mind the details. Plan ahead."* Another pivot and turn. *"If the plan fails, change it."* He stopped, faced her, and leaned closer, bringing with him an atmosphere of menace. *"If an asset becomes a burden, get rid of it."*

She cringed but never blinked. Leon backed away.

He spread his arms wide. *"What do you see when you look at us?"* Phaedra shrugged and shook her head. Leon pointed at her. *"Tell the truth."*

Mustering her courage, she replied, "A monster."

"Be more specific," he said.

Was it some kind of trick? Leon seemed to know what she would say, so why was he asking? She swallowed to get rid of the dry, sour taste in her mouth. "Something black and smoky follows you around," she said, keeping a wary eye on the beast's misty, snaking tendrils. Leon didn't react, so she added, "It's evil."

He tsk-tsked and waggled his index finger. *"Don't jump to conclusions."*

"It wants to kill me," she argued.

"Of course she does," Leon said. *"After all, this is a war. Fortunately for you, the decision's not hers to make."* He reached into his jacket pocket and took out a hypodermic needle. As he removed its protective plastic sheath, he said, *"It's time for you to take a little trip. Will you cooperate this time, or do we need the ether again?"*

She was too paralyzed with fear to respond. He took a small vial of golden liquid from his jacket's other pocket and poked the needle through its rubber cap, submerging the tip in the fluid. *"We'll take that as a vote for cooperation."* With a slow pull on the syringe's plunger, he filled its bottom quarter with the drug. *"Hold out your arm,"* he said, reaching toward her.

"No," Phaedra said. "You're supposed to use alcohol or something first, aren't you?" He stood in front of her, not moving, his mask reducing him to a cipher. She added, "You know . . . ? To prevent infection?"

"You got your first injection without it. You'll live." Anger crept into his voice. *"Now hold out your goddamn arm."*

Spooked, she did as he said and extended her left arm. He gripped her wrist and held it steady as he poked the needle into one of the tiny blue veins on the back of her hand. *"This will burn a little,"* he said. *"But only for a second."*

He pressed down on the plunger, and the drug coursed through her hand and into her wrist. It felt like cold fire under her skin.

She lost herself in a sensation of sinking and fading. As the room dimmed, she saw Leon's dark presence press in toward her—then it retreated. From behind, she thought she caught a glimpse of white light.

Darkness circled in around them until Leon was all that Phaedra could see. Leaning in as Phaedra slipped from consciousness, he asked in a weary whisper made harsh by the mask's speaker, *"Do you want to know a secret?"* As her vision blurred, he pulled off his disguise. "I really *hate* wearing this mask."

Tom ducked and stepped through the loose section of chain-link fence into the John Jay High School parking lot. He paused and held the section open for Erin, who followed him through the gap.

As she straightened, she fixed him with a dubious stare. "Want to tell me what we're doin' back here?"

He led her down the steps into the lot. "Looking for a clue," he said.

"Anything in particular?"

"Yes." He twisted the headpiece of his Maglite to the on position and turned it until the beam focused. Walking toward the fence that separated the lot from a below-street-level area behind the school, he swept the asphalt with his flashlight beam. A prismatic reflection caught his eye. "There," he said, already on the move.

She stayed at his shoulder as he hurried across the lot, which still stank of uncollected garbage in overflowing Dumpsters. He stopped beside a glistening patch of pavement that bent the flashlight's beam into a spectrum of color.

"An oil stain?" Erin sounded unimpressed. "That's your big clue?"

"No," Tom said. "It's my breadcrumb to the clue."

Keeping the light trained on the ground at an angle to light a wider area, he pivoted through a slow turn. Then his eyes found the metallic glint in the dark.

He jogged to the source of the reflection.

It was the coil of white and silver wire that he had seen just before getting his ass kicked twenty-four hours earlier. He picked it up and studied it with the flashlight beam aimed straight at it. "I knew it," he said.

Flustered, Erin asked, "Knew what?"

"Hold this," he said, handing her the light. She took it and kept it aimed at his hands as he pulled apart the white and silver twist. It unraveled into two small, wrinkled rectangles of paper—one white, one backed with foil.

"Gum wrappers," Tom said. "Folded and twisted exactly the way I saw Kolpack do it in the interrogation room." He looked over his shoulder at Erin. "It's some kind of nervous habit—he's quitting smoking."

"That'd do it," Erin said. "So he took the girl and helped the Russians set up their scam."

"Except it all went south. If we want to find her, we have to find him."

Erin radiated doubt with her lifted brow and a sideways nod. "Good luck with that. He's a cop—he knows how they find people, which means he knows how *not* to be found."

"What about the Scorned? Will they give him sanctuary?"

She shrugged. "Depends who he knows and what he's worth to 'em."

Tom's cell phone vibrated in his pocket. "Hang on," he said to Erin as he fished out the phone and answered it. "Hello?"

"Tom? It's Anna. Are you all right?"

"I'm fine," he said, bending the truth to keep her calm. "How're you?"

"How do you think *I am?"* she replied, sounding as if she was on the verge of a meltdown. *"All I'm seeing on the news is the*

bloodbath in the subway station. God help me, Tom, tell me Phaedra wasn't in there."

"She wasn't there," Tom said. "The Russians set you up."

Turning defensive, she asked, *"What do you mean they set me up?"*

He cupped his hand over the phone to avoid drawing attention from the people whose apartment windows faced the parking lot. "Anna, they lied. They never had your daughter. All they wanted was to steal your money."

She started to panic. *"Did they? Did they get my money?"*

"No," Tom said. "I didn't let them. It's still with me."

"Okay." She started to slow her breathing. *"That's good."* A bit calmer, she asked, *"Now what? If they don't have her, who does?"*

"I'm still working on that," Tom said. "But I just found a very good lead." He kept his answer vague because he worried that giving her Frank Kolpack's name might provoke her to do something rash, like go to the cops or the press without any evidence. Until he found Phaedra, Tom couldn't prove that he was right about Kolpack; the fact that he'd taken her didn't mean he still had her.

"Tom, I don't have anyone else I can trust right now. Please tell me the truth: Can you save her?"

"I'll do everything I can," he said. "I promise." He glanced at Erin, who looked as if she was getting impatient with him. "I have to go, Anna. I'll call as soon as I learn anything new."

"Okay," she said. *"I'll be waiting."*

They said good-bye, and she hung up.

As he tucked the phone back into his pocket, Erin folded her arms while staring at him. "You better have a plan after getting her hopes up like that."

"I'm working on one," Tom said, walking back toward the gap in the fence. From his pants pocket, he took out the prepaid cell phone that Anna had given him for the ransom exchange. "But first we have to wait for Kolpack to call."

"Now I *know* you hit your head in that fight," Erin said. "Why would Kolpack call us?"

He shrugged, as if it was obvious. "Why do you think? The money."

"You're kidding."

"Think about it," Tom said. "He just flushed his whole life down the drain. Now he's on the run with every cop and federal agent for a hundred miles on his tail. A guy in his situation could use a briefcase with twelve million bucks in it."

Tom pulled the loose fence open for Erin, who slipped through ahead of him. As he followed her back out to the sidewalk, she asked, "Don't you think a dirty cop like him has money stashed away?"

"Maybe," Tom said. "But not as much as we're holding."

They walked together, heading back to his truck. "Think he'll want it bad enough to risk calling us for another shot at a swap?"

"I'd say it's a fifty-fifty chance," Tom replied.

Erin shook her head. "I don't buy it. He wasn't willing to give her up for the ransom the first time in the subway. What makes you think he'd be willing to go through with the trade now?"

"He won't be," Tom said. "But he'll use her as bait to get the money."

"And risk walking into a trap? What if he's too smart for that? Guy like him would know to walk away."

It was Tom's turn to shake his head. "No. If he was gonna walk, he'd have done it in the subway. The safe call would've been to let the money go, but he went balls-out for the case.

Hell, he shot other cops for it. There's no going back after that." He threw a sidelong look at Erin. "Greed got the better of him once. I think it will again."

She exhaled a heavy sigh. "Hope you're right. 'Cause if you're wrong, that girl's as good as dead."

26

Frank turned Phaedra on her side and eased her onto the floor behind the driver's seat of his black Jeep. The girl was still unconscious from the injection he'd given her, but he knew she might awaken if he wasn't careful. He had given her a lighter dose than she'd had on the night he'd abducted her, because the Sages who were waiting for her would punish him if she showed up brain damaged.

Stepping around the luggage piled in his garage, he walked to the other side of the SUV and opened the rear passenger-side door. Leaning in, he grabbed Phaedra's shoulders and pulled her the rest of the way inside the vehicle. Quick tugs confirmed that the duct tape on her mouth and the cuffs on her wrists were secure. He grabbed a blanket off the backseat, unfolded it, and draped it over her like a shroud. Then he folded down the back seats to further hide the girl from view, and he closed the rear doors.

That ought to do it, he figured. If she stirred during the drive north, he could always turn up the Jeep's stereo to drown her out at tollbooths.

The beat-up old vehicle had a full tank of gas, and Frank had just topped off the oil for the fourth time in two weeks. He hoped it would be enough to reach the Canadian border without making any stops. *As long as my new passport doesn't trip any alarms, I should be home free.*

As he opened the SUV's rear hatch and started loading his luggage into the cargo area, his temper simmered. "I came so close," he grumbled, unsure whether he was talking to himself or the drugged-unconscious girl in his Jeep. "I had the damn case in my hands. Twelve million bucks, free and clear. And I fucking lost it." He tossed a garment bag on top of the pile. "Can you believe that shit?"

He slammed the rear hatch shut. "It's the Russians' fault," he said, walking back to the driver's door. "Trigger-happy shit-heads." He opened the door and got in. Slumped in the driver's seat, he continued rambling. "I had a quarter million in a rainy day fund that Viktor was holding for me. Guess where it is now?" He looked over his shoulder at the motionless shape under the blanket. "That's right—in the DA's evidence locker."

Staring out the windshield at the bare garage wall in front of the Jeep, Frank sighed. "I even did all the hard work. Tracked your movements, put the hit on your Sentinel, made up 'Leon' to take the blame if it all went south. All those idiots had to do was collect the money, and they couldn't even get that right." He shook his head. "All that work, and what do I have to show for it? Five thousand bucks."

A bitter chuckle quaked his chest. He'd invented Leon for two reasons. One was to launder money. Now he didn't even have enough to get himself stopped at the border. The other was so he'd have a traveling identity in case he ever got busted as a mole for the Russians. Now they were dead, and he'd outed himself in his failed bid for the case. He almost had to laugh.

His hand started turning the key in the ignition. The warning lights on the dash lit up, then he stopped.

He looked up and caught his sullen reflection in the rearview mirror. "Let the twelve million go," he told himself. "You've already tipped your hand. Making another play for the cash'll just get you pinched." He took a deep breath, closed his eyes, and asked himself, *How long do you think you'll live without it?*

Eyes downcast in Phaedra's direction, he considered his next dilemma. "The Sages told me to bring you in," he said to her. "But if I do, what happens to me? When I was a cop, they thought I was useful. Now I'm just another Seeker on the run. What if they decide I'm more trouble than I'm worth?"

Frank palmed sweat from his forehead and weighed his options. "As long as I deliver you in one piece, they might let me live. But if I also bring in twelve million bucks and give them half, they might let me live *in style.*"

It was a calculated risk, he knew. By now the NYPD and the FBI might be aware of Phaedra's kidnapping. For all Frank knew, he might even be a suspect in that case. Making another play for the ransom money after the fiasco in the subway station would be a very dumb move.

Facing the Sages of the Scorned empty-handed after a fuckup of this magnitude would be even dumber.

He picked up his disposable cell phone and stared at its keypad, in denial about what he had to do next. He'd shattered his personal cell phone in the subway tunnels to prevent the NYPD or the feds from using it to triangulate his position. This would have to be the last time he used the prepaid phone before ditching it. *Too much heat on this thing,* he brooded.

Dialing from memory, he called the phone he'd given to the Doyle woman, which she had handed off to the blond-haired enemy Seeker.

It rang four times before Frank's bane answered. *"Hello?"*

"It's Kolpack," he said. "You still have the money?"

There was a brief pause before the man replied, *"Why?"*

"Don't be stupid," Frank said. "You want the girl? I want the cash."

"How do we know you have her?" the man asked. *"You and your friends crossed us last time."*

Pinching the bridge of his nose, Frank said, "That was a mistake. It won't happen again."

"So you're saying you have the girl?"

"Yes," Frank said. "I have the girl."

"And you'll bring her to the swap this time?"

"Yes."

Another pause. *"All right,"* the man said. *"But we don't want another bloodbath like the one at Times Square. Someplace private this time."*

"Agreed," Frank said, knowing that keeping a low profile was in his best interest. Drawing attention was the last thing he wanted to do. "Where?"

"Ward's Island. Midnight. Next to the blockhouse under the first span of the Hell Gate Bridge."

Frank thought it over. Ward's Island sat in the East River, between Queens and Manhattan. Most of it was used for sports fields, but it also was home to a psychiatric center and a water-treatment plant.

The wooded area under the Hell Gate Bridge was an isolated locale even during daytime, and at that hour of the night there'd be no one around to interfere with the swap. Plus, most of the land near the bridge was made up of lawns, parking lots, and soccer fields that were wide open and fenced off. There'd be nowhere for the cops or the feds to conceal large numbers of vehicles.

Best of all, Frank could leave from the island directly onto the RFK Bridge, and from there he'd be away, heading north on I-87.

"Okay," he said. "Midnight under the bridge. And don't pull any tricks. I still have a police radio. If you call in the cops or the feds, the girl dies."

"Don't be late," the enemy Seeker said, and he hung up.

Frank opened his door, dropped the disposable phone on the concrete floor of his garage, and stomped the cheap plastic piece of shit till it was nothing but chips and splinters.

He inhaled, enjoying the dank, turpentine-scented air in the garage, then settled back into his seat and shut his door.

It was just after ten o'clock. In two hours he'd be up twelve million dollars and the Called would be down two Seekers, because he had no intention of letting them leave the swap alive.

With a turn of the key, the Jeep's engine purred to life. He triggered the automatic garage-door opener. As the portal behind the SUV lifted open with a rattling of chains and the hum of a motor, he smirked over his shoulder at Phaedra.

"Let's go get paid."

The night had gone from cool to cold in a few hours. Bitter winds had shredded the dome of clouds above the city, revealing a few bright stars in patches of black sky.

Tom shivered as he tucked in the tail of a clean shirt and zipped up his jacket. Erin tugged her trenchcoat shut and tied it at the waist, then turned up her collar against the gusts blowing in off the Hell Gate, a short and narrow arm of the East River that separated Randall's Ward's Island from Astoria, Queens.

From their vantage point on the sidewalk of Shore Boulevard in Astoria, the imposing steel architecture of the Hell Gate Bridge towered more than a hundred feet directly above them and stretched majestically away, suspended from one bank of the river to the next.

Tom leaned on the black cylindrical iron railing and peered across the dark, sparkling water to the far side of the river. That was where they would be risking everything to save a child they'd never met, in less than half an hour.

"I'm starting to wonder if this was a bad idea," he said.

Erin let slip a derisive snort. "Of course it's a bad idea."

"You got a better one? 'Cause now's the time."

She stuck her hands in her pockets. "Wish I did."

"Me too." He turned his head to look at her. "Promise me one thing."

Looking back, she said, "Name it."

"If you have to choose between me and the girl, save the girl."

Erin nodded. "Same goes for me."

"Deal," he said, and they shook hands. Then he looked at his watch. "Time to go." They turned away from the river and stepped back toward his truck, which was parked behind them. Holding up his keys, he asked, "Would you mind driving? I have to make a phone call." Off her nod, he tossed the keys to her.

He opened the passenger door and got in. Sitting on that side felt strange to him. By reflex, he turned in the wrong direction for his seat belt before he caught himself and reached over his right shoulder.

Erin climbed into the driver's seat and shut her door with a vigorous slam. She fastened her seat belt and started the engine. Seconds later they were moving.

Even as Tom dialed his home number, he had no idea what he would say to Karen. She worried about him enough already; how could he tell her he was going unarmed to a ransom exchange with a homicidal ex-cop? He hesitated as his finger hovered over the TALK button. Then he pressed it and lifted the phone to his ear.

It rang only once before Karen picked up. *"Tom?"*

"Yeah, it's me," he said. "I know it's late. Hope I didn't wake you."

She sounded vexed. *"Hell, no. I'm just sitting up enjoying my contractions."*

He replied with a note of alarm, "Contractions?" Erin shot a startled look at him from the corner of her eye as she drove.

"Relax," Karen said. *"It's not real labor, just more of the Braxton Hicks prelabor. They've been steady all day, since lunch. Doctor Nizolek says they're just softening me up for the main event."*

Letting go of a breath he hadn't realized he'd been holding, he said, "So, you're all right, then?"

"I suppose," Karen said, calming down a bit. *"I'm still pissed at you, though. You ought to be here so I can swear at you for getting me into this mess."*

Adding some charm to his tone, he said, "Hang on there. If memory serves, it took *both* of us to get you into this mess."

He could almost hear her crack a smile as she replied, *"Well . . . yes. Technically, I'd have to admit that's true."* Putting the edge back into her voice, she continued. *"But that doesn't get you off the hook for being out playing cops and robbers when you ought to be here at home, waiting on me hand and foot like you promised, buster."* Her voice trailed off into a melancholy silence that lingered between them. Then she finished, *"I just wish you were here to go through it with me. I miss you."*

"I miss you, too," Tom said.

"So when are you coming home? Are you almost done in New York?"

Tom knew then that he'd called Karen so that he might have a chance to say good-bye. But having reached the threshold of that soul-crushing moment, he couldn't take the last step. There was no way he could tell her that he might not live through the night. That she might awaken in the morning a widow and a single parent. That their son might be born without a father.

He took refuge in a lie of omission.

"Yeah," he said. "I'm almost done."

"When?"

"Soon," he said. "Tonight. I promise." His assurances were met with a long silence. "I love you, Karen."

There was fear in her voice, as if she sensed that he was hiding something terrible from her. *"I love you, too. Be careful tonight."*

"I will," he said. "Talk to you soon."

"Okay," she said, as if she were surrendering. *"Good night, sweetie."*

"Good night, my love."

They hung up.

Tom brooded in silence, staring at the phone in his hand.

Outside the truck, the Robert F. Kennedy Bridge was a blur as Erin accelerated down its mostly deserted straightaway toward the tollbooths.

She cast an apprehensive glance Tom's way. "You ready for this?"

"No." He gave her a bittersweet smile. "But I'm glad you're with me."

Mirroring his expression, she reached over and took his hand in a firm clasp. "That's what friends are for."

27

Tom heard Frank's car before he saw it.

Concealed in the dark behind an inside corner of a massive concrete bridge span, Tom was surrounded by knee-high dead weeds and spindly trees whose autumn-dried leaves rustled in the low, cold wind. Through that soft curtain of white noise he heard the low growl of an engine drawing closer on the deserted roads of Ward's Island.

Diagonally across a weed-choked clearing bisected by a well-worn path of tire tracks, Erin perched on a high, narrow ledge of the Hell Gate Bridge's graffiti-tagged blockhouse, around the corner from Frank's only avenue of approach.

Intense halogen headlights backlit the thick copse of trees that hid them from view. The beams bobbed slightly, and Tom listened to the changing sounds of the ground under Frank's tires—the crunch of gravelly dirt followed by the dry crinkling of old wood mulch, broken branches, and twigs that formed an eighty-foot-wide ring around the base of the blockhouse.

The sound of Frank's vehicle was momentarily drowned

out by the roar of an Amtrak train thundering by on the tracks more than a hundred feet overhead. Tom kept his eyes on the shifting headlight beams through the trees.

On Tom's right, a Jeep lurked forward through a gap in the trees. It turned in his direction. He ducked fully behind the corner of the massive concrete arch as the Jeep's headlights swept past his position.

The SUV followed the trail for a few yards, then stopped. All Tom heard for a moment was the idling of its engine. Then it turned off, and one door opened, followed by another. Next came sounds he couldn't easily identify—either of effort or a struggle—while the odor of exhaust fumes tainted the frigid night air.

Frank called out, "Show yourself."

"No!" Tom shouted back, his voice echoing off the myriad hard surfaces under the bridge, making it hard to pinpoint exactly where he was hiding. "First show me Phaedra!"

"She's right here," Frank said. "Have a look."

Can't stay under cover forever, Tom reminded himself. He peeked around the corner at the Jeep.

Tom had to squint against the glare of the Jeep's headlights, which rendered Frank and Phaedra little more than silhouettes in the shadows.

Phaedra stood next to the open rear door on the driver's side. Her hands were bound behind her back. A strip of gray duct tape covered her mouth. Frank was mostly hidden behind the door—but the muzzle of his semiautomatic pistol was clearly visible, inches from Phaedra's pale and delicate temple.

"Let her walk forward," Tom said, loud enough to be heard.

"Not until I see the case," Frank replied.

Reluctantly, Tom held the metallic briefcase in the open at arm's length.

Frank responded, "Open it!"

Tom brought it back behind the corner, flipped open the latches, and opened the case. Supporting it with two hands, he held it out again for inspection.

"All right," Frank said. "Bring it to me."

"I don't think so," Tom said, closing the case. "We'll meet halfway. You bring me the girl. I'll bring you the money."

"Deal," Frank shouted. "Start walking."

Tom took a breath for courage, then stepped into the open.

Frank emerged cautiously from behind the Jeep's door and prodded Phaedra ahead of him at gunpoint. They waded toward Tom through the billowing weeds, which were knee-high for the men and thigh high for Phaedra.

Lifting his free hand to block the Jeep's blinding headlamps, Tom could barely see anything at all. Phaedra and Frank were shadows in a flood of light, and the world around and beyond them was pitch-black by comparison.

When they were less than ten yards apart, Frank said, "Stop there." His pistol remained fixed on Phaedra as he glanced around and asked Tom, "Where's your friend? The *chica* from the clinic fire."

"Pointing a rifle at you," Tom said. "Which is why you have that laser dot on your chest."

Frank looked down at the crimson spot dancing on his torso.

He chortled. "Gimme a break. You think I don't know the difference between a targeting laser and a cheap laser pen you bought in a drugstore?" He grabbed Phaedra's collar and pressed his pistol to her head. "Tell your friend to cut the shit and come stand next to you, or I'll kill the girl."

The now-familiar cold pain of a lie twisted inside Tom's gut. "No, you won't," he said.

The fugitive cop wrinkled his brow at Tom, then lifted his chin and nodded knowingly. "Ah! I get it now," he said. "You're a lie detector. That's how you screwed us at the first exchange." Shifting the gun from Phaedra's head, he continued, "You're right, I won't kill her. But she's just as useful to me whether she can walk or not." He crouched behind Phaedra and aimed his pistol at the back of her knee. Raising his voice, he added, "Listen up, *chica.* Get your ass front and center, or this girl's limping for the rest of her short, miserable life."

There wasn't a hint of falsehood in Frank's threat. Tom looked over his left shoulder and nodded twice. The red dot vanished from Frank's chest, and Erin emerged from the trees and tossed aside her harmless laser pointer. She walked slowly forward and stood next to Tom.

"Put down the money," Frank said.

Tom set the briefcase on the ground, then raised both his hands in a gesture of surrender. Erin did likewise and followed his example as he took three steps back from the case. "All right," Tom said. "It's yours. Now let the girl go."

"I don't think so," Frank said.

His gun darted out from behind Phaedra's leg.

Fire blazed from the muzzle.

Deafening shots split the night.

Erin twitched and staggered backward as each bullet hit.

She fell on her back in the weeds.

Three more flashes and three more thunderclaps.

They felt like trains slamming into Tom's chest.

He felt himself fall, but he was gone before he hit the ground.

Frank's ears rang from the reports of his Glock. He savored the acrid tang of sulfur in the air as he watched white smoke snake from the barrel of his pistol.

Phaedra's terrified screams were muffled under the duct tape.

The enemy Seekers had each taken three hollow-point rounds in the chest, square in the center of mass. *Good kills,* Frank thought. *Solid.*

Taunting him, the briefcase stood in his shadow, unguarded in the weeds, reflecting a stray shaft of moonlight dappling through the wind-shaken trees.

Reaching up, he tore the tape from Phaedra's mouth. She let loose half a terrified shout before he slapped the back of her head. "Shut up. Stay quiet and I won't cut your face."

He unlocked her handcuffs, removed them, and tucked them back into their sheath on his belt. "Go get the case and bring it back."

She just stood there trembling. He gave her another smack on the back of her head. "Move it." As Phaedra took her first halting steps, he added, "If you try to run, I'll blow your legs off." He kept his Glock aimed and steady.

Phaedra tiptoed through the weeds, lit up by the Jeep's headlight beams, her shadow a dark giant looming ahead of her. As she neared the case, Frank kept his eye on the two downed Seekers, waiting for them to spring some surprise. He was certain that he'd nailed them, but there was no telling what some of the Called could do. It was best not to take chances.

The girl grabbed the briefcase and lifted it with both

hands. She moved awkwardly while carrying it back toward the Jeep, and Frank realized it must be heavy for such a young kid, especially one so slight of build. Her steps through the browned weeds rustled softly as she returned to him. He gestured to the Jeep with a tilt of his head. "Put the case on the hood," he said.

She strained to lift it above her shoulders and set it on the Jeep's front bumper. "Good enough," Frank said.

Frank watched her out of the corner of his eye and kept most of his attention on the two Seekers, who remained deathly still in the weeds.

Stop being paranoid, he told himself. He stood, holstered his weapon, and walked over to the front of the Jeep. Phaedra stepped away from him to the passenger side of the SUV as he opened the case and checked its contents.

All the bearer bonds appeared to be in place. A quick tally confirmed their value at slightly more than eleven million dollars—less than he'd hoped for but a hell of a good score all the same.

Underneath the bearer bonds was a prepaid cell phone.

He picked it up. It was just like the ones he and the Russians had used. He stared in confusion at the phone in his hand. Where had it come from? What was it doing in the briefcase?

It rang.

His whole body jolted with surprise. "Dammit," he muttered, recovering his composure. Curious, he answered the incoming call. "Hello?"

A woman's voice said, *"You should've let the money go, Frank."*

Frank froze as a pall of anticipation settled upon him. Then he dropped the phone and bolted for the driver's door of the Jeep.

The first bullet tore through the back of his shoulder. A split second later he heard the shot. His blood spattered across the open driver's door as he slammed into it. He landed face-first on the mulch-covered ground.

Marshaling his training, he drew his Glock and fired randomly into the trees behind him, then scrambled frantically into the truck. Only as he fell into the driver's seat and pulled his door shut did he realize that Phaedra was at a full run, heading toward the slain Seekers. Letting her get away would cost Frank dearly, but he had bigger problems at the moment.

He turned the key, and the Jeep's engine roared to life. Ducking for cover behind the dashboard, he threw the SUV into reverse and stepped on the gas.

The windshield spiderwebbed with bullet hits, turned white, then disintegrated, peppering his face with stinging shards of glass.

Frank yanked the wheel hard to the right, hoping to slip out of the woods through the narrow gap to the parking lot.

More shots hammered into his Jeep's engine. Gray vapor that stank of oil hissed up from under the hood.

He spun the wheel left. The engine whined as it pushed the reverse gear over the red line. Another rifle shot was followed by the bang of a blown tire.

Then the Jeep rammed into something solid. The rear window blasted in as the hatchback buckled, and the last thing Frank saw before he blacked out was the air bag hitting him in the face.

The rifle kicked hard into Bailey's shoulder as she put a bullet through Kolpack's shoulder. It felt righteous.

She didn't flinch as Kolpack drew his sidearm and fired wild shots into the trees above and around her. The woods swallowed his barrage with dull impacts. He clearly had no idea where she was. He was just wasting bullets.

Then he was back in the Jeep. The engine roared to life. Its reverse lights lit up the exhaust cloud billowing behind it.

Bailey verified that the girl was clear of the Jeep and her line of fire. As the vehicle started backing up, she sprang to her feet, emerging from cover in the woods with her M4A1 carbine assault rifle braced and steady. A subtle push of her thumb switched the rifle's firing mode to semiautomatic.

She blasted out the Jeep's windshield.

The Jeep swung through a sloppy turn around the corner of the blockhouse. Bailey put a few rounds into its engine block. A gray geyser erupted through its front grille. The Jeep swerved again, making a frantic bid for escape.

Aiming with care and patience, Bailey destroyed the front driver's side tire with one shot.

Rolling on flapping rubber and a hissing engine, the SUV fishtailed backward into a stand of trees and smashed to a halt.

Bailey kept her rifle targeted on the Jeep as she advanced on foot. She watched for any sign of movement inside the vehicle but saw none. When she stepped within a few yards, she saw that the air bags had deployed and knocked Kolpack unconscious. *I'd better take advantage of that while I can,* she decided.

Her breaths condensed into gray ghosts as she marched toward the Jeep. At the door, she lowered her rifle and pulled on the handle. It was locked.

She smashed in the window with the stock of her rifle, covering the dazed Kolpack with shattered safety glass. Then she slung her weapon behind her, reached in, and unlocked the door.

Working quickly, she opened the door and grabbed his left hand. She slapped one ring of her handcuffs on his wrist and locked the other on the now-empty window frame of his door. Then she leaned in, confiscated his handcuffs, slapped one cuff on his right wrist, and pulled his right arm under his left in a crisscross pattern that looked very uncomfortable. With a satisfying click, she locked the second set of cuffs to the door.

That ought to hold him till backup gets here, she mused.

As he began to stir, she frisked him and took his sidearm, spare clips, badge, and handcuff keys. Then she snatched the car keys out of the ignition.

Kolpack opened his eyes and regarded Bailey with a bloodstained grin.

"I need a cigarette," he said.

"I don't smoke," she said.

"There's a pack in the glove compartment."

"Thought you quit."

He coughed through a mouthful of pink spittle. "Quitting's for losers."

Bailey circled around to the passenger side, opened the door, and pulled open the glove compartment to find a pack of cigarettes and a lighter. She took them and walked back around to Kolpack. Standing in front of him, she pulled out one cancer stick, put it in her mouth, and lit it. White smoke curled away into the crisp night air.

She inhaled a bitter lungful, then exhaled a thick plume in his face. "Guess what," Bailey said. She flicked the lit cigarette off his chest. It exploded into sparks and fell smoldering at his feet. "You *are* a loser."

Black faded to gray. Silence gave way to a muted groaning of wind in the distance.

Deep, dull agony filled Tom's chest. His muscles ached and his gut churned with nausea. Throbbing pains threatened to crack open his skull from the inside. Breathing in hurt. Breathing out left him dizzy.

His arms and legs felt as if they were made of lead. He couldn't move.

Something rustled in the dry weeds beside him.

With great effort, he forced one eye barely open.

Phaedra kneeled between him and Erin, who weakly lolled her head in their direction. The young girl glanced expectantly at Erin, then looked back at Tom and said, "I knew you weren't dead."

Through a parched mouth, Tom rasped, "Only mostly dead."

"You'll be okay," Phaedra said. "Your glows are still bright."

Wrinkling his brow in confusion made his temples pound. "Our what?"

Phaedra looked nervously between Tom and Erin. "Don't you see them?"

Tom looked at Erin, who reacted with a pained smile. "She's a Seer," she said, and Tom understood: Phaedra was one of the rare members of the Called.

That's why the Scorned tried to take her, he realized.

The girl reached down and clutched Tom's hand. With what sounded like equal parts hope and fear, she asked in a whisper, "God sent you, didn't He?"

Tom didn't have to lie. "Yeah, sweetie. I think maybe He did." Offering her his own troubled smile of reassurance, he added, "But don't tell anyone about us. Make this our secret, okay?" The girl nodded in agreement. "Okay, then," he continued, stifling a groan. "Now run to the nice lady with the rifle."

Phaedra's face darkened with concern. "What about you?"

"We'll be fine," Tom said. "We just need to lie here awhile." The girl did as he'd asked and jogged back to Detective Bailey. As soon as Phaedra was out of earshot, Tom turned his head and asked Erin, "How're you doin'?"

"Shot," she said.

"Yeah," he said. "Me too."

28

From the backseat of the police cruiser, Anna could barely see what was going on.

She had been woken after midnight from a fitful slumber on her sofa by a call from the police, delivering news that had sounded too good to be true. A white and blue police car arrived at her door minutes later and with its lights flashing and siren wailing ferried her to the dirt roads of Ward's Island.

Leaning forward, Anna tried to peek through the diamond-patterned barrier that separated the front and back seats of the car. Ahead of them, a small fleet of vehicles had gathered under an imposing red-painted bridge. Hundreds of blue and red lights flashed, and helicopters' roving searchlights had turned the area around the bridge as bright as day. News vans formed a perimeter around the emergency vehicles, and video crews and photographers roamed the area in packs.

The cruiser stopped at the edge of the mayhem. A pair of uniformed cops opened the barricade. One waved the car through while the other waved away the press. As soon as they were through, the blue wooden barrier was moved back into place behind them. Searching the spectacle that enveloped her, all that Anna could see were more cops in uniform, people wearing jackets marked CSU or FBI, and what she guessed were plainclothes detectives.

Then the car slipped through a gap between some stands of trees near the massive concrete structure at the base of the bridge. A demolished Jeep was entangled rear-end-first with some skinny trees that had been rammed half out of the ground and now stood at a shallow angle, pinned under the Jeep's bumper.

A bloodied man was handcuffed to the Jeep's door and surrounded by cops wearing black combat gear and carrying rifles.

Several yards beyond that, two ambulances were parked. As the police cruiser rolled to a stop behind the red and white ambulances, Anna pressed her face to the window, hopeful and fearful, searching desperately for—

Phaedra! Her little girl! Her angel! The girl sat on the back bumper of one ambulance, flanked by two paramedics and a woman in dusty street clothes.

Her daughter saw her and jumped to her feet. "Mom!"

Anna's hands scrambled to find a door handle, only to find none. "Let me out!" she cried. "Open the door!"

"Hang on, ma'am," said the cop in front of her. He hurried out of the car and opened the rear passenger door for her. "Back doors on police cars can only be opened from—"

Anna didn't hear a damn thing he said.

She sprinted to her daughter in three long strides and swept her child into her arms. "Thank God you're all right!" she said, barely able to speak through her frantic sobs of joy and relief.

Tears streamed down her face, and she hugged her baby to her chest. She had to fight the irrational fear that this was just another of her wish-fulfillment dreams, another fantasized happy ending to a tragic story.

No, it was real. The beating of Phaedra's heart, her innocent cries of relief, the scent of her unwashed hair, the frightened clutching of her fingers on Anna's back. It was no fantasy; it was tangible. Phaedra wept against Anna's shoulder, and she released her tears onto Phaedra's.

My baby's safe! she rejoiced. *Thank you, God. Thank you.*

The paramedics kept their distance from Anna and Phaedra's reunion, but the woman with the dirty clothes and the gold detective's shield on her belt inched toward them. "Excuse me," she said softly. "Mrs. Doyle?" Anna opened her tear-filled eyes and nodded to the woman, who continued, "I'm Detective Katharine Bailey. I thought you might want to know that we recovered your money, as well."

"My what?" It took Anna a moment to remember the ransom. "Oh! That's great, thank you." It was good news, but as she kissed Phaedra's cheek, she knew it was only the second-best thing she'd hear today.

One of the ambulances pulled away and stopped on the other side of the clearing. The combat-equipped police uncuffed the bloodied man from the Jeep, secured his hands behind his back, and loaded him into the fire department medical vehicle. A paramedic inside strapped the prisoner to a gurney. Then the cops stepped out of the second ambulance, shut the doors, and slapped them twice. The hollow metallic echoes signaled the driver to depart, and the ambulance pulled away, passed the legion of cops and federal agents, broke through the media perimeter, and vanished into the night.

Bailey watched the departing ambulance, then turned back to Anna and said, "The briefcase and the bonds have to be processed as evidence, but the bonds can be returned to your lawyer tomorrow afternoon."

"That's fine," Anna said. "We'd just like to go home now, if that's okay."

"Sure," Bailey said. "We already have your daughter's statement. We can get yours tomorrow. I'll have a car take you home."

Anna planted another grateful kiss on her daughter's cheek. Then she wondered about Tom Nash and his female friend, who had risked so much for Phaedra at the subway station. Choosing her words carefully, she said to Bailey, "There were two people trying to help me save Phaedra. Do you know if they . . . I mean, are they . . . ?"

"I'm sorry, ma'am," Bailey said. She looked at the ground and didn't elaborate. Composing herself, she added, "We might have to ask your daughter some follow-up questions over the next few weeks. Will that be okay?" Anna nodded. Bailey waved over a cop in a uniform. "Take Mrs. Doyle and her daughter home, please."

The sandy-haired young police officer nodded to Bailey, then said to Anna, "Ma'am, if you'll come with me, we'll get you home in no time."

"Thank you," Anna said, carrying Phaedra as she followed the policeman to a nearby patrol car. She couldn't help wondering what had become of Mr. Nash and Ms. Morales. In her heart, she knew they must have played a part in Phaedra's rescue, but now it seemed as if she would never get to thank them.

Looking at her daughter in her arms, she silently vowed to say a prayer for them every day for the rest of her life.

She and Phaedra settled into the backseat of the police car. Helping the girl fasten her seat belt, she said with a smile, "Buckle up, honey. We're going home."

The anonymous strangers were waiting for Bailey in the woods by the river, several hundred feet from the bridge—exactly where they said they would be.

They leaned against two side-by-side trees, watching her trudge through the thick dry brush into the shadows. The man said, "Everything go okay?"

"It went fine," Bailey said. "Now would you mind telling me how you knew he had the girl?"

"Lucky hunch," the man said with a self-deprecating smile.

Bailey nodded at the transparent lie. "Sure it was." Looking around to make sure they were alone, she asked, "Why'd you call *me*, anyway?"

"I saw you at the precinct," he said. "You have an honest face. And since Kolpack took a shot at you, too, I figured you might actually help us."

He had a point. "Fair enough," she said. "How're you two feeling?"

"Been better," he said. He picked up one of the two Kevlar vests Bailey had loaned them at their previous meeting, under the bridge on the other side of the river. He tossed the bulletproof vest at her feet. "Could've been a lot worse."

His female friend lobbed her vest back to Bailey as well. It hit the ground with a dull *fwump*. "Slightly dented," the Latina said. "Sorry."

"No worries." Bailey rubbed her palms to ward off the cold.

"What happens now?" the man asked.

Bailey shrugged. "Kolpack gets patched up, then he goes to jail."

"I meant, what happens to us?"

She cracked a knowing smile. "You were never here." Noting their surprised reactions, she continued, "Phaedra's official statement is that Kolpack said he was bringing her out here to kill her and dump her body. As for me? I staked out the bridge on an anonymous tip."

The man nodded. "And the briefcase?"

"Last time I saw it, Kolpack had it," Bailey said. "There's no reason for me to think it left his hands since he got on the train at Port Authority. Besides . . ." She reached into one of her jacket's inside pockets. "I don't expect to find any usable prints on it except his." She took out and unfolded some papers she had photocopied back at the precinct and handed them to the tall, mysterious stranger. They were the inexplicably blurred and distorted photos and fingerprints from a John and Jane Doe arson report. "These are yours, aren't they?"

He showed the sheets to his female compatriot but neither said anything.

Their silence was maddening to Bailey. Were they government agents? CIA? NSA? Something even more secretive and exotic? How had they deceived and eluded the cameras and the scanners back at the precinct?

Anxious and desperate to know what was going on, Bailey demanded, "Who the hell are you guys? *What* are you?"

All she received in reply was the sheaf of papers handed back to her and two enigmatic smiles. The duo turned and walked away, shambling in crackling steps through the woods, their movements slightly hobbled and stiff from injuries.

Protocol required that Bailey at least hold them for questioning, treat them as material witnesses to Phaedra Doyle's abduction and the clinic arson, if not as prime suspects. They had never even told her their names, yet they'd persuaded her to loan them two Kevlar vests and to trust their tip about Kolpack.

It made no sense to Bailey. There was no reason for her to assume they were the good guys; there was absolutely no logical reason for her to trust them.

But she did.

Watching the pair melt into the darkness, Bailey somehow *knew* she was doing the right thing in letting them go.

She folded the papers, put them back in her pocket, and started the long walk back to her car. The strangers were gone—but something told her she would see them again. *Maybe then I'll get some answers,* she mused.

But she wasn't counting on it.

Dr. Kirti Sharma rubbed her eyes as she walked the brightly lit and antiseptic-smelling corridors of North General Hospital's first floor, her hands loosely clutching the ends of the stethoscope draped over the back of her neck. With only a dozen overdoses, domestic-violence injuries, rapes, and ambulatory crises since midnight, it was a quiet third shift in the teaching hospital's emergency ward.

Pushing a stray lock of black hair behind her ear and adjusting her thick-rimmed eyeglasses, she stopped and poked her head into the admissions office. "Tariq," she called out to the administrative assistant on duty. "Where's that ambulance the NYPD told us to watch for?"

Tariq swiveled his chair to face her and shrugged. "Like I know?"

"They woke me up thirty minutes ago," she complained. "It should be here by now. They said it was a GSW, right?"

"S'what they said," Tariq replied.

"So where is it? Time matters with gunshots."

"Do I look like the bus driver?" Shaking his shaved brown head, he turned away and said, "Call dispatch for their twenty."

Sharma sighed in disgust and moved down the hallway to the radio room next to the nurses' station. She swept her white lab coat with its overstuffed pockets behind her back and out of her way, grabbed the old-fashioned metal microphone, flipped the talk switch, and said, "North General to dispatch. Over."

"Dispatch. Go ahead, North General. Over."

"We need a twenty on the bus bringing in our GSW from Ward's Island," Sharma said. "It's late. Over."

"North General, unit one-three-five should be at your location now. Over."

"Yes, dispatch, we know it's *supposed* to be here, but it's not. Over."

The dispatch operator replied, *"North General, can you visually confirm that unit one-three-five is not on-site? Over."*

Sharma couldn't believe what she was hearing. "Dispatch, are you saying you want me to walk outside and look for the ambulance with my GSW?" It took her a moment to remember to add "Over."

"Affirmative, North General. Go out and take a look. Over."

"Okay, dispatch," Sharma said. "Going outside to look for your missing ambulance. North General out." She set the microphone on the table with a heavy thump, rolled her eyes, and heaved an irritated sigh as she meandered through the corridors toward the ambulance intake area.

Patients on gurneys were lined up in the hall like train cars. As she passed through the waiting area, four people in quick succession accosted her for immediate examinations. She shouldered past them, instructing each GOMER to tell his or her sob story to the admitting nurse.

Winter was Sharma's least favorite season, but she was grateful to step outside into the cold, clean night air. Sirens wailed, distant and plaintive, like coyotes in the city's canyons of steel and concrete. A quick glance up and down East 121st Street seemed to reveal nothing out of the ordinary.

Then she noticed a Fire Department of New York ambulance idling along the curb about eighty feet from the entrance. Its interior and exterior lights were off, but a steady cloud of white exhaust vapor billowed up behind it.

Sharma walked quickly toward the ambulance. Then she saw the number on its side: 135.

She sprinted the rest of the way.

As she reached the cab of the ambulance, she saw the driver inside, slouched in his seat, head drooped forward. There was a peculiar fog inside the vehicle that she feared might be its own misdirected exhaust. She opened the passenger door.

The charnel stench of burned flesh overpowered her. Only her years of medical training prevented her from vomiting on the sidewalk. She gulped a breath of clean air, then leaned back inside the ambulance, frantically waving away the smoke. As it dissipated, she saw that the driver of the ambulance had been burned to a crisp—but only his body was charred; his uniform was unburned.

A crude lightning-bolt S had been raggedly slashed across his chest.

Suppressing her impulse to run, Sharma climbed inside and put her finger to the driver's crispy throat in a desperate attempt to find a pulse in his carotid artery. There was nothing to find. The man was a cinder.

She clambered out and ran to the back of the ambulance. As she opened the door, a thick cloud of sickly sweet smoke from incinerated human tissue roiled out.

The second time was too much. She turned away as her stomach heaved its acid-soured contents onto the street behind the ambulance.

A minute later, after she had finished her surrender to emesis, she looked inside the back of the ambulance. The other paramedic's body had been all but melted in his uniform, which lay in a pool of rendered fat on the vehicle's stainless-steel floor. His chest, too, had been marked with a lightning-bolt gash.

There was no sign of what could have done that to the paramedics.

More alarming, there was no sign of the patient.

He was just . . . gone.

29

Tom followed Erin through the wrought-iron gate into the Conservatory Garden at the north end of Central Park. It was just after dawn, and the pale morning sun was at their backs as they strolled into the meticulously groomed green space. Sculpted hedges surrounded an immaculate lawn shining with dew. At the far end of the lawn, a geyser of white water shot up from a fountain flanked by two squat trees with lush crowns. All of it was sheltered from the city by thick walls of old trees.

Their footsteps echoed off the granite steps as they descended to the wide stone path around the lawn. Erin led him to the right, across the north walkway. As they strolled under the long, arched canopy of autumn-colored boughs, Tom asked again, "Are you sure he wanted to see *me?*"

"Positive," Erin replied. "Said to bring you here before you left the city."

His mind raced with anticipation of what might have prompted one of the elusive Sages of the Called to ask after him. "How'd he even know I was here?"

"I've learned it's better not to ask things like that," Erin said.

Every step reminded Tom of how much pain he was in. In addition to the scores of cuts on his neck, the welts on his face, the bite mark on his wrist, his beat-up nose, and his myriad abrasions and bumps, he now had three massive purple-black bruises from the impact of Kolpack's bullets on his chest through his borrowed Kevlar vest. If he hadn't been in such a hurry to put a hundred miles of road between him and New York and get home to Karen, he might have slept for a few days. Or a week.

He breathed the chilly morning air and was rewarded with the woody, grassy fragrances of nature. The garden seemed to be one of the few places in New York where one could escape from the noises and stinks of the city, even if just for a little while. It made him doubly grateful that he had been able to wash the subway stench out of his clothes at Erin's safe house the night before.

At the end of the north walk, another stone staircase led up to a gently curving pergola overgrown with wisteria. Beneath the tall wrought-iron trellis, low wooden benches were built into the arc of the stone rear wall, which was backed by an ivied slope and a forested knoll.

Guarding the north entrance to the elevated pergola was a tall, powerful-looking black man in his forties or fifties. He wore a dark suit, exquisitely shined black leather shoes, a crisp white shirt without a tie, and wraparound black sunglasses. His counterpart at the southern end of the pergola was a trim, twentyish blond woman garbed in vintage clothes from the late 1960s. Her ankle-length hemp skirt was overlapped by her tie-dyed shirt, some of whose brighter colors were echoed by playful streaks in the woman's hair.

Erin nodded to the male guardian as she and Tom approached. "Yo, Clean," she said with a flirtatious smile.

Clean didn't reciprocate. He put out one massive hand and gripped Erin's shoulder, stopping her shy of the stairs. His frown looked as if it had been hewn from obsidian. With a single sideways tilt of his shaved head, he signaled Tom to continue alone up the stairs. Tom nodded once to Erin, then climbed the steps.

Looking east over the pergola's low metal railing, Tom realized that there were two more people standing sentry in the garden. They had positioned themselves on the steps near the entrance at East 105th Street. Both were tall, thin men. One was white and dressed in blue jeans, a plaid shirt, sneakers, and a military-style fatigue jacket. The other man was Asian; he wore an all-black ensemble beneath a long leather coat.

Seated on a bench in the center of the pergola was a white-bearded old man with bronze-hued skin. Wisps of ivory hair tufted out from under his embroidered white kufi. He wore bleached-linen clothes. His hands were perched on the brass head of a lacquered wooden cane, which he held upright in front of him. As Tom stepped closer, the elderly gent said in a dry voice, "Have a seat, Mister Nash."

Tom settled onto the bench next to the Sage, who turned his head a few degrees—enough for Tom to see that the man's eyes were milky with age. "Mind if I ask your name?" Tom inquired, hunching his shoulders against the cold.

"Kalil," the Sage said. "You have questions."

"You could say that," Tom replied.

"I *did* say that," Kalil said with a wry smile. "Ask."

"I don't know where to start."

Kalil tilted his head toward Tom. The chirping of birds filled the pensive silence. "Perhaps I could ask you a question," the old man said.

Tom nodded for him to continue, then realized that the man couldn't see him and said, "Go ahead."

"Are the stories you told Erin true?" Kalil asked. "Did you really command entire crowds?"

"A few times," Tom said. "When I had to."

The old man nodded. "And bullets shot at you missed their marks?"

"I had a theory about that," Tom said. "I think something might have magnetized the girder next to me."

Another knowing smile lit up Kalil's wrinkled face. "Big magnet."

"Yeah, I know," Tom said. "But with all the power in the third rail, it—"

"And your gift," Kalil said, cutting Tom off. "You tell truth from lies?"

"Yes," Tom said.

"What does it feel like when it happens?" the Sage asked, leaning closer.

Remembering the sensations, Tom said, "Cold. Freezing, actually. It's like swallowing ice or getting frostbite on my ears."

Kalil grunted softly and nodded. "I see," he said.

Another silence stretched between them. A cool breeze whispered through the trees and blew dried leaves across the footpaths.

Tom asked, "What'll happen to Phaedra?"

"Ah, yes," the old man replied. "The young Seer." Turning a bit more in Tom's direction, he continued, "Since the Scorned obviously know who she is, we've taken steps to improve her protection. Normally, we'd have waited until Phaedra was older and reached out to her directly without telling her mother. But desperate times demand desperate measures. Fortunately, since all their money is already in untraceable bonds, relocating the two of them off the grid will be easier than it might have been."

Stuffing his hands into his jacket pockets, Tom said, "You mentioned 'reaching out' to Phaedra. Is that normal?"

"Yes," Kalil said. "When new members of the Called grow into their powers, we try to make contact with them as soon as possible."

"Then how come no one ever reached out to me?"

The old man's snowy eyebrows furrowed and arched, and a crooked grin tugged at his mouth. "Good question," he said. Turning back toward the rising sun, he added, "The truth is, we didn't know about you. You were hidden from us."

"Hidden? By who?"

"By *what*, actually," Kalil said. "Your Watcher concealed your bonding."

"I don't understand either part of what you just said," Tom confessed.

"I think you do. Maybe you know it by a different name."

Images flashed through Tom's memory. The blurred photos and scorched fingerprints. The wings in the fire.

"Is 'Watcher' another way of saying 'guardian angel'?"

Nodding, the old man replied, "That's one way of putting it. Some cultures call them angels; others call them djinn, or spirits of nature, or bow to them as gods in their own right. Our kind—the Called—hail from every faith and tradition, and some of us swear to none. But what we have in common is that each one of us is bonded, united on a spiritual level, with one Watcher. The unique qualities of our Watchers are what determine whether we become Seekers or Sentinels—"

"Or Seers or Sages," Tom said, reasoning it out. "Our Watcher determines the abilities we get, doesn't it?"

"Precisely," Kalil said.

"So what are the Scorned?"

The question gave Kalil a grim countenance. "People like us," he said. "Bonded with fallen Watchers—rebels and renegades, betrayers and deceivers. We try to aid humanity as the spirits move us; they exist to thwart us."

"But what do they want?" Too wound up to stay seated, Tom got up and paced in front of Kalil. "Do they have some goal besides messing with us? Why'd they take Phaedra? What was that about?"

"It's complicated," Kalil said.

"No kidding," Tom said, wondering what the Sage was hiding. "Erin said it had something to do with a bridge. What bridge?"

Kalil sighed. "Tom, trust me when I say that this is a discussion best left for another time." Pushing against his cane, he stood and steadied himself on shaking legs. "However, it won't do to send you home like this. We don't want your wife to worry, do we?" He reached out to Tom. "Take my hand."

Warily, Tom clasped Kalil's hand. A rush of warmth flooded through him—for a moment it felt a bit like being drunk. His vision blurred, and he became profoundly aware of his own pulse and breathing.

Then there was nothing but the low hush of air moving through dry leaves, and the cool caress of the morning breeze. All traces of pain had left Tom's body. With his left hand, he touched his face to find that his wounds had vanished.

"Much better," Kalil said, releasing Tom's hand. "I need to go now. But we'll meet again." The old man began shuffling away.

Tom called anxiously after him, "Wait! You said my Watcher concealed our bonding. Why would it do that?"

Stopping, then pivoting in small steps, Kalil looked back.

"First of all, 'it' is a 'she,' and her name is Armaita. The ancient Hebrews called her the Angel of Truth." He took a few halting steps back toward Tom. "We know her as one of the most powerful of all the Watchers—and one of the most secretive. She hasn't bonded with a human being in more than two thousand years. So if she's chosen this juncture in history to manifest on Earth . . ."

His voice trailed off, and he seemed to consider his words with care. Then he finished in an ominous tone, "It must mean that something truly momentous is at hand. And whatever that turns out to be . . . you'll be in the middle of it."

30

Erin walked with Tom from the garden entrance to his truck. He hadn't said a word about his conversation with Kalil or about his miraculous healing. She wondered whether he understood how rare such private audiences with a Sage really were.

"Learn anything interesting?" she asked, hoping he'd offer details.

"Mm-hm," he mumbled through closed lips, frustrating her further.

Their breaths trailed half a step behind them, catching the sun for a moment before dissipating into the brisk morning air. Tom seemed to be looking away into the distance, lost in thought. Then he said, "I guess my days of answering simple prayers and doing small favors are over."

"Maybe not," Erin said. "I still do my fair share of secret good deeds."

"What I mean is, it was never like this before," he said. "From now on, there'll always be the risk that something deadly's just around the corner."

She flashed a small, sympathetic smile. "Welcome to the big leagues."

They arrived at his truck. He stopped and faced her. "I just want to thank you again," he said. "For everything. I couldn't have done it without you."

"Any time, *papi.*" She reached out and straightened the collar of his jacket. "Got my number, right?"

"Yeah," he said with a nod. "You've got mine?"

She patted the left back pocket of her pants. "Right here."

"If you ever need my help, just call."

"Back atcha," she said, leaning in to hug him good-bye. Clenching him in a tight embrace, she whispered in his ear, "Sure you're up for such a long drive? Maybe you need to stay, spend a few more days in bed."

He leaned away and laughed. "You're shameless, you know that?"

She let him go and shrugged. "What do you want from me? I'm no angel."

"You sure about that?" He grinned, got into his truck, and shut the door.

The engine rattle-rumbled to life, and he lifted his hand in a farewell wave as he pulled away from the curb. Erin waved back as she watched him drive off, heading uptown on a mostly empty stretch of Madison Avenue.

She hoped she might see him again.

For his sake, she prayed she'd never have to.

Tom lifted his hand and waved good-bye over his shoulder to Erin. He looked up and caught her reflection in his rearview mirror as she waved back, then he watched temptation recede as he pulled from the curb and drove away.

The streets of Manhattan's Upper East Side were sparsely trafficked, and Tom guessed that it was thanks to the early hour. In no time at all, he had crossed 125th Street, merged onto the West Side Highway, and was cruising north toward the George Washington Bridge. According to the news-radio traffic reports, the bridge was the only one of the city's three Hudson River crossings that wasn't completely snarled that morning.

To his relief, when he reached the bridge several minutes later the only delays seemed to be for cars heading into Manhattan. The route out of the city was clear of traffic. He followed the signs to the bridge's upper level, and a profound sensation of relief filled his body as he guided his truck off the ramp and onto the long gray straightaway over the river to New Jersey.

The sun was at his back, and he had music on the radio.

Then he heard a whisper inside his head, a prayer calling out to him. Seven simple words in his wife's voice.

Please, God . . . bring my Tom home safe.

He had tears in his eyes and a smile on his face.

"Hang on, honey, I'm on my way. . . . I'm comin' home."

ACKNOWLEDGMENTS

As always, my first thanks go to my wife, Kara, who encouraged me for years to write this story, ever since I first mentioned the idea of it to her. Without her support, this story might never have moved beyond the concept phase.

The next step in this tale's creation owes its genesis to my trusted agent, Lucienne Diver, who patiently guided me through the development of its first-generation idea, and then shopped it around until it found a good home.

That home, luckily, turned out to be with my esteemed editor, Marco Palmieri, who has continued in his role as my literary sensei through the many stages of this novel's writing and editing. He has been my sounding board, my BS detector, my coach, and my friend.

Another editor who deserves thanks is Jennifer Heddle, who, after looking at my original pitch for this book, saw both what was wrong with it and what was right with it. Generously, she took the time to share her observations, and she coupled them with suggestions for making the story better—all of which I accepted and implemented with gratitude and without delay. I also received valuable notes and feedback from my friends Jaime Costas and Alan Kistler.

Fellow author and friend Dayton Ward helped me over a mental hurdle that had threatened to stall my entire creative process. To give credit (or blame) where it is due, he was the one who named my supernatural antagonists the Scorned. It was such a good suggestion that it bothered me only a little that he thought of it in less than thirty seconds after I had wracked my brain over that detail for weeks.

I also owe a debt of gratitude to Audra D. and the folks at the NYPD's Office of the Deputy Commissioner, Public Information, for technical advice and fact-checking. Also deserving of a tip o' the hat is Peter Dougherty and his website, nycsubway.org, which enabled me to research many details of the subway trains and the Times Square and Port Authority stations. Peter also provided me key advice about how to arm my villains in the subway sequence.

Thanks also go out to Father Damian Halligan from the St. Ignatius Retreat, for his counsel regarding my main character's Jesuit schooling and for his insights into the Jesuit philosophy as it might be applicable in a story such as this.

Lastly, I'd like to acknowledge the composers and their film scores that served as my sources of creative inspiration while writing this story: David Arnold (*Casino Royale*), James Newton Howard (*The Fugitive* and *Lady in the Water*), and John Ottman (*The Usual Suspects*). Furthermore, in an unusual twist for me, the album that served most prominently as a musical touchstone for this book was not a film score at all; I'm referring, of course, to *Snakes & Arrows* by Rush, whose song "Workin' Them Angels" is the source of this novel's epigraph.

Until next time, thanks for reading!

ABOUT THE AUTHOR

David Mack is the national bestselling author of more than a dozen books, including *Harbinger, Reap the Whirlwind, Road of Bones, The Sorrows of Empire,* and the *Star Trek Destiny* trilogy: *Gods of Night, Mere Mortals,* and *Lost Souls.*

Before turning his hand to novels, Mack's diverse writing credits spanned several media, including television (for episodes of *Star Trek: Deep Space Nine*), film, short fiction, magazines, newspapers, comic books, computer games, radio, and the Internet.

Learn more about him and his work on his official website, davidmack.pro, or visit his blog at davidmack.pro/blog.

He currently resides in New York City with his wife, Kara.